ACCORDING TO HELEN

ACCORDING TO HELEN

FLORENCE WALLIN

Grateful acknowledgment is made to the Republic of Greece, Ministry
of Culture, National Archaeological Museum, for permission to use
the photograph of a wall painting, "MYCENAEA" for the cover of
this book. It is number 11670, a female figure discovered in 1970 in
a house just inside the west wall of the acropolis at Mycenae, dated at
Late 13C BC

ISBN   0-9655948-0-7

PINE TREE PRESS, INC

PO BOX 172
Alexander, NC 28701

PRINTED IN THE USA

ACKNOWLEDGMENTS

Thanks to the readers, editors, inspiring thinkers, technical experts, moral supporters and everyone else who helped me with *According To Helen*. From among them I particularly acknowledge Michael Baumann, Albert Epp, Evan Farber, Bob Horn, Jean Johnson, Jeanne Marty, Anthony Papalas and Elizabeth Riorden. M. E. Witkowski designed the cover and map. Dershie McDevitt, Peggy Parris, Geraldine Powell, Virginia Sampson and Elizabeth Squire, colleagues in my writers' group, oversaw the growing manuscript in minute detail, and Margaret Beidler, Sirkka Barbour, Caroline Higgins and Penelope Niven listened to early chapters with heartening discernment. My entire family cared about the project and helped with their interest and suggestions, especially Franklin Wallin who shared in the adventure.

FOREWORD

This account of the story of Helen of Troy is found in the writings of Homer, Hesiod, and the fragments of other early story-tellers concerned with the Trojan War and its aftermath. It is easy to understand that, informative as they are, these tales often represent the era when they were written, about 700 BCE, more accurately than 1180 BCE or earlier, a more accepted time frame for the actual event. Scholarly evaluations and mythological interpretations added layers of information to the basic material. Archaeological sources brought crucial knowledge about the Mycenaean Age and enlarged our understanding of this advanced civilization and its disastrous decline.

Through the archaeological work of Marija Gimbutas and others, the Earth Mother was found to be the primary deity among the indigenous peoples of the Aegean area. John Chadwick, who helped decode the Linear B script on clay tablets in Mycenaean archaeological sites and wrote of his findings, agrees. Invaders were bringing in patrilinear religious forms that conflicted with the old matrilinear system. This confrontation is central to Helen's story.

As a featured player in the Goddess oriented religion Helen's choices and actions were motivated in plausible ways not acknowledged in the early interpretations. Rooted in a primitive awe of the magic of reproduction, females were endowed with creative power and the Earth Mother was a divine godhead. Recognizing the importance of the often suppressed, age-old, female religion fills in and illuminates the Mycenaean cultural picture. This fascinating convergence of mythology and archaeology sparked the idea for Helen's story. The first person telling permits an intimate look at her life in an effort to narrow the three thousand year expanse between then and now.

The language on the Linear B tablets is related to Homer's Greek, yet, as many proper names in Linear B were non Greek, fictional characters were often given non Greek names. The use of pre-Olympian Goddess names is in keeping with the era.

Though Helen, Castor and Polydeuces are often said to be from Sparta, the older designation for the place, Amyklae, was used to avoid an association with the Spartan ethic of Lycurgus which developed at a later time. In a section at the end of the book some sources and explanations are noted.

LACONIA GIRL

My feet touched the hard-packed earth in time to bursts of breath. The rugged terrain ahead showed no sign of the thieves' camp, only an upward trail with wooded rises and rocky outcrops. Tired as I was, I was determined to find them. Yet, the sun had slipped behind a mountain ridge stark against an orange and darkening sky. Impossible to continue in the dark, I would wait for moonlight to locate their fires. A wool mantle, tied hastily around my waist, was my sole protection from the approaching night cold.

Again, I brooded over the monstrous crime that sent me racing off into the wilderness. Again, I was outraged as I recalled that honored guests had insulted the Laconian people by desecrating a shrine and stealing a most sacred relic. Ahead of me on this very road, I would catch up to them and retrieve the precious image.

Early this morning the bridge over the river had thronged with festival visitors putting scores of sacred swans to flight. Great wings undulated across the dawning sky in a powerful hallowed throb. I had stopped to watch them on my way to the playing fields, thrilled with the day's excitement.

I saw my cousin Penelope and waved. She, too, was headed for the practice area where my older brothers were lifting weights. As I approached I saw their skin shiny with oil, their short hair, the same bronze color as mine curled tight to their heads.

"Hey, lazy one," Castor called to me, "this is a fine day to be late."

"We thought you decided not to race today," his twin, Polydeuces teased.

I had laughed, for it was very early in the morning, and I was rarely late and seldom lazy. My brothers had grown into men, and I admired their broad shoulders, their smooth chests evenly muscled, and their arms straining with the heavy bars.

"You be careful how you speak to me," I taunted back, "or I'll take you down."

They both scoffed as I knew they would. Though I was strong, I was slim and only as tall as their shoulders. When we were children, I could pin either one of them wrestling, if they vexed me enough, and if they giggled enough. I would never let them forget it.

Their keen resemblance made it hard to tell them apart. But they were different. Polydeuces was stronger and more quiet. He fought so cleverly with his fists that he was feared by all contenders in the ring. Castor had a way with horses. He owned a handsome band of Trojan racers that pastured in the fields beyond. We could see their flying manes as they cavorted in the dewy grass.

"Will it be the ebony pair today?" I asked. The black stallions were his favorite for the chariot race, but I knew one of them had strained a tendon.

Castor shook his head. "No, they are not ready. I've decided on the dappled mares. Those long-legged beauties will bring me luck today of all days. The Goddess will be smiling on all her beautiful running maidens—like you and Penelope." He grinned as our cousin joined us.

She was tall with pale skin and soft gray eyes. "I haven't won a foot race for so long, it will not be I who will be named High Maiden Priestess and Protectress of the Sacred Relic." She spoke in mock seriousness. I knew she might very well win this important race of the maidens and receive the honored titles. We had just completed our virgin-year studies in the temple, and the summer solstice festival celebrated our achievements of the sacred mysteries.

Penelope continued, smiling mischievously. "But, on second thought, I may beat you today. I had a premonition."

"You are a tease," I answered. "You're just saying that to rile me." I put my arm around her. "You know I would be happy if you won." Then I hugged her before I ran off, calling, "But I'll try my best to see that you don't."

We waved good-bye to the boys as we went to the women's quarter to rub oil into our muscles and stretch and exercise. Our race was to be the first event of the day.

"Did you really have a premonition?" Somehow I needed to know.

"Not exactly," she said, as I pulled off my tunic. "Though I did have a dream. In it you were hurt, and you went away for a long time." She sounded worried.

I was relieved. She had not dreamed that I had lost the race.

Sometime later we heard the call for the games' procession. We joined the athletes for the solemn march around the field as an announcer shouted out our names to a din of fanfare and cheering.

Our group of seven maidens walked proudly with heads up, our young breasts shining with oil, and our short pleated skirts belted around our waists. The excitement mounted inside me. In the royal stall Mother Leda and her husband, King Tyndareus, were with Penelope's mother and father and some visitors. Two men sat in special seats of honor, but I hardly noticed them, so preoccupied was I with the pageant. I waved at Mother, and she smiled back at me.

She was lovely, my mother, her movements soft, her brown hair silken; anywhere she went, she carried a quiet grace and welcome presence. I wished I could be like her, but I was quite different with my mop of bronzy curls and impulsive ways.

The race of the maidens was called. I crouched for the start and looked quickly at the other girls, our brown legs taut like a line of bows ready to release. I concentrated on the track ahead, on the expected signal. Crack! The blocks of wood slammed together, and I shot onto the course, assuming my running pace. We all kept together for the first straight-away. By the end of the second length, Penelope, Phiona and I were ahead, the others strung out behind. In the third, I pushed into a definite lead, but the other two did not falter.

The noise of the crowd intensified, and Phiona surged ahead as we rushed into the fourth length. In a flash, I was with her, Penelope close behind, and just as the finish line appeared at the end of the final stretch, I burst into an all-out effort. I soared with the falcons, passing Phiona, and crossed the finish line free and clear. Gasping for breath, Penelope, Phiona and I threw our arms around each other, thrilled with the competition.

An official led us to the royal stall where Mother Leda placed a garland of laurel on my head for being first, and honored Penelope and Phiona with laurel branches for being runners up. King Tyndareus smiled as he introduced the special guests, visiting kings. They congratulated me warmly, but I was much too excited to acknowledge them.

In making the presentation, Mother Leda spoke some words about the significance of the initiation of virgins. "This year," she said, her voice tremulous but clear, "the winner of the foot race, Helen, will be named, not only High Maiden Priestess and Protectress of the Sacred Relic, but also the Future Inheritor of Queenly Functions." A great cheering came from the crowd. "This means," she continued, "that the winner will someday become Queen in my place and the acting Goddess on Earth, here in Laconia."

I felt unequal to this honor. How could I take her place? I asked myself.

"It is unusual that the virgin chosen is the birth daughter of the present Queen. I believe it is an especially fine omen in the lore of the Goddess."

I smiled my pleasure at having made Mother Leda so happy. I heard such affection in her voice that I realized this festival was truly more, much more, than a footrace.

After Penelope and I had bathed, we donned white linen tunics bordered in blue and went to the royal stall to watch the games. Again, the visitors complimented us almost too lavishly. One, King Theseus of Athens, had sad eyes. The other, a Lapith from the North called King Peirithous, had black hair with streaks of white in it. They were strong and hard-looking and seemed younger than Tyndareus.

They had received a generous welcome including a feast that had lasted long into the night. They were so at ease with King Tyndareus, I assumed they had spent some summer holidays together, hunting and foraging the countryside as men liked to do. I paid little heed to their conversation, a mixture of comment on the games interspersed with common memories of old adventures. I was drawn by the excitement when Polydeuces out-boxed a clever contender from a distant province. Penelope and her parents left, and then Mother Leda motioned that she and I must leave.

As planned, Mother Leda went ahead of me to the sanctuary, and at noon, I would follow with a temple priestess. I stood below the stands in the cool shadows. The conversation of the Kings above me had changed, become more intimate.

"That girl of yours is magnificent," King Theseus said. "She radiates an indescribable grace—it shines from those fantastic golden eyes, and her smile—almost ethereal."

"It nearly makes one's heart melt and one's innards turn to mush. Holy Mother, she is truly stunning," King Peirithous said, "a perfect queen for any kingdom."

"Ah, yes," Tyndareus replied in that knowing way he had, "and you both need queens, do you not? What a tragedy, losing such fine wives." He waited a moment in respect for their wives now dead, I supposed. After a little he chuckled as though to himself. "She would be too much for either of you. She is young and beautiful with a mind of her own."

I had dismissed the words of the kings as lavish banter, but it perplexed me to hear my step-father admire me. He had never said I was beautiful before.

A great cheer burst from the stands and drowned out their conversation. After a spell one of the kings spoke again. "If I read things correctly here, Tyndareus, you could do well without her. A moon priestess will attract no end of suitors who would happily replace you." It was the Northerner speaking with his strange accent. "We would be doing you a favor by taking her away. Come, Theseus, let us draw lots for her," he joked.

All three of them were laughing, and I thought their humor foolish. I could hear them slapping each other on the back. "Well, it is a pleasant idea, but not this time," King Theseus said.

"Ah, I know," King Peirithous said. "We'll take the next best thing, a sacred relic. We would be doing you a favor, Tyndareus. We'll raid the shrine as we've done before, so often, in other places. Once those old things are gone, the people of the countryside will not be so tied to the Goddess. Isn't it time they gave their primary attention to Zeus?"

"To be sure, to be sure," Tyndareus agreed absent mindedly.

My guide signaled our departure. Believing these Kings to be jesting, my only concern was to secure the garland on my head. I followed the escorting priestess through the crowd of happy onlookers; some reached out to touch me, and, in my elation, I could not help but touch them back, taking a hand or grasping an arm.

When I reached the sanctuary at the river inlet, the crowd made way for me, and I entered the shrine alone. The cool dark interior was lit by torches on wall sconces. I followed the points of light, pausing when I came to the effigy. This ancient relic was believed to represent the Earth Mother herself. It was made of smooth wood thought to be oak or olive, but no longer possible to verify because the oil rubbed into it over the eons had turned it black as night. The torso was elongated with definite life giving hips and breasts. It rested on a rock pedestal, and a never-ending fire burned before it. A basket of snakes lay near by, coiling, uncoiling, arching and lowering, absorbing the Goddess energy. I bowed in deep respect, aware of my new responsibility.

I went out into a shaded courtyard, where I found silence, warmth and greenery. Arbors circled with vines formed delicate shadow patterns on the ground. The trees, leafed into fullness, still held on to some old blossoms, sweet with the promise of fruit to come.

My mother stood among the fruit trees at an omphalos altar near the lagoon. Her hair hung long on either side of her face, her white robe fell in folds around her.

The old priestesses assembled with her. One in particular, the most venerable of the seers, stood in front of the others. She was bent and wrinkled with age, and her eyes glowed with knowing.

Mother indicated I must be cleansed in the waters of the lagoon. Attendant priestesses helped me remove my shift, and when I stepped into the pool, water was poured over me again and again until my hair was soaked and I was thoroughly wet. Clean sand was rubbed gently into my skin until it tingled. More water rinsed off the sand, and I put my arms out welcoming the purification. I was dried with a linen sheet, anointed with a spicy oil and draped with a white robe. My feet and arms were bare. The laurel garland was replaced on my wet head, and my mother led me before the others. The sweet smell of early summer surrounded us.

On the altar a single creamy narcissus, perfect in bloom and stalk, rested near a bowl with a single perfect fruit, a pomegranate. As we stood, transfixed by the light, the voice of the old one commenced slowly and so low I could hardly make out her words.

She intoned the familiar story about a mother's joy in finding her long lost daughter, and the eternal renewal of womanhood through mother and daughter was celebrated again. Just as the mother passed to the daughter the fertility of the womb, the old woman handed Mother the fruit which she gave to me. I handed it back to the venerable seer, who took a knife and cracked it open.

The seeds spilled into the bowl, and she ran them through her fingers and gave the bowl to Mother, who did the same. Mother held the bowl for me and I felt the wet seeds strain through my fingers, some sticking to them. My mother took my hand and pressed it to my mouth. Some of the seeds rubbed off on my lips. Then, the old woman took the flower, the narcissus, by the stem. She put it to her lips and handed it to Mother, who did the same, then handed it to me, and I put it to my lips.

"The maiden beguiles the flower," the old woman said, as I felt the soft petals against the curve of my lips.

"The flower seduces the maiden," the old woman said, and taking the flower, she held it up. Some seeds from the fruit that were on my lips were now on the flower petals.

"The womb will be fertile, the seeds will bring forth fruit, the fruit will ripen and our harvest will be full," she chanted. After more words and some replies, the other priestesses sang a beautiful hymn about Mother Demeter's sense of loss as her daughter, Kore, returned to the shadowed underworld.

I was led back to the dark chamber, and we stood before the effigy where the venerable seer spoke ritual phrases to our Goddess Potnia, and we all fed the fire with sticks. The ones I put on had been treated with something, for they flared up more brightly than the others.

The service was over. I felt clean and aware of my womanly strength as I had never been before. I promised myself to be diligent in caring for the fires before the Goddess image and to continue to be part of her. What this meant for me as Queen, as Goddess Incarnate on Earth, or at least Laconia, I would have to think about later. I would have to find out from Mother.

Having donned our daily garb, Mother and I left our ceremonial robes behind and walked quietly away from the sanctuary and sat together in a nearby grove of sacred pear trees.

"Oh, Mother Leda," I said. "I will try with all my heart to merit this honor. You must help me learn how to be worthy of it."

"Darling Helen," she replied, reaching out to a cluster of wild daisies to pick one, "Did you feel the power in the temple?"

"Oh, yes," I answered, certain of my reply.

"Were you cleansed by the purification?" Mother twirled the daisy between her fingers then picked another.

"I've never before felt cleaner." I leaned back, looking up at the sky, but thinking of the cool water washing over me.

"Did the words of the Venerable Seer enlighten you?" She added another daisy to her collection.

"Yes. I understood it all." I felt pleased that it was so clear.

"Did you feel the beauty of procreation?" Mother looked at me then with the question in her eyes.

"It has become part of me." I looked away from her, feeling moved by my deep response. "I will be prepared for the sacred rites tonight," I said

"Yes," she agreed. "It is beautiful if you are ready, and I believe you are. Though there is no urgency for you to fulfill these rites tonight, you know."

"Yes, I know."

"And did you sense a force, a vigor directed to you from the Goddess effigy?" she asked.

"Not really," I said, in alarm for my failure. "I thought—the sticks—they were coated with something to make them flare up like that."

"The sticks were coated with nothing." Mother put the daisies aside. A slight crease between her eyes told me she was very serious.

I shivered in the afternoon heat. "Yes," I answered. "I did sense the force of the Goddess Potnia."

"You see." She laughed. "I cannot teach you anything."

"But, Mother, to be Queen?"

Mother stood and smoothed her skirt. She offered me her hand and helped me up. "Just remember, never take for yourself the divinity that belongs to the Goddess." We walked together in the shade of the holy fruit trees.

"You will know, darling. Do not worry."

I strode next to her, still uncertain.

"I must tell you," she said. "I dared not hope that you would be chosen today. Good things will come from it."

Suddenly, we heard a commotion across the meadow. We could hear people running, and shouts came from the sanctuary. We hurried back to the temple, and when we approached the shrine, we knew something was very wrong. Angry shouts came from all directions.

"They've taken it! They stole it!"

"Thieves barged in and ran away with it!"

The holy place had been desecrated, the Goddess effigy stolen. It was altogether true. Only an empty space remained where the sacred form had rested.

"It's gone, gone!" Mother cried, rushing about as though she might find it in some other location.

I moaned as her words made it true for me. "Oh, no," I cried, remembering the conversation between the guest kings plotting with Tyndareus. The Goddess figure had been taken, and the forever-burning fire snuffed out. The basket that had contained the snakes lay upside down beside it. Some of the priestesses had grabbed for the serpents, which now coiled around their arms or necks. One that had been overlooked slipped away as I watched. And the venerable, the ancient seer, lay stretched out on the dirt floor unnaturally still.

Mother bent over her and gently rubbed her hands, calling to her. "Come now, speak to us, speak to us."

I helped move the old one out to the courtyard. An ugly bruise on her forehead showed us the injury; she was unconscious, scarcely breathing.

"Bring cool wet cloths, some fresh drinking water," Mother instructed. She was so occupied that I could not interrupt her to tell her what I knew, that I had heard the plans being made to do this dreadful thing. I had thought it stupid, foolish banter. A terrible anguish enveloped me. I was the stupid one, so full of myself and my honors I had ignored the obvious signs of danger.

If I had spoken up, something could have been done to stop the theft, the defamation of the shrine, and the injury to the venerable one. I had been at fault for not alerting someone, and I had been at fault for not guarding the Goddess effigy. On the very first day of my responsibility, the sacred image had been stolen.

"What happened, exactly? I asked one of the priestesses.

"Men on horses," she croaked from a tormented mouth. "Two men charged up here. They jumped off their horses, ran into the shrine and took the sacred figure, and then they were gone." She put her hands on either side of her wrinkled cheeks.

"It was that fast," another said. "All over, away and gone, before we even realized." Her shaky hands groped vacantly.

As I heard their words, I understood the magnitude of my blunder; I must bring back the effigy of Goddess Potnia. I felt compelled to go after the thieves, and I had no time to spare. I borrowed a warm mantel carried by a priestess and told her what I planned to do.

"You must not," she protested, grasping my arm in a claw-like grip. I pulled away.

"Tell my mother," I said to her as she tried in vain to hold me back. I pressed her arm. "It is absolutely essential that I leave now. I must catch up with the thieves and bring back the effigy. I have no time to explain it all to Mother Leda."

It did not seem strange, nor would it to any other Laconian girl, to be alone in the surrounding hills, but I knew nothing of the hinterland. Furious at the outrageous act, driven by a pressing urgency, I took off running on the pathway heading north, my heartbeats and footsteps pounding in my ears. Although the thieves were on horseback, they would have to stop sometime.

GUARDIAN PRIESTESS

Their camp-fires burned bright in the darkness. With my warm mantle snug around me, I sat on a rock nibbling berries picked in the last light of day. When the lustrous moon appeared over the hills, I sidled wide of the thieves' camp closing with it from the far side, moving against the breeze that might carry my scent to the dogs.

How many were in their party? I knew of the two kings, each with a horse and some henchmen. As I kept in the path of the soft night breeze, the pungent smell of burning wood wafted to me. I stepped forward with care and had been lucky so far with the dogs.

I silently waited and listened. An owl hooted, and a bull frog croaked. I crept a few steps farther and stopped to wait and listen again. I heard a whinny nearby, and soon I saw the dark forms of horses staked outside the fire glow. Closer to the camp-fire the men were huddled in their animal skins. As I watched, a dog awoke and lifted its head, sniffing the cool air. In a few moments it settled again, stretching its neck out on its paws, inching closer to the fire.

I crouched behind a patch of thorny bushes and stayed as still as possible listening to the sleepers' snores. I made out the humps of traveling gear here and there under a tree, and I felt the luck of a moon maiden as I quietly moved to examine one bundle and another. Before long I felt the form of the effigy inside a sack that was tied around with cord, and with all care, I unwrapped the holy piece. I held the Goddess figure up to the night sky and turned it carefully as the different planes and curves of the oiled wood surface gleamed in the sacred moonlight. Magic power tingled through my arms and fingers, and I felt compelled to dance before her. I hesitated, briefly checking the humps and bodies around the fire; they were still as death.

I propped the sacred form against some bundles in a shaft of moonlight and solemnly circled around the figure. I dipped and turned, swaying to a rhythm inside me, as I stepped through the intricate pattern. I finished the ritual dance and bowed my head as though receiving a blessing.

I waited in a shadow. Someone moved restlessly. The wakeful dog stretched then settled again. I quickly re-wrapped the figure in the sack and tied it to my back and left. When I felt free and clear of the camp, I picked up the trail and headed towards home.

I stumbled once and turned my ankle, but I kept going until clouds sailed over the mountains and blocked the moon. Using whatever light was left to me as the clouds gathered and regrouped, I followed a stone-filled creek-bed up through brambles and broom. I tripped and fell on a slippery rock, ignored a scraped knee and kept going up and up until I came to a grove of wild olive trees. Here I found some shelter under an overhang in a smooth place some animal may once have used. I curled up with my arms around the precious bundle and fell asleep.

Sunlight warmed my face. I opened my eyes to the glare but squeezed them shut against the blinding brightness. I shivered as a terrible fear swept through me and reached for the sacred image and held it close. Had I seen correctly?

Had I seen figures, some people out there, just beyond my shelter?

I moved cautiously into the shadow and put my hand to my eyes to shade them. Three men lounged on smooth rocks and moss beyond some scrawny shrubs that screened my hiding place. One leaned against a boulder, another chewed on a piece of grass, his long legs stretched out in front of him. The third stood by, his hands held behind him. All three looked out at the view across the valley below. I recognized King Theseus and King Peirithous; the other must have been a retainer.

My heart raced and I tried to think of dashing away. Before I could begin to plan, a dog, a deer hound, wandered over to me wagging its tail. The dog swiped at my cheek with a gentle lick of the tongue, making me laugh despite the uncertain situation. I gently rubbed its ears.

"Why are you here?" I asked softly. "What do your masters expect from me?"

The pup's friendly overtures lessened my terror, and I forced myself to be calm. As I smoothed my tousled hair and put my tunic to rights, I reminded myself that these men, as recently as yesterday, had enjoyed our hospitality. These same men had desecrated a holy shrine, thereby insulting my people. I tried to believe I had nothing to fear, and it was they who had much for which to answer.

I stood, forcing courage and spoke, ignoring my parched mouth, hoping my voice did not betray my anxiety. "Good morning, sirs." I sounded much more certain than I felt. "I tried not to disturb you last night, when I retrieved the sacred Goddess image—you stole." My voice faded to a whisper. "I am sorry you found it necessary to follow me."

The three men stood tall before me with some semblance of courtesy. The retainer had signaled the dog that was now held attached to a leather lead. King Peirithous displayed a rough elegance in his softly tanned deerskins, silver wrist bands and with a gold ornament hanging from a leather cord around his neck.

King Theseus frowned slightly. His eyes, of a deep blue, had struck me yesterday as sad. Now they searched mine as though seeking an answer to some unsolvable problem. He was not so grand as the Northerner, but he exuded a natural grace touched with melancholy. "We can not explain away our rudeness," he said. "I am deeply sorry to have mutilated the holy sanctuary and insulted the hospitality we enjoyed in the palace of Tyndareus and Leda."

"Princess," Peirithous said, "once we thought it prankish to destroy sacred idols in the name of Zeus. We should have known better."

I was not impressed by their noble presence or contrite apologies. "Well, then," I said, hoping the conference over, "I will be on my way." I wanted to leave more than anything; my unperturbed attitude masked fear and anger. "I have far to go, and I have caused great concern at home." I walked into the clearing, clutching the effigy to me. "Certainly my brothers are on my trail. I will hurry along so as to meet them on the route." I turned to face the kings. "Admittedly, your actions are hard to understand. I fail in that, but I accept your apology. Now, I depart."

I stepped in front of them to find the narrow path winding down between the rocky mass.

"But, daughter, you need food and drink," King Theseus said. "We have brought fruit and bread and also cheese. Here, drink." He held out a skin beaded with cool drops of water. The servant spread a cloth and placed on it ripe cherries and pears. He laid fresh grain cakes on a board, then opened a crock of goat cheese.

Hunger gnawed inside me; my parched throat ached for water at the sight of the beaded sack. I hesitated. King Theseus flashed a smile, and I shrugged my shoulders taking the skin of water from which I sipped greedily. The three of us sat on the rocky ledge and ate our fill. The food was tasty and would sustain me for the trip back. I drank once again from the water flask.

Both kings watched me as though taking pleasure in my pleasure. "You are quite an astonishing young woman," Theseus said. "How did you manage to catch up with us?"

"And come into our camp without us knowing?" Peirithous added. "We followed your track at first light."

I could see expressions of admiration on their faces, but I was not pleased. All the pain of yesterday overwhelmed me, and I relived the moment when we had found the relic gone, the temple smashed and the ancient priestess smitten and motionless.

I shook my head and brushed at my cheeks, forcing back my wrath. No, I thought, I will have none of their pretty talk. "I must leave," I said. "Thank you for sharing your food." Now, I thought, get up and go, now.

Theseus motioned to the servant, who produced another skin. "Can we at least part as friends. Here, a sip of wine for friendship."

The servant poured some into cups. "None for me, thank you," I said, trying to be gracious in my refusal.

"Come," they insisted. "A sip to show we are friends."

"No," I insisted. "I do not need wine to prove friendship."

"Oh, it is only a custom. A sip will not hurt."

"No wine," I said stubbornly. I knew it could easily have been altered with a sleeping potion or poison. I felt desperate to part. I ignored them and started down the narrow rocky path. Almost at once everything reeled before me. Oh no, oh no, too late, I thought. I've been tricked. I fell into darkness.

I groaned aloud. I lay on some scratchy straw in darkness. My limbs ached, my head throbbed. What had happened to me?

Someone entered carrying a lantern. In the shadows I could see it was the retainer of Theseus and Peirithous.

"You are awake," he said in a raspy voice. His grizzled face peered at me from the shadows. "We were worried about you." He spoke kindly, but I knew he was a deceiver.

"Where am I? What happened?" My voice croaked like a withered old woman's.

"We carried you with us today. You were too sick to ride."

What nonsense, I thought. "You poisoned me," I accused, shaking with fury.

"Shh," he soothed. "Here, drink this. It is water." He held my head while I sipped from the cool flask. I drank deeply then fell back on the pallet.

"It was too strong. It wasn't supposed to make you so sick." He growled these words as he replaced the flask in his sack.

"What was it supposed to do?" I asked, angry, my voice clearer after the drink.

"Just make you sleepy. Now I will pick you up and carry you from here into a bathhouse where some serving women will bathe you and clothe you in clean linen. Then I will carry you, or help you walk, to a chamber where you can eat a little if you like, then sleep. Tomorrow you will be better."

With that he bent down and put his arms under me and picked me up as though I were a child. I was very tired, too tired to object. All happened as he said, and soon I was washed, wearing a clean shift and resting in a bed in a room with a window looking out at the night, where the moon's pale light shone in at me. The grizzly-faced servant of Theseus spooned hot gruel for me to swallow, and soon I was so sleepy I could barely speak. "What is your name," I managed to ask before I slipped off.

"I am called Pindros," he answered, and I slept.

The next morning I warily tested my limbs and joints for pain. My head was clear, and I stretched and breathed in the morning air. Resisting a formidable lassitude, I climbed out of bed. I felt shaky and weak, but the sight of the rough sack that had contained the sacred Goddess image lifted my spirits. I unwrapped the bundle and sighed in relief to discover the relic was just as I had left it.

Mystified completely by the events that had taken over my life, I felt immense gratitude that I was well and that the sacred image was with me. I splashed water on my face and as I combed my tangled hair, I looked out a window at a village set in a fertile valley. I dressed hurriedly and ran out of the sleeping room, down some stairs to a courtyard.

I sat on a low garden wall, for I was still weak. I admired some twisting grape vines and full leafy plants bright in the morning sunlight. Perhaps I could leave. Perhaps I could just walk out with my sacred bundle, and no one would care.

"Ah, the restorative powers of the young." King Theseus said from the shadow of a fig tree.

"I am quite weak, King Theseus. It is my need to know that brought me out so early. Tell me, please, am I a prisoner?"

I tried to be polite. The time for anger, if it flared, would come later. King Theseus sat next to me. He wore a gold band around his forehead and a simple tunic of soft stuff held by a wide belt. His sandal thongs crisscrossed up to mid-calf, and I could see the golden hairs on his tanned leg and the swell of powerful muscle beneath.

"Helen, you are my prisoner." He spoke quietly. His eyes looked into mine without flinching.

The time for anger arrived too quickly. It erupted from

me as I stood and faced him. "You have no right," I said, my voice rising. "You have broken every code of courtesy. I will not have it."

He stood and grabbed my hands, holding them in a vice, looking down at me, controlled. "You are young, but you have spirit and poise and intelligence, and stunning beauty, which will only increase as you mature. I am taking you to Athens."

Tears of indignation brimmed. "But I am to be Queen in Laconia, for my people and my country. It is all planned."

"It will be better this way. Come, the table is set out with edibles. Let us eat together. We have a long journey ahead of us. No tricks this morning, I promise," he said as we sat. I ate the cheese and olives, the grain cakes and fruit. I drank of the fresh water and knew the food would sustain me when I made my escape.

"We are in Tegea," Theseus told me. "From here we move quickly. We do not want to make too much of a spectacle in Agamemnon's country. Your sister's husband might not understand. We will even by-pass Troezen, my native place, where I rested for many days not long ago."

I received this information with inner confusion. My knowledge of these places was scanty at best. Were we really close to the Kingdom of Agamemnon, that brutal king who kidnapped my sister Clytemnestra to make her his queen? Kings must chose moon maiden queens to validate their kingship, but why must they kidnap them? And I was a prisoner. It was all too much. I must escape. They had ransacked the temple. And Tyndareus, King Tyndareus of Laconia, the husband of Mother Leda, had assented to their scheme. Did he think it a joke? Or, the worst thought of all came slowly, did Tyndareus want me kidnapped, spirited off to some other kingdom?

Silence seemed my only refuge. I could not speak to Theseus. I ate silently, ignoring him, resisting in the only way left to me. Yet King Theseus talked on, answering the questions that had been in my mind as though I had asked them.

"Peirithous has gone ahead to prepare our journey to Athens. He will arrange for us to cross Argolis Bay tonight. Tomorrow, we will head for the opposite coast, where he will meet us, having made all the arrangements for us to take passage across the gulf to Athens. As I said, we will skirt King Agamemnon's domain, for it might prove awkward were we discovered by some guard or other with his Queen's sister in our party."

If King Agamemnon discovered me, prisoner of King Theseus, would he help? I suspected he might not. Though an old friendship existed with Tyndareus, he had never shown any generosity to Clytemnestra's family. But if I escaped, I could find my way to Clytemnestra.

Theseus continued speaking, breaking into my scheme. "I must tell you something. Peirithous, he wanted you for himself. We usually agree on things; he too believes you will be a fine Queen some day." My eyes must have widened in disbelief. I studied a bee probing a rose blossom at my side. I felt unexpressed fury pour out of my eyes which I hid from him.

"Helen." He put his hand on mine, and I flinched but did not move. "I won you. We drew lots. It was fair, and Poseidon approves. Things go better for me when I feel his approval." I took a deep breath and held it. How could I contain my rage? He removed his hand, and I breathed more easily. He continued. "The sacred relic, for which you risked your life, will be in my care. I want you to know that it is yours forever, and that I will protect it as you would. You can trust me."

An eruptive expression of disbelief escaped my lips. I turned to follow the flight of the bee to another flower cluster.

Theseus continued. "I want everything to be as comfortable as possible. When will you be ready to leave?"

I turned to look at him with all the hate and fury that had gathered inside me. He held my gaze until, still not speaking, I stood and left him.

All day long I looked for a way to escape. The tortuous route led through narrow valleys and up scraggly mountain slopes. We rode in single file, Theseus in front and Pindros behind, and two other retainers behind him. The holy relic, wrapped in its rough cloth, was secured behind the saddle of Theseus. Somehow I would find a way.

My sister Clytemnestra and her husband, the high King Agamemnon, were close by, but I found no way to run off to find them. Agamemnon had kidnapped Clytemnestra after killing her husband in battle and murdering her baby. She was seventeen when she was brutally wrenched away to Mycenae. I had been horrified. That was five summers ago, and King Tyndareus had not interfered. He must have thought it suitable that Clytemnestra be Agamemnon's Queen. I remembered her as a wild beauty with flashing green eyes who disdained the running and jumping contests that had so occupied my energies. Mother Leda had been inconsolable for many months.

These memories gave me little hope. Saddened, I rode on. When the trail widened, I talked to Pindros. His raspy voice intrigued me. I learned that he was Cretan, that he had been a sailor on the ship that bore the Athenian bull dancers home so many years ago and had been a loyal servant to King Theseus ever since. A favorite story of harpers, I had heard it often, but never first-hand. Pindros described the young athletes, girls and boys, and the dangerous tricks they did in the bull ring. I visualized their somersaults and back flips over the sharp horns of the raging bulls. I looked at the figure of King Theseus ahead. Yes, in his bearing and movement, I saw lightness and coordination for such acrobatics. It was clear that Pindros worshipped his lord.

With the evening upon us, we came down from the mountains to the sea that stretched serenely before us in the twilight. I was bundled aboard a small craft into a passenger place under the bows. I fell asleep at once and was only vaguely aware of creaking oars and the vessel's movement as we crossed Argolis Bay. We reached the other side sometime in the middle of the night, but I was not disturbed.

Early in the morning I stretched and awoke, cramped from my awkward position. Food was shared amongst us. Theseus seemed preoccupied, and Pindros silently cared for my needs. Horses had been found, so we mounted and again took off on a dry and stony trail. The wild terrain was less difficult than that of the previous day. Stunted pine trees and thorny brush grew everywhere with rocky mountains looming high around us.

Escape was impossible, for I was closely watched at all times, and Theseus kept the effigy tied up with his gear. Despondent, I entered a dark and grieving place within myself. Even the efforts of Pindros could not draw me forth.

When we came to the meeting site on the coast, I suddenly wanted to bathe in the calm sea, to slip into the cool water and cleanse myself of the dirt of the trip and the anger and unhappiness that weighed me down. I slipped off my sandals and clothes and was fully submerged before Pindros or Thesus even noticed.

"You mustn't," Theseus called. "Come back at once."

I laughed for the first time in days, not in joy but in defiance. "Make me," I replied, splashing water and diving under like a dolphin as my bare form slid through the waves relishing the coolness. When I came up for air, I saw

Pindros. He was frowning with worry, but grinned when he saw me. I waved and splashed around before I came out dripping wet and naked, shaking the water from my hair like a dog, very close to where Theseus stood, soaking him, I hoped. I flopped down on the clean sand and dried off, trying to comb my hair with my fingers. I was still angry and sad, but I felt strong again.

When King Peirithous arrived aboard a small ship, he and Theseus congratulated each other that their plan had worked so well. I looked on with contempt as they joked and laughed. King Peirithous sought me out while King Theseus consulted the ship captain.

He led me aboard and pointed out a place of modest comfort where I would be protected from wind and water. "I leave you here, Helen," he said, as he ducked beneath the stretched skins, bending very low because he was so large and the space was so cramped. "I am not usually one for lengthy conversation, nor would I normally dare give advice to a young woman, particularly one as self-confident as you."

He sat cross-legged on a wood pallet next to me. "I have some important things to say, and time is short. Will you listen?"

I nodded my head in assent.

"Unfortunately for me, I lost the wager for you," he smiled wryly. "You will go to Athens with Theseus. You probably have no idea how exquisite you are."

"I have never thought about it," I answered, raging in inner turmoil at being the object of a wager. I hoisted myself up, resting on an elbow, and even though his expression held sincerity, I replied in cold, clipped words. "In Laconia we think other things are more important. A strong body, honor, loyalty..."

"That is part of your beauty," he interrupted. "How fine if you could always maintain such freshness." He paused a moment. "I must part company with you here. I know you are being forced against your will right now, but you seem to be someone who might listen to reason, so I thought I would try to reach you."

He grinned then, and his teeth were so white, his look so appealing, I could not help smiling back.

"I want you to know that to be a Queen in Athens is as great an honor as any woman could strive for. To be Queen to Theseus is an opportunity, not a sentence. You think he is old. He is just tired. His first wife, who was much like you, died long ago. He adored her. Their son, a boy to be proud of, was killed recently. The second wife of Theseus was bad for everyone and caused much unhappiness. She, too, is dead. For a long time Theseus felt he had nothing to live for, and he neglected his kingdom. Things do not go well in Attica. You could make him want to live again, and that would make all the difference."

He hauled himself up into a crouch. "I must be off. Good luck, my dear girl. I will pray to Hermes for you. You are both runners after all and..."

"Yes, I know," I said. Hermes represented a male phallus and he was also a God of male fertility. I did not need the care of Hermes. "May the Great Goddess enhance your life," I called in retort as Peirithous quickly left.

A drowsiness came over me with the dark cover of night, and I thought about the words that Peirithous had felt important to impart. My mind wandered to things Pindros told me about Theseus, and soon I fell into a sound sleep. I dreamed of the bull dancers, of a strong lithe boy with golden hair who jumped off a bull's flank in backward somersaults and did handstands from its sharp silver horns. I woke once, briefly, when Theseus came in to sleep on the other pallet berth across from me. I could hear his deep breathing, and I looked over at him. In the pale light from the moon, still large, his features were washed of time. His

ATHENIAN PRINCESS

In the rosy light of dawn I stepped ashore near Athens, longing for all the familiar sights of home. I looked across the wharf where fishermen unloaded their catch. A throng of early risers clamored for first choice, and carts and barrows filled the way. In vain I sought my brothers riding to my aid. All my life they had been at hand when I needed them, but now I could see only a far chariot winding down the steep path of a distant hill.

Melancholy hung over me like a cloak, and I felt wretched in my desolation. King Thesus had been recognized and warmly greeted, while I stood apart, aware of the curiosity in the eyes of onlookers.

"How may I help you?" Pindros asked, his gravel voice sounding to my ears like a bird's song.

"Oh, Pindros," I answered. He smiled at the same time that he blinked in a sort of double wink. Touched by his concern, I could not help answering his kindness with a tremulous smile of my own.

People edged closer. They watched my every move, and nodded their heads as though to help me.

"This is Helen," their king explained. "She is a princess from Laconia." The chariot I noticed had come for us, and Theseus ushered me into it as though I were indeed a princess and not a prisoner.

We proceeded slowly through cheering crowds, though a few watchers stood quietly as we passed. Cypress trees lined the way shading houses and shops. Higher we climbed, back and forth until we entered through a massive gate in a wall made of rocks. The lintel, painted a dark russet, showed a serpent wound about an olive tree. A great wooden door stood open, and in a moment we were through it into a courtyard. Huge red columns stretched before me, and I sensed, rather than saw, a Goddess representation within. I felt drawn to enter and pay homage to her, but Theseus did not stop. He led me past bowing greeters, and we ascended smooth steps of polished stone to another impressive doorway guarded by sentries. We walked through many corridors with wall paintings of dogs chasing boars; underfoot were decorated tiles of undulating waves and sea anemones. Pindros and a serving girl followed in our wake.

Finally we arrived at a large airy apartment with windows looking across the city. The washing room contained a tile tub for bathing and a table covered with unguent jars, boxes of ivory and sandalwood, ewers and basins for cleansing. Against the wall stood a chest, a bench and shelves of carefully folded linen towels. The sleeping room contained a bed of olive wood with a brightly woven coverlet in green and blue and gold, shades from outdoors.

"This is for you, Helen," Theseus said. "I want you to be happy here." He smiled, his eyes asking for my approval. "It is nice," I said. I did not add, "For a prison." But my expression must have spoken for me. He sent Pindros and the serving girl outside to wait.

"The serving girl is called Lani," Theseus said. "Lani will help you with everything, and Pindros too will be your servant."

I looked at Theseus with gratitude. "I do like Pindros," I said.

"No one is more loyal. You must understand he has my interests at heart."

"Well," I said, making light of my condition, "I am certain he is the nicest prison guard in the palace."

"I hope you will not always feel like this," Theseus said, his eyes alert to my grief. "You are not such a prisoner as you think. You have complete freedom to come and go within these walls. Also, my mother lives here. I think you and she will be friends, for she, too, is a priestess of the Goddess Potnia."

I did not comment about the mother of Theseus, but I thought it surprising that she was a Goddess follower.

"Pindros or Lani will go with you outside the walls to the running course," he added. All the time he spoke, Theseus rested slightly against the window sill, his arms folded easily in front of him. He smiled a little. "Come here, Helen," he bid me.

I moved to the window. He put a hand under my chin and held my face to the light. "Even when you are sad, you are lovely." His deep voice saying I was sad made me sadder. I could feel my throat swell and my chin tremble, but I was determined not to weep. I swallowed and swept a hand across my stinging eyes.

Theseus drew me to him and held me. He said soothing things to me; I was glad he could not see my face buried in his tunic. I could relax in his arms. I smelled the sea salt on his skin from last night's voyage, and the embroidered motif on his tunic rubbed my cheek. Even so, I wanted to stay just as we were. It was as though my unhappiness had become centered in my being close to Theseus. I felt warm and protected, and when he let me go a little, I pressed closer to him. I lifted my face to look at him, and his eyes burned with passion. He kissed my hot cheeks and lips, and I nestled deeper in the circle of his arms.

"Helen," he whispered, his face buried in my neck, "do you know what you are doing to me?"

I should have known, for I had mastered the lessons about procreation with the other girls in our temple studies, and as a maiden readying for the end of the virgin-year rites, I had learned carefully the many techniques of beguiling so as to entice a mate and to pleasure therein. I had learned well the beauty, and the Venerable Old One had prepared me with the narcissus and the pomegranate. Although I had missed the initiation under the full moon, perhaps I would have a different experience here.

Unable to do otherwise, I put up my face for more kisses, and I welcomed the intimate touch of Theseus' hands. I strained to mold myself to him. He picked me up without effort and carried me to the bed in the sleeping room.

"The Goddess wills it," I whispered.

He left me and went to the door where the servants waited. I heard him tell Pindros to inform his greeters that he would meet them in the great hall at noon. He asked Lani to bring ewers of hot water and leave them in the bathing room. He returned to the sleeping room, closing all the doors behind him, and he came to the bed and lay down next to me.

My tunic was easily cast aside as was his covering. His intensely blue eyes grew brilliant as he gazed at my naked form lying next to him. He gently stroked me, touching my lips, my cheeks, my shoulders, my breasts, as though he were touching precious jewels. He told me over and over that everything about me was exquisite, and he slowly kissed each place that he had touched. I was so overcome I became obsessed with loving him.

I ran my fingers over his brow and smoothed the creases in his forehead; I touched his muscled arms and explored the battle scars on his chest. He whispered that he had never before been so filled with desire. I knew the power of the Goddess was in me, for I felt my body flower of its own will, reaching towards him as though he were the sun, soft petals opening, enticing him into all manner of loving. We came together as though drawn by a divine force, and I nearly fainted with the pleasure of it.

I wondered, later, how I could possibly have forotten the ugliness of the temple desecration or the very fact that I was held against my will. But my only understanding then was the delirium of fulfilling the desire that burned inside me. After Theseus left, I napped and bathed. Lani mysteriously appeared with hot water, for the ewers she left earlier were long cold. My body felt beautiful for Theseus' love of it. I luxuriated in the bath. Lani gently massaged me with oil and carefully applied a spicy scented unguent on my skin. She dressed my hair, and I could see in the reflection of the polished metal that she had tamed it as no one ever had before. She opened a chest and brought out one carefully folded drapery after the other. She showed me mantles of many colors and patterns, all scented with rose petals. My simple girl's tunic would no longer do. I was now a woman.

"You choose," I said to her. She had a round face with dark brows and hair and olive skin. She moved quietly, and made few comments. I wondered about the clothes, but I did not ask her to whom they might have belonged. I smiled my appreciation as she held up a diaphanous robe of deepest blue. I stood while she draped me and softly belted the waist. Her eyes were bright with approval.

I looked out the window and saw that all was quiet in the late afternoon heat. The shadows were beginning to lengthen, and soon it would cool. I found my pack and unwrapped the wooden effigy, smooth and black, running my hands over its surface and turning it in admiration.

A knock sounded on the outer door, and Lani came to tell me that the mother of King Theseus, Lady Aethra, wished to see me.

I went to welcome her and curtsied as a girl would do in Laconia. Laughing at my own foolishness, I smiled. "I beg pardon, madam, I forget that I am no longer a child."

She stood in solemn scrutiny of me as my smile turned to doubt, and I waited for her to speak.

"No, you are no child," she said. Her voice was full of music. She stood tall and her hair, more brown than silver, framed a face with creased skin, high cheek bones and full lips. Her clear eyes expressed a knowledge of everything concerning me. Her next words, therefore surprised me. "I understand you are Helen, from Laconia," she said, not unkindly. "Do you mind telling me how you happen to be here?" I began slowly, but soon words tumbled from me. We sat together on a bench and I went on about the festival, the footrace, my mother and her proclamation that I was to be Queen, and the initiation at the temple. I told Lady Aethra about the theft of the effigy and my hasty flight to rescue it and about the poisoned food and my anger and how Theseus brought me here.

The wise eyes of Lady Aethra filled with sympathy, and she nodded her head for me to continue. I spoke again and told her how I had fallen into the arms of her son and into bed with him as soon as we arrived this morning.

"And what do you think of that?" she asked.

"It was the will of the Goddess," I said. "It must have been," I added uncertainly.

Lady Aethra did not comment on any of the things I had said. She asked another question. "And the effigy you rescued. Where is it now?"

I stood and went to the shelf where I had placed it. I removed the cloth for her to see. She drew in her breath and spoke with reverence in her voice. "It is very ancient and very holy."

She bent her head, and we stood together for many breaths, quiet before the figure. I felt a peace flood into me, and I, too, received the blessing of the Goddess. When I heard the sweet notes of an evening thrush, I looked up to see Lady Aethra studying me quietly.

When she caught my glance, she took my arm and led me back to the bench. "I must tell you something," she said. "When I was a girl, I, too, was a high priestess to the Goddess, and throughout my life I have been loyal to her, partaking in the rituals and ceremonies and doing my part, even though in both the house of my father—and that of my son—the sky gods are put before her. But lately I have come to a renewed understanding."

"What do you mean?"

"Let us go out into the garden, where I will try to explain my thoughts to you. It is lovely in the garden this time of day."

Lani held the door for us, and Pindros who was outside followed at a discreet distance. We sat near a pool, and I breathed in deeply the blossom scented air.

"Oh, this is exquisite," I said.

"My dear girl, your beauty puts the garden in shadow."

I had heard such polite words before, but my beauty or lack of it had little importance for me.

"Do you think you could be happy here, Helen?"

"I certainly did not believe it possible this morning." I answered. "But I feel at ease here with you."

"And my son?" she asked. I fear I blushed for the memory of my intimacies with her son. I had learned from the priestesses in the temple that rituals of copulation are natural and should be enjoyed, yet I cast my eyes down when Aethra mentioned Theseus. "He brought me wonderful pleasure," I told her. "Though I had not intended to leave my maidenhood quite so soon."

"Did he force you?" she asked solemnly.

I shook my head no.

She took my hand. "I think your presence here may be indeed the will of the Goddess," she said. "Helen, let us be friends."

"Yes," I agreed. "I feel we are already friends."

"Helen," Aethra spoke again. "I started to tell you—inside."

"Yes?" I prompted. I was curious about her thoughts.

"I have come to new understandings. I had always thought that one deity was as important as another. But, as I've grown old, I've seen too much cruelty and ruin come about through the jealousies of the sky gods who are ruled by the thunderbolt of Zeus. The Goddess stands for creation, and the sky gods stand for destruction." She hesitated, looking at me to see if I followed her.

I nodded my head, comprehending her words but not all the meaning.

"We are losing her," Lady Aethra continued. "Gradually we are losing her. Over the years she has become incidental. In most places it is only traditional observance that remains. When the old women in the sanctuaries die, no one will be alive to carry on." She stopped, looking at me again, seeking my response.

"But what does she mean to you?" I asked.

Aethra turned and stood silently before finally speaking. "She means a way for people to live in harmony. She represents a cycle of birth, life, death, and then always, birth again. What she means is too important to let go."

I quietly waited for her to continue.

"Helen," she said. "She is the Earth Mother. She is nature itself. She is the protector of the miracle of creation. The ancients understood it this way. We must no longer sit by while she is replaced with violence and destruction."

I was astounded at her vehemence. What she said made sense. "I do see what you mean," I answered.

"I knew you would. Any girl who would risk her life for the Goddess would understand."

I had never considered before that one could change or direct the nature of things. It was not one's destiny to do so. Or was it one's destiny to do so? Her words were perplexing, but her sincerity was moving. I wished to think about all she said and talk to her again.

The next day Pindros told me Theseus had gone off to meet with his northern leaders who threatened his kingship. No message had been left for me other than a small box which Pindros handed me. It contained a gold amulet with an owl incised on it. It was lovely and very old, and I wore it on a cord around my neck. I liked the feel of it next to my skin, and its touch reminded me of the touch of Theseus.

As the days passed, I went to the playing fields, and my body soon became supple and strong again. I raced with other girls and fell into casual banter with them and the men as we came together in our exercise.

Through Pindros my knowledge of healing became useful. He took me to a house at the edge of the city where a child and its shy mother lived together with other mothers and children. A baby moaned on a pallet in the shade of an arching pine. I knelt next to him speaking quietly while I folded back the light cover and saw his inflamed knee filled with a poison that would kill him soon enough. I called for the broad-toothed leaf of the elecamp flower and prepared a compress with boiling water. We changed it often and the little boy recovered. The child's mother thanked me with tears in her eyes.

"The Goddess has blessed your child," I said.

After this I was sometimes asked for advice at the running course for a pulled muscle or other athletic injury. And so it was that my advice was sought by a young man, Acamus, who had a breathing problem. I found him gasping for breath and helped him relax. He told me he had suffered with this condition since he was a child, and that it always came upon him suddenly.

His ailment reminded me of an illness endured by Penelope. Mother Leda had helped her by preparing a mixture of thyme oil and the flower of ephedra, but we could not find the plant here. An infusion of luvege seeds with hot water proved to be pleasant to taste, at least, and he drank it regularly.

Much to my surprise, I learned that he was the son of Theseus, and that he also lived in the palace. He came often to see me, and we became friends. He told me many stories about his father and about his older brother Hippolytus. Acamus was still so grieved at the death of Hippolytus that he could not speak easily about him.

I liked having a friend my own age, and when we exercised together, I teased him as I would my brothers. At first he was put off with my mischief but soon returned it in kind. We often ate with Lady Aethra at tables placed in the garden. The three of us made a happy trio with our jokes and lighthearted conversation. It eased the anguish of missing my home.

In quieter moments Acamus spoke freely before Lady Aethra, and she concurred with him that Hippolytus had been a remarkable young man. He reminded me of my own brothers, intelligent and kind, yet skilled in wrestling, the javelin, the chariot, and all ways of battle. He would have been the perfect king, but now he was dead. I could truly understand how Acamus must feel the disappointment of his father. The son who would be the perfect king, gone, and the remaining one, sickly and weak.

I studied Acamus quietly and saw a studious young man with a strong character. He was not a son to be ashamed of. Lady Aethra confided more to me when Acamus was not present. She told me how the mother of Acamus deceived Theseus. She had become obsessed with her step-son, fallen madly in love with him, and when he did not return her advances, she made it appear to Theseus that Hippolytus had ravaged her. The tragedy that followed left raw pain and brutal scars.

Then Lady Aethra said words that took me by surprise.

"I must warn you it would not be wise for the future Queen of Attica to be intimate with the King's son."

I gasped, for my friendship with Acamus was that only. I said as much.

"Helen," she answered, "it is charming that you are natural and unassuming, so lacking in guile. You enchant every place you go and everyone you meet. I would not say this, except that it is important that you be warned about Acamus. Since meeting you, he has grown in self-confidence and health, become manly in a way he never knew before."

"But I have not changed him. He had the possibility of being thus all the time," I protested.

"Yes, I believe so. All I say is that in the process my grandson must not become obsessed by you. He is already deeply affected."

"Our relationship will be that of friends only," I said somewhat coldly. Her words had stung. I had only his well-being at heart. In Laconia I would not be so misunderstood. "Besides," I added, "I have no wish to be Queen here."

"Ah, well, that may be beyond your determination. You are a born Queen. With you as his Queen, the people would believe in Theseus again."

When Theseus returned, Lani chose a beautiful cloth in shades of amber for me to wear. She said that it was the color of my hair, which she had arranged softly around my face, and the pale gold the color of my skin, so smooth after her massage with scented unguents. King Theseus who entered my rooms at twilight was bronzed from his days in the open. He turned as he heard me behind him, and I could see my own happiness reflected in his eyes as we looked at each other. He came to me and put his hands on my shoulders. At once I felt a warmth spread out from the place where his hands touched me to my heart which began to beat faster.

"Helen."

"Yes." I smiled. "How was your journey?" I knew he must be exhausted.

"I will tell you about it." I drew him to a window seat. "Pindros will bring food, if you like. He told me you had not supped as yet."

"Ah, that is a good idea." He sat back and took my hand. His touch again caught my heart beat. "How are you?" he asked. "Still lonely?" He put my fingers to his lips. "I hated to leave you so suddenly. I've thought about you constantly." He regarded me solemnly.

"I have been quite well," I answered, above all aware of the touch of his lips on my fingers. "Your mother and I have become friends. She is wonderfully wise. I know Acamus, too. What a fine lad, Theseus."

His eyebrows rose in surprise. I continued. "The three of us sometimes lunch together." I smiled at him, hoping he would relax a little.

Pindros and Lani entered, set tables for us and served roast fowl and spicy lamb. Some perfectly ripe pears and a fresh goat cheese were placed nearby. Theseus took up one of the gold cups filled with wine already mixed—and sipped. He ate sparingly of the food and talked. "I have been King in Attica for twenty years. My inner sight tells me it is time to step down. But I have no one to take my place now that my son Hippolytus is gone." His eyes clouded as he spoke. He would always yearn for what might have been if Hippolytus had lived. I listened, not mentioning Acamus again. I sipped my wine and tasted the fruit.

He spoke on. "I have had little energy to deal with the unrest in Attica, until now. That is why I went north to consult with Menestheus. It was his grandfather who was deposed by my father. We had constructive talks, and he will be no threat if things go well which they will." Theseus drank from his cup, his eyes now smiling over the brim. "I have renewed energy to rule successfully for a while longer if you will be my Queen. Together we will be splendid."

I looked away quickly. My allegiance had always been to Laconia where I understood the nature of things. All this must have been displayed on my face, for Theseus took my hand again. I clutched his in return. His voice was low, but his gaze was steady.

Pindros had removed the eating tables and lit a torch on the wall. He and Lani had disappeared. My eyes sought the place where the Goddess effigy rested in its niche. I stared as the flickering torchlight shone on its polished black surface and hoped for some thought or message that would help me see my way. I closed my eyes, and the words of Theseus washed over me as though from a distance.

"It is all arranged. The ritual for making you Queen, for marrying you, will happen in two days time. We will have a glorious ceremony. All the counselors have approved. They tell me you are already beloved by the folk. You have only to walk among them and people are won over by your gentle manner."

I remained as I was with my eyes closed. I had done nothing special. I scarcely knew the counselors. I opened my eyes, seeking the Goddess figure, which shone in the flares from the torch, no sudden insight or message revealed itself, and I realized I had no choice. I had no alternative but to do what Theseus wished. I was his prisoner. It was my destiny to do as he wished. But if I were to be Queen here, I would do my best. If the counselors thought I could be a good Queen without even trying, what if I put my mind to it?

I sat up and looked at Theseus. His gaze had not left my face. His hands held mine. "I really have no choice," I said.

"It will not be right unless you want it."

"If this is my destiny, I will accept it."

He breathed deeply, and a reflection from the torch danced in his eyes. He put his hands on my face, cradling it so that he could look at me carefully in the flickering light, and kissed me gently on the mouth. My lips responded to his, and the kiss became deeper. I could not bare to separate from him.

"Will you stay here with me, all through the night?" I whispered.

He drew back to look at me, and he nodded. He turned so that he could see me from every side. He groaned slightly and drew me close again. His hands were hard on my back needing to press me to him. With each movement my breath came faster.

He led me to the bed where he slowly removed my drapery. "I want to look at you without it," he whispered. He slipped off his clothes so that we stood naked in the soft, pulsating light from the torch. I could barely sustain the moment as we regarded each other without touching. Then, as if by some unspoken command, we came together and were directed by a divine passion that brought unimagined bliss.

Later, we talked quietly, then loved slowly, touching, exploring, kissing. Our mating had been sanctified with beauty; the Goddess was surely pleased.

I slept late into the next morning and went to the playing fields as usual. If I needed to be informed about my role in the coming celebration, I would be told somehow.

I donned the light shift Athenian girls wore for exercise, and ran hard. As I finished the last length, I saw Acamus at the side of the track. He beckoned to me, and when I joined him, I could see that he was worried.

"What is it?" I asked. "What has happened?"

"It is you who must tell me," he said. "Is it really true?."

I understood. He had heard about my becoming Queen. "Yes, it is true," I said. "I am to become Queen of Attica. Your father has decreed it."

His face took on the gloom of an approaching storm. "No, I will not have it," he said in a childish tone.

"Neither you nor I can do a thing about it. Just accept it. I have."

"It is not fair," he said, as though such things were ever fair.

"Perhaps I may do well at being Queen. Your father seems to think it is important."

"But, you, a Queen. You are so young."

I understood that he had never foreseen any possibility of such a thing. He really was such a boy. "Acamus, you must realize that I am here against my will. Did it not occur to you that I did not come here from choice? I have little to say about what happens to me. If I had stayed at home in Laconia, I would eventually have been a Queen there. You have never thought about who I am or what I'm doing here? Come along." I spoke in a gentle voice. "Now that you are in better health, you will be able to think of others more often, and not concentrate on your own problems to the exclusion of all else." I laughed a little to make my words light, but I hoped he had heard me. "Let us race. I'll beat you out and back."

I was tired from having just run the course, and he beat me by a length or two. He chortled gleefully and messed up my mop of hair as though he were petting his hound. Glad he was back to his usual self, I poked him in the ribs at just the place I knew would make him squawk, which he did. I ran off from him to join Lady Aethra whom I saw in the watching stand.

Before I could get my breath, she spoke. "I warned you about Acamus, Helen. Theseus was here with me, and we both saw the two of you. Whatever possessed you?"

Alarmed, I looked around and saw King Theseus just leaving. Someone had stopped him at the gate and detained him.

"Pindros," I called. The servant, standing to one side, came to me. "Please call your master." With a look on his face that said it was hopeless, he went after Theseus.

"Lady Aethra," I said. "Acamus and I were playing as I always did with my brothers."

I saw Pindros speak to Theseus. I breathed a sigh of relief when they both turned to come back to me.

I looked at Theseus as he approached. He was handsome, unsmilingly handsome. His stony eyes slid by me, their blue, cold and frozen.

I smiled at him anyway. I took his hands and drew him apart from the others, which was a brazen act in public. I decided to be direct. I saw little point in playing games.

"Theseus," I said. "Lady Aethra has tried to tell me that my friendship with Acamus might disturb you. I truly regret that I was so callous as to treat him as I would one of my brothers. I did not think how it might appear to you. I fear it is my nature to be thus, but please do not misunderstand it. I will try to curb such childish frolicking."

He looked at me, his eyes full of hurt. "Yes," he said. "I must consider that you are little more than a child." He paused. "Though it is indeed hard to remember, after..." His voice was hoarse, and he could not complete his thought, but I knew what he meant.

"The person you know so well," I spoke softly, "that person from our nights together," my eyes rose to meet his remembering our loving, "that is who I am."

We joined Acamus and Lady Aethra, and Theseus put his hand on the shoulder of his son and spoke to him. "I am glad to hear you are feeling stronger, Acamus."

The brown eyes of Acamus changed from hooded self-defense to bright response. "Yes, Father," he said. He looked directly at Theseus and stood straight.

"You and Helen have become friends," Theseus said. He was prevented from saying more, for at that moment he was interrupted by Pindros.

"A messenger, sir. He insists on speaking to you. Do you wish to see him?"

"Yes, of course," Theseus answered while beckoning the man to come forward.

Dusty from travel, the messenger rushed up to Theseus and knelt on one knee.

"Stand up and tell us what is so important," Theseus said to him.

The soldier stood and spoke: "An army is coming, sir. An army from Laconia. The Dioscuri are leading an army, here."

I felt dizzy. The words stunned me. I clutched Lady Aethra's arm, and she led me to a bench. She sat with me while I tried to make sense of this news. They did care. The Dioscuri, my brothers, were coming to get me. Happiness must have radiated from my face, for I was thrilled by the news. But to leave Theseus...

Theseus thought for a moment then spoke: "I will confer with the generals and go out to meet the approaching army. A parley might forestall a battle."

I could not help thinking that a parley should have been undertaken long ago. My brothers would think it too late for talk now.

"I will go with you," I said. "If they see me with you, they will understand that I am honored here. That will ease their anger. If we are seen together talks can be productive. I know my brothers well."

Theseus looked hard at me, and I could see that he noticed the animation in my face and eyes. Did he expect I should be sad to have my brothers come to rescue me, that I should, above all things, have made myself so at peace here in Athens that I would not want to see my brothers and return with them? Today I had a choice. Last night I had none. But...to leave Theseus. A terrible sadness overwhelmed me at the thought.

King Theseus nodded to Pindros, then turned to me. "For now, wait in your rooms. I will let you know what has been decided." He looked at his mother. "Stay with her, Mother." He beckoned to Acamus, and the two followed the soldier out.

Filled with foreboding, I watched them go. At the gate Theseus turned and looked back at us. I admired his bearing; I cared for him. Our eyes caught and held. Even at this distance I could see their astounding color. I stood with my lips slightly parted, wanting to call something, but no words came. He smiled a little, and a familiar expression came over his face, one of teasing and affection combined. Tears came to my eyes. Why would tears come to my eyes? I felt as though I would never see him again. I forced a smile and nodded my head a little, and he gave a sort of half salute before he turned and was gone.

APHIDNAE

I waited in vain for King Theseus to take me to Castor and Polydeuces. I raged in anger, detained in my rooms, until I was forced to leave Athens under guard without seeing my brothers. Lani, Pindros and Lady Aethra accompanied me.

On the trail north through high and rugged mountains I was constantly watched, but even so, I slipped away one night with the sacred effigy held close to me. Though I had outwitted the guards, I was stopped by a precipitous canyon impossible to descend. The guards found me broken in spirit and took me to my prison not far away.

The Fortress of Aphidnae was a forbidding bastion where King Aphidnus, a gentle old man, was my unlikely jailer. The fortress was one with the desolate mountains where my brothers could not find me.

Lady Aethra had been sent as my companion, and I cherished her company. Pindros and Lani became more my friends than my servants. Pindros' brusque manner and gravel voice masked a gentle heart, and Lani, her years scarcely more than mine, had knowledge of people and practical matters that was ageless. She cared for me as she did in Athens, although Aphidnae was a rustic place without luxuries.

I bathed in a swift mountain stream, not a tile tub filled from ewers of hot water. It was amid the boulders in the cold rushing waters that Lani first noticed my changing body.

"Helen, you must be with child," she exclaimed. "Your breasts—they seem to be swollen."

Her words had not surprised me. My breasts, enlarged, were extremely tender. Lani would know. I did not want to be with child. Tired and depressed, an additional darkness settled upon me.

"I suppose you are right, Lani," I answered. I remembered earlier talks with temple priestesses about procreation. Then, I had assumed, I would be filled with happiness on learning such news. I felt miserable. To be a prisoner in this desolate place and to be pregnant with no future. Why this, Great Mother?

I remembered Theseus the last time I had seen him. I remembered his boyish saucy salute. He believed that the delegation from Laconia was only a bothersome interruption. But word had trickled through to us of a battle amid much devastation. I wondered and waited, fretful and uncomfortable.

Lady Aethra and I spent long hours exploring mountain trails, but always with Pindros and one of the King's guards at hand. I wondered what she would say when I told her I was pregnant.

The mother of Theseus smiled an inscrutable smile. "How can I be surprised, Helen, when I know how you and Theseus were drawn to each other. The Goddess captivated you. She wanted this child." We sat on some mossy rocks near the roaring current. I spread bread crumbs for two inquisitive mountain jays.

"How do you feel?" she asked. "Are you content with this news?"

I looked at my still slim belly and sighed. "I have accepted the will of the Goddess," I answered, "but I feel only hopelessness."

"It will be a girl," she said. "The Goddess has arranged it that way." Her clear eyes gazed beyond me as though she saw something marvelous in the distance. "This child will be the beginning of a new way."

"How can this one simple life inside me have such import?" I asked, incredulous. She seemed to be carried away with her vision.

"Helen, your child, my grandchild, will bring light into the world of darkness that has descended over us. This birth will inspire people to follow Her ways again."

Aethra's words contrasted so to my feelings that they sounded humorous, but Lady Aethra did not make jokes. Often an aura surrounded her that was almost palpable. Seconds, minutes, time passed as we sat together, watching the birds and squirrels play in the trees.

Pindros' step cracked a twig and shuffled some leaves. "It is growing dark," he reminded us.

"Yes," Lady Aethra said, "we must return." She smiled as she took my hand and drew me up. "Another grandchild, and a girl. You make me very happy, my dear." We returned to the fortress.

Lady Aethra and I shared food with old King Aphidnus every evening. "I prefer to be up here in the heights where the hawks soar and the wind moans," he told us as we sat around the fire pit after our meal. His eyes blazed in the flickering light with his youthful memories, but his wispy beard and gnarled fingers signaled his frailty. He recounted tales of his hunting prowess as a young man and assured us that the wild bear and boar still roamed the mountain forests.

A bearskin rug in my chamber was stark evidence of an enormous beast with lethal claws and great sharp teeth, and one afternoon I saw a magnificent lumbering mother bear fishing in the stream with her clever offspring. It was then I decided never to attempt to walk away from the fortress.

As the weeks went by we took up hand work to fill the hours. Some colored threads and fabric were sent up from the town below, and Pindros repaired a loom he found propped against the wall of an abandoned store-room. Wool from the sheep that grazed the rocky heights above the forest was abundant. Whoever had idle hands helped comb the wool and twist it into thread on a spindle. None of us were expert, but soon we became proficient, and Lani sewed the woven lengths into cloaks that would keep us warm through the winter. On mine Lady Aethra embroidered a handsome pattern of leaves and vines in green and blue around the shoulders.

As we worked together, Lady Aethra talked of her dreams of a return to life under the Goddess. While listening to her, I thought about home and realized that most of the folk in Laconia practiced Goddess ways.

My mother officiated at rituals, cared for the sick, walked with her priestesses in the fields, loved the children and spread peace and beauty in her way. At mating rituals she had gone out into the bands of men where one among them was selected for copulation, and one among them was my father. One of the swan men was my father, not King Tyndareus. The story that Zeus appeared in the form of a swan and mated with my mother was face-saving for King Tyndareus; to have the chief sky god take over his father-function enhanced it. But it was a story. In fact Tyndareus was unable to secure either his fatherhood or his Kingship without my mother. Through talks with Lady Aethra, I grew to understand more and more about the forces behind the actions of kings.

Mother Leda had passed on to me, as future Queen, the powers of procreation and fecundity. And the Goddess had blessed me in mating. As future Queen in Laconia, the continuation of Goddess worship was up to me. I shivered as a gust of cold air found its way through the stony chinks of the castle wall.

Autumn turned into winter. The fires could not keep the fortress warm as gales whipped around and through the stone walls. When the weather cleared, we roamed outdoors in the meager warmth of the winter sun, but after a day or two the wind and rain commenced again. Pindros developed a hacking cough, and I took to my bed with chills and fever.

The figure of the Goddess rested on a corner stand in my chamber. The polished wood gleamed in the scanty light from the window slits, and when it grew dark the wall torches created undulating shadows that seemed to take the form of a great figure standing over me. I felt warm and protected, and I drifted off to sleep.

I dreamed of Mother Leda. As her face came close, her eyes brimmed with tears. I felt her presence, and I was a child again. She stroked my hair and hummed a tune. A great white light held us together, but gradually it grew darker. I watched as the light and Mother Leda disappeared, sailing away into the blackness.

A loud clamor, the noise of many voices awakened me. Darkness hung over my chamber and my head ached with fever. I heard a stomping on the stairs, a pounding on my door, and a great scuffling as it swung open. Heavy clad feet—an onrush of outdoors. Lani, nearby, held a taper, and I could see from its weak light the fear in her eyes. A terror filled me as two huge men, their cloaks swinging, the metal of their swords and scabbards clanging, moved towards me. Immobile with alarm, I could do nothing.

Even when I could see their faces, even when they knelt next to my bed, even when they spoke in familiar voices, the fear continued. I trembled with cold, and then I felt the warm touch of a hand as it grasped mine. Hope swept through me, and still I hardly realized. My body reacted before my mind, so disoriented was I.

My brothers—my brothers had come for me.

After my first joy at their arrival, we talked for as long as my strength would allow. I told them everything that I could think of about my time away. My words came so fast, and my thoughts were so muddled, they did not at once get a coherent picture of my experience in the wilds and of my time in Athens. But it was clear they had understood that I was with child.

"Helen," Polydeuces had said, sitting quietly next to my bed the afternoon after their sudden nighttime appearance.

I stirred at the familiar voice and smiled at him through a feverish haze. I felt his hand atop the rough blanket that covered me. He affectionately rubbed my shoulder then felt the bulge of my belly, impossible to ignore.

"What have we here?" he growled. The familiar distress at my pregnancy rushed through me. It was only when I felt well that I could happily anticipate the coming birth. Tears came easily with my sickness so that it was difficult to keep my voice from trembling. "It was the Goddess," I said. "She must have been happy that I rescued her sacred form and blessed me with child."

"I see," he said, taking my hand in both of his. "I see," he repeated. "Tell me more."

"She filled me with such a power, Polydeuces. We mated, Theseus and I. It pleasured us—we could not get enough of each other—and she blessed us—or me—I guess," I said, realizing that Theseus must be miserable, wherever he was.

"He told us that you were to be his Queen. Did you want that, Helen?"

"I thought my destiny was to be as it was for our sister in Mycenae, to be Queen of a strange country. I could have done it."

Polydeuces nodded. "Brother," I added. "My mating with King Theseus had nothing to do with becoming Queen or not becoming Queen. It was something between us, only."

"And The Goddess?" he asked.

"Oh, yes—the Goddess," I agreed.

When Castor came to see me he felt my belly and took my pulse and looked carefully at my skin and my eyes.

"My sister," he said, "you will have your child in about three lunar months."

"Yes," I agreed.

"But, you are weak, right now."

"Being a prisoner, even with nice old Aphidnus, is hard." I said.

Castor sat back thinking, one finger at the side of his mouth, his hand on his chin. "Helen, you must get well and try to regain some strength, for we want to take you down the mountain and away from here." He smiled to encourage me.

"Will we go home?"

"As soon as we can."

"How is Mother Leda? What happened after I left?"

Castor brushed back his burnished curly hair from his forehead. "It took too long to find out where you were, and it took too long to persuade Tyndareus that we should come after you."

"What changed his mind? And you haven't told me about Mother."

Castor never really answered my question. Instead he told me how they had defeated Theseus in a battle on the plains of Attica. They had been welcomed into Athens and installed Menestheus as King; it was my friend Acamus, the son of Theseus, who told them where I was.

"Was it a terrible battle? Were many injured?" I found it difficult to accept that men died because of me.

"It was bad enough, but I must admit, King Theseus did not have a warrior's temperament. He did not savor fighting as of yore."

"What happened to him?" I asked, my voice low as I smoothed the cover.

"He went away. Some said to an island where he has a house."

I put my head back against the pillow and closed my eyes, suddenly very tired.

"Helen, I will talk to your servant and to Lady Aethra and to King Aphidnus. We must all work to make you strong, for we will want to leave as soon as possible."

"Yes, I do want to leave," I whispered.

"Acamus, what a nice lad. He told us what good friends you were."

I nodded my head. Yes, Acamus and I were good friends. Castor quietly left the chamber.

I tried to visualize King Theseus, but I could not. Again tears rolled down my cheeks; no one could see them, and I was too tired to brush them away.

It took many days for me to become stronger, but even then I had little staying power and wore right down to exhaustion in no time. The morning, still and cold, boded well for our leaving. The ground would be hard under foot, easy walking over the usually mucky places. Only a handful of retainers, the usual winter guard, would be left behind in the fort. My brothers and their soldiers would lead us down the mountain to Aphidnae Town below. Menestheus ruled Athens, and Theseus had been banished.

Weakened by illness, I rode wrapped in my warm cloak with a bearskin over my knees. I sat in a basket chair strapped to a donkey's back. I wobbled about, lurching this way and that, thankful for the straps that held me in but hanging on for dear mercy. Lady Aethra also rode aback an ass just behind me. We understood that these surefooted mountain beasts were far safer for a steep track than the temperamental chargers of the horse-soldiers. Lani walked near me with Pindros who looked pale after his bout with illness.

The trip down the mountain was an agony of discomfort, thrown about as I was with every movement of the stubby footed ass, and it was a rare moment when the child within me paused to rest; it kicked and turned about most of the time. Everyone showed such concern for me I felt it rude to complain.

We stopped often, and at noon we shared a meal in a cypress forest. We sat on our cloaks on a carpet of pine needles and could see out across a great gulf far below. The sun filtered through high branches and a brook gurgled nearby.

I leaned against some bundles Pindros arranged for me and sipped fresh water from a clay cup. I closed my eyes and listened to the talk of others. I knew I needed to eat for strength, but it took so much strength to eat.

"I am honored to have you as my guests," Aphidnus said. "My family will welcome you into our town, and we will be happy to have you stay for as long as you wish. The bear men will arrange some games of sport."

My brothers liked King Aphidnus. He had done his duty honorably and was as happy as we were to give up being a jailer.

"We would enjoy some contests," Castor answered.

"Do you keep bears in the village?" Polydeuces asked.

"No, no," Aphidnus answered. "With us the bear is the glory of the forest. We do not often kill him for he is our symbol; we take care of him. Except for the festival sacrifice in the early spring, we kill only the old ones for their skins and sometimes for the meat."

I opened my eyes to see Pindros crouching next to me with some food.

"Here, Lady Helen, you must eat." He winked both eyes and made me smile.

I took the offered dish and tasted a gruel of grain and honey. I ate more to please him.

"Pindros, you must be weak from illness, too."

"I am stronger each day. I wish I were strong enough to carry you. Riding on that ass cannot be either comfortable or good for you."

"No," I answered, "but we will be down soon, will we not?"

"Yes, by late afternoon, I would guess." His rough, deep voice pleased me.

"Pindros," I said. "I have been told that Theseus has gone away, to an island. Do you know where it might be — an island where he has a home?"

"He has several, but it might be Skyros which is just over the sea across the isthmus." He stood and pointed out across the water.

"How close he might be," I whispered, for I was surprised. "Pindros," I said, excited by an idea that came to me. "You could go to him. You do not need to guard me any more. Would it be difficult to find passage to Skyros?"

Pindros considered my words. "It's true you don't need guarding any longer, but you know, I still feel I should be at hand to take care of you." He laughed from deep in his throat. "Ridiculous of me, isn't it, when you have these strapping brothers and their soldiers to look to your needs?"

"No one could be kinder or help me more than you have, Pindros, even my brothers, but I feel King Theseus needs you. He told me you had his interests at heart. If that is the case, I think you should go to him."

Pindros helped me up as the group reorganized to continue on. As he fastened the straps of the awkward basket seat, he paused a moment, looking up at me from under the brim of a hat that shaded his eyes from the bright noon sun. "Madame, if I sometime am not here, do not ask for me or worry about me. You will know where I have gone."

I nodded my head. Then, in a sudden afterthought I hurriedly untied the cord around my neck. "Here, Pindros." I handed him the little gold amulet incised with the form of an owl. "Give this to Theseus." He took it and put it inside his pouch, nodding in understanding.

We waited in Aphidnae Town for a propitious time to depart by sea. I made friends with Macaria, the priestess daughter of old Aphidnus.

I slept in a small dark hut, and early one morning something strange awakened me. My head was still fuzzy with sleep, but I could hear a heavy breathing, a licking, a nosing and chewing, something large, colossal. My heart pumped madly. I could not move even a finger or shout or whisper. My eyes, fixed on the black shadows in the corner, widened in disbelief as it began to move out of the blackness. Swaying with a heavy-footed lumbering, it came towards me. An odor of wild, dank moss surrounded me as the giant head of a beast bent down to me, sniffed and grunted. Stupefied with shock, I looked into its dull beady eyes, smelled its hot rancid breath, and felt its rough tongue on my cheek. Its long fur brushed across my face, and I was engulfed.

The great bear stepped over me and ambled out through the passage into the early daylight.

Almost at once figures rushed into my sleeping room. Macaria, the daughter of Aphidnus, knelt next to my bed, and Lani's voice called from behind a group of temple priestesses crowding in front of her. "Helen, are you all right?"

"Don't worry, Lani. I'm fine," I answered.

Macaria grasped my arm. "Oh, Helen, this has not happened for a long time. We watched it from outside. The great bear mother has blessed us. You have received the holy gift."

Still confused, I could make no sense of the words of the daughter of Aphidnus.

"Helen," Macaria went on, "today is the beginning of the spring festival. Not only did the mother bear come into the village and the temple room, she ate the honey-covered nuts, and most important of all, she stepped over you."

The golden light of dawn seeped through the doorway. It brought warmth, and my confusion was departing with the mother bear out into the spring day. I sat up and brushed the hair out of my eyes. My movements were awkward for my time was near, within the next few weeks we predicted.

"Macaria," I said, "have you any idea how it was for me? You should have warned me of this ritual. It was an enormous step, wasn't it," I said, looking at the great rise of belly before me.

Macaria smiled happily. Her flashing brown eyes were impossible to resist. "It's been so long. No one here can remember," she said. "I could have told you stories, of course, of the great bear mother actually stepping over a pregnant woman, but it did not seem worth alarming you."

"Well, what does it actually mean?" I asked.

Her serious tone sounded like a proclamation. "Here, among the bear people, it is the most splendid omen hoped for by every pregnant woman. The great she-bear knows. She has blessed you by stepping over you. You will produce a wonder child. She smells it."

The Goddess image rested on a flat white rock inside the temple garden. A thatch hut protected her from the wind and the rain and the sun, and a fire burned constantly before her while serpents lay coiled in a basket nearby.

An old seer groped randomly into the basket, choosing the serpent which came to hand. She held it up to the Goddess image and stroked it, asking important questions. Sometimes the snake licked her eyelids.

Lady Aethra, Castor and I sat with others watching the ritual. Polydeuces had gone to Laconia weeks ago and was expected back at any time. The garden, warm with the sun, was protected from the sea breeze by a tall hedge sprouting green shoots.

The venerable seer placed the serpent on the clearing as she had done every day of good weather since our arrival. So little had yet been revealed by the convoluted sensuous rhythms of the reptile about our future plans, that I was surprised when the old one's incantations took on a tone of importance. Of course it was the festival day, that was why she stood and made some signs and prayers, but her words were different.

She spoke in her old quivering voice and told us that we must leave. The ship, prepared for departure as it had been for so long, would take us by sea to our destination in less than two days. The omens were perfect. We must depart Aphidnae and our friends before another day had passed.

The virgin priestesses wearing bear masks danced around the circle with lumbering movements. One of them had been selected to go with other priestesses from coastal shrines to the ancient temple in Troy across the sea. Macaria had returned from her time in Troy two years past, and she was the last one chosen from here. It was for their departure as well as ours that the words of the venerable seer held meaning.

After I danced, more bear-like than anyone in my bulky state, I joined Lady Aethra and King Aphidnus.

"You are beauty to behold," Aphidnus said. "Nothing is quite so charming as a young woman in the last stages before birth-giving."

"And I feel well," I answered. "I enjoy being with you and your family. It is much nicer to be a guest than a prisoner." I liked the old man.

"We'll be desolate when you leave. I think you must stay for the birth of the child, even though the old one says it is safe to leave." He took my hand. I liked the feel of his thin hand and covered it with my other one in affection.

Lady Aethra spoke: "And you have little time, now."

"No, not long. I would happily wait here for the birth of my child. A sea voyage, even in good weather, does not appeal to me."

"Yes," Aphidnus said, "You must stay. And, besides, you can not leave before Polydeuces returns, now can you? You see? You must stay here."

His insistence pleased me, and I was quite willing to yield to his reasoning. I felt again the flood of happiness and well-being that seemed to be part of me these days.

Sometime later in the afternoon, when we had gathered at the cooking fire where the succulent carcass of a young bear rotated on a spit, and crocks of fish and grain cooked in the coals, Polydeuces and his party stirred up a commotion as their horses galloped into the village.

I hung back from those who rushed to welcome the arrivals, for I sensed something was wrong, very wrong. A darkness began in me, and soon I learned the reason why.

Polydeuces, dusty from the journey, looked over the assembled group. Castor had taken his horse's bridle, and my brothers exchanged quiet words. The eyes of Polydeuces passed over all the anxious faces until they found mine. His unfathomable look was devoid of humor or affection. He came to me and put his arms around me. I rested in his embrace and waited for his words.

"Mother Leda is dead."

The blackness came down upon me. He held me tightly. "What happened? Why, why?" I whispered hoarsely, clutching him.

He held me to him and spoke into my ear, his voice deep, nearly a whisper. "She had been very ill. Ever since you left, she had worried and been upset. I thought news that you were well would help. She died gratified that you were coming home."

"Why did you not tell me? I should have known." I pounded my fists against his chest.

He took my hands in his and held them tight. "You were too ill to be told."

I noticed the strain on his face and realized he had ridden hard for many days to get to us without delay. I pulled away from him and put my hands over my face. "I am sorry," I mumbled, "you did all you could."

Castor joined us, and we three went off to be together. We decided to follow the advice of the seer. Our ship left that night for a Laconian harbor a few days land journey from the Amyklaeon palace. I was now the Queen.

MIRACLE IN THE ARGOLID

I sat in the open with the oarsmen throughout the night mourning Mother Leda. Their dipping and stroking set up a cadence in the calm waters as we moved slowly southward. I rested against bundles strapped to the vessel's side, and when the half moon set, I sang a lament. My brothers' deep voices united with mine, and soon one sailor and then another joined in as we glided along under bright stars. Sadness was lifted from my spirit and the singing filled me with hope. At first light I wrapped my warm cloak close about me and looked upon the rowers still at their task. Their faces shone with a haloed glow.

We rounded Cape Sounion at dawn. Captain Thaos stood in the stern black bearded, young and strong. The rising sunlight outlined his form as he bowed before the high promontory in obeisance to the God of the seas. Bread was cast upon the waves, and I felt the power of Lord Poseidon as the oars were stowed the sail filled and the ship headed into an immense, empty silver gray expanse.

With the aid of my brothers, I joined Lady Aethra and Lani who, wrapped in furs, rested on wooden pallet berths under a tent-like shelter enclosed with skins at the back. Lulled by the gentle motion of the ship, I slept most of the day.

Late in the afternoon I was rolled about in discomfort. I awoke and saw, in the last of the daylight, that Lani had been sea-sick and that water had splashed into our sheltered space. I pulled myself up and, with my cloak about me, looked through a slit where the skins of our tent did not quite come together.

Spray blew across the bow, and wind moaned in the rigging. I watched in alarm as each rower, the captain, my brothers and their retainers all helped pull the great oars.

I opened the flap to see better, and the wind caught my hair with great soaking dollops of spray. I quickly drew my cloak to me and clung to a hull strut for balance. Castor noticed me and called between breaths.

"The wind—changed—coming from the south—we'll be blown—rocky shoal—trying to make—sea room—stay inside."

His powerful arms synchronized with those of the sailor next to him. The waves churned up foam as they slapped against the valiant little ship. Even I, who had little experience at sea, could feel the wind grow stronger as I watched.

I ducked my head down and pulled the flap shut. In the dimming light I saw Lani retch in misery, too weak to hold herself down. On hands and knees I crawled to her, taking great care to keep myself from being thrown about. I managed to tie her shawl around her and to the wooden pallet, then covered her with furs.

"Lani, are you all right?" I asked, my voice loud. It had grown darker, and I could no longer see her, but she uttered a low mournful sound in response.

I went to Lady Aethra. "Come, Helen," she said. "Climb up here with me." I grabbed for the covers from my pallet bed and we clung together wadded in the furs. The wind moaned, and water sprayed into our place with every lurch and pounding of the ship. The sound of the great oars was no longer part of the creaking, banging din.

Sometime later the tent flap opened. Polydeuces climbed into our space and crouched down next to me. It was too dark to see him, but his voice was raspy with fatigue. "We are carried along by the wind and sea," he said, breathing hard. Wetness from his clothes squeezed out as I held on to him. "We made it well past the reefs, thanks to the strong oarsmen and Lord Poseidon," he said. "By dawn we should be able to see where we will land. We may even be able to choose the place, more or less."

He leaned against our pallet bunk, exhausted. "Helen, how are you?"

"I am well, but Lani is sick. I tied her to the bed. Lady Aethra and I are together here."

"You mustn't worry about us," Lady Aethra's voice came out of the blackness clearly.

"No, madam," he answered. "If we are lucky, the wind may moderate, for we are heading up into a great bay."

After he had climbed back into the fierce storm, Lady Aethra and I lay in the dark and listened to the loud creaking of the boat, the pounding and clumping of cargo shifting about, and the shouts of the men trying to be heard above the howling wind.

"I think things are easier," Lady Aethra said.

I did not answer her. I was much more concerned with a searing pain that nearly stunned me.

"Oh," I gasped. The pain subsided and drifted away.

"What is it?" Lady Aethra said in alarm.

"A shooting pain, in my belly. There were some twinges earlier, but this was much different, much harder," I answered.

"Tell me if it comes again. Are you otherwise comfortable?"

I tensed in fear, trembling at the realization that my child was to be born. How could I manage it here? Comfortable? she had asked. Tears stung my eyes.

Lady Aethra put her hand on my great stomach and rubbed it gently. "Relax, Helen. It isn't likely to be for some time." Her voice soothed me, but another spasm began, an ache in the small of my back building to an excruciating hurt across my belly. I clung to Lady Aethra's arm. "Breathe deeply, dear, breathe deeply," she counseled. I tried to do as she said, but I panted shallowly in fright.

When the pain subsided, Lady Aethra sat up in the close quarters. The ship's movement did seem easier.

"Now," she said, "before the next one starts, get control of yourself. This baby will be born. We can do nothing to delay it. I will help you."

I hung on to her all important words and kept breathing deeply, but a new pain hit sharply, and I lost the rhythm. In the midst of it all, the tent flap flew open, and Castor entered in a commotion of wet clothes and noise.

"It is the barest beginning of the new day," he shouted, "but we have no choice. We will be beaching the boat within minutes. There may be rocks or some other obstacle. You must be prepared."

"Well, we have no choice, either," Lady Aethra said sharply. "Helen will have her baby, soon. Her pains have started, and they are strong."

With the flap open, snapping back and forth in the wind, Castor was just visible as a shadow that halted suddenly at Aethra's words then turned and called out through the opening, "The baby will be born this day. Find shelter ashore as soon as possible. Find shelter ashore for her."

He came to me and wedged and braced himself on the edge of the pallet berth. He put his arms tightly around me and held me fast. Lady Aethra was pinned against the side of the ship. Suddenly, there was a massive lurching and scraping, an abrupt jolt and sudden stop. Castor's arms kept me from pitching about, but I heard Lady Aethra call out in pain as her head struck hard against something. I had no idea how Lani had fared. I heard a scrambling and pounding outside, and the pain rippled through me, so much pain that I groaned in agony. Castor continued to hold me securely through it.

"Holy Mother, be merciful," he shouted out.

In a muddle of confusion, soaked by the sea water that gushed in through an outright break in the hull, I was manhandled out to the open, somehow passed to Polydeuces and another man standing below knee deep in the surging breakers. I felt stinging grains of sand whip my face as they carried me across the rocks, through brambles, to a fisherman's hut. Behind it was a lean-to, where they set me gently down on a bundle of nets spread out and over-laid with skins and covered me with fur. I could hear the waves continue to pound on the beach like Castor's white-maned mares galloping ashore at regular, unending intervals, just like the pain rolled through me.

Soon, my brothers were with me. A fire crackled outside the lean-to, and a cauldron of water hissed and steamed on it. Lani, looking wan and exhausted, smiled down at me. She wiped the perspiration from my forehead and brushed my hair back. She helped me remove my wet garments and covered me with a fur, warm from the fire. Lady Aethra had also been carried here and lay near me, unconscious from a head injury.

Lani, too weak to help me further, sat by me and instructed Castor and Polydeuces in midwifery. Though skilled in the healing of wounds, they had no experience in attending a human birth. The pains wracked me so that I thought each time I could not endure another. Lani was much relieved when I felt the urge to push. "Helen, this is why you have been working so hard. Do as your body tells you. Push as hard as you can." She wiped my face with a damp cloth. "Sir," she instructed Castor. "it is time to place her in the birthing position."

Castor held me under the arms and pulled me up so that, leaning against him as a support, I sat on my haunches. The pushing pains became powerful, taking over my whole body in the straining. Sweat poured from me. Each effort seemed like the greatest possible. And then there came another, and another. Finally, when I thought I could bear no more, I felt excruciating pressure.

"I can see the head, just a bit," Polydeuces said.

An overwhelming force came over me, and I nearly fainted. I leaned against Castor in exhaustion as I felt the baby's head emerge.

It was thus, on the shores of Argolis Bay, in the midst of a wild south wind, that my child was born. Polydeuces received my daughter as she came into the world. He examined her as she took her first breath and cried out lustily; he held her upside down by her feet, and the blood rushed to her waving arms and bawling face.

Castor helped me lie back down on the skins.

"Be careful, Lani said. The after-birth is still to be born, and the cord of life is attached to the child."

"As beautiful as her mother," Polydeuces said.

"Here," Lani instructed. "Place this linen loosely around the babe; gently put her on her mother's belly."

He did as she said. I could feel a warm little person who, moments ago, had been a part of me inside, was now outside of me, not inches from her former comfortable living place. It felt good to me, and I ached to hold her. She was covered with ooze, her little limbs waved about in random fits and starts, and she wailed loudly with her new voice.

When the birthing tissues appeared, Polydeuces tied the cord of life and cut it.

"Now," Lani said. "The after-birth must be cast into the sea, and the babe will be sure to have a smooth transition from dark to light, from death to life."

Polydeuces found some seaweed to wrap it in and took it away. Lani patted the baby gently with water to clean her, then dried her and anointed her with oils found in our belongings, and finally wrapped her in cloths. The little bundle was handed to me, and I held her close. She stopped crying. I looked into her solemn little face, her blue-gray eyes held mine for a moment, but I knew she did not see me. Her little lips parted in a big yawn, and she went off to sleep. I lay in bliss, holding her quietly, until I, too, drifted to sleep.

I awoke and remembered that a daughter had been born to me. In the slanting light of early evening I thanked the Goddess, whose image had been placed near me. A ceremony for the baby must be offered during any of the five days before the moon was full, which could be now or in the next few days. Then, unable to restrain myself, I sat up, cautiously, to see my child. She nestled in a fisherman's basket at my feet, awake, for her tiny arms were waving.

I looked around the sheltered space within the lean-to and saw that it had been turned into a proper room. The ground had been swept clean, pallets from the ship had been brought here, and I was, in fact, on one. Another was nearby, and a form I recognized as Lady Aethra rested on it. The fire that had been started just outside burned still, for I could see its flame through an opening in the ships sail, which had been draped across the wide unprotected side of the lean-to, leaving a narrow entrance. The wind had subsided, and the gentle sound of lapping waves replaced the wild pounding surf. I stiffly moved to my baby. Tenderly, I picked her up and held her close. I studied her, unwrapping her to see her torso, her arms and legs and fingers and toes. She was complete and wonderful. I held her close and smelled her and put my cheek next to hers and kissed her. She made funny faces with her mouth and began to make little grunts and cries. I carried her back to my bed, climbed under the furs and held her close as I hummed a tune, but she continued to fuss.

"She's hungry, Helen." The weak voice came from Lady Aethra who must have been watching us.

"I hope we did not wake you, Lady Aethra." I was concerned for her head injury. "How do you feel?"

"In truth, I feel a bit dizzy. I shall rest here until I feel better." Her voice faded away, and I looked over to her, but her face was in shadow. She spoke again. "My, but you've done yourself proud, haven't you? What a fine child. I do believe she is hungry, though. Put her to your breast, dear."

"But I have no milk," I said.

"It does not matter; it will come. Her sucking will help."

I opened my shift and held the child close to the tip of my breast. I was astounded for the contact excited her. Her tiny mouth sought something, unknown. As soon as I placed the nipple in her mouth, she quieted and started sucking.

"It's a miracle," I said, beaming at Lady Aethra, so pleased with myself.

"A miracle," she repeated, then was silent.

Evening shadows had begun to fall. I was about to call out to someone, when a figure came through the lean-to entry. It was Lani, she carried a lantern.

"Ah, you are awake, Helen," she said in surprise. "And the baby too." She found a hook in the wall and hung the lantern on it, a soft flickering light fell over us. Lani and I watched the suckling child.

"She's perfect, isn't she?" Lani commented. "And you seem fine, for all you've been through." She put her hand on my forehead and looked carefully at me. "Yes, you are cool to the touch, and your eyes are clear. It is quite remarkable." She laughed a little. "To look at us, one would think I suffered more than you."

"You Lani, you helped me even when you felt so weak. I am glad you are better."

"Yes, I have recovered, but not so Lady Aethra. She is still unconscious. She must have received a very serious blow to the head."

"But," I said, "she spoke just a moment ago."

Lani rushed to the side of Lady Aethra. "Are you awake, Lady?" she said in a loud voice. "How do you feel?" There was no response from Lady Aethra.

"Her eyes are open a bit, and she is moving about," Lani reported. "I wonder if she is in pain. Lady Aethra," she repeated, "wake up, wake up."

Lady Aethra restlessly thrashed about and mumbled. Her voice suddenly rose in pitch and she spoke out clearly: "It's a miracle."

"Oh, poor thing," Lani said. "I'll get her some water." She turned to me. "Would you see Captain Thaos? He is waiting to talk to you. He has a message for you."

"Why, of course. He may come in." Lani left, and almost at once the drapery across the entry was pushed aside, and Captain Thaos stepped in. His manner, at first apologetic, changed when he saw me. I held the child to my breast, still. I realized that the evening had darkened and lantern light illuminated us and probably nothing else. I tried to smile at him, to make him feel easier. He put his hand to his eyes and fell to his knees.

"Captain, you have a message?" I asked.

Eventually, he lifted his head and spoke. "The Goddess is present. I felt a marvelous divine force all through the night. It was with your brothers, who guided us here, and now I see it personified before me." Again, he bent low to the earth.

"Arise, Captain Thaos." I spoke seriously, not wanting to demean his thoughts. "Indeed, the Goddess is present. Her image rests on a standard just near you. She helped us all to pass through this day and last night."

He glanced at the Goddess image; a dull sheen emanated from her form. He looked back at me. "The Goddess presence is before me, and I am much moved. My men felt it when we sang together. They received your touch as a blessing. We felt it when the Dioscuri inspired us to row beyond our strength into the wind around the rocks." His voice was low and full of emotion. His words came slowly, and he cast his eyes down. After a moment, he stood up as I had asked. His gaze of adoration fell upon us, and he bowed his head in the very manner he had done in glorifying Lord Poseidon at Cape Sounion.

I spoke after a few moments of respectful silence. "Captain, I am honored by your esteem. Come, come forth to see the babe. She is sound asleep, now."

He did as I asked and stepped to the side of the pallet bed, the light from the lantern including him in its glow. His dark head and beard contrasted with the whiteness of the light. The baby's head rested against me, the soft curve of her cheek pink from her exertion.

"Have you a message for me?" I asked.

He stepped back a few steps. "Yes. I am to tell you that your brothers are away for several days. They have gone with a small party to the citadel of Mycenae."

"We are that close, are we?" I asked.

"Yes, our landing place was fortuitous, for that purpose anyway. The Dioscuri will return with help so that you can then be taken to your sister in comfort. I have been put in charge of the camp and would like to know how I may serve you."

"Ah, I understand." I paused a moment. "Captain, will you answer my questions? I am very concerned about the men and the ship. Have they food and fresh water? Was the ship destroyed? What of the fisherman whose place this is?"

"The fisherman must live in the village. He has not been seen. As for the ship, it can be repaired, and the men are well enough supplied with food and water."

"Captain, will you continue on to Laconia?" I asked.

"That will depend on your brothers," he answered.

"Well, as for me, I will not mind resting with my sister in the comfort of her house for a time." He did not respond to my thought. "My sister is Queen of Mycenae. I have not seen her since we were children together."

He seemed to relax a little and even chuckled. "Not so long ago at that."

"Why, I am fifteen, now," I replied indignantly, sounding like the child I so recently banished from my soul. "I have completed my virgin year priestess studies. I was made guardian priestess."

"A virgin birth!" His eyes took on a luster. "A miracle," he said.

"No, no," I hurriedly interrupted, annoyed for having said anything about myself. I searched his black eyes and spoke firmly. "This child indeed has a father, a fine man, although I fear she will never know him."

"Ah," he nodded his head. "I understand, but the men may not. The sailors are even now preparing a shrine. They have found a suitable sheltered place on a rise looking out over the bay. The shrine will be dedicated to Potnia, to bless the child and in thanksgiving for the safe haven we have found here."

"How considerate" I said. "It would mean much to me to have my child's naming ceremony there. Will it be ready before the full moon, do you think?"

He smiled. "Ah, that will please the sailors—I'm sure the shrine will be prepared very soon."

Lani returned and went to Aethra's side.

Captain Thaos stood. "I will leave you now." He backed out, his head lowered.

From the darkness where Lady Aethra lay, her croaking mumblings rose in intensity, and her words carried clearly through the dusky evening. "A miracle, a miracle."

With my brothers and her serving boy, my sister came into our camp a few mornings later. We heard the lumbering cart pulled by oxen well in advance of their arrival, time enough for Captain Thaos and me to go out to meet them. Polydeuces and Castor were on horseback; Clytemnestra and her servant rode in the conveyance.

Her sweeping glance flicked over Captain Thaos and me in instant appraisal and settled on the baby. What did she think? I felt years older since leaving home, but I must have appeared to her like an ill-bred girl in my simple tunic with my hair a tangle. The baby nestled in my arms, awake but quiet. My milk had come plentifully, and she had just finished suckling.

Polydeuces helped her down from the cart. Clytemnestra was before us, and I realized we stood eye to eye, although she did not look at me. "Greetings, my sister," I said.

Her hair was black as night, and long coils hung down around her shoulders. She wore gold necklaces and bracelets, and her costume of rich material was tightly belted. Her eyes were lined with cobalt, and the tips of her full breasts, which could be seen through the folds of her drapery, were touched with carmine.

"The hospitality of Mycenae is yours," she answered, regarding me directly, briefly. She turned to Polydeuces at her side. Her voice high and sharp. "We will return at once."

"My sister," I said, "I look forward to resting in your house and being with you, but I must beg you to wait to return until the end of the day." I stopped and looked from one to the other of my brothers and sister. I could not help but smile as I continued.

"We have planned a joyous celebration. The sailors who brought us here have constructed a sanctuary to be dedicated to the Goddess. It is beyond." I turned and indicated the coastal path. "We, here, have all fasted this morning.

Lambs have been sacrificed, and we will feast after celebrating the creation ritual. It is, fortuitously, just the right time, before the full moon." I looked at them, expecting compliance, understanding, even joyful agreement.

My brothers nodded, but my sister looked angry, a deep crease appeared between her brows.

"It will not be possible. I must return."

Oh, no, I thought. I cannot leave until evening, but neither could I spurn the hospitality of my sister. I turned in anguish and found myself facing Captain Thaos who looked on with compassion. He would understand and explain matters to the others, but even so, I could not leave now.

I turned back. When I spoke, my voice was very low. "Death and rebirth. They always go together. Mother Leda, our mother, and my daughter," I said. "Our sailors have done this beautiful thing. They revere my brothers, and they adore the child. The people from the fishing village are inspired by the story of our voyage. They have offered the lambs, and they, too, will come."

I looked up at Clytemnestra, for I knew what I had to do. "I am so sorry." I sought her eyes but did not find them. "I would like to have been with you, but I cannot go away now, after all they have done."

"Clytemnestra," Castor urged. "If you had known, you could have arranged for this. And, think, to have all four of us together to honor Mother Leda. Send the boy back with a message."

My sister looked to Polydeuces for affirmation. He nodded his head. "Very well," she said, tossing her head so that her hair cascaded down her back. She walked off to speak to the boy without another word to me.

The shrine was a simple place in the rocks on a hillside. Clumps of cypress trees that grew out of stony soil sheltered it. Yellow-flowered broom lined the ascending path and purple crocus dotted the land as it fell steeply to the deep turquoise sea.

I had bathed in warm water and scrubbed my hair which was then combed out while still damp. My skin was rubbed with scented oil, my tunic was clean, and over it I wore my long cloak woven in Aphidnae castle and embroidered by Lady Aethra. Lani and Lady Aethra also wore their cloaks, the perfect garment, for we had no other.

Afternoon sunlight flooded into the sanctuary, warming the smooth white rocks. Iris and lilies, cleverly arranged in niches, announced the coming celebration. The mouth-watering scent of roasting meat wafted across the still air.

Lady Aethra, still very weak, would lead us in the ritual, and, at my request, she had chosen a name for my daughter that pleased me well. Iphigeneia meant "inspiring leader," fulfilling Lady Aethra's own foreknowledge for the child.

The white disk of the nearly full moon rose slowly before us in the mellow sky. The fisher-folk and sailors came bringing flowers, shells, Goddess images carved from drift wood, and smooth egg-shaped stones. They settled themselves easily just outside the sanctuary, as did we, inside. The ancient Goddess image rested in the central position. Lady Aethra, leaning on a staff, her voice weak, led us through the dedication to Potnia.

The child, in her basket, had been hidden behind a screen to protect her from death during the devotions to Mother Leda. When lady Aethra sang the notes for the sanctity of the new life, the sailors joined in. I brought the child from behind the screen and placed her on an altar-like rock before the Goddess. Lady Aethra put her staff aside and held up her arms in supplication and spoke of miracles.

I suppose every birth is a miracle. But Lady Aethra could not but mention the hopes she had for my baby girl. Her name, Iphigeneia, was bestowed and blessed, and Lady Aethra made much of its meaning: divine leader of a strong new race. The sailors and the fisher-folk uttered holy sounds and fell to their knees.

The baby was handed around to an awkward young sailor, an aged grandfather, to a wide-eyed village girl. Each took a turn gently examining the tiny fists and soft cheek. Clytemnestra took Iphigeneia from Polydeuces and looked at her for longer moments than most. Suddenly, tears squeezed through my sister's free hand that covered her face, and sobs wracked her body although she did not make a sound. Concerned by her distress, I gently took the child from her. When Lady Aethra moved on to the next prayer, I put the baby to my breast where she settled at once to the nipple and sighed in contentment between sucks. I smiled down at her. The daylight was fading, and the moon had grown silvery in its rise.

CLYTEMNESTRA

The baby slept in Lani's arms as we bumped along in the ox cart. My brothers, on horseback, rode nearby. Clytemnestra sat on the far side, away from me, but in the darkness she spoke, explaining her silent sobs in the shrine.

"When I held the infant in my arms—it seemed for a moment that—she was mine." Clytemnestra's voice quivered. "It is twenty days since my baby died."

"Oh, no," I was shocked.

"Six weeks old. Her breath—irregular. I knew from the first that she could not last."

I felt a terrible grief. "How dreadful for you," I whispered. "The ceremony of new life—I understand." I silently thanked the Goddess that Clytemnestra had one blooming child. "Castor tells me your daughter Electra is a lively girl."

"Oh yes, but..."

"But nothing can replace your baby," I said aloud. I agonized for her and reached out to her in the dark, but she shrugged off my hand.

"The wet nurse has much milk. She still feeds her own little son. Perhaps for Iphigeneia..."

I did not answer. I could not imagine anyone else feeding my baby. "We will be leaving very soon, you know," I said.

"No. You must stay," she insisted. "Wait until Lord Agamemnon returns from Troy. I think his brother will be with him. Menelaus has been across the seas for over two years. They might be offended if you do not wait to greet them. They are expected any day."

I did not know what to say. I felt a desperate need to leave, to flee before I had even arrived.

"He, Agamemnon, he so wanted his own child. He will be grieved," my sister continued.

"But Electra?" I asked, astonished. "Surely...." My sister remained silent, and I could not read her face in the dark.

"No—not his child." Her voice was so low I could barely hear her. "I was pregnant..."

Again she was mute. I explained for her. "I see. Electra is the daughter of your former husband, whom Agamemnon killed." I shuddered at the thought of the murder by Agamemnon.

"...and my small boy," she said after a long silence, in such a low voice I had to strain to hear her.

I seethed in horrified anguish as I visualized the brutal deed: Clytemnestra being dragged off to be queen in Mycenae after the killing of her husband and son.

"Electra was safe in my womb," her voice trailed off.

A distant light shone out of the black night. The great gate of Mycenae ominously appeared in the leaping shadows of huge torches. Licking tongues of fire illumed two lions on either side of a single pillar. Their forelegs were raised, and their heads turned outward watching our approach. Suddenly, I felt a pervasive evil, and the rumored tales of a curse on Mycenae's rulers seemed borne out and frighteningly close at hand. 'The curse on the House of Pelops,' a harper had called it. I remembered one story in vivid detail. Murdered children were served up in a stew to their father at a false reconciliation between Atreus and Thyestes, power-mad brothers. This same Atreus was the grandfather of King Agamemnon.

All of the events in my life, since the impulsive chase to rescue the Goddess image, were nothing compared to passing through the Lion Gate of Mycenae. A palpable sinister force emanated from the huge carved rocks of the massive wall and the awesome guardian beasts.

Other than a sentry guard, we saw no one as we traversed the empty ways in the dark of night. I said goodnight to my sister, and a silent servant showed me to a commodious apartment. Lani brought me my baby to suckle, and then we slept.

I awoke to the hungry squawks of Iphigeneia, and I could see the light of the new day through the doorway. I sponged and oiled the babe and tied in place a new bunch of sun-dried grass from the basketful Lani had placed near the clean swaddling clothes. I wrapped her, put a shawl over my shoulders and carried her out into the new morning.

A secluded garden terrace, with a balustrade on one side, overlooked a complex of structures spread out below. Houses, offices, warehouses, treasuries, and courtyards fell away to meld with orchards and distant pathways circling away among the hills. Golden morning light enhanced the warm tones of the building slabs and flagstone pavements, and I sat amidst a serenity that spread through me to the child, who contentedly fed at my breast. My fears about the evil House of Pelops and Atreus had dissipated.

Suddenly I heard scuffling steps. The terrace gate slammed and my brothers appeared, unannounced. Dressed in traveling leggings and riding cloaks, their masculine presence filled the garden. Their movements were charged with strength as the morning light caught their bright hair brushed back behind their ears. A flutter of anxiety began in me. They have had bad news.

"What is it brothers?" I asked.

Castor answered, pulling up a seat. He touched the baby's cheek gently, though his eyes never lost their troubled glitter. "We leave at once," he said, all the time looking at the baby. "My retainer, the man Stanus who rushed to

Amyklae almost as soon as we beached the ship, returned here an hour ago. He told us of trouble at the Messenian border of Laconia. The cousins are making mischief. Lynceus and Idas have chosen to stir up the old dispute." His eyes were hard. "But that isn't the worst. It appears that Uncle Icarius has joined their cause. He is organizing an insurrection against Tyndareus. Stanus believes our own soldiers are involved."

My mind raced ahead. I was Queen of Laconia. I too should be in my own land. Part of the problem was the absence of a Queen. "Yes, go now," I said. I could see how everything had fallen apart. Castor and Polydeuces had been away too long. Tyndareus could not hold the army together; he had never been a soldier. Without Mother Leda he had lost the loyalty of the people. She was their leader in spirit, the Goddess presence in Laconia. Now I was that presence, and I felt a great responsibility fall upon me.

"I should be with you," I said aloud. "I could reawaken the folk to their loyalties. I am Queen now."

"Yes, Helen" Polydeuces replied. "You have become a legend among the people, a heroine because you rescued the Goddess effigy. They know of this and tell the story to each other. When you return to Amyklae with the effigy, you will be welcomed almost as the Goddess herself. You are the Queen, as Mother Leda knew full well, not even a year ago."

Castor came close to me. "It is right that your babe is foremost in your life now, but..." He paused. I waited. "Yet, if you could manage to leave soon—it would help us—help Laconia."

"Iphigeneia—bring her with you, or leave her here, perhaps—yes—you must come. You are Queen of Laconia, and your country needs you," Polydeuces added.

Castor and Polydeuces stood. They glanced at each other, exchanging a silent understanding. They must depart.

"I will do as you wish," I said. "Go now, as you have planned, on horseback. I will send a runner below to fetch Captain Thaos. We will plan my departure by ship."

"You could sail down the coast and be in Limera harbor

in two days. We will be in Amyklae by tomorrow evening to assess our next move and organize an army. Then we will go directly to the border."

"You are not to concern yourselves with me. We will meet again—when we meet again." I smiled bravely for their benefit.

"We will send someone—someone will be in Limera to greet you," Castor said.

Then Castor winked and Polydeuces saluted. They left in a flurry of scufflings and closings and were gone. I sat with my baby as before. Nothing had changed except that she nursed from the other breast. Everything had changed.

Long after Iphigeneia fell asleep, I stayed on in the garden imagining my arrival in the strange Laconian harbor town. I would find the village leaders and priestesses and announce myself. Iphigeneia would be carried in her sack on my back. I would feed her when she was hungry, and Lani would help. It did not seem difficult.

"But, Helen," Lady Aethra said later when I had told her this news. "You must think of the child; she will be much better off staying right here. It is calm compared to another storm at sea, and who knows what terrors await in Laconia? You may have to move quickly, sleep without proper shelter. War and destruction may abound. That is no place for a newborn babe."

We sat with Clytemnestra in her apartment. Dissent from Lady Aethra unsettled me. She had seemingly recovered from the blow to her head, but the steady counselor I looked to had become nervous and difficult.

My sister held Iphigeneia and seemed distressed because she cried. "Iphigeneia is hungry," Clytemnestra said. "I'll call the wet nurse."

"No," I answered. I heard a cross tone in my voice. "She just finished suckling." I leaned over and took the infant to me. She continued fussing, which was unlike her. I opened my shift. She found the nipple and stopped her crying at once.

"The baby is welcome to stay here," my sister said. "After all, we are prepared for a child, and the wet nurse is at hand." Clytemnestra's eyes were sincere as they found mine.

Lady Aethra could not stop voicing her concerns. "I find it difficult to understand why you feel you must do this thing, Helen. But if you must go, do leave my granddaughter here. Your sister has the perfect solution. It will be a temporary arrangement. I will be here to see that all is done to your liking."

"Lady Aethra," Clytemnestra explained in an unusual, sisterly way, "Mother Leda designated Helen as her successor. In Laconia this means much more than just an honor. She represents the Goddess and Helen is Queen of Laconia.

"Ah, yes," Lady Aethra said, "it is reassuring for me to understand that such adoration for the Goddess is still possible in some places."

My sister smiled engagingly. "Helen, as the daughter of Mother Leda, you must accept your responsibility, but leave the baby. We will see that she is cared for."

I tried hard not to immediately counter her. Was she right? Iphigeneia would have good care. It would be for a short time only—and Lady Aethra was, after all, the child's guardian and teacher—and grandmother—and it was my sister's house. What luck, in a way, to have this opportunity, just when I needed it.

The baby started crying again. I put her to my shoulder and patted her gently. I stood and walked out onto the terrace and sang to her. I could not leave her behind. I could not give up my child. Despite all the good reasons to leave her, I could not.

Lani approached to tell me that Captain Thaos had come to talk to me. I reluctantly handed her the baby and went to greet him.

Captain Thaos knelt and bowed his head as I approached. I urged him to rise and led him out to the garden so that we could talk. His black eyes were as wise as I recalled. "Captain," I said. "My brothers received word of strife in Laconia. They left this morning. I, too, must go home. What are the possibilities of leaving by ship?"

"Excellent, my Queen. The ship has been repaired. We have only to clean and load her with provisions to depart."

"Then I will leave as early as you advise. However, I would not chance another storm."

Thaos stroked his beard. "As we will follow the coast south, it will be easy to beach the ship if we need shelter. Also, if down-drafts develop from the high coastal mountains, we need only stay in close to shore to avoid the heavy seas farther out. All in all, I believe it will be a comfortable voyage for you and the baby."

"Your words relieve me," I said.

"May I ask?" he paused. "Will you have an escort?"

"Lani will be with me," I answered. "We are safe with you and your sailors, and when we get to Limera, I—will be in my homeland, where I am Queen."

"Very well, then. We will leave tomorrow at dusk in the calm night sea."

After he left, I stood at the balustrade and watched until his small party disappeared on the seaward road far away. I stayed on and watched the patterns of the dappled light through the trees. I had no wish to join Lady Aethra and my sister and subject myself to more of their talk. I watched the activity below and wondered about Lady Aethra. Had the blow to her head changed her?

Lost in thought, I did not realize at once that an approaching line of men and horses could be seen far in the distance. Twenty or thirty riders followed a double line of chariots, and behind them a less defined group of carts and heavily burdened horses. The sun caught flashes of metal, but I could make out few details. It must be King Agamemnon and his brother returning. When I went to tell Clytemnestra, I met with a flurry of activity and knew the household had been informed of the King's return.

I went to my own rooms, where I found Lani, but not the baby. "Iphigeneia was sleeping so quietly that your sister put her in her chamber," Lani told me.

In her apartment, Clytemnestra, freshly dressed, looked beautiful. Her hair was wound in golden bands, and the rich jade-colored fabric of her robe was carefully draped and tightly belted to reveal her exquisite breasts, the carmine tips jutting forth. Her eyes glittered and a frown appeared and vanished when I entered.

"Where is Iphigeneia?" I asked. My voice sounded hard and cold.

"They return, Helen. A messenger arrived from the King."

"Yes, my sister, I saw them from the garden overlook." I forced myself to remain calm. "Where is the babe?"

"I put her in the nursery," Clytemnestra answered as she examined herself before the polished metal. "She was so fussy, the wet nurse gave her a good feed. She is sound asleep. Why don't you just leave her where she is?"

"How dare you—without my permission." I could not believe what she had done. "Where is the nursery?" I demanded. Anger flooded through me.

"Oh, Helen. It won't hurt the child. It will do her good. In there," she said, indicating a doorway through which the servants passed. "I must go below," she said over her shoulder, as she rushed out into the courtyard.

At the end of the passage that led to several work rooms, I found the nursery, a large chamber where light flooded through the window, and where Lady Aethra sat on a comfortable seat looking out into a peaceful garden. The babe slept in a pretty basket which rested on a special stand in a shadowed alcove. At hand was every possible necessity for her care: neatly folded piles of fresh white wrapping cloths dusted with rose petals, jars of unguent and flasks of clear oil for her tender skin, ewers of fresh water and sponges for her bath and heaps of the softest sun dried grass to absorb her infant wastes.

I looked at her sleeping so calmly, so content. Her little breaths were even and her cheek a healthy pink. Just looking at her made my breasts tingle, and I realized it had been several hours since I last fed her. I reached for one of the folded cloths to press against my chest, for milk oozed from me. I picked up the baby and held her close. Suddenly all was right again. I looked over at Lady Aethra, who nodded and smiled at us. We sat next to her. The baby slept on soundly, but eventually I saw the little eyelids open.

"I doubt that she's ready to feed, Helen," Lady Aethra said.

"How long will it be?" I asked. "I'm more than ready; my breasts are overflowing." I put the nipple into the mouth of the babe. She sucked as usual for a few minutes then stopped. The breast had not been emptied and the other was painfully full. The baby cooed and looked around.

Lady Aethra and I laughed together at her sweetness. "She is a dear, isn't she?" Lady Aethra said. "I don't see how you can leave her, Helen."

I repressed a sharp retort. Why had she assumed I would leave the child, especially after all our talk. "I plan to take her with me, Lady Aethra," I said, insisting that she understand. "I can manage. I have much milk and Lani to help."

"Perhaps," Lady Aethra said. "Dear Helen, I believe you can do anything you set out to do. I have great faith in you." Her words took me by surprise. I was prepared to counter her. She put her hand on my arm, and I felt again the old closeness.

I realized then, deep in my bones, that despite my most fervent wish, I would leave the baby here. Although Captain Thaos had relieved my mind of the dangers of the sea voyage, no one could know what peril awaited in Laconia. The baby continued to coo happily, looking about her. Eventually, I put her to the other breast for a few minutes, and then she fell fast asleep. I gently replaced her in the basket and returned to Lady Aethra.

I could not manage to be brave any longer. Tears filled my eyes. Lady Aethra sensed my decision and took me in her arms and tried to comfort me. I cried softly into her shoulder. Still clutching the cloth I had used to quell my full breasts, I dabbed at my eyes.

"I have known her for such a short time; she is everything to me."

Lady Aethra nodded and stroked my head resting against her. "Helen," her voice was low, "I said before that you are capable of doing anything you set out to do. You will be able to do this difficult thing, too. You will be able to go away and leave your child behind, for her own good. You are strong, Helen. You know what is right. It is the will of the Goddess, now, isn't it? It was her will that brought us here among your people, so that you could leave with that knowledge."

Gradually my sobs quieted. "You will bring her to me, as you promised?" I asked.

"Of course. You know I will."

"You will see that she is not overly indulged, as I suspect is the way in this household?" My voice was clearer.

"Yes, dear. I will do as you wish."

"She must come to me as soon as things are settled in Laconia," I said, sitting up. "I will be leaving tomorrow at dusk. I want to feed her and care for her myself until then."

"Yes, dear, you must do all of that and get to know the wet nurse, begin to wean the baby from your milk. A gradual change is best for the baby and for you—less painful for you. I know of some balm that might help. I will try to find some for you."

The advices went on. I looked at Lady Aethra. Had she, in fact, returned to her true self?

"How are you, Lady?" I interrupted her. "Have you recovered? Are you truly able to take this on?"

She nodded just as the door opened.

Clytemnestra entered the room, exuding bountiful goodwill. "We've been looking for you. My husband wishes to welcome my sister and Lady Aethra to Mycenae."

I stood, surprised that we would be sought out. I tried to smooth back my hair, suddenly very aware of my rumpled appearance. My eyes must be swollen from crying, and my tunic was scarcely presentable, still unfastened for feeding the babe, my breasts almost fully revealed.

For the first time in my life I was abashed as male eyes inspected me. Lord Agamemnon and another man, both imposing figures, stood before us. I supposed it was Agamemnon in front and his brother behind. The King's dark eyes frankly slid from my face to examine my open tunic. His skin was brown, and his stern, thin-lipped mouth did not smile. He spoke correct words of welcome.

I forced myself to regain my poise without hurriedly closing my tunic. I refused to permit a lecherous stare to disturb me. "We gratefully accept your hospitality, my Lord."

King Agamemnon nodded and moved aside. I faced his brother who was called Menelaus. He had bronzed skin and short cropped brownish-red hair. I noticed a smile crease at the corners of his mouth that did not disappear when he was serious.

"My personal regrets that you have been put to such trials," he said in a clear voice.

"Thank you," I answered. "I hope your long journey was well rewarded."

"Yes, no matter the success or failure of the journey, it is always a reward to be home." He smiled pleasantly.

"Regrettably, my brothers found it necessary to leave this morning. I'm sorry that they did not have the opportunity, as I have, to see your Lords." My words were meant for both men. Menelaus bowed his head in acknowledgment, but Lord Agamemnon did not hear me. He stood with Clytemnestra at Iphigeneia's basket regarding the tiny form. A wave of regret washed through me for their dead child, and I felt pity for them. Lady Aethra fluttered about.

"I know the Dioscuri, my lady," Menelaus said. "Indeed, I would prefer to meet them in the polite surroundings of my own halls than on the battlefield."

"Sire, they will be on the battlefield soon enough. There is trouble at the Laconian border with Messenia."

"Ah, Idas and Lynceus," Menelaus said in understanding. "Still at their games, are they?"

"Yes, our cousins have chosen their time well, for we have all been gone far too long." This brother of King Agamemnon was an agreeable person while King Agamemnon was all barbs, thorns and condescension. He turned from Lady Aethra and his wife to speak to me; his brows rose in disdain.

"Well, little sister, you are not to worry. If your big brothers have gone off and left you, here are two others who will take their place," he smirked. I could not reply to such nonsense and remain polite. I held my head a little higher and returned his gaze, reminding myself that he had a right to be embittered just now.

"Come," he nodded to Clytemnestra and Menelaus. He bowed to Lady Aethra and left.

"We will see you tomorrow at the festival," Menelaus said in parting, following his brother.

Clytemnestra remained behind. "Helen, I have given Lani some robes and drapery for you. They are yours, a present. Find something pretty to wear tomorrow and take them when you leave. Have you decided...?"

"Yes, sister. I will leave the baby in your care. Lady Aethra is her guardian and teacher, as well as her grandmother. She is to be consulted in all things. You and Lady Aethra—" I found it difficult to speak.

Clytemnestra's face broke into a radiant smile. "Oh, I knew you would see reason." She hugged me quickly. "Iphigeneia will be fine here."

Lady Aethra helped me find the old fisherman's basket, and together we arranged little Iphigeneia in it and carried her back to our chambers.

I relaxed in scalding bath water, and afterward Lani rubbed scent and oil into my skin. Refreshed, I fed the baby from both breasts, and when Nimea, the wet nurse, appeared, I gave her the baby to finish feeding. I was secretly pleased that Iphigeneia fussed and did not take to the change.

In the alcove chamber, before the Goddess image, I offered my silent thanks for her care. The sheen from the dark smooth wood glowed in the evening light and I felt deep regret that I could not leave the sacred form behind to watch over my babe.

In the morning we organized our departure and Nimea and I shared the feeding of Iphigeneia. Nimea told me how to bind my breasts to stop the making of milk. She warned me that it would cause great pain for several days.

Later I dressed to attend the King's welcome home celebration. From my sister's gift of beautiful weavings and rare fabrics, we chose a delicate cloth the color of ivory decorated with gold thread. Lani draped it about me and belted it in the fashion of Mycenae. We found golden bands for my hair and long dangling earrings.

To stay with my child this last day would have insulted my hosts. I would honor their hospitality in the most queenly way I could manage. Laconia deserved my best.

Lady Aethra, looking stately in a rose-colored robe, and I were escorted by a guard through many bright frescoed passages and stairways to a games field where banners flew and throngs clamored for the athletes. We joined Clytemnestra who was installed with some others in a viewing stand. Draped in a diaphanous flowing robe of blue and silver, she pointed to the competition. "Look, brother Menelaus is about to throw the discus." I could see him out on the field, stripped of all but his heavy belt and loin cloth, his strong shoulders shining with oil, his beard and head caught red by the glint of the sun. The round stone whirred low and landed fair. King Agamemnon, conspicuous in his purple cloak and golden headband, stood with the jury of referees.

I excused myself once to be ushered back to my apartment to feed my baby, and when I returned the celebration had moved to the great hall in the central palace.

I waited at the entry with the guard, and in a moment Prince Menelaus was beside me.

"Come, Helen. We have a place waiting for you."

I smiled my thanks and he led me to the center bank of tables where we joined the King and Queen, Lady Aethra and other nobles and retainers. We sat before a spread of juicy slabs of lamb, cheeses made from the milk of sheep and goat, baskets of bread, date and plum cakes, cooked apples and figs. Servants filled our cups from a wine bowl well mixed.

My sister and her husband exuded a royal brilliance. I caught Clytemnestra's eye for a moment when she spoke to her husband behind her hand as though they might be overheard, although the din of conversation and feasting was almost deafening.

King Agamemnon stood and called for quiet. His voice carried authority as he spoke of his sojourn across the waters. "This festival hails the return of Prince Menelaus who has been away over two years tending to affairs in Miletus," he said. "And it welcomes Lady Helen from Laconia, sister of our own Queen, and Lady Aethra from Athens, mother to King Theseus." He raised his arms in the air in a gesture of welcome and motioned for us to stand. A great cheer rose up, and after order had returned, he spoke again. "This is not the time to tell you the details of our journey, but I wish to say, ever so briefly, that though our mission in Troy was not what we had hoped, our brother Menelaus has succeeded well in Miletus, and today we celebrate."

Musicians played, and a group of brightly dressed young men formed a circle and began to dance in precise steps to the slow throbbing of beats on a skin stretched over a hollow gourd. Their movements became ever more complicated as did the tones from additional gourds added to the first. The compelling rhythms brought others to the circle. From behind me, Menelaus whispered in my ear. "Come, let us dance."

The music and tempo took us as we moved in cadence. We turned and bent, forward and back, always in step. Menelaus and I danced perfectly together. The more complicated the beat from the gourds, the more intricate were our movements. It was a joyous expression of some inner power that could have continued on and on. I lost myself in this enchantment for a rapturous spell, until I began to tire from so much exertion after so recently giving birth.

"It is time for me to leave," I managed to say to Menelaus, as we passed close by in the circle turn.

He nodded, and in a moment he had led me apart from the dancers.

"My ship departs at dusk," I told him, and it will take several hours to get down to the sea. The ox and cart will be waiting."

"I will accompany you," he replied.

All was confusion. Lani was busy with the trunk, and Nimea held the fretting baby. I took the child to the sleeping room and sat in the alcove window seat, rocking her and murmuring to her. I did not give a thought to Menelaus, who was in the outer room with Lady Aethra and Lani.

The sweet babe nuzzled into me as I suckled her for the last time. I told myself once again that it was for her good that I leave her behind. My eyes brimming, I let Lani take her. I stood while Nimea bound my chest so tightly, in a length of white linen, that my breathing was possible only in shallow breaths.

I finished dressing. The oxen and cart waited, the trunk and bundles loaded, and the Goddess effigy carefully wrapped. I held and kissed Iphigeneia one last time, and with damp eyes I lifted my chin and bid good-bye to Lady Aethra and Nimea.

Menelaus waited for me. "I will see you to the ship," he said. I nodded, unable to speak. Lani sat in front with the driver. Menelaus and I sat in the seats set for us in the cart, and I gradually composed myself outwardly; inwardly, my spirit agonized. On the way out of the city Menelaus found a mount for a faster return. It was tied on to the cart and trotted along behind.

"Helen," Menelaus said. "Please, I am so sorry for your grief. Lady Aethra explained some of it to me."

I tried then to tell him, but it was difficult. "You see," I finished, "I must go home as I am now Queen."

"The ways of worship are changing everywhere, are they not? In Laconia too, I dare say, though clearly, you are the hope of your homeland. You must be careful." He paused a moment, then asked, "Do you have the Goddess image with you now?"

"Oh, yes. Right here," I answered. "Would you like to see it?"

"I would," Menelaus said, "if it's not too much trouble."

The old fisherman's basket that had most recently been little Iphigeneia's cradle now held the carefully wrapped wooden effigy. "We must be very quiet. This is not a curiosity, you know. It is an object of adoration."

Carefully I unwrapped the protective covering of the precious image. Kneeling in the cart for balance and for a proper posture when encountering the Goddess image, I held it with both hands before Menelaus. I bowed my head slightly in obeisance, and my hands felt the smooth wooden surface, the gentle, curving form. I felt the tingle of Goddess energy in my finger tips. We were both silent, and I sensed he, too, had felt something of her power. I said a quiet prayer, and when the moment had passed, I wrapped it up again and placed it in the basket.

When I looked at Menelaus, he was studying me. "I see why you were chosen, Helen." His words were spoken softly, and solemnly. I smiled my response, for I felt his good will.

"In Miletus where I have lived recently, temples and cults for the Goddess are everywhere, but I have never felt so moved by her as in this wobbly vehicle with you."

I settled myself against the back rest. "Tell me," I asked, "are the Sky Gods worshiped as well in Miletus?"

"Yes," he answered, but nothing like the Goddess." All along the coastal area and inland too, she is worshipped. In Troy the Goddess has a unique place. As long as her images—and there are many—are revered, the city will flourish."

I remembered the maidens from Boeotia who served in a temple in Troy for three years. I wanted to learn more about

Troy, but I could see that we were leaving the hills, and the glistening sea spread out below. I looked for the ship.

"Well," I said, in a final explanation, "you see why I must leave Iphigeneia behind. I cannot take a baby into a land at war. I thought I could, at first. I planned to, but–Lady Aethra and my sister persuaded me otherwise.

Menelaus, his voice uncertain, asked a strange question. "Helen, why does Agamemnon believe Iphigeneia is his child?"

"I do not think he does," I answered, astonished. The very idea alarmed me. "Agamemnon and Clytemnestra expected a child, but my sister must have explained at once that her baby died," I said. "Iphigeneia is so obviously mine. How could she not have told him?" I remembered what my sister said about her husband's wish for his own child. "If he so believes, he must have misunderstood," I said, seeking to make some sense of his question.

"Ah, yes. He has misunderstood," Menelaus agreed.

"You will do me the honor of seeing that he understands. Certainly, he cannot now still believe such an error."

Menelaus shrugged. "I suspected he was overjoyed in thinking she was his child."

"Yes, but you must inform him of the truth. Lady Aethra, Nimea, the wet nurse, my sister all know the truth. Now you know the truth. You will not let this misunderstanding remain." I spoke firmly, my voice rising in panic even to my ears.

We had reached the beach. The oxen stopped, and Lani climbed down from her perch. Before I could descend, Menelaus put his hand on my arm, and his light brown eyes held mine. "You must listen. You must know that as I learn of your mission in Laconia, your grief in leaving your child, I want to help you. With your permission, I will do all in my power to do your bidding."

His words reassured me. "Please, yes, please make certain your brother has no misconceptions about my baby."

"Tell me one thing," Menelaus said. "Who is the father of Iphigeneia?"

"Theseus of Athens," I answered without hesitation. I could see Captain Thaos approaching. The ship appeared to be readied. "Lady Aethra, his mother, will tell you anything more about all that, if you want to know."

Menelaus did not reply, for Captain Thaos had come to greet me, looking about for the child. I took his outstretched hand to descend from the cart. When I stood before him, he did not bow his head as usual, his black eyes searched mine in concern.

"I left Iphigeneia in the care of my sister and Lady Aethra," I said in explanation to his unasked question. "Is all prepared for departure?"

"Yes, my Queen," he answered, a small crease between his eyes indicating his lingering concern.

We watched our trunk and boxes hoisted aboard. Lani and I sat on the rug placed for us, and the craft was pushed out beyond the surf.

The captain took his place at the tiller and the men bent forward as one to the oars. Menelaus stood for a long time as the craft moved away. He waved once or twice and finally turned to mount his horse and head back to the citadel of Mycenae.

MOTHER LINE

Limera's stone cottages spread round the harbor and dotted grassy hills above. Dark hulls of boats cluttered the beach; some, moored to anchor stones, bobbed quietly in protected waters. It was a welcome sight at the end of a tedious voyage. Lani and I watched as lines were thrown to men ashore, and our craft was pulled neatly up on the beach.

Lani carried our cloaks and the small bundle for our night at sea, and I carried the fisher basket. It held the sacred image, wrapped and secured, along with the other precious tokens from the dedication of Iphigeneia in the seaside shrine. Before we left the ship, I showed the sailors how I cherished their gifts.

"But the child, Lady," an oarsman said. "The basket is empty without the child."

I could not help the waver in my voice or the mist in my eyes. "The child is safe with Lady Aethra and my sister in Mycenae." I spoke bravely, but I was in an agony of remorse without her, and my feverish breasts ached with the making of useless milk.

We debarked the vessel, and I looked about in hopes of seeing a messenger sent by Castor and Polydeuces. Other than a few workmen who nodded a greeting, I saw no one but an old man with a spotted dog tugging on a leash.

Suddenly Lani rushed to the old man with the dog, and they fell into each others arms. It was Pindros, dear faithful

Pindros, gone to be with King Theseus, here to meet us. I waved as they came closer, the silly hound bounding about. Pindros, his face creased in smiles and brown with his years in the sun, was as welcome to see as anyone could be. His eyes swimming, he knelt before me.

"Oh, Pindros," I said, over and over while the ridiculous black and white puppy jumped about.

"King Theseus sent you the pup," Pindros said rising.

Later we sat over cups of hot broth served to us in a small inn, a simple stone building with dirt floors swept clean, where Pindros had awaited us since the previous afternoon. A table and chairs were brought to a porch that looked out on the courtyard where travelers unburdened their animals.

"I had been wandering around the palace quarters for six or seven days when I heard the Dioscuri had returned. I sought them out, and it was a lucky thing, for I was the very person to come to meet you."

"Indeed yes, dear Pindros," I said.

Gradually the news came out on both sides. In Skyros, Theseus, living under the protection of King Lycomedes, had welcomed Pindros. But as the time neared for the birth of our child, Theseus insisted that Pindros rejoin me and serve me in the name of King Theseus of Athens from that time on.

"He gave me gold for this purpose," Pindros said, holding out several heavy pouches for me to take.

"But it is for you to use and look after," I said, touched by this gesture. "You who have accepted the trust will know best how to use it."

"If you say so, Lady," Pindros replied, "I will do everything possible to warrant your faith in me." He returned the pouches to his sack.

"You already have done, Pindros." I solemnly stated the unalterable fact.

Somewhat abashed, he bent down to rub the pup's ears. "The animal's mother was your favorite deer hound. His father is a great molosian belonging to King Lycomedes."

If King Theseus understood feelings of loss, and he would if his own were any measure, he would know our spirits would be lifted by the silly beast.

I looked into the pup's black eyes and scratched his ears. His short white coat was covered with black spots of different sizes that looked like the black stones I had seen on the coastal shore of Laconia as we sailed under the high stark mountains. Skyros means stone, I thought.

"Skyros," I said. "He will be called 'Skerri,' unless you have another name for him, Pindros."

"No, I was told to have you name him, and you have. Come, Skerri, sit. Sit down." Pindros shrugged his shoulders as Skerri ignored his command. "It's a good name, I think, and we will make him into a good dog."

"And is King Theseus well?" I asked. My voice sounded no different than usual, but I feared for the reply. He shook his head, and rummaged in his sac. He handed me a leather pouch.

"He received your gold amulet with happy surprise and here is what he sends in return." Out of the pouch fell a small ochre-colored ceramic bird decorated with black chevrons. A rawhide cord ran through a hole for its eye.

It felt warm as I touched it and examined it.

"It is ancient," Pindros said, "something passed on in his family."

I put it around my neck and felt at once close to Theseus. I thought how I would one day give it to Iphigeneia, a solid, true gift from her father. I looked away, too full of emotion to speak.

"Pindros," I said when all had been told, "did you sense unrest in Laconia? What did my brothers say to you?"

"Ah, Lady, the invaders have made forays from the mountains. Your brothers were reorganizing their army. My instructions were to escort you to Amyklae, but to emphasize the need for you to show yourself to the local people. Take the time at every opportunity to tell how you rescued the sacred image and let them worship before it. Icarius has fled, King Tyndareus is ill and not a threat."

I nodded just as Captain Thaos and another man entered the inn, and Lani and Pindros left to fetch our boxes. The puppy's antics made us all laugh so that any ceremony of introductions was impossible.

Eventually I learned that Timolos, a man with a big smile, led a band of seafarers. He also had a way with animals, for Skerri calmed and rested quietly at our feet.

"My Lady," he said, not looking at me and somehow taking on Captain Thaos' attitude of deference. "I welcome you to Laconia and offer my assistance. How may I be of help to you?"

I thought a moment, looking out into the hills. "Would people here wish to listen to me tell the tale of recovering the Goddess effigy, which was taken from the temple in Amyklae last spring?"

I picked up the basket resting on the table at my side, the precious object within. "I have brought it all this way," I said. "It holds much meaning. Perhaps the folk would care to see it, to worship with it, to gather together around it."

The eyes of Timolos widened as they slid from the basket to my face and back to the basket. His head lowered in awe.

"Queen Leda passed her guardianship and Queenship to me that same fateful day. Now that she is gone, I represent the sacred power. Queen Leda bequeathed it to me."

"Oh yes My Lady. Everyone here would want to see you and hear you and pray with you. Even those who follow Poseidon and Zeus would want to be with you." With his head bowed, I could barely distinguish his words.

"Friend Timolos," I said. "Could you arrange such a gathering or take me to someone who could?" I held my hand out to him.

He held it a moment. "Yes, I will do both. I will go now to the shrine and seek the Venerated Priestess. I will tell her of your presence."

She was small and shriveled with red rimmed-eyes. Her claw-like hands clutched a knobby staff, and she stood, bent over in front of the shrine, its white stones gleaming in the sunlight. Her welcome was more suspicious than friendly, her voice dry and cracked.

"May Potnia watch over you," she croaked. "Who is it who visits the holy shrine today?"

"Honored Mother," I said. "I am Helen, daughter of Queen Leda. Timolos, the harbor master, has told you of me. I have come from across the sea, and I have many things to tell you."

She led me to a grove of green-black cypress trees surrounding a spring. We sat on a stone bench in the lush shadowed cool, where I placed the fisher basket next to me. She offered me sweet water, and I rested and drank and felt a welcome peacefulness. I listened to the hum of bees and watched a golden oriole perch on a fig tree branch.

"Mother," I said, hesitant to break the spell. "Have you heard about the sacred Laconian image?"

"Oh yes. When I learned of its despicable theft, I gave up. I had no more strength after that." Her dull eyes seemed to see beyond our quiet place. "Once, long ago, I made my own pilgrimage to honor her. It was the most important thing I have ever done. To think that she could have been so degraded." The old one shook her head in disbelief.

I arose and removed the figure from the basket. It felt solid as I looked once again upon the dark smooth surface, sensed again a tingling response to this archaic relic of mystery. I carried it to the old priestess and knelt before her.

Her vision was so poor and the copse so shadowed that she did not see me clearly. She put her hands in front of her, and I placed them with mine on the figure. I heard a sharp intake of breath as she felt the smooth wood. The palms of her hands moved over the image, and tears glistened on her wrinkled cheeks.

We sat thus until she spoke. "Come, daughter." The old priestess led me into the shrine, where we placed the holy statue in a niche lighted by rays of sunlight from cracks in the roof. It gleamed as the light above changed with the movement of tree branches and the power of the place spread around us. Later she brought a pot of flaming oil and set it on floor stones before the holy figure. The old one seemed to became stronger as she performed these tasks.

Each afternoon people came to visit the shrine and as the sun slid behind the mountains, I told them about the ancient statue.

From town to town we gradually made our way towards home. In each village we brought the folk to the Goddess again. Word of our journey swept ahead of us, and we were often welcomed at the edge of a town and led by maidens to the holy shrine. A journey that could have taken two or three days took weeks. Ignorant of affairs at home, anguished by the absence of my child, we continued.

"Pindros, Lani," I called. We stood on a promontory that overlooked a winding river as the happy yelps of Skerri echoed over the hillside. A cloud of delicate gray-green olive groves below changed to the dark jade of pines in the higher reaches, and golden grasses at our feet intermingled with the pinks and yellows of wild flowers. "Those are sacred waters," I said. "It is the Eurotas River that nourishes all of Laconia."

After crossing the river, we came to a town where a group of young people met us and led us through the village. We entered to the hubbub of late afternoon when villagers stirred and came together in the coolness. Vendors uncovered their wares; clay jugs and ewers were set out; metal workers' knives and daggers glinted in the lowering sunlight; hunks of lapis from the quarries of Krokeai were polished to a sharp intensity of breathtaking blue.

A flock of black goats pushed through the narrow ways, urged along by a scruffy-haired goat-herd singing in a high voice. We passed a garden where men talked in the shade. Four or five, dressed in rough leather riding garb, lounged at the entrance and sipped their wine, watching the busy scene.

As we passed, a large fellow pushed into the road to impede our passage. "Here she is," he crowed. His dusty face was well enough made but his manner was impudent. He smiled at our discomfort. "It's a Goddess," he announced as his lewd eyes slid over me.

I made an enormous effort to ignore him. Pindros, leading the ass burdened with our bundles, gave the animal a sharp blow with a stick, so that it bumped the brute aside and knocked him off his feet. We passed by without a change of pace or blink of the eye, and the ruffian was hauled away amidst hoots of laughter.

The sacred figure reposed in a rocky sanctuary protected from wind and rain by a gigantic chestnut tree, a resting place for butterflies. They clung to the bark of its gnarled branches in such numbers as to change the tree's original color and shape, unless one looked close enough to notice the thousand quivering wings.

Resting from the day of travel, I sat with Skerri near a pool in a quiet garden apart from the visitors who were beginning to arrive. Lantern light flickered in the settling darkness, and out of the shadows I heard a strange chant.

"Gorgophone, Queen of two kingdoms, whose mother was Andromeda, daughter of Cassiopea, daughter of the Neriads, whose father Perseus was son of Danae, daughter of Hypermnestra the Danaid, protectress of sacred waters...."

Who could be reciting the mother-line that I had memorized in the nursery. This was not a family ritual. Alarmed, I searched the shadows for the speaker. I saw no one, but I joined in, picking up the cadence. "Whose grandmother was Anchinoe, Queen of Chemmis in Egypt, who carried the wisdom of the seeds and the planting."

I stopped as a young man stepped out of the trees. He carried himself with poise, and came to me. His brown hair was pulled back and tied at his neck, and his eyes sparked a piercing intelligence, or was it a wariness? I recognized him.

"You were among the ruffians who accosted us on our way into town this afternoon. By what right do you recite the mother line of Gorgophone, my Grandmother?

"By the same right as you. Gorgophone is my grandmother."

"You claim we are cousins?" I asked, thinking quickly who this might be. "You are either Lynceus or Idas," I stated, "but they are engaged with my brothers in a border conflict between our countries."

Skerri, tail wagging, sniffed the intruder's feet. I sat straighter, for a vision appeared in my mind of a time in the past, a time when I was a child. Boys played together at wrestling, then ball throwing. One flung the red wooden ball up into the clouds and the other leaped high to snatch it; neither missed the step of an intricate foot pattern which was part of the game. A big clumsy boy jumped in to play, but he mis-timed the move and was hit so hard that he later had a great purple bruise on his arm. Enraged, the injured boy jumped on Polydeuces and when Castor pulled him off, the lout turned on him with his fists. It was still another boy who stopped the ruckus, and I now knew to whom I spoke.

"You must be Lynceus," I said, "or else Idas has changed mightily since that family gathering when you apologized for him."

"My regrets, Cousin Helen," the visitor said. "Idas still misbehaves. He is so strong he feels he does not have to be civil."

"And it was Idas who was knocked asunder by our ass?" I asked, not hiding my smile.

"Yes. We have come on a mission of reconciliation, and bring a message from your brothers. Idas did not believe it was you we saw in the village. I am certain now, for no one else would know the mother line of Gorgophone."

I could not speak, his words surprised me so. "My brothers?" I finally asked. "You come from my brothers?"

"Yes. Idas was to have come with me, but he sulks in embarrassment after his disgrace this afternoon."

"Does he still know nothing of apologies?" I asked.

"No, nothing. It is I who always make his apologies. And I do so now. We heard a Goddess had been seen, that she was coming here. Everyone was talking about it. He never thought that the simple party with the ass—could be you. He is chagrined and sorry to have insulted you."

"Come closer, Cousin Lynceus. Enough of meaningless apologies. I will hear one some day from his own lips. Come and sit with me and tell me about my brothers, and what has happened between you and them that you carry their message. Did you meet in battle? What have you to prove to me that what you say is true. Why did you threaten our borders in the first place?"

Lynceus came forward. In the meager lantern light he handed me a wrist band made of gold. "Castor said to give you this."

I recognized it as one bestowed upon my brother by Mother Leda at his manhood initiation. It represented the wearer's honor, and he never removed it. I took it and put it to my lips, and wound it twice around my own wrist. I felt Lynceus spoke the truth.

I waited for him to explain further. He sat on a bench facing me and scrutinized me carefully as I did him. I was curious about this legendary cousin who appeared out of the woods with this incredible tale. He spoke finally, in a precise voice.

"It started with your Uncle Icarius. King Tyndareus, who over-stays his Kingship, has ill used his brother. He has ignored Icarius, his co-king. With the death of Queen Leda and the absence for so long of the Dioscuri, Icarius came to us for help.

"King Tyndareus has never been sensitive to his destiny," I said, thinking about how Theseus had put it. "A wise king once told me that a king's duty is to understand his fate. He must know his appointed end and act on it."

"And did your 'wise king' act as his own words instructed him?"

A vision of Theseus standing on a high cliff looking out at an endless sea came to me. The great wings of a lone eagle sailed slowly downward, golden in the sinking sun. I shivered, realizing that my vision was of Theseus before his death.

I answered, hearing a tremor in my voice. "Yes. He was wise and courageous." Skerri cried out in his sleep. I picked him up and calmed him. "I fear King Tyndareus does not see it that way," I said. "But what of the Dioscuri? What happened in battle? How did you settle the matter?"

"Well, to be brief," he explained, "they hid their army just over the mountain pass. How they got there so quickly I do not understand, for we expected to engage them on the plain, not in the mountains."

"They surprised you," I said, unable to hide my gratification. "Did you have a terrible battle?"

"It was bad enough," he snapped. "They flung their arrows just as we passed. Their soldiers were hidden behind rocks and trees in the heights. As our men were downed, they came at them with their axes. Many were killed." Lynceus was clearly unhappy. His was an honest telling, I believed.

"Did you not fight back?" I asked, letting the words speak themselves before I realized their rudeness.

My cousin's agitated pacing stopped in mid-stride. He turned towards me and said decisively, "Yes, we fought back, and your brother Polydeuces was sorely wounded. Idas managed a solid blow with his dagger. The right arm of your brother may never be so strong again, provided it mends without putrefying and killing him."

I stood, alarmed.

"Lady, you know how Polydeuces likes to box. He may find that sport a difficult one after this." He almost smirked.

I held Skerri close to me. I beseeched Lynceus, trying hard to ignore his gloating. "Where is my brother? What happened to him?"

His tone changed. "After we surrendered, we guided your brothers and the other wounded to Leuctron where Leucippus, my uncle and King of Messenia lives. He offered them hospitality and provided Polydeuces a quiet place for rest and recovery."

"Was Polydeuces feverish? Did they have ointment or herbs for the injury?"

"He was being looked after by Leucippus's daughters, who are priestesses and trained in healing. Hilaeria found wood wort to mash and mix with oil and apply to his wound."

"Ah," I said. "That should help."

"Leucippus lives in a great house overlooking the sea amidst terraced olive groves. It is a hard day's journey from here over treacherous mountain passes. We will return as soon as you have received our message, and we have a reply from you."

My brothers were so close. Would it also be wise for me to journey to Leuctron I wondered. "Was Polydeuces able to participate in the talks? Tell me of King Leucippus." So many thoughts rushed through my mind at the same time.

"We met for talks of accord on a terrace shaded by arbors that looks out over the gulf to the west. Leucippus prefers this place to all others. He is an old man, eager for Idas or me to replace him so that he can retire." Lynceus paused, as though about to enlarge on that situation, then smiled and continued. "He is a peace loving man, a sincere follower of the Goddess Potnia. He did not encourage us in this latest dispute."

And Polydeuces?" I reminded him.

"Ah, Polydeuces," he said. "A reclining chair and bolster had been placed for him. He rested easily, I believe. His wound was bound and Hilaeira hovered near in case of need."

"How did he look, was he terribly weakened?"

"His eyes were a bit glassy, but his tongue was as cutting as usual. If he had not strength, he did not admit it to us."

"Ah, no, he would not admit such to anyone," I murmured "Please continue."

"We agreed to cease our forays into Laconia, and to hold further meetings to sort out other problems. It has always been our hope that our lands might be reunited, as in the days of Gorgophone."

I was struck by the thought. Again I nodded my head, taking in all that he said. "And how do you hope to accomplish that?" I asked.

Lynceus sat again. Torch light flickered on his face and illumed the space around him. Skerri stretched lazily and walked around to Lynceus, who obligingly scratched the dog's ears as he spoke.

"We counted on Icarius, you see, and now perhaps diplomacy. We wish to make marriage agreements between us. For instance, if Icarius's daughter Penelope married Idas, she would, as a moon priestess, endow Idas with the royal power he needs to become King, and at the same time, unite our lands."

My immediate thought was to warn Penelope of such a match for her own well-being. To marry such a brute would mean certain discord and grief. The political ramifications of the plan were unacceptable, as my brothers must have indicated.

"If that is your question to me, I know you are here falsely. My brothers would never entertain such a plan."

"You are correct. Thus our mission is to you, my lady, for they assured us that the Queen in Laconia choses the King, and that you are the Queen in Laconia."

It was convenient for both of us that we spoke in near darkness, for surely a flush of embarrassment flooded his face. I ascertained that it was he who wished to become King. He explained quickly. "I do not know what the procedure is for chosing a King, but at that time I would offer myself. To even make such a suggestion now," he said, hurrying his words, "is outrageous, for we do not know each other at all. I ask only that you do not preclude me as a candidate. Remember, it is the bringing together of two strong countries that share Goddess wisdom and were once united. If you permit it, I will take the message back to

Leuctron that you have not precluded me as a possible King, and we can continue with our talks."

I quietly considered his words. What inspired me most was his notion of returning to the realm of Gorgophone. I could see that a political union of Messenia and Laconia might be very useful. Someday, when I was Queen in Laconia, I would chose a King.

"You may tell my brothers," I said, "that when the time comes, I will not rule you out as King. Is that the message you wish to carry back?" I asked.

"Yes, that is it," he said, nodding. His eyes gleamed in the reflected light.

"Then let us be friends, Lynceus. You are welcome in our country. In the meantime, what of the daughters of King Leucippus? Would not a good match be made between them and my brothers? Has that possibility been considered?"

Torches were lit and placed in holders lighting the path to the sacred image. Splashes of light washed over us. Lynceus stood purposefully. "I believe it is something that may have passed through their minds. Phoebe and Hilaeira are very beautiful. It would be a still stronger bond between us if such marriages took place. One of your brothers might be King in Messenia."

"Perhaps," I answered, "but they do not strive for kingship. It has grown late. Our conversation has instructed me about many things. Tomorrow afternoon I invite you and your party to return. At that time I will speak to the folk about the figure of the Goddess Potnia, and I will give to you my own token of honor which you can take back to the Dioscuri. It will identify me in their eyes, and my message will be believed."

We walked together to witness the holy effigy. A zephyr whispered through pine branches; I bowed my head, at peace as I always was in the mysterious presence. I looked once at Lynceus and saw in the torch light that his eyes, so piercing, now rested on the form in curious contentment.

As the sun's rays began to slant long across the sky, Pindros invited the visitors into an orchard clearing to sit on the grassy banks of a shaded hillock. I saw that Lynceus and Idas were with two or three companions. I waited amid some ancient pear trees, their fragrant blossoms wound into a garland for my hair. Barefoot, in a simple white drapery, I welcomed everyone and told the story of the effigy.

"In the very beginning of time before time," I said, "the Great Earth Mother alone was the endower of the magic of procreation for all of nature's beings. Her essence roamed everywhere, and it inhabited an ancient olive tree. The sacred wood received her power, and her form was revealed in the curves of the tree trunk. Her face, lifted in adoration, her nourishing breasts, her fruitful pelvis, were brought forth with all care by a carver blessed in vision."

I told them how this one effigy had become a fertility idol of powerful meaning worshiped throughout the ages until it became the holiest of holy figures in Potnia's shrine.

"Everyone in Laconia knew of her," I said. "Your parents, grandparents, great-grandparents and ancient grand-parents all worshiped this very same figure. Some of them journeyed long distances to kneel before her, to feel her power for themselves, to interpret her messages in the various ways she chose. Lord Zeus and Lord Poseidon, coming later to our land, pay her heed in all they say and do. Some of us have chosen to give more loyalty to these new Gods, but none of us will ever dismiss the power of Potnia, who holds the secrets of nature within her and endows the magic of procreation for all of nature's beings."

I told them of the day when, by winning a foot race, I was given the momentous responsibility of becoming her guardian. I told of the sacking of the temple and my chase to retrieve the effigy. When I came to the part about entering the camp of the thieves at night, how I found the image among the saddle bundles, I went to the fisher basket on the altar rock, and removed the holy form from its protective cloths.

I held it high for all to see and rubbed my hands lovingly over the smooth oiled surface, then I set it with care on the rock where gnarled branches, thick with pure white pear blossoms and shiny dark leaves sheltered and adorned it; their slight movement in the breeze constantly changed the shadow and sunlight patterns that slid across the form.

"I unwrapped the sacred effigy, just as I have done here," I said. "I placed it in a shaft of moonlight and propped it against some saddle bags. A feeling of glory flooded through me, and I was compelled to dance the steps of her adoration in the moonlight as the thieves slept around a fire."

From somewhere near the pear trees, Pindros tentatively sounded sweet notes from a flute, then stronger, and I danced again before Potnia's sacred form. When I finished, I stood quietly with my head bowed, and the people were quiet as well.

I spoke again. "The sacred image embodies the power of Potnia herself, the essence of life-giving creativity, the very blessing of the ripeness of mature fruit and a full harvest. We are her children living together in her way."

I stopped speaking for some moments, letting the presence of the figure before us be felt by all. Then, I invited them to come close, without hurry. "There is time for everyone to see her," I said. "There is no need to press; she will be here for you."

As they came forward, some fell to their knees; others gently touched her. I seemed to be included in their awesome respect and felt profound affection for them.

As Lynceus and Idas and their friends approached, I wondered if Idas would be insulting. Lynceus touched my hands in unspoken regard. The dark brown eyes of Idas looked deeply into mine. "Little Helen," he said, as butter-flies flitted about his shaggy head, "please forgive my brutish behavior of yesterday."

They moved on just as a child grasped my hem. "I touched her, the Goddess," the little boy said.

"Yes, The Goddess," a man's voice repeated. "I was in Amyklae that day; I heard the Queen say the words."

I looked upon his work-worn face and reached out for his hands and felt the calloused palms before he moved on.

"She is the new Queen."

"She is the Goddess here in Laconia."

"The Goddess."

SWANS

Skerri ranged ahead of me on the high trail above the swollen river. I walked over grassy paths, looked down at the boulder-strewn embankments, smelled the scents of spring and listened to the bird song in the bright new leaves. Lani and Pindros, with the ass, fell behind.

When I saw the first swan, I knew I was close to home. As sunlight broke across the peaks, I stopped to watch the great white wings undulate slowly and come to rest in a shallows at the river's edge. Its gracious neck bowed into a curve that might fool the unwary into believing such magnificence harmless, but I knew its bill was lethal and its killer-wings harbored mutilating knobs in their tips.

I held out a piece of bread from a nibbled breakfast loaf and called. The swan circled above me, then swooped down in its flight to gently take it.

"I must be dreaming," Pindros said as he and Lani caught up with me. "Wild swans don't feed from people's hands."

"Some do, Pindros. Some swans are that tame," I said. "Mother Leda brought gentle swans to Laconia when she married Tyndareus, and their quality exists still. We will soon be home."

Skerri barked, but kept his distance when more swans appeared. I tried my luck again in calling, and one took the proffered bread, and others seemed curious and flew close to me.

The bread had long given out when I caught the first glimpse of the city. Houses and workshops spread out below, and the river wound around and through it past the games fields and sanctuaries.

I waved and called to Lani and Pindros and told them about the distant town. I retrieved more bread from the lunch basket tied to the back of the ass and ran ahead on the wide path that descended to a lower road used by farmers and herders and the swan men. I continued to feed and talk to the swans, cooing the deep-throated sound that attracted them. The air was filled with their seldom heard, throaty calls and the whir of their wings in flight. I walked quietly hoping not to excite them. It was as though they passed along a secret message to each other. I had never seen anything like it before among swans.

People appeared and stared at the sight. Little children hailed each other, staying far from the wide-spread wings. I took in all the sights, breathed in all the aromas of the marsh grass, of the potter's oven, of the cooking oil. The royal house, cresting the far hill with the mountains behind it, would be my destination after seeing the Goddess image once again where she belonged.

With a tingle of excitement, I saw Penelope at the head of a group of priestesses waiting to welcome us. They came as had other priestesses in other towns, but I could not call or speak for the fluttering din and guttural coos of gathering swans made it impossible. The sky was white with their waving wings, and the river inlet at the temple site, normally tranquil, teemed with hundreds, their gliding white forms moving serenely.

I stood upon a large rounded boulder at the edge of the water and crumbled up the last of the bread and held it towards the mighty gathering of birds. Some was taken from my hands, and the rest I spread out before me.

The ancient seer appeared at the temple portal, leaning on a staff. Penelope stood by to aid her, but the old one seemed possessed of unnatural strength. Her voice, at first harsh with age, took on a tone that could be heard above the din of the birds.

"Helen has come back to us. She has brought with her the sacred form that protects our place and blesses our seeds and our life. Helen has returned to us . . . Helen, the Goddess, Helen the Queen."

She raised the arm that was not supporting her on the staff, and, at that moment, voices from the crowd echoed her words, "Goddess! Helen! Queen! Helen the Queen."

The swans, as though they were one instead of hundreds, spread out their mighty wings in an incredible wave, a slowly accelerating oscillation, a thunderous lifting up and away.

Penelope, her gray eyes excited, rushed to greet us.

"My dear friend and cousin," I said as we embraced. "It is true, it is Penelope, and I have come home."

"Helen, you cannot know how we have longed for this moment. And with the effigy?"

Pindros untied the fisher basket from its place on the back of the ass and handed it to me.

"Yes," I said to her and the others who gathered around. "I bring back Laconia's sacred effigy to Potnia's holy sanctuary."

"We are prepared for you," Penelope said. "The Venerable One is waiting."

"I am so happy she is able. I am eager to go to her, but I must purify myself before approaching."

"She said to tell you to come at once. She said to tell you that we will conduct a proper ceremony at a later time. Now, we want to welcome you and return the sacred image to its place."

The Venerable One waited in the dark recesses of the shrine where the holy image had rested through the eons. I carried the fisher basket and followed Penelope.

The old one sat withered and thin to one side surrounded by her priestesses. A white hooded cloak was wrapped around her, and she leaned on her staff. Her eyes, the lids wrinkled with time, glowed like coals. I knelt before her and felt her hands rest on my head with a loving caress. I stayed, receiving her blessing, feeling her potency rush through me. When she removed her hands, I raised my head and filled with awe and love, I looked at her. She nodded in unspoken approval.

I held up the fisher basket for her to see and placed it next to her on the bench. She put her hand on it and beckoned to Penelope who, with another priestess, gently lifted the figure and unwrapped the layers of protective cloth. Together they placed the sacred form in its wall niche where light from roof slits fell upon it, enhancing its oil-rubbed contours of fecund belly and fruitful breast. Snakes, quiet in a painted bowl on the floor, began to squirm and arch, and the assembled priestesses sang a joyful song of return that echoed sublimely throughout the shrine.

As the old one listened, she picked up one by one the other things in the basket, the gifts of shells and carvings for my babe given by the sailors and fisher folk at her naming ritual. "What are these, my child?" she asked.

Distressed by the meaning of these gifts and the emptiness in my heart at the absence of Iphigeneia, I lowered my glance and turned away.

She bid me rise and sit next to her on the bench and tell her my story. This I did while she held and fingered one of the carved figures. I tried to be as truthful and as brief as possible. I told her of my capture and my time in Athens. I told her of King Theseus, Aphidnae, my pregnancy. I introduced Lani and Pindros and told of their unfailing loyalty. I told her of my brothers' help, of Lady Aethra and her impassioned belief that Iphigeneia was a divine child and a new leader.

I left much unsaid, much that she did not need to be told. I ended my recitation thus: "I learned my procreation lessons well, Holy Mother, although they were practiced out of our tradition. I love my child more than anything else in the world. I want her to be brought here as soon as possible".

The old one closed her eyes and put her head back in meditation. "Let us see if the Goddess has a message for us." She spoke to Penelope; my cousin and another priestess knelt before the holy figure. Penelope reached into the bowl of snakes; two curled around her arm. The other priestess smoothed the sand on the floor with a whisk of twigs. She brushed it into the traditional pattern, and one after another, the snakes were put down. They wriggled and slithered, leaving marks that we had all been taught to read. I knew without the interpretation by the Venerable One that the Goddess held me in esteem. I had to look to the old one for the rest of the message, for I must have misunderstood it.

I saw a sadness in the old eyes that confirmed my worst thoughts. Iphigeneia would not be coming here to me, the message said. But it was unclear. It could not mean that. It most decidedly could not mean that. Another interpretation would explain it.

I managed to keep my worries to myself. In fact, I did not even admit to myself the possible meaning of the message. I carried through with the courtesies and formalities of the return of the effigy excusing myself as soon as possible. Relieved that the sacred image was now safe where it belonged, I hid my grief and worry about my baby as we made plans for a great feast and jubilation, a celebration for the return of the Goddess effigy.

Yet, in leaving, I knelt down next to the aged one again. She put her hand on my head in affection. "I will contact our temple in Mycenae," she said kindly, her voice quavering and weak. She understood what was bothering me. "They will tell me about the child."

"And I will send a messenger to Mycenae. As soon as Pindros is rested from our journey, I will send him to Lady Aethra. He will bring her and the child back. I will do that." I made my voice sound happy and expectant.

The eyes of the Venerable One held much grief, but she smiled in sympathy as she nodded assent.

The royal Amyklaeon palace, where I grew up, commanded a fine view of the mountains. Fertile lands around the palace were abundant with olive groves, grape arbors, fruit trees, and grain fields. The Chief Steward, who had thickened noticeably through the middle in my absence, welcomed us with all the flourish a returning princess could expect. Servants smiled their greetings and came to kneel or touch me in deference. I introduced Lani and Pindros, explaining that Lani would attend me in my quarters, and that Pindros was also my personal attendant.

The Chief Steward bowed his head and assured us that he himself would show them about. I told the Chief Steward that I would go to my chambers to refresh myself. "And the King," I said, "please tell King Tyndareus I have returned and that I will call on him shortly."

As we walked through the passages, I looked at the great house with new eyes. The stonework was even, the mosaic smooth, the designs minimal. Rich, showy presentations were not the Laconian way. Even Tyndareus, preoccupied as he was with power, did not display substance to prove it. It felt good to be back.

At the welcoming room the guard stood before the doors with his legs planted firmly apart, holding the double ax before him in both hands. His military tunic and cape were of white and blue, and he wore a band of braid around his forehead. His eyes smiled recognition as he announced me, then told me to enter.

Tyndareus sat in a throne chair placed before the large window looking out at the groves and houses that spread before him down to the river. His back was to me so that I could only see his balding pate, strangely vulnerable as I approached from behind. The scalp was brown and his white hair which started above his ears had grown much longer than I remembered. Mother Leda was not at hand to remind him to have it cut.

I had washed and rubbed my skin with unguent and felt fresh. Lani said I glowed with health. I had donned a fresh white tunic with a golden leafy border, and Lani had arranged my hair, rolled it back neatly and secured it with a gold comb. As an after thought, I decided on a mantel of filmy gold, one from the box of Clytemnestra. I wished to appear a woman in the eyes of Tyndareus, not the carefree girl he remembered.

I came before him and knelt in deference as was the custom. With my eyes lowered, I waited for his words. When they did not come, I spoke: "It is I, Helen, Father Tyndareus." I had never before called him Father.

As he still did not speak, I looked up and saw that his eyes remained focused on the distant view from the window. He had aged years since my parting. His skin was wrinkled, his body bent in his chair, as though he could not sit straight. One hand trembled all the time. I put all formality aside and took his trembling hand in mine.

"Father Tyndareus, it is Helen," I said, loudly. "I have come back." Finally his filmy eyes slid to mine, and I saw a spark of recognition.

His voice, when he spoke, cracked with weakness. "Oh, Helen," he said as though he had seen me just yesterday. "I saw the most amazing thing. The sky was filled with swans. It was astounding."

"I saw them too. They came to meet me as I came home, up the river valley. It was as though they knew me. I called to them as Mother Leda taught us when we were children."

"Ah, Leda," he said.

"I know," I answered. "It is terrible not to have her here."

He looked at me with an acuteness I almost recognized.

"Do you want to hear what happened to me, what ordeals I experienced since leaving?"

"You ran away," he said, his voice stronger and harder.

"It was the day of the summer solstice games, nearly one year ago," I reminded him. I seemed to have his attention so I continued. "I won the foot race. It was the most wonderful thing that ever happened to me. Mother Leda made me Guardian of the Effigy, and then, a very special thing for her to do, she made me Inheritor of all Queenly Functions."

His eyes glowed a little then. Had he really forgotten? Did he really remember now?

"King Theseus and King Peirithous were visiting. They stole the effigy. It was some sort of prank, I guess. For me and for Mother Leda and for the Venerable One it was malicious destruction."

King Tyndareus remembered. He even put his hand over his mouth to hide a grin that came unexpectedly to his face. I ignored it and continued.

"As Guardian of the Effigy, I went after it. That is why I left."

"That was foolish." His voice was sharp with disapproval.

"Perhaps," I agreed. "I caused much trouble for many people. I should not have been so impulsive."

"You have always been thus," he answered, in a less severe tone. He sat straighter in his seat, but the trembling persisted in his hand. I suspected he had been very ill.

I smiled. "I did retrieve it. It has been returned to the Temple of Potnia this day."

He looked at me with the old coldness.

"I fulfilled my obligation to the Goddess," I said, and then I took his hand again. I knelt on a cushion at his feet, not in servitude, but so that I could be closer to him and speak more directly to him. I did not want to offend him, but I knew I must state my purpose. I put his hand on my cheek and held my head so that he could look into my eyes closely.

"I am prepared to become Queen, as Mother Leda intended. I hope you will help me, but first, you must rest."

His eyes closed, and a few tears squeezed from them. Truly, he was tired and ailing.

I continued. "The Dioscuri have made peace with the Messenian cousins. Things will go well now. You have served with loyalty." I wanted to remind him about his duty, that he would offend the Great Goddess and Zeus himself, if he persisted in his kingship, but I could not. It was not for me to say it.

"It is time for you to rest," I repeated. My voice and the repetition of words seemed to sooth him, for he put his head back against the chair and closed his eyes.

I sat with him, still holding his hand, and told him more about my time away. I assumed my brothers had kept him informed about Iphigeneia, so I told him about Clytemnestra.

"She would like to come home to visit you," I ended. His eyelids fluttered.

"I think she is lonely. Her husband is often away, and she has no true friends." He nodded slightly.

My voice did not change in tone as I went on to more practical matters. "I will move into the Queen's apartment in a day or two. The temple priestesses have planned a joyous celebration of return for the Goddess image," I said. "It will coincide with the summer solstice games. Then I will act as Queen for the first time in public. But I will take up my duties here at once."

I leaned over and put my cheek against his. He had never before been needy of affection, at least from me, but now he leaned against me and appeared to welcome it. He had always depended on Leda. Now he could depend on me. I spoke as she would speak, and he had understood.

I called to the guard at the portal.

"King Tyndareus would like to be helped to his chamber," I ordered. "Please call his servant."

Soon a little man, who had served King Tyndareus for many years, rushed in all a-dither.

"King Tyndareus is ill," I said to him, "the guard will help you lead him to his rooms."

Together the two men helped the weak and shaky Tyndareus. I followed behind as they went through the passages to his apartment. I entered with them and waited in the ante-room, while he was made comfortable in bed.

"Now," I said to the guard, when he reappeared, "I wish to speak to the healer and to the Chief Steward. Please report to me as soon as you have contacted them." He bowed and left, not questioning in any way my authority. I breathed in deeply and waited for the valet who, I remembered, was called Spiro.

"How is he?"

Spiro, bowed and told me the King was sleeping. "Tell me," I asked him, "has Tyndareus been ill for long?"

"He has never really come back to his former self since Queen Leda died."

"But this weakness and trembling," I said, "it is more than just grief."

"We could not direct him—I hope you understand. He was King and no one could tell him—anything."

"Ah, yes. I do understand. Thank you, Spiro, for being so loyal and so helpful to him for these many years. Perhaps he would recover faster in the country."

Spiro's face brightened. "He is happiest in the country. He loves his orchards and his vines. It would be good for him to rest at his country estate, but..."

I smiled at him in appreciation. "Spiro, you make all the arrangements. I believe he will go there now."

"Ah, Lady Helen, if you ask him I believe he will."

The next day King Tyndareus left for his country house to rest. I was not certain that he thought of his exit from the seat of power as permanent until his parting words—hesitant and weak.

"If you are—to be Queen, Helen—you must have a King."

"Yes," I agreed. "Some day I shall choose a king."

The old man could not sustain a conversation for very long. "I will put my mind to it," he breathed. "Could be very important for us—who we choose."

From all reports he settled into country living with ease, and I hoped he would not dwell on the selection of a new King. I was not ready for that. I was making my way carefully, and as far as I knew, I had not yet alienated anyone.

Pindros left for Mycenae to fetch Lady Aethra and Iphigeneia. Lani and I moved into the apartment of Mother Leda with Skerri whose puppy antics provided constant amusement. His silliness made me laugh and took me out of my somber gloomy concern over my missing child.

Daily I took Skerri on a lead into town to greet the folk and mingle with the artisans and vendors. I spent time at the playing fields and exercised with the athletes.

I met with counselors. I used the conversations with the chiefs of departments, and sometimes their assistants, to learn about the organization of the palace, the holdings and the farther provinces.

The nobles who managed the holdings and the Governors of the provinces were all responsible to the palace. I was shown the stores stashed in lower chambers; huge tubs full of olive oil, wine, wheat and barley. The bronze ingots used in smelting, as well as for trading, were stacked in rows. Alum for dying fabric, amber for funeral rites, ivory, copper, tin, silver and gold all itemized, all accounted for. Records of barters, supplies, weapons, seeds were all kept on clay tablets filed away in marked baskets.

One of the assistants named Arneus, a serious man concerned with trade, talked enthusiastically about his work. His vision extended well beyond the palace walls, for he saw possibilities for acquiring goods from distant shores through negotiations. "We are fortunate that our most exportable product, marble, is located near a port. We send as much away as we can quarry."

"I noticed our Laconian stone, the green flecked with yellow, in the royal chambers in Mycenae," I told him.

"Ah, yes. It is beautiful and easy to work, always in demand everywhere: Athens, Corinth, Crete, Troy, Miletus, and even north through the Hellespont if it were not such a difficult voyage."

Arneus had long tapering fingers and a finely shaped head made evident by a receding hairline. His youthful face, smooth and brown, could not disguise a profound intelligence. I would remember him.

I visited the Goddess Shrine every day and conferred with the Venerable One and her priestesses.

"I have received a message from the sisterhood in Mycenae," she said to me one afternoon. My spirits rose; my baby would be sent to me.

"What does it say?"

"It is a simple reply to my inquiry, Helen. You must not raise your hopes."

I did not listen to her warning. "Tell me, tell me," I pleaded.

"This is what it says. 'A new aura of happiness exists with the birth to the King and Queen of the beautiful child, Iphigeneia.'"

I was devastated. I refused to accept the implication of the message. Penelope became my sounding board. "Wait until Pindros gets to Mycenae. He will put it straight. Lady Aethra and Clytemnestra will have to tell the truth."

Penelope sympathized. "Helen, I feel deeply for you. I cannot begin to imagine your pain."

Just telling her brought back the joy of my few days of motherhood. "It was wonderful. She was mine. I created her." Numb with the sorrow of loss I kept on.

Penelope accompanied me on many errands. We visited other temples and were received by the priests of Hyakinthos and Hermes with cordial warmth. I felt it of the greatest importance to accord them full honors and obeisance.

I realized that one day Penelope might replace the Venerable One if she so chose.

"Dear Cousin," I said. "Your own future will be decided one day soon. What does your destiny tell you? You could be named Superior High Priestess when the Venerable One passes on, and what a splendid leader you could be.

"Yes, Helen. I see truth in the insights you have gained through Lady Aethra. I could take on the devotional duties of Superior High Priestess and work together with sisters in other temples to keep our ways alive." Her eyes glowed with a passion, a commitment she would carry with her whether she became Superior High Priestess or not.

"But you ask me what my destiny might be," she continued. "I feel that another fate is in store for me. I will take a husband sometime, I think. I will leave here. That is what I feel."

"Oh, Penelope," I rushed in. "Lynceus is a fine person. It would be a perfect match. Along with our new alliance, think how such a union between you and Lynceus would bring Laconia and Messenia together?"

"Helen. What you say is true, but perhaps it is for you to choose Lynceus. It would complete things for both places."

"Perhaps." I answered.

Pindros returned, and although I had been watching for him daily, his arrival was unexpected. Awakened early one morning, I threw a shawl around my shoulders and rushed to the door of my apartment to find him alone. Still dazed from sleep, I looked for the child. "Where is she, where is she?" I asked, smiling foolishly in anticipation of seeing Iphigeneia.

Dusty and tired from the road, his smudged face held grief for me, and soon I knew.

"Iphigeneia is well," were his first words, brief and to the point. He continued speaking in a slow and deliberate voice, preventing my anticipated outburst of alarm. He stood with his legs apart, his hands clutching his staff, the deep creases in his face deeper for his fatigue. His brows, always wild, shadowed his tired eyes, but could not hide his burning concern.

"I was received by Lady Aethra, who is well and sends her warm greetings. She tells me the baby thrives and is the delight of King Agamemnon. Queen Clytemnestra, your sister, is as a mother to the child."

He must have memorized these phrases on his long trek back for I detected no expression in his voice, and he knew how they hurt me. He went on telling me how well she fed at the breast of the wet nurse, what a happy baby she was, and finally, he lowered his eyes and in obvious anguish, said what I dreaded to hear.

"Never, for even a moment, did anyone consider giving your baby to me to bring to you."

I could barely restrain my rage. I paced about the room, brushing at my stinging eyes, wringing my hands.

"How can this be, how can this be?" I implored my faithful friend and servant. I longed for my Iphigeneia. I wanted her with me, next to me. I wanted to hold her and to love her.

"The Goddess omen was right," I moaned. "Why, oh, why should it be so?" I did not expect Pindros to answer; it was not for him to either explain or console me, but he could not but try. Our regard for each other was such that he would speak, and I would listen, or the reverse if such were the case.

The deep rasping voice went on. "Somehow, my dear Helen, you must accept your destiny. Perhaps it is a test for you, perhaps it is something you are not to understand, but I fear it is to be."

This despicable message was expressed with such kindness and sympathy that I had to turn away and cover my face for the tears that welled. Anger filled me. "I am trying, Pindros. I have done and am doing what my destiny demands. I am becoming a Queen here, and people are accepting me. I have returned the Goddess effigy and the folk are grateful and inspired by her return. In the process, I gave birth to a beautiful child, my child. I will not give up my child." My words were brave, but my voice quavered.

Pindros walked to the window to watch the activity of the morning below in the vineyard as the cultivators began their work. I noticed how tired Pindros looked as he leaned against the window opening. His loyalty and service could never be questioned. I must not vent my anger at him. "Come, Pindros. Sit here next to me. You must be exhausted. Lani will bring some food and drink for you. Tell me more. Try to tell me why you have reached such a conclusion. It is important for me to know why you believe my child will never return to me."

He joined me on the bench as I suggested, clearly relieved to rest his weary body. Lani brought in a table and placed a jug of wine, some bread and cheese before him. He ate and drank then spoke quietly.

"King Agamemnon, the overlord of many lands, has great power and strength. He has decided to be the father of Iphigeneia. Whether he knows, or even suspects he is not, makes little difference. His daughter by Clytemnestra would fulfill his destiny, insures his right to power, and he will not give her up."

He drank from his cup. I considered his sober words. He turned to me, speaking again. "To cross or challenge King Agamemnon would be unwise. As Lady Aethra has told us, Iphigeneia, for reasons we know not, is outside the usual. Lady Aethra sent you this message. I repeat it as she said it. 'It is the fate of Iphigeneia that is in charge. It is yours to let it be so.' Lady Aethra is convinced of this."

"Ah, of course, Lady Aethra. She convinced you of this?"

"She has convinced me of much more than this. I have come to believe in her mission, and yours, but my opinion is of little importance."

"How did my sister receive you?" I needed to speak of something else. "It is my sister who planned this whole scheme to deceive me. I will never forgive her."

"You would not want to be in her place. She has no authority as Queen. Her husband does not respect her. She is very proud of the child however. And the King–he carries the baby with him among the people, holding her up so all can see her."

From then on I could not let that vision go. It tormented me. I could see the proud King, strutting about the palace with my daughter in his arms. I promised myself that I would never give up my motherhood of Iphigeneia. Someday I would have my revenge and bring her back where she belonged. But, what of the child? She would never know me as mother. She would not change all of her loyalties just because I might suddenly come into her life.

The notion that it was the fate of Iphigeneia that directed events, finally made me understand. A woman will give up anything for her child, but even the child herself? I thought of Theseus and Tyndareus, and felt for them and their decisions of personal relinquishment, their decisions to step down from kingship. I vowed to have more consideration for Tyndareus.

I took my fearful problem to the Venerable One. After consulting the Goddess Potnia through the snakes and other auguries, she said to me: "Helen, you must not let this great injustice direct you or your life. It will destroy you, or it will enhance you. You must find the even path."

QUEENLY FUNCTIONS

Tyndareus, frail, but with the keen intelligence of former times, returned to Amyklae from his country home for the summer solstice celebrations. We sat on the terrace in the evening, and his servant rushed about pouring cool wine and arranging his footstool.

Moonlight flooded the garden, permitting me to see clearly the old man's satisfied smirk as he spoke. "It won't be long, I daresay, Helen. Soon they will come, these young men who want to be King here. We must receive them with the finest hospitality. I've sent out the message." His voice held all the warm tones of pleasure.

My easy reply covered astonishment that he had made this move without discussing it with me. "It all comes faster than I expected," I said. "Tomorrow will be the first time I appear in public as Queen. Perhaps the people will not accept me in place of Mother Leda." His very brashness appeared to me a sure sign that I was not yet Queen. I kept my anxieties out of my voice. "Lynceus will be arriving from Messenia tomorrow with Castor and Polydeuces and their brides. Perhaps he is the first of the suitors. Maybe the only one. Idas will not be with him."

Tyndareus chuckled and sipped from his cup. "The line of Gorgophone is not all flawless I fear. Idas is a brute. But Lynceus does not displease you, I gather."

"I do not yet know him, but the idea does not displease me." I tried to be frank with Tyndareus when possible. Most of my thoughts could never be shared with him, for I knew him to be dishonest when it served him and to use information about people given in trust, against them. Talking about Lynceus was safe.

"Lynceus may have qualities that would make him a fine king." And he is an impassioned follower of the Goddess, I thought.

"He may be a good lad, but with the marriage of the boys to the two girl cousins down there—we have done enough to placate Messenia."

"Perhaps," I said, "I am eager to meet Hilaeria and Phoebe."

"Ah, yes. They are opposites, I have heard. One is fair and the other dark, and they both mindlessly adore their mates."

His words surprised me and made me laugh. "How do you know so much when you are all but isolated out there in the country?" I neither understood nor liked his prying.

"Oh, I have my ways." He laughed.

"In any case," I continued, "remember that with Lynceus as King, Laconia and Messenia would become bound together as never before." I waited for his response.

He made a sound from deep in his throat which sounded more negative than positive.

"Oh Father Tyndareus," I went on, "I am not saying I would actually choose Lynceus, but certain of his qualities would make him an excellent possibility. We can't just dismiss him."

"Yes, all the honey-dripping Goddess nonsense, I suppose," he countered quickly. He paused, then spoke more slowly. "It will pass, it will pass. The folk are all stirred up now, but it will pass."

This time I remained silent. I did not say that if I could manage it, the way of the Goddess Potnia would be the way of the future. He was not prepared to hear that from me.

"My dear girl," Tyndareus said, his voice stern, the warm tones replaced by sharp edged emphasis. "Most important of all, you must not forget Agamemnon."

"Oh, Agamemnon," I said in scorn. "He will not tell me who shall be King here. He does not frighten me. I know him."

"Let's hope so," he said gently. I suspected Tyndareus did not say all that he thought about the High Overlord Agamemnon. We sat in silence thinking our own thoughts.

"I have reason to dislike him," I finally said. "I have accepted—am trying to accept—that it is the fate of my daughter to be in Mycenae, in the house of Agamemnon, the fateful House of Atreus." I had not spoken to Tyndareus of Iphigeneia before this. My brothers had kept him informed of the facts.

"You have decided correctly," Tyndareus replied. We were again silent for a few moments, and then he added, as though from his own experience, "Such decisions are difficult. That old nonsense about the grandfather, Atreus, is just the imagination of the storyteller. Don't pay any attention to it."

We sat again in silence. I did not wish to say more about this painful topic.

"Well Helen," Tyndareus said. He yawned. "It is time for sleep. Do not worry, my girl, you are the Queen. As soon as we have a new King, I will fade away into obscurity."

Would he, indeed? I wondered.

With the help of Spiro, he hauled himself up. Then he turned to speak again: "But in the meantime these ways I have, these people who tell me things, my loyal retainers, I will keep them on."

I stood as Spiro took the elbow of the old man to guide him. I went to his other side and took his trembly hand. "I am happy for your recovery," I said, pressing his arm, "and I appreciate your help."

We stood at his door. Spiro had entered and was placing an oil lamp in a holder. I kissed Tyndareus lightly on the cheek. "Good night, Father." Since his illness, this term had come easily to my lips.

He took my hands, and we looked into each others' eyes. We were of a height, as he had shrunk these last years. "I wish your mother could see you. You have her strength and her grace, Helen," he said to me in a quiet voice. "Leda's grace—your own beauty. I've fallen victim to it—as has everyone around you." He squeezed my hand with his strong one. "You have courage too. It is hard for you without the child. I know." He turned to leave me, then remembered something. "Don't worry about all my loyal retainers who tell me things. You have them too. They are all around you. It is but for you to recognize those whose judgment you can count on—and to use them."

The summer solstice celebrations were the first of many pageants and ceremonies that dignified my Queenship. Penelope, with other Temple priestesses, had led the virgins in their initiation rites of procreation. They set fire to a great pile of wood and debris in a cleared open space. It was a fire of fertility and the joy of the return of the fruitful daughter from the underworld. The maidens threw seeds into the fire and danced around it and jumped over it to absorb the procreative energy present in the burning. Soon they were joined by young men of the male bands.

I felt myself becoming a part of the ritual, but more in longing for my lost daughter than in welcome for a returned one. I swayed and moved alone in my grief. We danced for hours under the stars in the warm night. I discarded my warm cloak and my single silvery drape swirled about me. I threw off the belt, an encumbrance, and kicked off my sandals. Barefooted, I twirled to music which came from a flute player who fit his notes to my rhythms.

Finally, the fire burned low, the dancing ended. The virgins and young men had long disappeared to the mating place for the enticing ceremonies. I retired to my own bed and heard their music and frolicking late into the night. I felt a restless longing to be with them that kept me awake until the pink edge of dawn appeared in the eastern sky.

"It was lovely," Penelope told me later. Her eyes found a focus above me as she remembered. "The moonlight—it fell upon us with a silver sheen. The summer breeze—so tender to the skin, and—the musicians—there were musicians." She looked at me, her gray eyes large. "They were unusually artful this year. Or perhaps last year, at my own initiation, I was too nervous to notice. The musicians, their clever strumming and piping intensified the ritual dancing. I think we all felt it. Her eyes dropped. It was stirring—seductive." "Who were your partners?" I asked. I wanted to hear more.

Her voice recovered its usual timber. "Men from the band of horsemen," she answered. "They were beautiful," she smiled mysteriously. "At least they appeared so to me then." She laughed. "I would not know them without the magic of the moonlight."

I could not help but remember the previous year and my own initiation with Theseus. Was it actually a year ago when all this began? It seemed so short a time, but when I thought of the changes wrought to my life—it was an eon.

I forced myself to think of the sacred effigy and rejoiced anew that it was back. My greatest responsibility for the summer solstice rituals had been in Her ceremonial return to the Goddess Shrine. My Queenship was confirmed within myself. I would walk as a Queen, live as a Queen, behave as a Queen and think as a Queen. I was Queen of Laconia, and whatever I did, I did as Queen—and the Goddess would be part of it.

My brothers and their brides arrived in time to take part in the games, as did Lynceus. Phoebe the fair and Hilaeira the happy is how I thought of them. Phoebe and Castor, Hilaeira and Polydeuces.

These two girls, sisters to each other and cousins of mine, lost no time in performing their temple duties. They took part in the Ceremony of Return and joined the group of young women who daily served the Goddess and moved among the folk dispersing Her care.

Polydeuces and Castor became counselors to me and continued with their military leadership. Uncle Icarius, father of Penelope, brother to Tyndareus, and betrayer of Laconia, had not returned to Amyklae.

I hoped Lynceus and Penelope might form a friendship, but neither was interested. Penelope devoted herself to Temple affairs, and Lynceus devoted himself to me.

He followed me about and we had much to say to each other. He knew about administering people and government, and he proved valuable as I worked through my new responsibilities. His agreeable smile and quick eyes charmed me and his light humor amused me. We often relaxed together or exercised together, stretching, leaping, running. He had a strong, well-muscled form, which pleased me.

"I don't want to rush things, Helen," he said one morning when we were resting, stretched out on some flat rocks near the river after a vigorous run on a track that led out across the fields and hills. "I have decided to leave here when the suitors begin to arrive."

"Lynceus, are you certain that is wise? I would be happier if you stayed." He was my true friend, and I felt I wanted my friends about with so many strangers expected. I sat up and looked at him, his eyes closed in the brightness of the sun. He was handsome and kind. He and I were more than friends.

He looked up at me, his arm shading his eyes. I could see their deepest blue reflecting the sky, the river, the color of his tunic. He sat up and took my hands. "Let me offer my suit now. Please know I wish nothing more than this. If you will accept me, I feel in my bones it would be right. We would be an extraordinary match. You give to me a deeper richer hue that enhances what I am or could ever become. If I offer to you any small part of what you give to me, we would be indomitable. Our union would create a marvelous presence that might not please the High Lord Agamemnon but would be splendid for both our lands."

"Lynceus, I..." His words stirred my heart as well as my mind. I believed him and wanted to reach out to him, to touch him.

"You are not to reply now. Of course you must wait to meet the others. I understand. I just do not want to be here and have to watch it all."

"Thank you, Lynceus," I said. "I don't know what will happen, but I believe you are correct, we would make an extraordinary match."

If it had not been for my longing for Iphigeneia, I could have been happy during those summer months. Often my brothers and their wives, Lynceus, Penelope and I went off together into the mountains to swim in the lakes and picnic leisurely in the shade of some giant oaks. We talked and sang and danced.

At these happy times, I wondered if my acceptance of Iphigeneia's fate, my giving in to the argument that it was her destiny to live with Lady Aethra, my sister and King Agamemnon, was the right decision. The visions of war with Messenia, danger, fighting and disaster here in Laconia, that had persuaded me to go against every instinct I possessed towards my child had proved to be absurd, and never more so than now.

The sun filtered through layers of green in the trees and the sound of laughter and happiness rang through the clear air from the limpid lake where others cavorted in the cool waters. My brothers were happy in love, and our enemy, Cousin Lynceus, had become a dearly cherished friend.

"Helen, you are quiet today," Castor said as he and Phoebe joined me in the shade where our picnic waited. Castor's hair was damp from swimming, and he had tied a linen towel around his hips. Phoebe's long wet tresses twined like serpents around her breasts.

"The water is so refreshing." Phoebe said. She looked like a water nymph. She smiled, wrapping herself in a linen sheet.

Castor sat down and reached for a handful of grapes. He tossed them up, one after the other, each to land perfectly in his mouth.

"Missing your babe, aren't you?" Castor asked.

"Yes, I must admit I am," I replied. Phoebe had wandered away to dry off.

"Here at Deep Lake I have so many happy memories from our childhood," I said to Castor.

"Yes, I remember how we came every summer with Mother Leda."

"And sometimes Tyndareus would come and Uncle Icarius and his family," I added. "It would be nice to bring our children here, wouldn't it?"

"Ah, yes. We will do that, eventually."

"Castor," I said, "I can not help but think how unnecessary it was for me to leave Iphigeneia." My voice cracked.

I did not want to unburden myself, and the others were approaching. I forced a smile.

"Think of her as being in the arms of Potnia. You must try to remember that it was all Her plan. Can you not accept that?" Castor put his fingers under my chin and forced me to look at him. I saw a handsome face with the kindest eyes in the world, caring about me.

"Yes," I said, willing myself to believe it. "Yes, I can," I whispered, regaining my poise as others came up wrapped in their linen drying-sheets, pushing their wet hair back from their faces.

They must have felt the poignancy of our interchange for they became silent until Polydeuces took up his wine cup.

"Let us drink together so as always to remember this time," he said. "Is it not remarkable that such tranquility has come to us? I believe this harmony represents a new communion with the rhythms of the earth."

"It surely seems so today, if not all the time," Hilaeira said in her lovely lyrical voice. She spread a cloth on the ground, and everyone eventually found a place around it. I sipped my cup with the others, wanting to share their feelings.

Penelope had tied her drape around her hips. Her long wet hair, held back by a band tied round her head, hung in tendrils down her back to her waist. She had found fresh figs in the food sacks and arranged them in a basket for our picnic, along with grain cakes, cheeses, slices of cold lamb, and the delicate white meat of shredded swan mixed with oil and spices. "I believe what you say, Polydeuces," she said. "It is as though we were all directed in the same way; it is an energy we have within ourselves—and it is Helen who has empowered us by bringing home the effigy and by her person."

Lynceus, his bare chest and shoulders bronzed and smooth, turned to me: "You are Queen, Helen. And you are what a Queen should be." His words were serious, and his meaning so profound that I could not speak. I was relieved to see the familiar face creased in a smile. Water drops still stuck to the fringe of dark lashes around his clear eyes.

I was moved by their confidence in me but aware that this time of leisure would not last. "Many guests will arrive before long to end these happy days," I said. "They come to vie to be our King, and we will all be occupied with duties then."

"Will they wonder why Castor and Polydeuces do not become King and co-king, as happens in most other lands?" Phoebe asked. She lay back on one elbow, delicately nibbling a morsel of the swan meat. The sun cut through the rustling leaves of the oak above, catching her brilliant hair in a shiny aura that spilled onto the golden skin of her bare shoulders and breasts.

"Ah, what a good excuse to give them a lesson," Castor answered. He sat cross-legged next to his wife and ate a fig, which he used to accent his words as he continued. "I will tell them that to be King is to be the Queen's mate. It is the Queen who possesses the mysteries and renders the cycles of life which we celebrate." He bit into the fruit, wiped his mouth with his hand and made an appreciative sound as he tasted its succulence. "These new kings who seize power for themselves do not understand; they destroy exactly what it is they seek."

Polydeuces poured the wine around. His face was in shadow as he leaned back against the trunk of the oak. "A king who achieves his kingship by military victory, or by kidnapping a moon priestess to fulfill merely the form of our traditions will rule as despot."

"You might be describing Lord Agamemnon and our sister," I reminded him.

"Yes, and so it is." We were all silent with the implication of his words. "A despot forcing his will on everyone is exactly contrary to the desired way we want to live together—in agreement with nature, with the earth cycles of begetting, growing, dying and rebirth, venerating this life force our Queen represents." He nodded to me and emptied his cup.

"Ah," I said, sorry to break the beautiful spell. "I must remind you that we are unusual. These princes who will come here to vie for kingship, will they understand us, or will they wish only to usurp the power?" No one answered my question.

VISITORS IN AMYKLAE

My brothers, magnificent on their matched white stallions, their golden muscled arms and legs taut with strength, rode out to welcome the first arrivals from Salamis. Lani and I watched them from my window. One was a giant of a man; the other seemed still a boy who sat his horse with style. A feast was offered in their honor for which I prepared carefully.

Pindros, in his tunic of the Athenian guard, escorted me to the receiving room. My brothers awaited me in the ante-chamber dressed in formal attire. I walked across the smooth stone floor and sat in the carved chair at the far end. Pindros took up his place behind me. Almost at once our guests were announced. My brothers ushered them in and stood before the stone benches at either side of my chair. Ajax and Teucer of Salamis entered, and I watched them approach in the light of the wall torches.

I do not believe I had ever seen a man so large as Lord Ajax. My brothers, whom I had always thought perfect in form, stood not much above his shoulder. The veins of his arms webbed his muscles like sinew, and his thighs were so thick he adjusted his gait to accommodate their bulge. He held his head tilted to one side, emphasizing a great proud jaw. A band of gold around his head kept his hair in place, for there was much of it, brown, crimped and long. His beard was trimmed to a point, and as my eyes moved upwards I saw thick, well-formed lips, a wedge of a nose, and dark eyes that slid from mine on contact.

His half-brother Teucer, dark of skin and hair, lithe in his movements seemed to be about fourteen. He clearly acted as a subordinate to his older brother.

"Welcome, Brothers from Salamis," I said. "You have made a long journey to visit us, and we open our house to you."

Ajax spoke with a muffled speech and had difficulty returning my gaze. This man must be shy, I thought. How extraordinary, for he is in command by his presence alone.

Teucer grinned, flashing very white teeth. He returned my gaze with what I took to be admiration. "Yes, your lady. The mountains seemed higher and rougher the closer we got to Amyklae. We accept your hospitality with pleasure." I liked his enthusiasm.

"We have brought many gifts," Ajax mumbled.

I looked up at him towering above me. "I thank you, Lord Ajax, for all the people of Laconia."

"Oh Lady, but these gifts are for you." He had such a look of distress on his face I felt sorry for him.

"You honor me, Lord Ajax," I said. "We will deal with the gifts later." I would refuse them, of course. I could not become so obligated to any suitor.

I stood. "Let us mingle with the others who await you." I put one arm on that of Ajax, and the other on that of Teucer. "We have games planned for the next days, Sires."

Ajax mumbled something which I took to be assent.

"Oh, yes," Teucer said.

"What is your favorite event?" I asked him.

"For me, I am an archer," Teucer answered.

"And your brother?" I inquired turning to Ajax. The huge man seemed to relax a little as he told me that he wrestled, that he threw the javelin, that in his youth he ran in the footrace, but now his specialty was to lift the weights.

"I will look forward to seeing you do so," I said. "Our athletes practice every day, and I, too, am often at the practice fields. Maybe we can run together some morning," I suggested.

A look of surprise overcame Ajax, and a harsh sound escaped his throat, which I did not at once recognize as laughter. "I do not run with women," he croaked.

I laughed with him, for it was a ludicrous image—the two of us running together.

All of the suitors were not so flustered as Ajax who found the near nakedness of Laconian women athletes upsetting. Teucer on the other hand felt no qualms, and he and I, in my Athenian shift, ran the course together every morning of their visit.

Ajax performed well in the competition. No one could come close to him in lifting the iron bars that had been acquired from far north Epirus. Teucer revealed a happy nature that appeared to be oblivious to his brother's plodding mind and undue self-pride.

"You are very loyal to Ajax, Teucer. He is a lucky man to have such an admiring younger brother."

"Oh no, Lady Helen. I am the lucky one. Why, my brother Ajax is the strongest man in the country. I serve him with honor."

"You have fine qualities, Teucer. You are smart, quick, you speak well and you think well. I don't believe that you must always be second to Ajax."

"Now you sound like my mother. But my father says it is good training to serve Ajax."

"Ah, yes. It is wise to take advantage of your opportunities. I think I like your mother. Is she like you? What is she called?"

We sat together in the shade of the garden at the edge of a cool pool. Silver fish darted about in the dark depths, turned green now and then by an intermittent sun released from milling clouds.

"My mother," the boy said looking at me, "is called Hesione. She is from Troy, the sister of the King." His eyes followed the movement of a hawk in the sky. "My father fell under her spell when he was in Troy on a special mission. He was not able to make a marriage agreement for her so—well—he just took her." His eyes found mine again, and he laughed. He found the story amusing.

My hand dabbled in the water. I could see our shadows reflected on the rippled surface. "I am sure your mother cares deeply for you. Have you ever asked her about it? Did she want to leave, or was she taken against her wishes?"

"Oh, Mother is happy, now. There may have been times when she was angry. But she is happy now," he repeated. A perplexed frown lingered on his face. "You would like her," he said. "I wish you could meet her. She would be so happy if Ajax brought you home as a bride; it would give her a beautiful companion to talk to and to be with."

"Is she lonely, then?"

"Yes, that's it. I do believe she is. Lonely."

"I would like to know your mother. My own died not long ago, and I am lonely for her." I stood up and brushed off my robe where some dried leaves had settled. "You see, I am taking her place, here in Laconia. I am Queen now, and anyone I choose to marry will come here and be King."

"Ajax would like that," he said, his eyes warm and approving. "Oh, that I were a few years older."

"Teucer," I said. "You are only two years younger than I." And much more of a man now than Ajax would ever be, I thought.

The leisurely pace of entertaining visiting princes ended abruptly, for suitors began to arrive in such numbers that it became difficult to house them properly or to entertain them with the glory they were due. Diomedes came from Argos with Sthenelos. Another Ajax came from Locris, called Little Ajax though he was as large as Diomedes. King Idomeneus and Lykomedes came from Crete. King Menestheus came with Prince Acamus from Athens.

When I saw my friend Acamus, the son of King Theseus, I could not restrain myself from embracing him. He was taller and stronger than I remembered. "You are a vision come to life," he said. His brown eyes seemed to consume me.

"You appear to be in excellent health, Acamus."

"I am indeed very well." His smile was infectious, and I looked upon him with pleasure. "Helen," Acamus said more soberly, turning to introduce Menestheus. "Here is the King of Attica who comes to further my cause. He brings the good wishes of all of Athens."

I turned to King Menestheus. I saw a man of medium height and stocky build with a square face and blunt features. He had a wiry crop of short brown hair and a beard cut short as well. His eyes held no particular light, but he mouthed the proper words, and I said a silent prayer for the shade of Theseus as I tried to welcome him with the honor and courtesy he deserved.

Patroclus from Thessalia came the longest distance. He had set up camp outside the city and did not depend on our hospitality for the keep of his retainers. He was a cousin to Ajax and Teucer and quickly entered with them into the games competition. He was most courteous and endeared himself to me at once for his consideration. Fair in complexion with yellow hair, he possessed sharp brown eyes that missed little.

"My Queen," he said in meeting, "I have come a long way to put forth my case and hope not to be a burden to your house. Please tell me what it is that I may do for you."

I thanked him, and a few days later I responded to his request for it was unusual among our visitors. "I ask of you a service, Sire." I said to him one evening. "I must go out into the country tomorrow, for I wish to consult with Tyndareus, my father, who is in retirement on his farm. I would like some company. Will you so honor me?"

He bowed his head in acceptance, and the next morning early, we rode together with several of his retainers and some of ours.

Pockets of snow were still visible in the high mountain peaks that dominated the sky. We let our frisky horses canter in the coolness, then we walked them, riding abreast and chatting comfortably. Patroclus was interested in our Laconian ways. I spoke freely, for I sensed his sincerity.

He told me about his land. "I live on a rich plain, where fields of golden grain are surrounded by great mountains, and herds of galloping horses thrive on hilly grasslands."

We came upon the orchards of the country home of Tyndareus, then the terraced vines and finally his house surrounded by trellises and arbors. Other horses were tethered in the courtyard, I noticed. A servant called for grooms and sent someone ahead to announce us. In a few moments we were led into an inner courtyard where Tyndareus and a stranger sat in the shade of a fig tree, a small table holding a jug and some cups between them. Did I see an expression of wariness cross the old man's face? He held out his hands in greeting.

"Well, well, Helen, this is a surprise. And, please, let me welcome your companion. Prince Patroclus, is it, from Thessalia?" He turned to introduce the stranger, a man with light red hair and strong features. "This is King Odysseus, a suitor from Ithaca and the Western Islands. He has stopped here on his way to Amyklae to give me his greetings, as we are old friends. Come, come sit in the shade. Rest yourselves."

He clapped his hands, and chairs were brought. A servant bringing a bulging skin covered with little beads of water poured cups for us. Another carried one of wine which he added to the water in our cups. We were all smiling and talking in a matter of minutes.

"Helen," Tyndareus asked, "have you come to make an announcement? Have you brought your chosen prince for me to meet?" I saw such teasing in his eyes that I responded in like manner.

"Prince Patroclus may indeed be the right choice. He has been kind in his wish to serve me, so I enlisted him to come with me today."

"My dear girl, what is the urgency?" Tyndareus asked.

I felt hesitant to speak openly before the two visitors. Patroclus, I felt, would understand, but I had no knowledge of King Odysseus. Nevertheless, I spoke up.

"Many princes, several kings, and their accompanying retainers are now in Amyklae. Frankly, it is becoming difficult to care for so many. I think it is time for you to join us. I believe the process of selection should begin."

"Oh, Helen, Helen," Tyndareus said, thinking the entire situation very amusing, for he laughed until tears came to his eyes. "Who has come?"

I named the roster of guests. "And King Agamemnon and his brother arrive today, and others tomorrow. Just what did you say in your message, and how long will this continue? Father Tyndareus, you initiated this program; now you must come back with me and help take care of it."

Still finding the situation amusing, he dabbed at his eyes with a square of linen. "I will set out for Amyklae tomorrow," Tyndareus said. "You should be honored, not distressed."

Odysseus had a unique way of speaking, a cadence to his words that was slightly musical. It made one listen. "It seems the combination of the Kingdom of Laconia and the beautiful Queen Helen is so alluring that it draws princes from all lands." He smiled engagingly, and we all laughed with him.

"Well, it may be a nice gathering and an opportunity to have some games and contests," said I, "but I'm sure to find it difficult to select a king. Perhaps it would be useful to have other meetings while so many are here, some meetings about common problems." I had thought this often, but had not voiced it before. "In that way I would see the princes engaged in serious matters and get an idea about their strengths as leaders."

Servants served us lunch, and the talk changed to food and drink and lighter subjects. Cicadas thrummed, and the sweet scent of ripening figs pervaded the air. Goat cheese, round brown loaves fresh from the oven, perfectly ripe pears and wine were all provided by the country estate of Tyndareus.

Patroclus told of his long journey from Thessalia, ending his tale by saying, "My cousin Achilles wanted to come with me. He is just a youngster, but extremely strong for his years and talented. Unfortunately, his mother would not hear of it."

"Teucer would have liked another lad for company," I said. "You are all cousins, are you not?"

Before he could answer, King Odysseus spoke up. "Yes, we are all cousins one way or another, all of us—that is, if we are descended from the daughters of Atlas." He smiled once again.

I found him agreeable and awaited his next smile, for it twisted his lips in laughter and made his bright blue eyes crinkle until they were just slits through which they shone.

"And we are," we said in unison.

To my delight, Odysseus smiled again and then drew himself up for more serious words. "Well, as we are all family, so to speak, your thoughts earlier on, Helen, have stayed with me. Perhaps, in addition to the momentous decision for you and for Laconia concerning your visitors, they should be alert to the fact that it is a rare event in a different way. I don't imagine so many royal leaders have ever been at one place at the same time before. It would, in truth, be a moment to talk over matters we all care about. Matters we could agree upon and pledge our word upon. And Helen would have some good debates to listen to that would help her make a choice."

"I would approve of that," I said at once. Tyndareus and Patroclus eventually agreed with the general idea.

After lunch Tyndareus showed Patroclus who was particularly interested in vine culture about his estate, while Odysseus and I rested in the cool shade of an arbored terrace near a pond where some of Mother Leda's pet swans nested. I made the sound in the back of my throat that attracted the birds, and in a moment their wings spread and beat in the air. Two of them landed near our shady place. They came close and took some bread from my hand. "My mother loved the swans," I told Odysseus. "She taught all of us children how to call them. They are special here, where she most liked to be."

"I feel the charm," Odysseus commented. "A reverence of the place and the birds, or perhaps it is you who creates that aura."

I felt no need to reply, and we sat quietly until Odysseus broke the silence. "I suspected as much," he said, crossing his legs, relaxing in his chair. "My journey here is a sham. I am defeated before I start."

"Why ever do you say that?" I asked. "You have made this long journey; you will be welcomed and honored as you deserve." I could not understand his attitude.

"Ah, but you see, beautiful Helen, even if for some incomprehensible reason known to yourself alone, you chose me to be your King, it would not work: I cannot leave Ithaca and live here. I am a King, not a prince." He sat up, resting his elbows on his knees and chuckled inwardly. "I had a notion I could talk you into coming with me. After all, I reasoned, you do have two princely brothers who are natural kings, are they not?"

"They are everything one would want for Kings," I agreed. "They have recently married moon priestesses from Messenia. It is possible that they may be called to the country of their wives for Kingship, but that is not their ambition—to be Kings."

"The traditions of the Goddess are accepted seriously here in Laconia," King Odysseus said.

"My brothers and I as well as most of the folk in the country follow Her way."

"Yes" he twinkled, "Laconia is noted for being a bit backward."

I laughed, agreeing. "You are right, and is Ithaca so different, so accepting of Zeus and his thunderbolts?"

"Well—now that you ask—there is Goddess worship everywhere. One just accepts it without really thinking about it. Followers of Zeus are more likely to be young men who hope to fight battles."

"And women?" I asked. "What about the young women?"

Odysseus answered, "Come to think of it, Zeus does not have much room for women. When it pleases him, he simply takes over a Goddess shrine." He stood and walked about. "The truth of it is," he said, standing before me, "we do honor the Goddess in Ithaca. We practice many rituals and traditions still. My father believes the old religion is fading because we lack young female followers to carry on."

"Oh," I said, seeing an instant answer to their problem. "Then you must marry a moon maiden. We have an active shrine here with young women who would suit your needs perfectly."

"Do you?" Odysseus smiled. "That brings us back to why I am here, I believe." He sat down again in his chair, an impish grin on his face.

"You are clever" I laughed. "As you so clearly realize, I will not be going home with you, but yes, yes, you need not go home without a bride." Then I spoke too soon. "If you are looking for someone to regenerate the fading Goddess culture, Penelope would be perfect for you."

"Tell me about Penelope," Odysseus said, obviously interested.

"Penelope is my cousin. She is my closest friend, and I would miss her dreadfully if she were to go so far away."

"Well, now, that sounds too good to be true. She must be very ugly."

I had been half joking, but I realized this might be a serious conversation. "Penelope is absolutely lovely—but" —I laughed, trying to make light of the exchange—"I am not in the business of arranging marriages. And besides— I've changed my mind. Several others would do for you. Phiona, for example. No, you must not take Penelope away from here."

We did not speak further about Penelope, for Patroclus and Tyndareus returned and we prepared for our departures. "I will be with you tomorrow," Tyndareus called as the three of us rode off.

As Lani readied me for the welcome of King Agamemnon and Prince Menelaus that evening, she lamented the absent Iphigeneia. "If only they had brought her with them, and Lady Aethra as well." She held up the filmy silver and white robe interwoven with a pattern of faintest pink. She had altered it slightly during the day so that it would drape perfectly when held by the silver side pin. It must have met with her approval for she laid it aside and knelt next to me, taking my hand. "How difficult this is for you."

I repeated words to her that I had said often before, but they still rankled. "It is the will of the Goddess: the destiny of Iphigeneia is to remain in Mycenae with my sister and Lord Agamemnon. Lani, you have said so yourself, as has Pindros, my brothers, and the Venerable One. All of you have said it is Her will." I spoke the words bravely enough, but I quietly anticipated my meeting with Menelaus. He would tell me about my daughter. Had he not pledged to do my bidding?

Lani handed me a long silver earring studded with pale pink stones. "You do it," I said, tilting my head. She attached one earring; I turned my head, and she attached the other. She wound silver bands in my hair and held the robe for me to slip on.

"Now let me see you," she said. I stood and turned for her. "Yes, it hangs well; the earrings bring out that slight bit of rose pattern in the fabric, and that trace of rouge on your cheeks was a good idea, too. "Looking into the polished metal mirror, I saw that she was correct. My cobalt-lined eyes looked back at me. I held the mirror at arms length and saw that the robe covered me modestly, yet, through its fine texture my breasts and shoulders were very nearly as revealed as on the playing field.

"Why do we bother with all of these preparations?" I joked. "I may as well go unclothed?"

"Yes," Lani beamed, "it's just right.

King Agamemnon and Prince Menelaus entered the receiving chamber after my brothers and bowed formally.

Prince Menelaus bore himself well, standing at his brother's side. His russet-colored mantel and gold-trimmed tunic were a shade or two lighter than his wavy hair and beard, both cut short. He carried a heavy sword embossed with copper which hung from a studded belt. He looked at me with inquisitive eyes. The edges of his mouth curved up in greeting. I nodded and smiled in return.

King Agamemnon lifted his gaze from an acute examination of the open work of my robe. He made no effort to hide his animal stare. His blue mantel and tunic were trimmed in silver, and his sword was silver-sheathed, his belt of silver studs. His black hair was pulled back into a tight knot, and his black eyes, deep with buried memories and hidden deeds, held mine. I returned his look, curious to discern the person within and the workings of his peculiar mind, refusing to let him demean me by his rude and bestial manner.

I spoke: "You are welcome, brothers. I hope you have brought news of my dear sister Clytemnestra, my friend Lady Aethra, and the infant Iphigeneia."

Prince Menelaus stepped forward. "We are honored to be here, Queen Helen, and we do bring greetings. Your sister Clytemnestra regrets she could not accompany us here. I fear she was sadly indisposed by illness."

I nodded. How could I expect my child to come with them when they would not even bring my sister. "Father Tyndareus, her brothers, and I are greatly saddened. We hoped very much that she and the baby would return to her home place for a time of family pleasure and reacquaintance."

King Agamemnon's brow furrowed. "We regret any grief caused to you by our house." He bowed his head slightly in deference, then said, "I will see to it, Sister, that such a visit occurs when Queen Clytemnestra is well." His flat high-timbered voice bespoke of giving orders more than pleasant conversation. He continued: "There may be many opportunities for family visits in the future," he smiled, "for I am here to join my brother in presenting his case to you to become your consort and to be made King of the Laconians."

I nodded, accepting his words, wondering if he spoke from the heart. "Come, sirs", I said. "A feast awaits in the dining hall. Friends and colleagues from far places are eager to see you. Let us join them. This evening we will feast and dance. Tomorrow we will enjoy games in the afternoon, for in the morning we will gather for some sincere exchange of ideas and opinions."

I held out my hands, nodding to my brothers who stood at either side in front of the stone benches. They came forward, and we led the way out, Agamemnon and Menelaus followed.

"Don't forget," Castor whispered as we left, "the Over-lord is not an unwanted guest. It won't go well if he feels insulted."

"Flatter him, just a bit," Polydeuces said in low voice.

I realized I had been less than cordial in not choosing Lord Agamemnon and Prince Menelaus as my escorts. We entered the great hall where a din of boisterous conversation came to a sudden halt as we were announced.

I moved first to Tyndareus whose chair sat on a dais so that he could look out upon the gathering and the royal visitors could pay him homage. Nestor of Pylos and his son, Antilochus, stood aside as I approached. Antilochus was a light-haired young man who ran past all the other early morning runners with ease. The royal team from Mycenae moved slowly towards the dais.

"Good evening, Father Tyndareus and visitors from Pylos," I said. "Forgive me for interrupting your conversation. I believe you were in the midst of some important talk."

Nestor, tall, with a balding head of wispy gray hair, a lined face and thin features protested. "Oh, no, my dear."

"My old friend has been telling a marvelous story," Tyndareus said. Continue, Nestor, I beg you."

The nasal voice of Nestor took up the thread of his tale. "If you insist..."

I realized at once it was a very detailed account of a test of strength concerning Antilochus. I glanced at the young man who reddened as he felt my eyes. He was clearly embarrassed to be the subject of his father's bragging.

I felt his relief as Agamemnon and Menelaus came forward at that moment. They bowed with respect, first to Tyndareus who seemed happy to see them, and to Nestor who introduced his son.

Tyndareus spoke warmly and held out his strong hand. "Welcome, Agamemnon, and welcome, Menelaus. It is with honor, indeed, that we receive the strongest amongst us, the king with a ready army for any need. But it is a pity that my daughter Clytemnestra is not with you. I long to see that girl—and the child, tell me about the child."

I silently thanked Tyndareus for asking the question. I watched Agamemnon closely as he answered. "Electra is now five," he said, "a serious girl. The baby, Iphigeneia, is a chubby, happy little person. She likes to have me carry her about, and everyone fusses over her." He spoke naturally. Once his eyes met mine, but they did not linger, nor could I detect any unstated hidden knowledge. Could Agamemnon feign this fatherly image? I wondered. Could he truly believe that Iphigeneia was his child?

Menelaus turned to me. "How was your journey home from Mycenae?" One eyebrow arched in concern.

"Not at all difficult," I answered. "The border fighting with Messenia was resolved with friendly accords."

Servants carried in large trays of food. Tyndareus stood with the aid of his staff and signaled that it was time to feast. "Come, sit with me tonight," I said to Menelaus.

He nodded, and we were able to continue our conversation amidst the confusion of people and servants milling about.

"Lady Aethra sends you special greetings," Menelaus said, walking behind me.

"I hope she is completely well now." I turned to take his arm.

"She is strong and assumes her responsibilities with Iphigeneia very seriously."

"And my sister? She accepts this?"

"Your sister accepts this."

We were quiet as the traditional calf bones and waste were offered to Zeus. Tyndareus sat with Agamemnon. Menelaus and I sat with King Idomeneus of Crete and Lykomedes, his son.

"You have chosen well this evening," Idomeneus said after the prayer. "It is good luck, you know, to sit with Cretan cousins."

"But you are not from Crete," I said to Menelaus.

"Ah, but yes. My mother was the daughter of Catreus."

"And we his nephews," Idomeneus explained, including Lykomedes, a shy youth who let his father speak for him. Idomeneus had brown teasing eyes and a smile that flashed the heart of a genial man. His mature face showed lines of strong character, and he was exceedingly graceful in manner.

"One can always use luck," I said. "I am pleased to be your dinner partner in any case, though my luck usually comes from being a moon maiden, a priestess of the Goddess."

His eyes glowed. "Then you are doubly lucky tonight, he added. "You will be pleased to know that The Goddess has been reawakened in Crete. After many years of being repressed by Zeus, she is back in the minds and hearts of the folk. In the further lands on either side of us in central Crete,

Goddess worship is as strong as it ever was." He smiled pleasantly, turning to Menelaus. "It actually reminds me of the ardor for The Goddess we noticed in Miletus."

He spoke to me. "We are old friends, Menelaus and I. We have spent many months together away from home. Though we are cousins, I know Menelaus like a brother."

The congenial conversation continued as food was brought and taken away. Wine cups were filled again, and the musicians started up a rhythm. Dancers of the Brotherhood of Swans appeared in white plumage. Everyone focused on their intricate gliding steps, their magnificent undulating wings, and the final mating ritual battle.

Maidens entered dressed in simple flounced robes and performed the spiral dance, and then others too began to dance. I turned to Menelaus. He nodded his head and hand in hand we joined them. I recalled how well he and I danced together in Mycenae. It was not just happenstance. We could not err. I lost myself in the music, swaying and moving to the rhythms. I closed my eyes and let the excitement of the tempo carry me along. Menelaus gripped my hand as we kept the step; we each sensed the movement one to the other. I had never found a dancing partner who pleased me more. Our dancing in Mycenae had been ever so brief that afternoon, before I had hastened away to ride in the cart pulled by the oxen down to the sea, away, away from Mycenae, away from my child.

I broke with the circle and still holding the hand of Menelaus, I led him away from the dancers, out onto the terrace. I sought a private place at a distance from the revelry. I sat on a stone bench under the branches of a poplar tree. A gentle breeze rustled its leaves, and the moonless night sky glittered with stars.

"Please, Menelaus, sit here with me."

"Of course," he said, and sat down.

I came directly to the subject that haunted me. "Has Lord Agamemnon been informed that Iphigeneia is my daughter?"

"I tried to tell him, but he would not permit me to do so."

I could not see Menelaus in the darkness, for even with the many stars overhead, we were in shadow. I could hear regret in his voice. "But, how can that be?" I asked, even as I knew full well that such a man as Agamemnon could direct a conversation by interrupting, becoming foolishly distracted, or insisting in an overbearing way on addressing another topic.

Menelaus replied: "He has clever ways. I believe he does know, or he prefers to act as though he does not." Menelaus did not attempt to cover his own lack of success in getting this matter straight with his brother. "Helen," he added, "it was not possible for me to carry out your wish. I had hoped to be your servant in this, and I failed."

I spoke after a bit, my voice low and even. "I must then believe that Lord Agamemnon, for reasons of his own, has decided that Iphigeneia will be his child. He gives no credence to the truth. And everyone around him who knows differently permits him to carry out this subterfuge." My last hope had vanished.

He put my hand in both of his and touched my fingers lightly. "I know my brother. I know his mind. I know that he will do as he wishes, no matter what." He let me grasp the import of his words before he continued. "I know also, that I regret more than anything that has ever happened to me in this world, that I was unable to carry out the mission you asked of me."

A great weight settled on my heart, darkening a part of me forever. All hope vanished, even my secret, illogical hope. Now I must accept, in all ways, that my baby was gone.

With my silence Menelaus said, "I watch the child. I play with her. She is well cared for, and I know she is happy. She smiles often, and Lady Aethra says she is alert and very intelligent."

Menelaus could not know how his words stung. "Please, no more." I spoke sharply, but the anger drained out of me with my harsh words. "It is too painful," I whispered.

"You are very brave, Helen," Menelaus said.

I was suddenly filled with bitterness and self-sorrow. "Very brave, yes. One must be very, very brave to be Queen in Laconia. Oh, fabled luck! Where are you?"

Shamed by my outburst, I sat on, silently. Menelaus held my hand. Finally, his voice low and hesitant, he said, "I must tell you, I admire you. From the first time I met you, I knew you were a woman different from all others. I could not imagine anything more glorious than being husband to you. I would care for you. I would help you. I would worship you." His words washed over me. I felt little response. I was not thinking about husbands.

I stood again, and he, too, stood. We faced each other, and he put his arms around me, drawing me close to him. For some reason, I was unable to move. It was as though I watched the two of us from some distant place. I rested in his embrace, it felt comfortable, safe and warm. I did not resist as he put his head down and kissed me gently on the lips. It was a simple kiss, warm and pleasant. "I will see that you know Iphigeneia. That you are with her often. Remember this when you make the decision."

I still remained quiet. When we walked back to the others, I forced a bright face, and soon we parted. Then I was drawn off by Prince Acamus. Over the shoulder of King Odysseus I could see the back of Prince Menelaus as he and King Agamemnon joked with King Nestor and King Idomeneus.

TO CHOOSE A KING

Benches arranged in the great hall faced a three-legged table at which my brothers and I sat. Penelope, Hilaeira, Phoebe, Father Tyndareus and other notables were grouped in chairs at the side. The Kings and Princes arrived amidst noisy talking. Few wore swords, but some had daggers fastened to their belts. Their dark-colored tunics and mantels were brightened by gold or silver head bands and neck chains. When the gathering was more or less settled, Castor explained the nature of the meeting and then he turned to me.

"Queen Helen, will you address this gathering? We would hear your expectations of our talk."

I stood and put my hands on the table to prevent them from waving around in nervousness and spoke. "Honored Kings, Honored Princes, you celebrate our country by your presence. One of you may become King here. All of you are regal in bearing, keen contenders on the playing fields, brave and valorous on the battlefield, and gifted in different ways." I paused as an undercurrent of muffled laughter broke out amongst them. I smiled with them and continued. "I have made many fine new friends these last weeks and renewed several friendships from previous times." I saw Acamas nod slightly. Lynceus, who had returned a day or two past, stood at the back of the room with his arms folded across his chest. He nodded, but he did not smile. Menelaus, sitting apart from Agamemnon, raised an eyebrow in an expression familiar to me even in our short acquaintance.

"All of these friendships are precious to me. I must choose a King for Laconia. He who will be best for Laconia will best please me." Again there was an undertone of good-natured joking. "Because I know little about you in matters of state, it is my hope that your talents may be revealed in these discussions this morning. I would like to hear your opinions. I would like to see in action that part of you that is so vital to kingship.

"My brothers will ask some questions to start the talk and will interfere if someone speaks too long or disagrees too ardently. I hope we may discover some profound agreements."

I took my seat to clapping hands and stamping feet. There was still much talking and laughing, and I feared this was not to be a serious affair.

Polydeuces stood. His presence quieted the outbursts. "In our deliberations about today's gathering, we noted things about this group that we share commonly."

They were listening to him. King Agamemnon sat with King Nestor, his demeanor was serious and suggested disapproval.

"King Agamemnon of Mycenae, powerful Lord of ships and armies, honors us by his presence here, and we hope he will speak freely. We have no intention of overstepping conventions." Polydeuces smiled and nodded toward Agamemnon who scowled—"This session is not intended to cause dissension."

Agamemnon looked from side to side. A stiff nod of his head meant the meeting could proceed.

"We increasingly have entered into trading arrangements with each other and with countries not represented here. My question for discussion is, in what way can our trading efforts be improved by a group alliance?" Polydeuces waited as the shuffling feet and clamor of voices subsided. For a moment I believed no one had anything to say.

Then King Idomeneus of Crete stood. "When you bring up the question of trade, my brothers, it is ever so natural that some one from Crete must speak." Idomeneus, by his very nature, presented a powerful presence. Intelligence snapped from the fire in his black eyes.

"Cretans are sailors. Foremost of all peoples it is the Cretans who are sailors. It is we who held the secrets of navigation long before anyone else. It is we who brought bronze from Cyprus, gold from Egypt, and took back your oils, your perfumes, your grain." He looked at his fellows. "We were once the sole traders in Greece, but now there are many. It is my observation that there are too many of us plying the same routes." As he paused, I could see some listeners nod their heads in agreement. "To answer your question, Polydeuces of the flying fists, we could help each other by cooperating, not duplicating trips with half empty vessels."

To my ears he spoke well, and his message made sense, but Idomeneus was a king. The Prince, Lykomedes, of Crete, his son who could be king here sat mute, uninspiring as a future king. To my surprise, it was Prince Acamas of Athens who stood next. Polydeuces recognized him, and Acamas spoke:

"Queen Helen, my colleague princes and their kingly mentors, I do not wish to be too forward among this august gathering, to rush to speak, for I am very young, and it would be appropriate for me to listen first to my elders." I remembered that he and I were the same age; he was sixteen. He stood straight, and his strong voice projected clearly.

"For two reasons I speak now," he continued. "Queen Helen has asked that we who would be her consort show themselves in kingly matters. For the second, I must say that

I, too, am of Crete, grandson of Minos as is King Idomeneus. As you all know, it was my father, Theseus of Athens, who made the alliance with Crete that opened the way for the rest of us to trade."

As he spoke, I could not help but remember the tales Pindros told of the heroic deeds of Theseus in Crete. It was much more than the making of an alliance; it was the downfall of Crete that Theseus undertook. It was a tactful reference on the part of Acamas, and I credited him with diplomatic skill.

"With the heritage of these two traditions behind me," Acamas was saying, "seafarers and the alliance makers, I would offer a new suggestion. That we distinguish trading from plundering. To trade is to make an honorable agreement, to represent ourselves fairly, and to do what we say we will do. If we all agree to this, we will not only develop confidence in each other, but we will build a reputation of honest negotiation, and others will seek us out for trade.

"Too often the same parties who wish to trade do not hesitate to commit acts of piracy when it pleases them. This undermines the trading effort and is damaging for future trust. If we here could agree to an oath amongst us to stop this, it would be a good beginning."

Immediately there was a clamor of voices, and everyone spoke at once. As Polydeuces attempted to regain order, I thought about the words of Acamas and believed that there was truth in them.

Prince Patroclus stood at the back when he had been noticed by Polydeuces, who, with a calming motion of his arms, had quieted the group. Patroclus smiled like a boy. He stood tall and strong like a man, but there was a glint of humor in his dark eyes. "Brothers, I know what you are thinking. Prince Acamas wants to take our pleasure away from us." He grinned and rubbed his hands together. A great hubbub of approval came from the others "Why should we not do as we want?" He waited a moment looking around the room at each face, all waiting for his next words. "Because," he said, his voice now serious and low, "because, it defeats our purposes. It is expensive and wasteful; it causes bad feelings, and destroys trust. If we here agree not to plunder and pirate each other, we would all be winners."

I thought how people could agree on this. It was only a matter of making it formal.

"Just imagine," Patroclus continued, seemingly enjoying the experience of speaking his mind to such a group, "that we can count on one and another as true allies and partners." He paused slightly, and his little-boy grin returned to his face. "Do what you want to with outsiders, with Cyprus, with Troy, with Egypt, but with each other, we will not plunder nor engage in piracy." He raised his arms to finish, and the grin came again. Everyone cheered.

Patroclus truly has a way with words, and a way with people, I thought. I remembered our day together in the country, and it came back to me that he was also a considerate man. He was handsome with his yellow hair and black eyes.

The crowd quieted, and Polydeuces nodded to someone. At first I thought it was Ajax of Salamis, but he sat on his bench like a dolt. It was Teucer, his young half-brother who stood to speak.

Brave Teucer, confronting this body of seasoned warriors looked so young, my friend Teucer. "I would agree with what has been said," he commenced. His voice had a nice cadence even though it was more the voice of a boy than a man. He stood with his legs spread and his hands on his hips to present himself forcefully. "It makes little sense to enter into serious trade arrangements and then rob, steal, burn and rape those you do business with. At least among us, we can agree to stop that practice and the practice of kidnapping women, particularly the practice of kidnapping moon-priestesses to be queens. If we can make agreements for trading goods, we can also make arrangements for marriage. We should add this to our oath."

Teucer sat down. His speech was short, but he spoke with passion. Ajax looked at him, completely unable to hide his astonishment. After all, Ajax's father had kidnapped Teucer's mother. Was this boy insulting their mutual father? The jaw of Ajax rose a degree higher as he looked down from lofty heights on this brother of his. A look of fury spread across Ajax's face; he stood and lumbered forward, eyes clouded in anger.

"What is all this talk?" he gasped. Debate was not his strength, I knew. "Soldiers are not meant for talk. Soldiers are meant to fight. To win a battle is to take what others have lost whether it be gold, food or women. That is how it has been, and that is how it will be." His wide, wild eyes did not focus on anyone. He spit out words from a dark hole of a mouth, his beard covering any sign of lips. When he finished, he gave a sideways shake of his head toward Teucer and stalked out, his great thighs rolling and his greaves creaking.

There was total silence. I looked at Teucer, who sat alone. One could feel the shame spread through him for causing his brother anguish. Finally, he stood and walked out without looking at anyone. I felt so for the boy that I wanted to run after him. Castor must have sensed my anxiety, for he put his hand over mine, and I did not leave my place.

Odysseus stood next. He must have found the whole episode amusing for his eyes crinkled, and he smiled his lopsided smile. "Honorable brothers and beautiful Queen sister, I believe we have had enough discussion for one day. The idea that we here can talk together without rancor is important. I propose we gather again tomorrow." He left his place and came forward. He wore no metal at all, so his movement was agile and cat-like. He was nowhere near as large as Ajax, yet his body was strongly muscled so that he projected an aura of immense strength. He faced the group, his head upraised, his reddish beard jutting out. He spread out his arms to Agamemnon. "If Lord Agamemnon finds this a wasted effort we may wish to alter our suggestions." He addressed Agamemnon directly. "Sire, are these just word games, or do you find this meeting useful?"

I suspect Agamemnon had hoped to sit out the entire meeting without saying a word and then dismiss the whole effort as nonsense. Now, he had to speak. He stood at his place, turning so as to see the others. Always stern of expression, he did not smile nor attempt to win his audience with graceful speech. The harsh timber of his voice carried to all corners of the room. "I see no reason to stop," he barked, "though I strongly doubt agreements will be kept."

After Lord Agamemnon resumed his seat, Castor stood to relieve Polydeuces as arbiter. His gold wrist bands glinted a moment in a shaft of light as he placed his hands on the table. He waited for the clamor of voices to cease, then spoke:

"We will continue. The sun is not yet high enough in the sky to call us to our games. We have heard statements that stimulate us to think further on the subject of trade and agreements amongst us. Who else has wise words to offer?"

The silence lasted a long time. Menelaus sat with his head down, looking at his hands, concentrating as though he would rise to speak, but it was Lynceus who stood. Since the arrival of so many guests, I had found no moment to welcome Lynceus back. The comaraderie we had established earlier in the summer had ended suddenly with his parting.

"Lynceus, Cousin, please come to the front where we can see you and hear you," Castor said.

Lynceus pushed his way to the front. He answered my smile with a curt nod. He looked fine in his dark blue tunic that exactly matched the color of his eyes. His dark hair, pulled behind his ears, was held in place by a leather band around his forehead.

"My message is one of conciliation." he said. His voice was low but gradually took on vibrancy. "Everything we have heard thus far seems reasonable. First, that we cooperate in our trade. Second, that we not plunder and pirate each other. Third, that we not kidnap priestesses for queens. Despite the anger of Great Ajax, we should agree to this. Many of us have used this method of finding queens; Salamis is not alone." He glanced at the High Overlord Agamemnon, but did not refer to him.

I thought he had finished. I approved of what he said. He spoke well and had the concentrated attention of everyone. When he did not return to his place, there was a stirring, but it was silenced as he spoke again. "There is another idea to add. I believe it is reasonable and feel you too will see it that way. We must not desecrate religious shrines, for in so doing, we incur the deep animosity of those who worship those deities and the deities themselves. Divine retribution of some sort was, in the past, always to be feared and avoided. Lately it has become prankish and sportive to desecrate places of worship. Some people seem not to fear retribution. Whether or not there is or is not a punishment, the desecration is wrong. I would add this to our list. That we do not destroy religious shrines in each other's country."

Of course I thought the suggestion of Lynceus excellent. It was just what was needed for the protection of our Goddess worship. He did not specify any particular deity or shrine. I wondered how the others would see it. Lynceus quickly returned to his place at the back of the hall, and now someone else would be heard.

Little Ajax stood at his place and spoke up quickly, in agitation. He was very different from Ajax of Salamis I knew by now. He never flaunted wealth by wearing showy pieces of gold and silver and his tunic was always of simple un-dyed linen. He competed admirably in the games, for he was one of the finest spearmen and fastest runners—no one to give way to others in the sports arena. His brown hair grew in whorls creating a great mass around his head. I had spoken with him several times, and our conversation was always memorable. I learned that his country held to the old ways, much as they did at Aphidnae. In fact, they held religious rituals in common, and Locris, too, sent girls to study with the priestesses in Troy. He had a pet serpent that often twined around his neck, and his eyes teased when he told me that it followed him everywhere. I laughed to myself as I realized he was not wearing his serpent today.

"My Lord Agamemnon, Queen Helen, Kings from all places and fellow Princes, I am little known at home for my tempered speech. I beg your pardons, but I am often told that I argue too much and have no patience. Now that I have given away to beautiful Queen Helen that I possess these hideous faults, I also give away, I fear, any weak chance I may have had to be chosen as her consort. Thus, I have nothing more to lose if I continue with this confession. I support Prince Lynceus in his suggestion that all refrain from shrine desecration."

He stopped speaking and looked about him. He smiled sheepishly at all of us. "It is convenient that the other Ajax, kin to me in some manner lost in time, is away just now, for he would not approve of my words. I will say them quickly in case he may return. We in Locris, and I, more than most, follow the ancient Goddess worship with solemnity. I cherish the life-giving power of her womb and her blessed nurturing of the seeds of the earth. Each of her images is holy, and the desecration of one is the destruction of life. I bow to Zeus, to Apollo, to Poseidon because I do not wish to offend those who think highly of these Gods, but for me it is the Goddess." He then cast his look upon me. "To me, Helen is a Goddess in person."

I felt strange, embarrassed even, and knew not what to do. He returned to his place.

The room was still. No one moved. His words had touched me, but the purpose of our gathering seemed to have changed.

Menelaus stood. "We have talked enough, I think. If it pleases Queen Helen and the Dioscuri, I suggest we think about our discussion here today and come together again tomorrow. By then an oath will be drawn up that we can sign. Brothers, Dioscuri, please name two or three here who will put the oath together, two or three of your chosing. Do you agree, all of you? Please speak up if you do."

"Aye." "Yes." "Go ahead." "Yes." There were no dissents.

The following day the kings and princes met again. The oath, prepared by King Odysseus, Prince Patroclus, and Prince Diomedes included all of the points raised in the discussion plus one more. A courtesy pledge for each to honor me, Queen Helen, in all things and to come to my assistance if ever they were needed. It was a friendly sort of thank you and commitment to friendship which I found endearing. Every prince and every king selected a white stone to place in the jar. There were no black ones. Every king and every prince agreed to this oath now scratched in clay.

I would announce my choice for king at the evening's feast. I spent the day alone, mulling over the decision, anxious that I choose correctly. In the presence of the holy image in the shrine, I found quiet and calm, and my quandary was eased. I left knowing not the name of the man I would choose to be king, but that I would decide well.

I wandered out into the hills with Skerri and strolled among the juniper and oaks. Myrtle spread at my feet and gradually my mind quieted. My brothers had urged Prince Acamas, for they thought a closer tie to Attica desirable. Tyndareus urged Menelaus, for he always wished to please Agamemnon. I thought of these two, and others. Lynceus, Patroclus, Little Ajax, Teucer, all had become my friends, and earned my admiration. Odysseus, a possibility, had taken himself out of the running. We would probably lose Penelope to him. A good thing for her, and for him, but I would miss her.

Did I prefer any one of them above the others? If I had not experienced mating with Theseus, ah, if I had not mated with Theseus, I would not know to ask the question.

Patroclus, a nice man and clever. We would be good together, I thought. His lively humor, his natural care for others, his bright mind all pleased me. I liked his kind face.

Lynceus, we were comrades. There was nothing about which we could not talk, and his adoration for the Goddess would help keep her in the minds of our people. Laconia and Messenia would join together as in the days of Gorgophone, but the Dioscuri had made a satisfactory alliance with Messenia through their marriages. I felt sad, for Lynceus and I cared for each other in a profound way.

Little Ajax, too, worshiped the Goddess. He was wild and amusing, and no doubt correct when he said he argued too much and was impatient. I saw no political advantage to a partnership with Locris.

Acamas was a strong possibility. I knew Athens and Attica. A political partnership would help both countries. Politically, we would become a balance to Mycenae, which might not please Agamemnon. To displease Agamemnon would not be a deterrent, to my way of thinking. Acamus had matured, and I liked him.

Menelaus did not impress me in the discussions. He was not skilled at kingship. He had been unable to confront Agamemnon about the true parents of Iphigeneia. He has been too much in his brother's shadow. Yet, he had lived away for years and might be more his own person than I realized. But he came from the House of Atreus, which is marked with the curse of infamy. My sister is Queen to Agamemnon and is restrained in all ways, of little help in that quarter.

What advantages would result from chosing Menelaus? Closer ties to Mycenae might be helpful. Anything to receive the approval of the most powerful High Lord of Mycenae would be to the good, despite my personal dislike of him. Menelaus was easy and sometimes witty, and we danced together as though we had practiced for days and days. We shared a physical coordination that could enhance our mating.

Unbidden, an idea at the back of my mind came forward. The vision I tried to keep out of my thoughts demanded my attention. I saw my sweet child, my babe Iphigeneia. Now she must be able to sit up. She could laugh and play. Her hair, was it dark or light?. Was it straight or curly? What color were her eyes now?. Could they be like those of Theseus? How I longed for her. To marry Menelaus would make contact with her easy and natural. "That is no reason to select a king. No reason at all," I said to Skerri who looked at me and barked a response. I forced my child out of my mind and concentrated on my friend, Acamas.

I dressed carefully. It was the time of all times to be queenly. A robe of exquisite woven threads of gold was draped to reveal, rather than cover, my breasts, which were also accentuated by the heavy gold necklace of Mother Leda. A golden diadem fit snugly in my hair, and long golden earrings swung as I walked. My skin had been rubbed and oiled so that it too glowed golden.

At the announcing ceremony I sat in the chair of the queen with Pindros attending as my guard, and my brothers flanking me at either side. I spoke to the assembled suitors, honored by their cause. I would present each with a ring of gold incised with the wearer's totem. The man I chose to be king would be given a ring of gold incised with a swan.

One by one each suitor came forward, and I placed a golden ring upside down on his forefinger, requesting, as I did so, that he not look at it until the trill of the flute sounded.

Everyone in the room stood before me in silence. I looked around at my own family, the visiting royal kings and princes, the leaders of the divine orders, including Phiona from the Goddess and the high priests of the shrines of Hyakinthos, Zeus, Poseidon and Hermes. I saw the solemn members of the esteemed Council, consisting of the governors of the provinces, the leaders of the military and the administrators of the government.

The princes returned to their places. A more handsome and distinguished line of young men could not have been found anywhere. I gazed upon each, and, as they looked back at me with expressions of hopeful expectation or acceptance of lost desire, I felt completely humble and immensely honored.

I nodded, and the notes of a trilling flute floated around us. I watched each prince study his ring, and when Menelaus looked at his, he raised an arm into the air and shouted a victor's cry. His brilliant eyes found mine and his happy smile warmed my heart as he immediately came to stand before me.

I saw his bronzed face and his thick, red-brown hair held in place by a dark green and gold band. He wore a tunic of the same color green trimmed in gold and an emerald studded gold belt with a golden dagger at his waist. I took his hand, and, together, we walked to the dais amidst much cheering and clapping. Happiness and pleasure graced the features of Menelaus as we continued to gaze upon each other. His lips parted in a broad smile, and he turned from me to look out at his comrade princes, not in victory but in pure delight. All of them offered generous congratulations. They were urged to remain for the wedding, which was to take place in one week.

I let myself be caught up in the frenzy and excitement of the nuptial rituals. Wedding gifts beyond measure in beauty and value were received and displayed. We were married late in the afternoon in the town center with a blessing by all the priests and a placing of floral wreaths on our heads. The entire community reveled, feasted and danced. Led by children who threw flowers in our path, Menelaus and I walked among the people, accepting their affection. When I danced with Menelaus on the night of our wedding, we moved together so perfectly it was as though a divine moment had been given us. We celebrated with others long into the night, but finally we fell exhausted into the marriage bed in the Queen's apartment.

Despite our need for sleep, the will to mate was more urgent. Our first shy fumblings kept us awake. We whispered and kissed and touched each other, and I felt happiness descend upon me. I would help Menelaus become a good king. We would be fruitful and our land would prosper. We would abide by the oaths agreed to by kings and princes alike. I became more and more aroused by our lovemaking and soon became lost in its intensity and fulfillment.

I awoke from a deep sleep at daybreak and saw a rosy line of dawn behind the hills. I stretched languorously recalling the pleasures shared with Menelaus the night before. I turned to him and watched as he slept, his muscular form stretched out next to me, his face strong and handsome, even in repose. I resisted an urge to wake him, feeling sleep wash over me again. As I looked out at the brightening sky, I closed my eyes and remembered that sometime soon I would again see my adored Iphigeneia.

THIRTEEN YEARS LATER

From the terrace of my summer house I looked across the river valley and watched Menelaus and his brother ride off to hunt for game. The final day of the visit of the Mycenaean family—I sighed, regretting the necessary parting with sweet Iphigeneia. I heard her soft laughter and that of eight-year-old Hermione float across the hedges. The little boy cousins must still be fast asleep.

I returned a wave to the distant figures and felt disturbed at Agamemnon's displeasure. We in Laconia refused to support him in building fortresses in the outreaches of the Peloponnesus. And he was interfering in Crete with his military, to which we were decidedly opposed.

"Will you have breakfast here in the garden, Queen Helen?"

"Oh, yes Lani. Please." Still in my sleeping robe, I breathed in the fresh scents of morning and turned as a new servant girl set my place at a stone table under a hanging willow.

"Come Lani, join me. We have not relaxed together for so long.

"Yes," Lani said, "as soon as I fetch the hot brew."

I sat down to goat cheese and bread, figs, plums and spring water, although I did not eat. My eyes roamed the secluded garden surrounded by flowering euphorbia hedges.

At an ivy-covered wall I could look out at the massive mountains, constantly changing in light and season, forever present. This morning the ridge was starkly etched against the early morning sky caught by the first rays of the sun breaking from the hills behind me. I had not to leave my chair to imagine the valley below, for I knew the sight well. The river wound around spreading its gift of water to the orchards, olive groves and fields of grain; it could be a torrent or a trickle.

The royal palace overlaid the first high hill across the river, where farewell feasting for King Agamemnon and Queen Clytemnestra would be celebrated tonight. Its vast basement and sub-basement store rooms were filled to bursting.

A shrine to young Apollo on the other side of the rise of the palace could not be seen from here. The young god had moved into the holy place of Hyakinthos, ancient and wise deity of male fertility.

Way down the valley to the south my brothers had constructed houses. Their families were in Messenia for the summer, but Castor and Polydeuces had returned early in honor of our visitors and would join today's hunt. The Dioscuri knew the feeding places for game, and Agamemnon might leave tomorrow happy with his hunting prowess.

Lani sat opposite me and poured scalding liquid from a steaming jug into our cups, the mint aroma pungent and welcome.

"Mama, Mama, are you there? Can we come in? It was Hermione with Iphigeneia, on the other side of the hedge.

"Yes, darlings, come through at the wall path." I met them as they entered the garden. Hermione's face was alight with curiosity, her hair always a mop of tangled reddish curls until someone smoothed it.

Iphigeneia's light brown hair shot through with golden tones waved becomingly around her face. Her blue eyes alert to the new morning smiled at me, as did her full lipped mouth showing even white teeth. In mind and body she possessed a composure unexpected in a girl of thirteen.

"Good Day, Auntie," she said.

"Good Day to you, Iphigeneia," I said as I knelt down to hug Hermione. I put an arm around Iphigeneia. "Have you had enough breakfast. Look, here are some figs and a plum."

Hermione scrambled from my embrace and ran to the table and took a fig. "The plum is for you," she said to Iphigeneia.

"And it is just ripe," Lani said. "You will like it."

"Thank you," Iphigeneia said. She walked gracefully to the table to take the offered fruit. Her rough woven child's play dress graced her lithe form as though it were designed by an expert seamstress. Her slim tan legs were long so that the tunic ended well above her knees. She would make a good runner, I thought.

"This morning," I said, "Pindros will take me into town to visit the temple and the royal palace. If you girls would care to come with me, I would like your company."

"Oh, yes, please," Iphigeneia said, wiping plum juice from her chin with her hand. "I want to see the Goddess effigy one last time before we leave. Lady Aethra told me that it was the most important thing in all of Laconia."

"I want to go with you, too," Hermione chimed in.

"Good," I said. What could be finer than to have my daughters like each other, even if they knew not that they were sisters.

"I regret that Electra did not come," I said to Iphigeneia, "and also that Lady Aethra did not feel up to the journey."

"Electra refused to come." Iphigeneia said. "I don't know why, but she managed to persuade Papa to permit her to stay behind."

"Well, in any case, you must give Lady Aethra my personal regards. She was a very good friend to me when I was a girl." Lady Aethra's role as teacher was a success. Surely, the old lady must have some of the same regrets as I concerning the secret of her granddaughter's parenthood.

"She has little endurance, you know," Iphigeneia replied.

I visualized the older woman as she must be now, fragile physically, but still strong in character. The vision of Lady Aethra, as she was the first time Menelaus and I visited Mycenae after our wedding, came to me unbidden, for it was a scene I longed to forget, but could not.

In a flash I lived over again those terrible moments. I had been so full of suppressed anger at the theft of my child that it was a trial for me to be civil. My brothers and my husband had convinced me that it was in the best interest of all for me to accept the situation, accept that Iphigeneia was the daughter of my sister and Agamemnon. In my mind I did so, but not in my heart. On that first visit to Mycenae, it was Lady Aethra who received the full force of my bitterness.

I looked out to the mountains remembering. Iphigeneia, then just beginning to talk, was in the garden with her nurse. Her hair, lighter than it was now, shone gold in the sun; her face, bright with curiosity smiled at me as I knelt down to her. "Rose," she said, pointing to the blossom on a bush. "Smell," she said, as she carefully leaned toward the pink petals and sniffed their scent. "Smell," she demanded, and I obligingly smelled the flower. I studied her, examined every detail of her perfection. I saw the bloom on her round cheek. Long dark lashes fringed the penetrating blue eyes of Theseus and rosy lips parted over eight pearly teeth. I took her hand and looked at the plump fingers, the lines on the palm, the nails pink and clean. Suddenly, I was overcome with grief and stood quickly. It ached to smile, but I did so.

I kissed her briefly and rushed into the nursery. I had a vague image of the little girl watching me leave with a puzzled expression on her face, then toddling off to another interest.

I had hoped to be alone to regain my composure, but Lady Aethra was there, organizing something. When I saw her, all of the rage I had buried deep inside me came to the surface. "Oh," I muttered in surprise and went to her and shook her. She stood before the window; her white hair was neatly pinned at her neck, her drapery of a mottled blue and lavender became her. I accosted this dignified woman, worthy of the greatest respect. "How could you," I groaned and shook her again until the pins fell from her hair and her eyes widened in alarm.

"Helen, Helen, dear," she uttered, her hands flailing uselessly as I took great handfuls of her loose hair and pulled hard. "You knew, you planned it all the time," I fumed. Her hair was wild, and tears of pain streamed from her eyes. I saw her start in surprise as she looked behind me. I released her and turned to see Iphigeneia and the nurse looking at us with horror.

I buried my face in my hands, overcome with shame. In a moment Lady Aethra's arms were around me, and I wept into her shoulder, just as I had done in this room once before. The nurse must have taken the little girl quickly away for they were gone when I finally stopped sobbing.

"It has been hard for you," she said.

"I should have insisted," I mumbled. "No danger for her existed in Laconia."

"But you couldn't know," she added, her voice almost a whisper. I sat up to right myself, wiping my face and smoothing my hair. "I'm so sorry, Lady. I beg your forgiveness. I do not imagine it was your doing that keeps my child and me apart."

"No, my dear," she said, covering my hands with her own. Her kind eyes beamed a loving regard all through me. "It was the way of the Goddess."

These words had not helped me in the past, nor did they now. I did not reply at once. I stayed on for a moment, looking about me, realizing what a lovely room had been created for Iphigeneia, the painted furniture and sheepskins on the tiled floor.

I looked up at Lady Aethra, whose hair was re-pinned, and who had picked up her work of smoothing and folding Iphigeneia's pretty little tunics before placing them in a clothespress. "I will leave you now," I murmured. "Thank you for your understanding."

Ashamed of my outburst and downcast because my longed for time with my child would not erase the pain and longing that plagued me, I returned to the garden and watched her from a distance. I memorized everything I could about her, for I knew I would never be her mother.

"Is something wrong, Auntie?" Iphigeneia asked with concern in her eyes.

Brought back to the present, to the lovely morning and the anticipation of an outing with my daughters, I could only rejoice. "No, nothing that we can change," I said.

My hand reached for the ceramic Bird Goddess amulet I wore around my neck, the token Theseus had sent to me after our parting. I had always promised myself that I would give it to Iphigeneia.

"Darling Iphigeneia," I said, undoing the clasp of the gold chain on which it hung. "Will you accept this amulet, this sacred, very ancient bird? You would please me by wearing it."

"Oh, Auntie," Iphigeneia breathed. "I would be so honored." She turned so that I could put it on her. "What does it mean."

I closed the golden clasp and put my arms around her for an instant. "Lady Aethra knows the lore of the ancient Bird Goddess. Ask her when you return. Remember it is a symbol of my love for you."

Pindros, white haired and slightly bent with age, waited for us next to the pair of spirited brown mares attached to the chariot. His face glowed as he settled the girls in the seat.

"Hermione, my pet, and Iphigeneia, her eyes—uncanny, isn't it?" He spoke, with his back turned to the girls. I nodded, for sometimes it was as though Theseus himself looked at me through the penetrating sea-blue eyes of Iphigeneia.

High Priestess Phiona received us in the Courtyard of the Virgins, where twenty-five maidens learned the mysteries and rituals, the serpent magic, the procreation blessings for the planting of seeds, the harvesting of fruit: all the wisdom for understanding the abundant earth.

"Dear Phiona, this reminds me of our own days of training to become priestesses. It was much simpler then, was it not?"

Phiona, her rosy cheeks and jolly smile belying her serious position as High Priestess, agreed. "It was easier with so few of us and so few old ones to teach us."

"I am nearly their age," Iphigeneia said. "I would like more than anything to become part of this group next year when I turn fourteen. To be a priestess to the Goddess—and to be near you, Auntie." She turned to Phiona. "Please, Honorable High Priestess, could I become a novice?"

Phiona smiled. "It could happen, little one. Talk to your temple priestess. You would be welcome here, I assure you."

Back in the chariot on the road to the royal palace, Hermione and Iphigeneia chattered while I thought about the wondrous pleasure of having Iphigeneia here as a temple maiden. It was such a beautiful thought, that I lingered over it much too long before one ugly fact of reality interrupted my dreaming: Agamemnon would never permit it.

The jowls of the Palace Steward quivered in pleasure as we approached. He seemed to grow stouter every day. His skirts swished with each heavy step as he lumbered along to the great hall which was being prepared for a lavish evening entertainment. Flowers and garlands bedecked the tables that had been set up to seat one hundred guests. Musicians practiced with flute and lyre on a raised platform, and the kitchens were astir with activity. Sacrificial ceremonies had taken place earlier, and great chines of lamb, pig and calf were placed on spits. Cauldrons of grain, herbs, and dried fruit simmered very slowly over low fires. Bakers pounded dough into loaves, and baskets of grapes, apples, pears and plums were being culled, washed, and arranged for each table.

"All is proceeding very well, Chief Steward. I know we will have an excellent feast tonight," I said, just as Arneus, the controller appeared to usher me to the cellars.

"May we wait for you outside?" Hermione asked. She knew from other visits that discussions with Arneus about the production of olive oil did not interest her.

"Yes darling, of course," I agreed.

Iphigeneia and Hermione left with the Chief Steward as Arneus led me to the basement storerooms. He was unusually animated. "We have a fine opportunity, Lady Helen," he said, as we stood at his work table surrounded by stacks of bronze ingots needed for making weapons and tools, while ranks of great storage jars stretched before me. They were filled with olive oil, marked for their different flavors, wine, marked for its age and grape, and different grains, marked for strain and quality. At least fifty huge ceramic bowls filled with chunks of lapis from Laconian quarries waited to be graded and sorted and put into different sized covered boxes that would be used for trading. Unseen was the precious gold and ivory from Egypt and the Laconian mined silver which was stored away in treasure vaults. In further rooms were chariot parts, finished leather for harnesses, sandals and shoes, leggings, parts of furniture, sacks and more. Shelves of work from our finest potters filled others. Wine jugs, cups and urns of many sizes, formed, decorated, glazed and kilned, were all accounted for and itemized by Arneus and his scribes.

Arneus stood tall beside me. His bald pate gleamed amber in the torch light, and he could not restrain a smile of pride. "I realize you are busy with guests, but it is important to tell you of a recent development." He glanced at me for my reaction.

"Yes, what is it. What has happened?"

"One of our most reliable sea captains has brought news from Troy. They wish to trade horses, foals, which they know we want, for Laconian green flecked porphyry stone."

I nodded. This information alone was not unusual. Castor had a stable bred from Ilium mares, and Laconian green and red porphyry stone had been used in Troy, as well as other distant cities, for years.

"The special part is that they will reduce the usual levy charge, if we respond at once."

"It sounds too good to be true," I said, skeptical of the news. I recalled how Troy, situated at the head of great travel routes to the Asian hinterlands and at a control point to the Hellespont straits into the Black Sea, charged heavily for use of its port. "The tariff to enter the harbor at Troy has traditionally been a burden for seafarers and caused limitless strife and retaliation. How do you know this and why would they do this?"

Arneus smiled. "Here is Captain Thaos to tell you about it himself. Come."

"Captain Thaos?" I said, pleased. "Is he here?" Arneus led me into a workroom where scribes were busy with tablets and wedges at the far end near a window. Captain Thaos came from behind a cluttered table and knelt before me.

"Captain, I am overjoyed to see you." He stood and I took his hand.

"To actually be in your presence again," he said, "is my eternal hope come to pass."

He appeared very much the same man I remembered from our sea voyage fourteen years ago, save a few white hairs in his black head and beard. His brown eyes seemed to gather in the light around him and refocus it wherever he looked. I turned to Arneus and explained. "I had the special privilege of being a passenger the first time Captain Thaos commanded a vessel."

"I gather it was a memorable passage," he said.

"It changed my life." Thaos spoke without explanation, and it was clear none would be given. I thought briefly of Iphigeneia, who was so near at hand. I would like to have him see her.

"Tell me, Captain Thaos, how long have you been sea captain for Laconia?" I asked.

"For ten years," he answered. "Such an opportunity was an unimagined privilege for me."

Captain Thaos, my old friend who long ago pledged me his service! "I have full confidence in you," I said. "Tell me, Captain, tell me about the proposal you bring to us from Troy, how did it come about?"

Thaos spoke: "My Queen, I have made several voyages to Troy this spring and summer, always following the practices laid out: no raids and no stealing of treasure goods while in foreign lands. My crews have never been guilty of pillaging crops or robbing lambs, even if we do run short of food while we wait for favorable winds."

Arneus nodded his head, and I listened, fascinated. Thaos was not as tall as Arneus, but he commanded a vital presence.

"Our cargo, this last time, was fifty stirrup jars of scented olive oil in exchange for fifty bronze ingots. We hurried the process for the weather was fine. If we had been stranded there with high winds, as is very often the case, we would have had to pay in pottery, olives, or holy stones each day we lingered. And if we decided to leave port and beach the boat in some protected place down the coast, outlaws would have attacked us, and not only robbed us of everything, they would have killed us had we resisted. I was surprised when the harbor master told me that I was wanted in the palace." Thaos paused.

Arneus used the moment to draw up chairs. "Please, let us sit," he insisted.

Thaos continued. "I was taken by chariot to the great walled citadel. The huge gates stood open and we entered into city streets alive with people going about their affairs. I was taken to the palace on a hill. It stood all beautiful and glistening white in the afternoon sun. A servant met us in a large court yard and ushered me through walkways to a meeting with the controller in an office out-building."

"What did he say," I prompted, eager to hear the full tale. Thaos stroked his black beard. "He told me the Trojans appreciated the honesty of the Laconians. He said they wished to trade for more of the porphyry stone, the green Laconian stone. I have some tablets, or rather I gave Arneus some clay tablets, with the exact amounts put down."

"And you understood it?" I asked Arneus.

"Yes. It is very clear. It is a large amount and will take at least three ships to haul it."

"He was insistent that it be sent at once." Thaos said.

"Is this possible?" I asked.

"Yes, it is possible." Arneus answered.

"Why," I wondered aloud, "are we suddenly given such special treatment by the Trojans?" I speculated about Troy. "It is a long and difficult voyage from here, in any season, but particularly now with the north winds of summer to confront."

"Yes," Thaos agreed, "and the screaming winds must moderate before any vessels can depart, particularly to the north through the straits, which I have never done. Ships must wait for exactly the right moment for this passage and often seek shelter on protected beaches while waiting. Sometimes Trojan farmers are forced aboard to provide extra rowing power for the short difficult pull through the straits and into the Sea of Marmara. And a strong northern current is always present, even with no wind at all. The best way is to seek shelter in the protected port of Troy, where, unfortunately, the king always demands a high tariff on any vessel coming or going."

"And he is willing to discard this custom for us?"

"That is what I was told," Thaos answered.

"In return for our quick service," I repeated.

"Yes," Thaos said. "They will charge us no levy, even if we are held up with bad weather and cannot leave."

"It is written in the clay tablets," Arneus said. Also, if we deliver the stone sooner than the one month specified, they will permit our ships to go on through the Hellespont straits with no charge at all."

Thaos sat back in his chair. He had told us most of his story, and was content to let Arneus provide the final details. "Oh, one more thing," he said. "I have brought two particularly handsome colts, gifts of King Priam, to assure good will. I left them in the care of a faithful groomsman in Limera. A field of sweet grass is their home pasture until you decide their future."

I was mystified by such a turn. "How remarkable," I said. "We will send someone to bring them here." My thoughts turned to the Hellespont Straits. "It will take much planning for us to go on through the Straits. We would have to carry trading goods in addition to the stone for Troy. Would we go to Varna to trade, or is some other city on the Black Sea a better destination?" I had only vague notions of the land around that huge body of water.

Arneus seemed to have thought it all through. "Thaos has not mentioned that we were promised extra rowers for the difficult passage against the current of the Hellespont. Also, as for cargo, I believe we could take as many crocks of oil as space permits, as well as the holy stones and lapis from Krokeai, which is rare. The holy stones are precious and should make good trading in Varna for gold beads, or even sheet gold. Also, we can resupply in Troy. Isn't that correct, Captain?"

Thaos nodded. "Yes, my contact said that would be possible." Again, I gasped in wonder.

"This is most astonishing," I said.

"Yes," Arneus agreed, "and if we decide to do it we have no time to lose. We must ready our ships at once." He had worked it all out. Excited now, he spoke hurriedly. "Forgive me, Queen Helen. I took the liberty of directing Captain Thaos's ship to proceed at once for the loading of the stone. If for some reason you do not want to pursue this opportunity, we have only to cease the loading." He waited a moment to see that I was not upset at his overstepping his authority. "I have also given instructions that two other vessels be called in for this service. If we agree to this request from Troy, we will be positioned to take advantage of it."

"You are a master of planning, Arneus." I realized that I must decide at once. "We will move ahead with this trading venture. Continue with your plans, Arneus, and, Captain Thaos, you must leave to oversee the preparations."

I had more words for Thaos, serious words. I stood to speak. "Captain Thaos, once in the Black Sea, it will be your mission to make as propitious trading agreements as possible."

Thaos stood also, with bowed head. "I have sailed to many strange lands and know the dangers of being an outlander. I have, with experience, become proficient in the art of negotiation. I say this not in pride but simply for your information."

It was time to leave, the girls were waiting. "I will be going then, Arneus," I said. "I hope to see you this evening."

"I am honored to be included in the farewell feast." His eyes lowered in respect.

I turned to Captain Thaos. "You will be in my mind and heart. May Potnia watch over you."

Captain Thaos bowed low as he received my words of parting. "If it does not inconvenience you, I will see you out," he said.

"Yes, please do."

We emerged into the light of day just as Iphigeneia and Hermione rushed into the courtyard. "We've been to the Temple of Apollo-Hyakinthos," Hermione said between breaths. "We watched a sculptor."

"He carves a likeness of Apollo," Iphigeneia added. Their cheeks were pink from the heat and from running.

"Some priests showed us where we could sit and watch," Hermione explained. Suddenly, she noticed Captain Thaos and became shy.

Iphigeneia, having nodded her head to Captain Thaos in a hurried gesture of courtesy, continued with the morning's adventure. "The priests hope it will draw visitors to their shrine rather than the shrine of the Goddess Potnia." As she finished, she spoke directly to Captain Thaos. She must have sensed his interest. Her full lips parted in a brilliant smile. "But I do not believe worshippers will ever give up adoring the Goddess effigy, do you?"

Captain Thaos, I could see by his expression, suddenly realized who she was. I went to the girls and stood between them, preparing to introduce them. Before I could do so Thaos spoke:

"Iphigeneia, you have been singled out by the Goddess Potnia." His voice took on a resonance of pronouncement.

His black eyes focused on her, compelled her complete attention. "Your birth, divine, a miracle. I was present and felt Her power at your ritual dedication in a shrine on the shores of Argolis Bay." He stopped, lowered his head and stood quietly before her. We were all still; the sacred moment was impossible to interrupt. Then he raised his head and spoke quietly. "The Goddess light will shine through you."

Iphigeneia stood still, stunned by the gravity of his words.

Captain Thaos turned and walked quickly away.

Even after a touching good-bye to Iphigeneia later that evening, and even with many other vivid memories of her, it was the vision of my daughter caught in a moment of reverent awareness with Captain Thaos that would return to me over and over here after.

My private garden, the terrace outside my chamber, was bathed in pale moonlight. I had shed my finery, unpinned my hair, slipped in to a light wrap and stepped out to this quiet place of beauty. It was well that the family from Mycenae slept in the royal palace tonight and would be off before dawn. Our farewells had been said. Agamemnon seemed content and had spoken words of warm appreciation for their agreeable stay.

The only moment of discontent I had noticed all evening was directed at my brothers, who had drawn around them a group of admirers from the Mycenean retinue. They performed clever sleight-of-hand routines we knew well but always enjoyed. They somehow managed a new twist with such dexterity and wit that we were all amused. All but Agamemnon. Perhaps I alone noticed, for everyone's attention was drawn away from him. A look of such naked hatred flashed across his face that a terrible blackness engulfed me. He cast this evil leer upon the Dioscuri. The next moment it was gone. Had I imagined it? The warning that made my heart pound, my breath come in sudden gasps, and a haze of darkness fall before my eyes was not imagined. I forced myself to attend the harper's stories and buried the incident, for then.

In the night garden I recalled the moment and shuddered. Lani would soon bring a warm drink; Menelaus would join me, and perhaps we would begin to recapture the tranquility of our own life again.

I stretched, inhaling the aroma of the night blooming moon flower. I had just seen Hermione, clutching a rag doll made for her by Iphigeneia, and Nikko both fast asleep. I had brushed back his fair hair and traced the curve of his round cheek. Potnia had blessed my devotion by giving me Nikko, a boy child who filled my heart with his laughter. Born under some special sign, he was a golden child of beauty and health.

This afternoon Nikko and his cousin Orestes laughed in excitement as they rolled colored wooden balls. Clytemnestra appeared as Nikko rolled his yellow ball, and he and Orestes ran after it. My sister and I watched our sons disappear in a cluster of cypress trees.

"Our boys are good friends," I said to her.

"Yes, it's been nice for Orestes to have a playmate so close at hand. Nikko reminds me of our brothers when they were babes. Menelaus must adore him."

"He does, even though Nikko is a child of the Goddess. Like Mother Leda, I often participate in the procreation rites. After Hermione, the fatherhood of Menelaus failed us, although not for a lack of mating. We pleasure each other greatly, and someday..."

"Of course, Clytemnestra said, "It is the curse of Pelops and Atreus. The sons of the house of Atreus will produce no offspring."

I could not reply for the boys demanded our attention, but I wondered if Orestes was a child of the Goddess, also. Had the curse of Atreus struck Menelaus, as Clytemnestra suggested? He had been sick with the swelling disease after Hermione was born. Was this the curse of Atreus? We had no more babies until I took up the practice of observing the sacred rites of procreation.

"Here is some hot mint brew," Lani said bringing me back to the garden and the scent of the moon flower. She set a tray on the table. "Was the farewell feast a success?"

"Oh, yes," I answered, not daring to utter my dark concerns aloud. "King Agamemnon had a happy day's shooting and the harper sang stories of Herakles and Perseus, comparing them with Agamemnon himself. The musicians were particularly good so that the dancing was inspired." I let myself relax and enlarge on the evening. I sipped from my cup and rested back on the reclining bench. Lani sat in a chair to hear more. "Do you know that my sister and I danced the awakening dance, just the two of us?

"No," Lani said, "tell me."

"It was not planned, it just happened, as those things do, sometimes." I heard my voice light and enthusiastic. "Clytemnestra looked splendid. She wore a diadem of gold and jewels in her sleek black hair. Her robe was exquisite and she moved with a style and dignity of her own." I pulled my wrap around me.

"It was meaningful for the rest of us, as well." The tall form of Menelaus was outlined in the shadows near the bed chamber. His voice had taken on an unusual fullness. "Truly, Lani," he said, "it was a sight to behold. The two sisters danced together, so different yet similar in uncanny ways." He walked slowly over to the table and poured a cup of brew for himself. He sipped it a moment, then turned to Lani, who was about to leave. "You should have seen Helen,

Lani." He flashed me a smile that I caught in the meager light, but his eyes were in shadow. He continued talking to Lani as though I was not present. "She danced the provocative awakening steps in a glorious golden aura." He looked up at the sky and strolled about, still talking. "Helen's hair, her skin, the golden pendants, earrings and arm bracelets that adorned her, and, particularly, her drapery, an amber shade that floated around her, or clung to her, she was breathtaking, Lani," he paused. "My beautiful wife."

Somehow he was talking to me now, and Lani had disappeared. He set his cup on a table and sat on the edge of the reclining bench facing me. His eyes shone dimly in the pale moonlight. I reached up and touched his face, his lips. He took my hand and looked at me intently although he still spoke as if Lani were present.

"Lani," he said. I heard his voice catch. "How many times have I said to myself, right now, this day, this moment, she is the most beautiful she will ever be. No one could be more beautiful than she is now." All was still, except for the night sounds of crickets. "And then, a next time always occurs, as it did tonight."

I trembled as he put my hand to his cheek, then to his lips.

"I have never seen you so absolutely shining, so glorious, so lovely, my dear Helen, my wife, as you were tonight." His passionate voice made me swallow, for my mouth was dry, and I felt a lump in my throat. The fine fabric of my wrap felt coarse against my breasts, and a sweet ache had commenced deep within me. I sat very still and restrained an urge to reach up to him, for the moment was too precious to interrupt. "Her graceful arms, her slender shoulders..."

He edged forward on the reclining bench and stroked my arms. He opened my wrap and cupped my shoulders in his hands. His arms slid under my back. He held me firmly as my wrap fell away.

"Her lovely breasts," he whispered. I arched my back to his embrace. I reveled in the feel of his wandering lips.

A feverish urgency commanded me. "Let us go inside," I whispered. The bench was hard and our positions awkward. Reluctantly we pulled ourselves apart and entered the open doorway of the sleeping chamber. I quickly slipped out of my wrap and lay down on our marriage bed. I watched him remove his cumbersome sword and other paraphernalia, and then he was next to me. The soft light from the night sky fell across us and I felt a compelling eroticism begin to infuse me. With every touch we were carried into an ever more sensuous state of consummate joy; we fell asleep in each others arms. Later, I looked out at the sky and saw that the moon had set. In its absence the stars glittered more brightly than ever.

TROUBLE AND GRIEF

Castor's hair, though longer in winter, glittered brighter than ever as he spoke to the assembled members around the council fire.

"I have requested this unscheduled meeting to hear a messenger from Western Crete."

Polydeuces' forehead creased in worry. Three governors from neighboring provinces stirred in their seats, and Counselor Arneus smoothed his hand over his bald head. I sat in the chair of the Queen, the high seat carved from wood, painted a deep red and decorated with golden serpents. Colorful wall designs brightened the dull morning, despite the downpour outside.

"Let him come in," Menelaus said from the King's chair opposite. His gold ring, the sign of his Kingship, flashed in the meager light of the burning coals.

Castor nodded to a sentry and a slim stranger entered wearing a rough woven tunic with a wide leather belt. Intense fatigue marked his shadowed eyes and drawn mouth.

"Here is Sileus from Kydonia" Castor said.

The stranger smiled briefly, and spoke in a low, steady voice that masked incredible words. " We in Kydonia are peaceful farmers and fisher folk who continue in the old ways of honoring and caring for the gifts from the earth in gratitude to the Great Goddess. Our Chief, my father, sen⁺

me here to tell you that our most sacred shrine at Aptra has been destroyed."

I interrupted. "But Aptra is an ancient holy place, a center of the Goddess mysteries, of priestess lore and training. Destroyed?"

"Raiders came by sea with torches and swords." Sileus continued. "Nothing was spared. Precious relics, holy carvings, tablets marked with sacred writ. All broken and burned. Twenty-five priestesses were murdered, some raped, some charred beyond recognition, all run through with swords."

His recitation stopped. An awful silence filled the room. "And who committed these grotesque deeds?" Polydeuces asked.

"It was Idomeneus," Sileus replied. His hands clenched. "He has been sending raiding parties to attack our towns and shrines for months, but nothing like this, ever before. We captured some who told us that King Idomeneus intends to bring Kydonia under his rule, and that he hopes to destroy every evidence of the Goddess Potnia in Crete while doing so."

I shuddered, reminded of how King Agamemnon urged us to join Idomeneus in putting down the Kydonians as he had. I looked over at Menelaus whose eyes were cast down.

After a heavy silence Telestes spoke. "I am Governor of Scala," he said. "It is a southern Laconian province with strong ties to Crete. We have heard rumors of these atrocities."

"Yes. These things happened. They are not rumors." Sileus looked around at the circle of listeners. "I have come to ask for your official cooperation. If you send soldiers to help us, these secret attacks will be exposed and Idomeneus will back down."

Council members stared in shocked silence at the charcoal fire in the great circle hearth. It burned red on a mound of accumulated ash packed into an oval, like the egg-shape of creation, inspiring their judgments with holy truth.

Finally, I spoke. "Friend and neighbor from Kydonia, the murder of the priestesses at Aptra and the destruction of the Sanctuary and all its sacred holdings is an outrageous act that reveals a malicious scheme. It is more than the sport of rough hoodlums who topple relics in unplanned forays."

"Queen Helen," Sileus said, his anguished face suddenly warming. "It is your example that gives us strength when we listen to our harpers tell of a beautiful girl who rescued the stolen effigy of the Goddess Potnia."

I bowed my head acknowledging his words, but my mind raced on with unspoken thoughts. Is this Agamemnon's plan, to destroy the whole of the Goddess religion? What could we do to deter him? Gather together a great army from Messenia, Laconia, and yes, Arcadia too, and move into Kydonia and put down Idomeneus? But that would be breaking with Agamemnon. Yet, the tradition of the Goddess is widespread and, though formerly in decline, a resurgence of her worship has begun.

My musings were interrupted. King Menelaus was speaking.

"...and so before making a major commitment of soldiers, I suggest we send an envoy or several envoys to King Idomeneus. I have known him for many years, and will go to reason with him. If the Dioscuri or one or two of the honored governors would accompany me, so much the better."

There was more discussion and in the end it was decided that King Menelaus would travel to Knossos with Polydeuces and the Governor of Scala.

I bid my husband good bye in the nursery where I attended little Nikko. The baby lay still in his bed, his cheeks flushed, his eyes feverish, and a rash covering his chest and back.

Menelaus entered dressed in his leggings and warm traveling cloak. He knelt next to the cot and put his hand to the boy's cheek.

"Don't go, Papa," Nikko said, a tear in his eye.

"You'll be better in a few days, Son."

"Stay, Papa," Nikko said, lifting his arms for his father to hold him.

Menelaus carefully wrapped the covering fur around the child and picked him up. He held Nikko for a few minutes, speaking softly into his ear about riding their horses as soon as the weather improved, "...when you are fit and strong again," he said, giving him a hug and putting him back in his bed.

Nikko contentedly closed his eyes. I nodded to the nurse and left quietly with Menelaus, my thoughts turning to his mission in Knossos.

We walked together along a corridor to the courtyard where his horses and retainers waited. I brought up my worries about Idomeneus again, and he responded as he always had. "I know Idomeneus. I truly believe I can change his mind."

"But Idomeneus is trying to please your brother. I see no other reason for him to ravage shrines. He isn't the sort of man to do that."

"Nor does Agamemnon gain by waging war on Potnia," Menelaus replied. Weak sunlight filtered through the window covers. The rain had stopped for now, but it would be cold traveling.

"He hated it, you know," I said. "Agamemnon hated the tranquillity he felt here last summer. He was envious of our happiness. He dislikes my brothers and is menaced by our ways. I feel his violence and his jealousy."

We had reached the side doorway to the courtyard. Menelaus turned to me, his hat in his hands. "No, he is not an easy man, my brother. My salvation was always to go away from him. My years far from his house were not unhappy. But my greatest salvation of all was to come here and live with you." Our eyes met and locked in a mutual regard filled with emotion at our parting. He kissed my lips, and I leaned against him for a moment. "Take care, dear one," he said as he pulled his hat down snugly over his ears, drew his cloak around himself, hurried out to the waiting party in the courtyard and rode out through the palace gates.

I slowly walked back to the nursery thinking of his final words. "My salvation was always to go away." he had said.

Nikko continued to waste in fever. Neither poultices to draw out the poison from his rash nor herbal brews mixed with peppermint helped. One day he would be better, and the next his fever would flare alarmingly.

Baby Nikko was not alone in his sickness. Small children and old people were taken the worst. Thanks to the Goddess, Hermione had suffered only a light case. I called on others who were ill, consulted with Phiona and meditated with the Goddess. I had put off meeting with Arneus several times.

Pindros, who had taken to his bed, dissimulated his misery when I called at his neat chamber. He managed the double wink, his habitual sign that all was well. But I knew differently.

His skin was hot and the whites of his eyes were pink with illness.

"He takes good care of me," Pindros croaked, speaking of his boy-servant who was in training for future duties in the retinue of the Queen. "He follows your instructions, you need not worry."

"Of course I worry about you," I said. "You are my dearest friend." I sat on a chair near his bed and took his hot hand.

"I feel better to have you here," he said. "How is Nikko?"

"The same," I answered, trying to be lighthearted.

"Oh, the poor babe," he said. "You are beside yourself with worry about him."

I nodded, unable to trust my voice.

"But this plague does not kill," he said, trying to make me feel better. "It just takes time."

I could not reply, for several children had died. My eyes stung at the thought of the little girl who went off into a deep sleep, for which everyone was thankful; but she never woke up. And Castor and Phoebe's third child, a girl babe was very ill.

I whispered, "Only rarely." I hoped he had not noticed my dismay, but he had.

"Oh, so it is a killer, is it?" He sighed. "If it takes me, I am prepared." He smiled wanly and suddenly started coughing. He gasped for breath just as the servant-boy rushed in.

"Please, wait outside," he said. "I will care for him."

I stepped back as the lad of thirteen or fourteen deftly put his arms under the bulk of Pindros and raised him up. He held some eucalyptus oil on a linen cloth to the old man's nose which eased the coughing. I went out as I heard Pindros breathe deeply.

In a few moments the boy came to me. He was thin with big hands and feet. He had a mass of brown hair that fell over his brow, and intelligent green eyes. "He wants to see you," he said, his voice ranged from high to low.

"Thank you," I replied. "What are you called?"

"I am Meriandynus."

"Have you learned much from Pindros?" I asked him.

"I have tried, my Queen."

"Do you honor your teacher?" He continued to look past me as he would have been taught, but I could see a spark of emotion in his eyes.

"He is like a father to me," his eyes finding me for a brief flick of the eyelash.

I sensed a steadiness and loyalty in the young man. In a rush of intuition I wished to reward him. "There is no one I value more than Pindros," I said. "He has trained you well, and I feel that you have many of his virtues. Continue as his aide and when he has recovered, you will come to me as an attendant."

"Yes, your lady. I will do as you say."

I returned to Pindros, who rested with his head raised on bolsters.

"I beg your pardon for my rude behavior," he whispered.

"I like your boy," I said. "He must begin his work in my quarters when you are well." The old man was pleased.

I sat on, trying to instill him with strength. I knelt by his bed and thanked the Goddess for Pindros, for his loyalty, his unfailing friendship and wise counsel.

As Nikko improved, I arranged an evening meeting with Arneus. Dressed in a double wool tunic and leggings, Nikko played with his blocks near the hearth in the welcoming room of the Queen's apartment. Hermione practiced embroidery stitches under a lamp, and we both listened as Nikko told us a story of bears that lived in a house in the forest. He addressed us with such clarity for a child of three, that it made me smile. Pale from illness, the fire glow shone on his cheeks and cast a sheen on his hair.

Arneus was announced. "Thank you, my friend, for coming here."

"It is my wish to serve you," he replied. Flashing Hermione a smile, he commented, "I fear our discussion will be of little interest to your charming daughter." He must have remembered her disinterest in conversations of goods and trade.

"Today I will not mind," Hermione said. "I am stitching a wonderful scene of deer in the forest." She looked delightfully pretty in the light from the oil lamp.

Arneus directed his attention to Nikko. "Perhaps we will make an accountant out of you," he said, as he sat next to the boy near the fire. He listened carefully as Nikko explained the intricacies of his building. I was in no hurry to bring up our business.

Nikko began to rub his eyes. "Come, darling," I said to him. "Climb up here on the chair with me. Put your head in my lap." He nestled down in my arms and put his thumb in his mouth. As he closed his eyes, I brushed his hair back from his forehead. His skin felt cool to the touch.

I gave my attention to Arneus, who had risen from the floor by the fire and taken a chair opposite me.

"A message arrived several days ago," Arneus commenced, his voice deep, unemotional. "The trading party has completed a successful venture to Varna on the Black Sea, but has been detained in Troy because of the weather. Captain Thaos says that they have been received with courtesy."

"This is good news," I said. I rearranged Nikko into a more comfortable position.

Hermione moved closer and sat on a cushion near the hearth. "Is it terribly dangerous to sail into a stormy sea?" she asked, her eyes wide with interest.

Arneus ran his hand over his smooth bald head and leaned forward resting his elbows on his knees. "Sailors have told us of their adventures. The lucky ones who do not perish are blown far off course, and sometimes it takes them years to find their way home. Some may live in an unknown place for the rest of their lives."

He turned to me. "There was another message. It is for you."

"For me? But from whom?"

"I believe it is from the Trojan Queen. I was told by Thaos to give it to you myself."

The Trojan Queen? I felt like rising to take the tablet and try to decipher it, but I did not want to disturb Nikko.

"Please, Arneus, can you tell me what it says? I am curious."

"I will try," he said, reaching into his sack. He gently removed a tablet wrapped in protecting cloths. I saw the familiar oblong shape. 'Most honored Helen, Queen of Laconia,' it says. "Your beauty and your courage are known in every realm. Your name is consecrated in our sacred shrines. We are inspired and blessed by your deeds. Hecuba, Queen of the Trojans.'"

What could it mean, this message from the Queen of the Trojans?

"I believe this message is a hint as to why our ships are given special treatment in Troy. It is you who have made this possible, Queen Helen." Arneus's voice had lowered in reverence, he who always thought in terms of numbers.

I looked down on my sleeping child and stroked his head. A cold chill ran through me. Nikko was unnaturally still and his lips were blue. "Oh, no, " I moaned as I lifted him up. "Nikko, Nikko," I called, shaking him gently. Hermione ran over to us and Arneus took him, patted his cheeks and moved him back and forth. He thumped him on the back, but Nikko did not breathe. His pretty head hung lax, and his limbs sprawled loose. "We must not give up," I said, feeling the panic rising. "Hermione, call Lani, prepare a hot bath." She ran off.

"Hang him upside down," I instructed. I could hear my voice becoming shrill. Arneus did as I asked, but there was no coughing, no crying.

Lani rushed in and took the child. I could see from the despair on her face that she thought he was gone, dead.

"He will awake in a moment," I insisted, hoping my words would make it so. The alternative was too terrible to consider. We hurriedly placed him in the hot water bath but it did not help. Lani wrapped him in a linen sheet and strode about jouncing him, talking loudly to arouse him.

I could not bear to see the futility of the effort. I took him back and carried him into my sleeping room. No lamp burned but a dull sheen from the shuttered windows outlined his cot next to mine, its covers still in disarray from his fitful tossings, and the lullaby chair in its usual place. I sat with my baby in my arms rocking and singing the songs he loved, the ones that made him laugh, the ones that put him to sleep. Silent tears rolled down my cheeks and I prayed to Potnia. Please, Holy Mother, make your decisions clear to me. Why, oh, why must my children be taken from me? Why this golden child so blessed with gifts, your gifts?

Much later, Lani came in. "Arneus has remained," she said. He wishes to know how to serve you."

I had forgotten about Arneus. "Thank him, please," I said. "Tell him there is nothing right now."

She nodded. "I will tell him." Then she knelt next to me and put her hand on the baby's cheek. "This perfect child must be prepared for his long journey to Elysium. Give him to me now, so that he may be washed and scented and draped."

Reluctantly I gave up my Nikko. She took him away, and I lay on my bed in the gray shadows with my eyes open.

How much later, I do not know, Hermione tiptoed into my chamber. She stood and looked at me until she could see that I was awake.

"Oh, Mama," she wailed.

"Come darling," I said, indicating a place next to me. She crawled up on to the bed and nestled in my arms. She asked of me the same questions I had asked of the Goddess.

"Why did Nikko have to die? He was recovering, and he was so happy."

"We cannot know the answers, Hermione. Perhaps there are no answers. Perhaps there is no reason." I could find no consolation for either of us. She sobbed in my arms, and my tears came again. Eventually she found respite in sleep. I held her, listening to her even breathing, cherishing the life that was my daughter.

Castor and Phoebe's sweet infant, Locasta, died that very night. Three days later we stood together as the tomb of the royal family received the flesh of our loins.

Other deaths claimed my presence. Hollow-eyed and numb, I went from funeral to funeral. The day after I told Pindros of Nikko's death, he too succumbed. Meriandynus told me how the old servant had sipped hot broth, "and when he handed me his cup, he put his hand on my arm." The boy's eyes glistened with tears. "You know how his voice was, deep and rough?"

I nodded. A fulness in my throat prevented me from speaking.

Meriandynus continued. "He told me I was a fine young man." 'Keep on with your learning,' he said. "He was tired and nodded off to sleep." The boy's eyes, green and bright, sought mine. "He awoke again and took my hand. His was smooth and bony and I realized how thin he had become. Then he looked very serious and said, 'Learn from her, she will teach you in a myriad of ways.'"

I was sad but pleased that the last thoughts of Pindros were of the Goddess.

'Follow her,' Meriandynus continued. 'Follow Queen Helen in all things.' Meriandynus covered his face with his hands for a moment. "Those were his final words."

Gradually the plague wore itself out. Numbed by the deaths and tragedy that had overcome everyone, I dared not believe that it might be ending. Even sitting with Lani and Hermione in the warmth of a sunny corner of the courtyard on the first bright day in many, I could not let go. It was here that Polydeuces found me.

I stood when I saw him alone. Where was Menelaus? I felt no welcome in my heart, only despair. Hermione rushed to her uncle, who hugged her. "How grand to see such a blooming girl." he said.

She put her hands on either side of his face. "Oh, Uncle. You have come back." She giggled happily. "And is Papa with you?"

Polydeuces glanced at me before answering. "No, my Hermione, not today." I could see that he was travel-worn and weary. "I came home to Vapheio late last evening," he explained. I looked into his golden eyes and saw pity. "I was told the whole of it. I know about Nikko and Locasta. Castor says the plague is over." With one stride he came to me and engulfed me in his arms. I felt his strength and clung to him, my face buried in his embrace.

"Where is Menelaus?" I asked.

"Menelaus has gone to Delphi to consult the Oracle."

I straightened, startled. Menelaus to Delphi?

"Word of the worsening plague reached us," he tried to explain.

"Did he know that Nikko...?"

"No. Only that many had died. He asked me to tell you that he took advantage of a ship's departure the very day

Telestes and I started for home. He must be in Delphi by now."

"You mean he went to Delphi to get help to stop the plague?" I asked. "And he still knows not that Nikko died?" I shook my head in confusion. "And the plague seems to have run its course. Our news will be devastating for him when he returns." I listened to my brother.

"Menelaus was sorely tried," Polydeuces continued. "Our meetings in Knossos were not fruitful."

The sun disappeared under gathering clouds, and I wrapped my cloak around me. "Tell me," I demanded. I must know what happened.

We moved to a bench. "Idomeneus and Menelaus are like brothers in the way they share memories and joke together. We were entertained in splendor." Polydeuces could not continue to relate this experience sitting at my side. He walked back and forth, his rust colored cloak swayed with each step.

"I know they are old friends," I said. I have always liked Idomeneus. I am not able to believe he would wantonly destroy the villages and holy places of worship. There must be some explanation."

"What it comes down to is this, Helen." Polydeuces put a foot up on the bench and leaned forward, demanding my full attention with his penetrating eyes. "It is a plan to unify Crete as it was under the old empire. It means that the entire island, not just the central province, would be under Mycenaean power. It is a beginning step in regaining the wealth of Crete. Zeus with his thunderbolts and Poseidon with his power over the seas will replace the Goddess."

"My worst fears are confirmed," I said. "I suspected Agamemnon."

"Idomeneus demanded that we support him." Polydeuces resumed his pacing. "It was I who told him we could not." He shrugged his shoulders. "I reminded Idomeneus that

Laconia has had long-standing connections with Western Crete from earliest times, linked as we are by stepping-stone islands and generations of contact. I told him that any vandalism, anywhere, that could be identified as a purposeful assault by his soldiers on Goddess places would be unacceptable to us. To do this in his own land is one thing. But to move into other lands, in stealth, to murder innocent followers of the Goddess and destroy her sacred objects is not only vile and indecent, it would be stopped."

"What did he say to that?" I asked. His words stirred me.

"He said something about Kydonia being part of his land."

I thought how surprised Idomeneus might be when he encountered the well-organized resistance of Sileus and the many people who were flocking into Western Crete to help.

"We must activate our coalition with Messenia," I said.

"Yes, and alert our friends in Arcadia, and send envoys to our allies in Aetolia, Locris, and Boeotia."

Later, after Polydeuces and I walked to the family tomb where we honored the dead children, I wondered about Menelaus. Could his loyalty to his brother be stronger than his loyalty to us?

BLAZE, O BLAZE

I awoke with a start. In the dim light from the outer chamber I saw his shadowy form while my heart beat fast with shock.

"Oh, my darling. How I have longed for you." he murmured.

"Menelaus." His mouth on mine prevented more words. The kiss became deeper and longer until my whole body was aflame for him. We clung together quenching the thirst brought on by separation.

Our passion spent, we lay in silence. Soon he breathed the even breaths of sleep, but I lay wide-eyed until dawn. When I heard the subdued sounds of a servant leaving the ewers of hot water in the bathing room, I arose and quietly washed and rubbed my skin with an unguent prepared from the oil of jasmine. I combed my hair and put a warm robe over a fresh long-sleeved tunic.

I requested a hearty breakfast be prepared and returned to the sleeping room, where I opened the shutters and sat in a chair next to the bed. A vulnerability, natural to sleep, was present in the face of Menelaus. Could this be a face of cunning? I did not believe so.

Suddenly his eyes flew open, alight with questions. I knew what they asked. I brushed aside a sudden spring of tears and held his hand. "Nikko is dead," I whispered.

He pulled himself up, covering his face and the anguish of his grief with his hands; sudden sobs wracked his bare muscular chest. While he struggled for control, I talked. "Hermione is fine. Others, many others, died. Sweet baby Locasta. Pindros. It has been a terrible time. We lost eighty-five souls in Amyklae alone."

"Nikko," he said, spreading his fingers through his hair. "Please, I wish to know about it?"

I told him, feeling the baby's special aura as I spoke.

"He died in your arms?"

"Yes, in his sleep."

We ate on tables overlooking the garden. The bright morning promised a fine day. Early buds swelled the branches of the cherry trees, and a beginning yellow-green showed everywhere. "Polydeuces delivered your message and informed me of your journey to Delphi," I said, "and he also told me of Knossos."

Menelaus did not respond. His downcast expression was unrelieved by anger at Idomeneus or a contentment at being here with me. How could he feel anything but grief right now? Finally he sat back and looked at me. "I leave again tomorrow."

"Where will you go?" I asked, astounded. "Are you not concerned about Laconia? There is much stir about sending soldiers to Crete."

"They should not interfere in Crete," muttered Menelaus "Potnia is losing out. Zeus, Poseidon, even Apollo are everywhere. Even in Delphi young Apollo is present."

"In Delphi?" I asked, stunned. "But Zeus honors the Pythia and Oracle, the highest religious sage anywhere."

Menelaus explained: "Apollo's priests and acolytes are in charge. They bring the questions to the Oracle."

I could not understand.

"I will tell you from the beginning," he said. He spoke quickly with few embellishments. "After leaving Crete and passing Cape Malea, we had fair winds that continued up the west coast and around into the Corinthian Gulf. Several young priests of Apollo were my shipmates. They told me how their small shrine in Delphi had enlarged. Some said Apollo had slain the old Pythia. Others that she died naturally. A young priestess has taken the ancient's place."

I tried to follow the rapid accounting.

"After landing on the northern shore we went by foot through olive groves, slowly approaching an escarpment. Black crags spired over green forests. We climbed steeply to a high ridge that brought us to an awesome valley below beautiful snow-covered Parnassos. The crags we had seen from below where wild eagles soared, loomed over us. The rocky heights rose from two great rocks separated by a beautiful gorge. From far into the chasm, so narrow it was nearly impassable, a fountain gushed clear cold water. In its deepest recesses, I was purified."

I listened as though Menelaus told an age-old story. "And you were taken to the Oracle?"

He sipped from his cup and told me more. "I was taken into the sanctuary by Apollo's priests. After ritual celebrations, I asked my question. "What can I do to abate the plague in Laconia?" The new Pythia listened to me behind a screen.

"I waited for the answer in the seclusion of a remote garden surrounded by great rocks. I sat on a mat, and for hours I looked at the few blades of grass and moss near a seeping spring. I splashed my face and head and drank the sacred water from my cupped hands.

The longer I sat, the more I concentrated on the things in the garden: the texture of the moss, pebbles of varied oval shapes. In the wetness, they glowed with a subtlety of rose or tan or gray-green that cannot be justly described. My eyes were overwhelmed with a beauty that would have been unnoticed in a larger setting. I felt such peace that it was an interruption to be called to hear the fateful answer.

"I was led back to the sanctuary where a priestess, sitting behind a gauzy veil, spoke. Her voice resounded from the rocky hollows behind her.

"'The plague is not in Laconia, it is within you. You will find self-knowledge at the tomb of Lycus in Troy, where, after a significant sacrifice, the curse laid on you by your grandfathers of the House of Pelops and Atreus will be stemmed.'" Menelaus sat, his eyes glowing.

I was moved by his serene certainty. "Lycus was a disciple of the Goddess in Messenia," I said.

"What do you know about him?" Menelaus asked.

I repeated a story Hilaeria and Phoebe had told about a wise man, who walked about the land in the garb of a simple shepherd and taught the meaning of Goddess worship.

Menelaus nodded. "I must follow the instructions of the Oracle, Helen. The teacher, Lycus, has something to tell me."

"I understand why it is important for you to go to Troy, as the Oracle has instructed. But..."

"I will go tomorrow," he repeated.

"But, Menelaus," I said. "The plague in Laconia is over. You can wait. The King of Laconia is needed here, now."

"I believe that you and the Dioscuri can manage without me."

"We may decide to take action that your brother Agamemnon will not sanction. If you disagree, we need to hear from you."

It was as though I had not spoken.

I tried to reach him again. "As you well know, Idomeneus has no intention of stopping his raids of Kydonian towns and Goddess sanctuaries. The Council agrees, and we have contacted Messenia and Arcadia. We are outfitting our soldiers, readying supplies, mapping strategies, preparing departures. We should have our combined armies in Kydonia within ten days."

Menelaus shook his head sadly. "I am grieved to hear of these plans for war. I do not agree with these actions." He paused and looked at me, and my heart sank, my worst fears borne out.

"The King must not leave at this time. You are needed here." I clung to his arm, my voice low with emotion. Could he not understand this terrible act of disloyalty he was forcing upon us? It could not go unaccounted for. I felt my cheeks pale at the thought.

"It is best I leave here tomorrow as I plan." He actually smiled at me. "Carry on with your war, but I will have no part of it. Now, let us go to the tomb of Nikko. Where is Hermione?"

Fitted with a soldier's tunic, mantel and helmet, I accompanied our forces and those of Arcadia to the southern gulf. I rode a white Ilion mare, and General Leontes of Arcadia, lean and hard, with an intelligent wit, rode his great war horse along side me. "What a show this is, Queen Helen," he said, as we looked upon the hundreds of foot soldiers, grouped into their male bands of the swan, the horse, the ram, stag, dolphin or bull, spread out as far as we could see.

"To go into battle in the name of Potnia makes war significant," he said. "It is exhilarating to have such a glorious cause."

General Leontes and I watched from a hill as the Messenian forces joined ours. "It was She that brought these famous enemies together," the General said.

"And was the enmity between my brothers and their Messenian cousins so well known?" I asked.

"Oh, indeed, yes," he answered. "Castor and Polydeuces are heros everywhere. Idas and Lynceus too. What a waste it was to have these endowed young men at each others throats."

Castor and Polydeuces controlled their excited stallions with tight reins. Lynceus, commander of forces, and Idas now King after wedding an Aetolian princess, called out a fierce battle cry and galloped down a hillside circling around until they could pull their mounts to a stop. All four animals reared in frenzy. Finally, amid shouting, the four beckoned to General Leontes who joined them. The gathered armies gave a huge cheer and soon out-vied each other in demonstrating colorful routines and marching expertise.

At night around the fires we told stories, and I often danced the ritual homage to the Goddess. I thanked the soldiers, feeling an overpowering gratitude for their devotion.

One evening I looked to Lynceus who sat quietly by. "Come for a walk under the stars." He arose, and we left the firelight, wending our way through groups of soldiers until we were far down the shore. "I value your friendship, Lynceus," I finally said. "Does it exist no longer?"

His silence continued for many steps before he spoke. "My feelings are so much deeper than friendship. I was determined to remain quiet, but perhaps you should know my thoughts."

"Yes, I should."

"I believe Menelaus was the wrong choice—those many years ago." His voice had lost its edge and now sounded very sad. "You and I—the two of us could have done marvelous deeds for our countries. Under the aegis of the Goddess we would have outshone even Agamemnon." He stopped walking and stood to face me. "My feelings are not of a lack of friendship, but of regret." The night breeze came in off the bay and bits of stars and a piece of moon showed under moving clouds. "Where is King Menelaus now?" he asked.

"He...I..."

"It doesn't matter," Lynceus said. He reached for my hands, and we stood together under the stars, unspeaking.

The next day I said good bye to the five leaders as they each boarded one of the last departing vessels. The intelligence in General Leontes' eyes was clear to read. We are doing the correct thing, they said. He smiled, and I clutched his hands.

Idas, too, took my hands and a deep feeling of care filled me. Lynceus's perceptive look told me that he understood me completely. "And are we friends?" I asked.

"Always."

Castor's golden eyes filled with the fun of our teasing, which was also care. "It was right that you were here, Helen." He enveloped me in a great hug.

Polydeuces was sober. His eyes shadowed some of the uncertainties we all understood. "Do not wait here, Helen. Return to Amyklae." He hugged me briefly.

I made the age-old sign of Goddess protection and as the ships left the harbor sent her blessing after them.

Messengers brought news of the strife in Kydonia each day. Our forces had spread out to crucial sites, raiding parties had been captured, prisoners had been taken. Our three pronged army marched over the pass into Idomeneus's territory carrying banners of truce and met with his commander and representatives. I waited to hear that the threat to Kydonian Crete had ended.

When the wonderful tidings arrived, all of Amyklae celebrated. In a few weeks they would be coming home. The orchards and grain fields burgeoned with potential harvest. Children ran about with blooming cheeks and high spirits. I received word indicating that Menelaus would leave for home soon. Phiona told me she had heard that Iphigeneia had entered the Shrine of Potnia in Boeotia to commence her virgin year training with my friend Macaria. How happy I was!

At home games and feasting had been put off until our men returned. As soon as they were on the route home, final preparations would begin. It was with a great thrill of anticipation that I was told a messenger had been sighted.

I waited for him in the courtyard of the Royal Palace along with several Counselors, Governors, the Adjutant who covered the military business here, Hermione, Hilaeria, Phoebe and their children, Phiona and the Priest from the Apollo-Hyakinthos shrine.

When the messenger entered the courtyard, his horse was wet with sweat. I recognized the young rider. Usually correct in decorum, on this occasion his eyes were wild. When he saw me, he fell to his knees, his lowered head showing his tangled black hair. I had trouble hearing his words.

"Speak up," Arneus said, annoyed at this poor display.

"While deliberating together after their return to Laconian soil in the bivouac they used for their consultations..." his voice faded.

"Yes, yes go on...." Arneus insisted.

The boy's eyes, pleading and frightened, found mine. "From out of nowhere, bandits—they had daggers—all of them—all five commanders—slain, dead." He managed to get out the final words then broke down into wracking sobs.

Uncomprehending, we stood mute, unable to take in the horror. Arneus broke the spell and called for servants to lead the messenger away. Cups of water were passed around to the would-be welcomers nearly faint with shock. We clustered together asking the unanswerable questions. How? Why? What happened?

I put my arms around Hilaeira and Phoebe, picked up Neria, the youngest child of Polydeuces, and held her close. We went inside and were served hot broth, still unable to grasp the meaning of those terrible words.

I could not believe my brothers were dead. I could feel their powerful presence just by thinking about them. There was something impossible about it. They still lived. They must!

Lynceus, my special friend, loyal, exceptional Lynceus with the glittering eyes that could see through to truth. Lynceus! His name echoed in my head like a cry for help. And Idas, King Idas, and General Leontes, who marched for the glory of the Goddess. I could not accept it. There was some mistake.

Like a heavy cloak, a protecting shield fell around me and resisted the onslaught of reality that lingered beyond the shadows awaiting its time.

Arneus and the Advocate came to me. The officer, called Volos, had been a contender on the athletic fields as a young man. He had thickened in figure but remained loyal and competent. His dark eyebrows grew together over small brown eyes. "I will leave at once with a unit of soldiers to meet the returning army," he said. "Do you have instructions for me?"

"I will go with you," I replied. "I must assay for myself what has happened." Moved to action, I paced around as ideas came to me. "We will leave at first light. If there are prisoners, I will interrogate them. I must speak to everyone who witnessed this unspeakable crime."

Early the next morning I dressed in my soldier's tunic, wrapping around me my warm cloak the color of wine. I went out into the brisk morning to meet General Volos and his soldiers. As usual, Meriandynus was my aide.

Late the next day we saw our returning armies spread in disarray all through a wide valley. Foot soldiers stumbled along, unfocused. Officers on horseback rode together making no effort to organize their units. From a high point on the slope of a hill where all could see him, General Volos hailed them. "Stop here for a rest," he called out. "Senior officers report to me at once."

I cantered my horse out among the soldiers. "Take heart, men," I said. "You have proven yourselves in Kydonia. We are proud of you." I rode on down through the disordered units trying to reach most of them with my voice, at least. "Look sharp, fellows, you have done well," I called. Then on to others, galloping about and stirring them up, shouting at them to pull themselves together. My cloak billowed about me, and my hair came loose from its restraining bands.

Towards the end of the line I saw the supply wagons pulled by oxen. I approached cautiously until I found what I sought. Three wagons at the very rear were attended by two officers each, on horseback. The vehicles were pulled by horses; blue and white colors fluttered from staffs attached to two of the carts. Arcadian colors of green and white drifted over the third. The Messenians would have separated from the main army earlier, hauling their own two wagons of death, their own tragic cargo of slain leaders.

The unit stopped, and the officers watched me without expression. I walked my horse around until I saw each shrouded body lying across the flooring; they were such big men.

I gave the orders. "Remove them. Spread covering on the ground over there under the oak tree and place my brothers on it."

As I waited I spoke to a man near me, a leader of foot-soldiers. "Tell me in your own words what happened." The first body was lowered to the ground.

"Strangers, thieves, bandits, came into our camp. They went into the shelter where our leaders conferred and murdered each." The soldier spoke quickly. He brushed the sweat from his brow and rubbed his beard. The shroud was being removed.

"Were prisoners taken?" I asked the same soldier.

"Yes. Three were killed, but we have two others. Both are wounded."

I did not answer, for the wrap of Castor had been taken away, and I knelt down next to him. His nude body had been washed, but blood from a killing wound in his abdomen had seeped so that the stench was sickening. I put a neck scarf over my nose and looked upon his face. I touched his cheek and felt his lip. I saw the closed eyelids, the hand so carelessly resting at his side. I nodded to the attendants, and they carefully wrapped him up again.

The wound of Polydeuces was in his throat. His head had very nearly been cut off. I took his stiff hand in mine and examined the intricate details of the folds of the skin and the cut of the nails. I stood and gave the motion to remove him.

My brothers were dead. I no longer disbelieved it. Feelings of horror and grief churned within me, nearly escaping the cold protective emotional shield that permitted me to continue. I clenched my teeth and stood straight. "Who killed them?" I asked the same soldier I had spoken to earlier. He did not answer but nodded to another. I turned to see General Trophonios, the officer who would have the highest command next to General Volos.

"Queen Helen," he said, bowing low. "Your presence here is"... His voice trembled. "To return to Amyklae like this," he mumbled, indicating the soldiers cast down in grief, the demoralized men strung out in disorder. "Thank you for coming. It is more, much more than we could have hoped for."

I noticed his own despair, his tangled brown hair and watery eyes. I did not reply to his welcome. "Who has done this?" I asked him. "General, who has done this?"

"We believe the murderers are renegade Cretans. It must have been some act of revenge," General Trophonios said.

"I will see them."

"Of course." The general took me to a wagon covered over with a scrap of cloth. Two men, both filthy in ragged loin cloths were tied back to back around a central post.

"Please untie them and give them some water," I said to the General, who passed on my orders.

General Volos had joined us. "Queen Helen, are you certain you wish to confront these men?" he asked me. His fresh tunic and mantle amidst the chaos and filth of death reminded me of how little time had passed since my brothers had lived. Now and forever more they would inhabit a distant past where excellence had been the touchstone.

"Yes," I replied. I was determined to uncover their secrets. "Let them come down from the wagon. Take them to that shady copse near the rocks where I noticed a spring." I proceeded with certainty.

Meriandynus and I followed the pair as they were led away. The older gray-haired fellow limped along, and the other had a bandage tied around his head.

"I will have my aide with me," I explained to the generals, indicating Meriandynus. "You may post guards at a distance if you fear there may be trouble. I prefer to speak to them alone." I counted on a gentle approach yielding far more than punishing blows.

The generals nodded but frowned in disapproval. I ignored them as I joined the prisoners.

"Please, sit down." They found places on pine needles under the cypress trees. I spread my cloak on a flat rock and sat on it. Meriandynus stood behind me. "I am Helen, Queen in Laconia. I have no interest in hurting you. I will see that your wounds are cared for."

To Meriandynus I said, "Please fetch clean cloths, containers of water and any balm or medication that might be at hand."

He bowed and left.

"Have you been asked many questions?" I inquired in a kindly manner.

The two prisoners looked upon me in wonder and nodded.

"And what were you asked?"

The older man looked down as he spoke. "They wanted to know who we were."

"And what did you reply?" I asked the young man.

"That we were Cretan," he answered.

Meriandynus returned with two bowls filled with water from the spring and clean cloths and the medicaments I had requested.

The older man rested against the trunk of the oak tree, his legs spread out in front of him. The creases of his brow and cheeks were encrusted with dirt.

"May I examine your injury?" I asked him.

He nodded, and I saw that the ankle of his outstretched leg was badly swollen and discolored. I put two fingers under his foot and pressed upwards. I was relieved when he did not yelp in pain. Then I turned the foot one way and another and touched the swelling itself. I could tell that it was very sore.

"What are you called?" I asked him.

"Langoulous," he answered. His red-rimmed eyes were full of amazement as he watched me.

I soaked a cloth with clean water and washed his foot gently. I dried it as carefully and covered the swelling with the balm, then tied a clean cloth around the ankle and foot. "You must not put your weight on this foot for several weeks," I said as I washed the other foot. "I will have some crutches fashioned for you."

The young man studied me as I put a clean damp cloth to the face of Langoulus and smoothed away the grime. I kept my hands on those of Langoulus and looked deeply into his eyes. He returned my gaze. "How many days since you have last been in Mycenae?" I asked him.

His eyes widened. "We have been away two weeks," he said, his voice uncertain.

I released his hands and went to the young man and knelt next to him. "I will clean your wound."

I cautiously removed the filthy rag from around his head. A deep gash on his temple was crusted over with dried blood. I carefully washed the area around it, cleansing the dirt and dried blood from the wound itself, permitting it to bleed freely. I held the washing cloth to absorb the blood before I applied the healing salve. After that I tied a fresh strip over the wound and around his head. I took the cloth and rinsed it and poured clean water on it and bathed his face, his eyes, his mouth. I took his hands and wiped them with the damp cloth. When I finished, I put my hands on either side of his face and looked into his eyes for a long time. He returned my gaze with one of reverence.

"Why did you lie about being Cretan?" I asked softly.

His eyes flooded with tears.

"I would like to hear your stories," I said to them both. I beckoned to Meriandynus to come closer, for I wanted him to hear everything. I arranged my cloak on the ground near them, so that I could see them clearly. "Please, commence."

I waited patiently and Langoulous spoke. "We were part of a specially trained Mycenaean force that learned to move around enemy territory without being seen and to hide for days on end in the mountains and forests without leaving any trace."

"And you," I asked the young one. "You were in this group?"

"Yes," he answered. "I have not been in the army very long, while Langoulous here has been in many years."

"Ah yes," I said, recalling that in Mycenae a large army was kept in readiness for war at all times.

"What happened when you had completed your training?"

Langoulous shifted his position a little and awkwardly moved his injured leg.

"We were sent to Crete, to Knossos, where we joined soldiers of King Idomeneus."

I nodded and turned to the younger man.

"How are you called," I asked him.

"I am Racius."

"Racius, did you participate in such raids in Crete?"

"Yes." His eyes brightened for a moment, then sobered.

"So you felt your training was beneficial? You succeeded in the destruction of religious shrines and in raiding wealthy houses."

"Yes, my lady," he answered with some pride. "We succeeded very well. We also helped train Cretans for this task and eventually were sent back to Mycenae."

I looked to Langoulous, who nodded agreement. "We had returned home after our mission to Crete when we were suddenly called back." His tired eyes held steady.

Racius was ready to continue. "This mission was different. We were told to follow the movements of the Laconians."

"How did you do this?" I asked, trying to keep the emotion out of my voice.

"Just as we did before. We watched their camps and their movements, but we did not show ourselves in any way."

I did not comment, but I could envision the scene.

He continued his tale. "We were told to follow the leaders, the Dioscuri and King Idas of Messenia and his brother and General Leontes, even to their homeland and to do away with them, all of them." His voice caught, and he looked away from me. "You see, we were following orders."

I looked upon him with sorrow that he should be given such orders. "And you carried out these orders?"

"We did. Five of us landed from the sea on Laconian soil at a secluded rocky inlet. We hid ourselves, going out one at a time to scout." Racius stopped speaking. His voice had grown weak. He coughed and drank some water from a ewer Meriandynus had placed by his side. He looked to Langoulous to continue.

"How did you infiltrate the camp so easily?" I asked.

"Lady, it was quite easy. Before we left Crete, we had managed to accumulate items of identification from the different armies. We had an Arcadian helmet, a Laconian mantel and colored bands, Messenian colors and a mantel, also. The camp was huge. We could walk about for short periods, if we were careful not to engage anyone. We discovered the bivouac where the leaders met. We each slipped into the tent when it was empty and hid until the five of them gathered for a meeting. It was one evening after the meal. They were relaxed from friendly bantering and toasts of wine. We had drawn lots. Each one of us had..." He stopped. He looked up into the tree above him. I followed his glance and saw the leaves sparkle in the sunshine, and the blue sky beyond, pristine in its purity.

"You must continue," I said. "I must know." I looked to Meriandynus, whose face had taken on an expression of disgust.

"Who did you kill?" I asked Racius.

"One of the Dioscuri. I could not tell them apart," he said.

"How did you kill him?" I asked.

"I crept up behind him and cut his throat, quickly."

"That was my brother Polydeuces," I told him

"And you, Langoulous," I said. "Who did you kill?"

"The big fellow from Messenia. King Idas. I stabbed him in the back, over and over. He turned and lunged at me and threw me to the ground where I twisted my leg, and then he fell on top of me, dead.

"And Castor my other brother, how did he die?"

"He had time to grab his dagger and struck me on the head," Racius said. "But our comrade sliced him deep in the groin."

I had learned what I had come to find out. My head was swimming with the effort to remain calm, to keep my emotions in check. The sunlight ricocheted through the leaves in a dizzying glare. There was something else I must ask.

"Do you know where your orders originated?" I mumbled.

"Of course, from King Agamemnon. He instructed us himself."

I sat for a moment to gather strength. "Thank you for telling me the truth. You will be treated justly." I nodded to Meriandynus who assisted me to rise. I stood, striving for balance. I took the arm of Meriandynus, and we slowly walked towards the two generals who awaited us amidst a group of soldiers and horses, from where they had watched me with the prisoners. Guards passed us, bowing as they did so.

"They will take the prisoners back to their jail," Meriandynus said.

I stopped and called to them. "Wait, please. The older man has hurt his foot, badly. Do not let him step on that foot, and see to it that he has crutches as soon as possible. They are to be fed and treated well. Do you understand?"

The guard put his hand to his forehead in assent and bowed.

When we reached the generals and the other soldiers and horses I waited, gathering my strength, still using the arm of Meriandynus for support.

"I have their story," I said. "My attendant, Meriandynus, listened carefully and will report to you every detail."

I stood next to a great black horse with a white mark on its nose; it nickered and lowered its head so that I felt a nudge from its soft muzzle. The generals stared at me, their eyes were full of questions, and I wanted to tell them everything.

But a vertigo came over me and my control began to slip away. The horse nickered again, and suddenly I realized it was Castor's horse, his favorite for marching. I wanted to throw my arms around his neck, but he was too tall. I grabbed his mane with both hands and buried my face in it. "Blaze, O Blaze," I cried again and again. I could not hold back the terrible flood of anguish and loss any longer. It engulfed me, raging through every part of me. "Blaze, Blaze, O Blaze," I said over and over. Deep sobs seized me and tears poured from my eyes. "O Blaze, Blaze."

GUEST FRIENDS

Back from his pilgrimage to Troy, my husband sat with me in the garden of our summer home. The blooming euphorbia hedge reminded me of the previous summer of Agamemnon and the gathering clouds of trouble.

"Did you receive a message at the tomb of Lycus?" My voice sounded insincere to my own ears.

"There is much to tell," he answered.

How we had cherished each other. Now I felt bereft of affection. I saw a handsome man before me, whose eyes expected my understanding.

"Again you come home to news of death," I said. "It is not a pleasant way to welcome you." I relived for a moment the pulling back of my brother's shrouds. I looked away at the mountains, hazy in the heat, and a pungent aroma of ripening fruit drifted up from the orchards below.

Menelaus came to me. He took my hand and pressed it so hard I almost protested. "Helen, Helen. My ears cannot take in such brutal tidings."

He had been home one full day. Exhausted, he had slept long, and when he awoke I told him briefly the barest of facts. "Meriandynus was with me," I had said. "He will tell you details of my brothers' murder. You understand that I do not wish to do so."

Menelaus, stunned, had reached for me, but I turned aside. I called for Meriandynus, and in my presence he had begun the recitation. I escaped to my loom for I did not wish to hear more.

Pressure on my hand brought me back to the present with Menelaus. I adjusted my position. "Come sit, there is room for you. Tell me about Troy, and I will try very hard to attend."

He sat facing me on the reclining seat. How many times in the past had we conversed in this way?

"First, please, Helen, I want to share your grief. They were such vibrant, incredible men. I cannot believe they are dead. I cared for them as I cared for my own brother."

The mention of his own brother filled me with silent rage. Later, later we would talk about Agamemnon.

"We will go together to their tomb. Now, continue with your travel tale." My voice sounded as though I spoke to a little child.

His brow furrowed in anguish, his mouth, an agonizing slash. He sighed deeply. "I will try. But, dear, dear Helen, this seems most unimportant in the face of our tragedy here."

"Tell me," I prompted. Did I want to hurt him, punish him? I wondered if I could actually listen to this story. I would try.

"Troy is a great citadel surrounded by stone walls accessed through towering gates. It commands a high place overlooking a rich plain to the east and the sea to the west. It is very wealthy."

His voice was crisp and resonant. I liked listening to its cadence; I could imagine well the city overlooking a rich plain. He compelled my attention with his eyes.

"I was welcomed by King Priam with much celebration. As envoy from Laconia, I was received with special honor. Indeed, Helen, Laconia is thought of highly in Troy. The trading overtures are mere symbols of their goodwill."

"Did you meet the Queen?"

"Yes, often. She is a tall, serene woman, grave yet full of life and light. She sends her greetings, especially to you. Helen, Troy is a place of the Goddess. Everyone worships the Goddess in one form or another. There are images, palladiums they call them, holy representations of the Goddess that are sacred. One in particular is said to have dropped from the sky when the city was founded and will always protect Troy from destruction."

He stood up and wandered over to the ivy-covered wall that looked out across the valley. As I watched him, I thought of the tall, serene woman full of light. I would like to know her.

Menelaus turned to me. "Sometime I want us to go to Troy together. There are many princes and princesses. Hector, the eldest, is commander of the military, and there are beautiful daughters, and other sons. I believe Alexandros, or Paris, as he is called, is the most talented. Prince Paris is coming here with the trading ship. Oh—I failed to mention—they are sending a trading ship here. If I had known of the tragedy—he must not come now. I will meet him in Limera and explain." He sat down again.

"Perhaps we should make him welcome," I said. "He will understand if our feasts are subdued. We would not wish to refuse him after coming all this way." Could we make a fine prince welcome in our house without the Dioscuri? I asked of myself. We would have to try.

"Let us think about it," Menelaus said. "We have time. He expects to stop in Salamis to call on his Aunt Hesione, mother of young Teucer."

"Ah, yes," I said, remembering Teucer's tale of his mother's becoming Queen to Telamon, kidnapped by him and carried away.

"They will bring horses and copper gained from their inland trading routes into Asia. They continue to want our green and red marble and holy stones."

"What about the tomb of Lycus?"

He shook his head. "I spent many hours every day at his revered tomb. Although I contemplated and worshipped, I could never achieve the focus that I did in Delphi. There was no oracle to lead me. I sacrificed some fine lambs and cattle, and waited for a sign." He shrugged his shoulders. "One day a young girl came by and sat with me. She looked like a tree nymph; her long tangled brown hair had leafy twigs wound in it. We did not speak, but on leaving she came to me and said, 'If you wish to find contentment from the corruption of your grandfathers, give of your self as Lycus gave of himself.'"

"Who was she?" I asked, startled, for surely this was a sign.

"I do not know. She wandered away, and when I looked for her, she had disappeared."

"Does it mean that you must don a rough cloak and go into the wilderness to teach the message of the Goddess?" I could not see Menelaus in a simple shepherd's habit, wandering from hamlet to hamlet.

"No, I'm sure not." He smiled at the vision. "It is an outlandish notion, dear Helen. There may be some other explanation, but that is not it." He slapped his hand on his thigh and stood again.

I lay back and followed the flight of a hawk soaring above. "It may be very easy," I said. "It may just mean that you follow Goddess ways. Not half way, but wholly. Perhaps, Menelaus, it does not mean that you go into the world as a nomad teacher, just that you give all of yourself, as did Lycus."

"If what you tell me is the correct interpretation, Helen, it is not effortless at all. You make it sound as simple as donning a new cloak." He walked about with his hands on his belt. "I have always done what was necessary to appease all the gods and goddesses. That should be enough. I am not the sort to become a holy man."

I could see that he was not. "No," I agreed, "but that should not matter. Remember, this advice was given you so that the you would become free of the infamy of the House of Atreus."

"Yes, the House of Atreus and all of its crimes," he said, sitting down again at my side, facing the garden, his arms resting on his knees. "Its murders and cannibalism, its fratricides and infanticides. Oh, that I would free myself of its infamy." He spoke as though talking to the ground at his feet.

I believed I understood the problem Menelaus could not manage. I believed I had suggested a solution for him. I believed he was unable, for the present, to follow the advice he received at the tomb of Lycus. Now I must find out if his confusion about this matter had influenced his actions concerning Laconia. Had he betrayed us?

"Meriandynus did not tell you the complete account yesterday," I said. "He left out something at my request."

Menelaus picked up a small branch fallen from the shady willow above and fingered the leaves. "Oh, what was that?" He turned to me.

I sought his eyes. "He did not tell you that the prisoners confessed to taking orders to murder the five generals directly from King Agamemnon."

Menelaus abruptly turned aside, "Oh, no," he murmured. "I don't believe it. To murder your brothers, he would not do it."

"The prisoners did not lie to me. I will take you to their jail so that you can talk to them, and you, too, will believe them." I arose and went to the stone wall and stood with my back to Menelaus, attempting to calm my rising anger. I traced the course of the river, a silver band winding among the fields, and felt a terrible pain of realization that Menelaus could not accept or admit the truth about Agamemnon. I turned to face him. "Menelaus, my husband, how can we believe in you as our King when your loyalty to your brother is greater than it is to us? You avoid your duties as King in Laconia." I stood straight and spoke to him as a Queen, not as a wife. I held my head up; a light summer breeze caught my hair and ruffled my drapery.

"No, no. Helen, how can you suggest such a thing?"

"It is absolutely imperative that we solidify our relations with Messenia and Arcadia. Who is King in Messenia now? Are the Arcadians still our allies? Are you prepared to organize the army against Mycenae? It may be necessary. General Volos and General Trophonios deal with these problems, and I have become very much involved as well. I do not believe you have given our situation a thought."

"I have just returned. I am just learning about it. You asked me to tell you about Troy when I wanted to know about Laconia." His imploring tone did not go well with me.

"You have four more years to complete your great-year as king," I said. "It would be wiser for you to step down before that." I spoke calmly. I saw that he was alarmed. His eyes were wide with surprise and a questioning expression wrinkled his brow.

I continued. "Perhaps this is what you were meant to do, Menelaus. Perhaps this is what the message meant. You are to make a sacrifice to remove the stigma of the House of Atreus from your soul. The sacrifice is to give up your Kingship in Laconia and go out into the world to seek the truth. If it cannot be under the auspices of the Goddess, so be it. You must do it anyway."

Menelaus looked at me in disbelief. "Helen," he whispered.

"As for leading the military, you cannot be counted on when action against Mycenae is involved. And it is very likely that Agamemnon will find reason to test us now that the Dioscuri are gone. We must prove to him that we have the strength and the will to continue our protection of Kydonia, and more if it is needed. You are unable to do this. You will come to see that it is best that you step down. If, in the process of your search, you reach understanding, then return here and resume your Kingship."

"Helen, you are in shock from the death of the Dioscuri. You do not know what you are telling me. You cannot send me away." His words hung on the air.

Lani entered the garden. "Please excuse me for inter-rupting you," she said, "but a messenger has come from the retinue of a prince, a Trojan prince, he says. Will you see him?"

Menelaus and I looked at each other in mutual concern; the Trojan Prince Paris must be arriving here very soon. "Please," I said to Menelaus. "We will talk later. Think about this. It is the only way..."

"How can you? This is madness." Menelaus muttered, striding about in anger, his hair in disarray, his brows drawn together over his glaring eyes.

"Yes, Lani, we will see him," I said. "Take him to the welcoming room."

"Come" I said to Menelaus. "We must arrange to receive Prince Paris as best we can."

"Heaven help me," Menelaus moaned. "Now you expect me to behave as though you still have trust in me."

I could understand his confusion. "Yes. I expect that of you. Let us not discuss this topic again until the Trojan Prince leaves us."

We feasted under the stars on a summer evening with flickering torches to light the tables. Two Trojan princes, not one, had come to our house. Prince Paris, tall and full of life and light, was as Menelaus had described his mother. His friend, Prince Aeneas a vibrant person with thick dark curly hair cut short, carried most of the conversation with Menelaus. The three men knew each other and had recently broken bread together in Troy. The Trojan visitors had been reluctant to accept our hospitality. They had learned of the death of the Dioscuri as soon as they had touched the shores of Laconia.

"We will not impose on your kindness at this time," Prince Paris said. "We condole with you. The Dioscuri were marvels, renowned everywhere."

"We care not to intrude," Prince Aeneas said. "We will pay our respects and depart."

"Thank you." I answered. "Though our spirits are low, we are not prepared to ignore visiting princes. If you will forego celebrations in your honor, we welcome you to our house for a quiet visit. Troy is friend to Laconia, and Laconia friend to Troy. Please stay."

Now, on this pleasant evening, I realized the absence of Castor and Polydeuces intensely. It was as though they sat here with us but could not be seen or heard. I found it difficult to put on a face of interest and pleasantness. Lani had made me presentable in the white drapery of mourning. I wore no jewelry and silver bands kept my hair in place. We were in the central courtyard surrounded by gardens and arbors. The sweet breath of summer caressed us, but I felt empty and alone.

"Perhaps you could help me." The statement was an intrusion. I looked at Prince Paris, who had spoken. His low voice had not disturbed the discussion between Aeneas and Menelaus.

"How?" I asked, more with my eyes than my voice.

A servant filled wine cups and another placed fresh fruit on the table, pears and grapes.

"I wish to be purified," he answered, his face in shadow. "Your husband encouraged me to come here for that purpose. As he searched for peace of mind in Troy, I so search in Laconia."

His words brought me out of my deep melancholy. His eyes, some shade of gray, reflected the flaring torch, searing the hurt within me. "If I am to help in your purification, I must know the cause," I said. "Perhaps it is something too private to talk about with a stranger."

"It is perhaps easier to talk about with a stranger," he replied.

I waited, not knowing if he chose to tell me more.

"My cousin Antiphus has charming children. My favorite was Antheus, a handsome little boy who liked to play games of battle. In one such game, with toy weapons, there was a mis-step. Antheus tripped and fell upon the child-sword I held and was impaled to death. I will never forget the look on his face as he beseeched me to make it right. It was only a game, after all. He died in my arms." His voice broke briefly and was quiet.

Now tears welled and spilled down my cheeks. I, who had developed such control for my own grief, wept openly at hearing another's. I turned away, hiding my face, mastering my outburst. "I am so sorry," I gasped, wiping my eyes with a linen square. "How they must have suffered, his parents. And you, I understand your need." I sorrowed with him in his terrible pain. More grief, even more grief, was there no end?

Aeneas spoke with anticipation in his voice. "Menelaus tells me the game in the mountains here is bountiful. He will take us hunting, Paris, tomorrow if it pleases everyone."

"I will stay behind," Paris said. "That is, if Queen Helen will direct me in the rites of purification. I told her of my grievous offense for which I seek absolution."

"Yes. You must do that first, of course," Aeneas replied. "But I will join you, Menelaus, if you are willing."

Menelaus nodded, draining his wine cup before refilling it. "Yes, we will get an early start. I promise you a brace of partridge before noon."

Aeneas and Menelaus were well up into the forests by the time Paris and I, on horseback, rode down into the valley to the sanctuary of Potnia. We dismounted and tied our horses to a post, then walked along a path marked by willow trees.

"This shrine was once home to the Goddess effigy which is now in a safer location on higher ground," I told him. "I will leave you in the care of priestesses who will help with your purification. After your cleansing in the quiet lagoon, follow the path of white stones and enter Her hallowed place. Rest there in silence until I come for you."

"I have never felt so clean," Paris said later as we sat together on stone benches in the orchard outside the Goddess shrine. "I will stay here for the prescribed time of three days."

"Is Potnia a familiar deity for you?" I asked him. His light brown hair, with some strands tinged white by the sun, fell over his brow. His eyes, gray and changeable, brightened. In the daylight, at peace after the rites of purification, they were the color of a plover's breast. He put his head back and laughed. My question pleased him.

"Queen Helen. I all but nursed at the bosom of the Goddess."

I was puzzled but curious.

"You do not know me," he explained. "I grew up a shepherd on mountain pastures. I ran free with the beasts and learned the lore of the heights. It was as though Mount Ida's verdant hills were the breasts of the Goddess, for they nurtured my body with honey and milk, and my soul with beauty. She taught me the wisdom of the wilderness. I know her moods of weather, how to build shelters from the trees, and fires from dried twigs. I know flowers and plants and help them grow and multiply. I know her creatures, large and small, and how to trap the fox and avoid the bear."

As I listened, his eyes grew dark with his memories but projected an astonishing light that forced me to look aside, so penetrating was its focus. "I thought you were a Prince of Troy," I said, "not a shepherd boy."

"I am both." He laughed. "As I grew, I became fleet of foot and strong of arm; my skill with the bow was uncommon among the country boys. Once I had the temerity to participate in contests at Troy, where the sons of King Priam took second to my first in most events. The truth was told me: I too was the son of Hecuba and Priam. Because of a soothsayer, who predicted dire consequences at my birth, I was given to the shepherd of the royal flocks who left me on a rocky mountain outcrop to perish. This same shepherd found me later, thriving in the care of a she-bear. Unable to leave me in the face of such a favorable omen, he took me home with him and raised me as his son."

"And you were received back into your birth family?" I asked.

"Yes, but not without difficulty. I knew little of the customs and habits within the royal house and drew derisive abuse from my brothers and sisters for my loud voice and lack of ceremony. My father hired a tutor for me, and eventually I was tamed. Mother Hecuba enjoyed the unexpected perceptions of a child of nature and encouraged me to express my simple observations of all that I encountered in my new surroundings. As these conversations were of little interest to others, she and I grew into the habit of having long talks together in her apartment. I cherished these moments alone with her, for she is blessed with a warmth and brilliance that inspires me. In my naiveté I failed to realize that her interest in me further antagonized my brothers and sisters. If I had not been so successful in competing in their games, I might have gone far away from Troy and never returned."

Prince Paris looked out across the orchard where we sat, apparently not seeing of the fruitful trees for the vision that was in his mind.

"Even now I return often to my boyhood haunts." His teeth flashed as he smiled, bringing me into his happy memories. "I go to my friend Oenone, a shepherdess and nymph daughter of the River Oenus. We frolicked together as children and were initiated together into the sacred ceremonies of procreation. She has become a priestess to the Goddess, is renowned for her healing, and lives with her son in a hut where I am always welcome."

"You are a man of two lives," I said to him, envious of his idyllic escape into childhood when his royal duties became burdensome. I stood, for it was time for me to leave.

"Soon we must talk together about our two countries," I said, "for we have many common interests." I arranged my mantel on my shoulders. Again I caught the brilliance of his eyes as he watched me. The planes of his face were flat, yet the bony highlights of his cheekbones were sculpted curves. His eyebrows made perfect arches over those astonishing wide-apart eyes, arches darker than the fawn-shaded hair of his head. I could understand fully why his parents were so taken with him.

When Prince Paris had completed his purification rites, he and Prince Aeneas accompanied Menelaus, Hermione, and me to the tomb of Castor and Polydeuces. With several grooms, Meriandynus, and other servants carrying fresh-cut laurel branches, we wound down a precipitous path through the orchards and vineyards to the valley floor and followed the river south to their homes in Vaphio.

The stone houses of the Dioscuri dominated the crests of twin hills and glowed golden in reflected sunlight. Spiky cypress trees interspersed among the orchards and olive groves around them.

Polydeuces' oldest boy Tarsas, with a retainer, waited for us on the road to guide us. The tomb was dug into the side of a hill, its doors stood wide. "It is still under construction," Tarsas explained. We walked through a narrow passage to the vaulted chamber containing two graves. The interior of the tomb was lit by oil lamps set at intervals around the sides of the vault. Facing stone of Laconian green marble, each piece decorated with gold spirals, was being put in place by masons who quietly left when we entered. I felt chilled and put the shawl I carried around Hermione.

I could not help but think of the other tomb, the ancestral family tomb, which held eight graves. I knew it particularly well. At my wish and that of Castor, the grave of Mother Leda had been opened to receive the remains of Nikko and Locasta. The marble marker covering the well-like opening of Mother Leda's grave had been pried away and the debris filling the well had been removed. The two babies, with their favorite toys and golden cups and rings, had been gently lowered to rest in her skeletal arms, still covered with royal gold encrusted linen. The well-shaft had been filled again, the stone slab, wreathed in woven branches of shiny leaves of laurel, replaced.

A new tomb had been deemed necessary for The Dioscuri. They had died in the service of the Goddess, and their gentle strength and humble courage was greatly honored. The brutality of their demise swelled the unbearable feelings of loss to their families and followers. Visitors came regularly to pay them homage.

The burial had taken place as soon as the graves were prepared, the tomb constructed around them. Personal adornments, jeweled belts, gold and silver arm bands and neck chains, ceramic containers for eating and washing, their similar gold bull-catching cups given to them by Mother Leda, had all been buried with them because they held the aura and identity of each. As they were born together, they died together and were so buried.

We all placed laurel branches around the graves and then stood in quiet respect. I closed my eyes and could see Castor and Polydeuces in my mind and feel their brightness in my spirit. I almost smiled, for their presence always made me happy.

"I depart tomorrow," Menelaus said to Hilaeira in response to a question. We sat at tables set in the garden of the palace of Castor and Phoebe. The shade of old oak trees protected us from the sun, and colorful pink cystus bushes and evergreen hedges enclosed the space.

A sudden concern washed across the face of Hilaeira. She glanced at me, and we both awaited his explanation. Hilaeira, dear friend and sister, knew well the worry that the absences of Menelaus had caused us. Lines of fatigue and shadows of grief dimmed the bloom of her radiance.

"It is a sign I received. I must go away. I shall accompany Aeneas." Menelaus had drunk well of the wine. As the light breeze caught the leaves of a branch above him, dappling shadows made him appear first to be joking, then to be crying, expressing my feelings of loss at having him leave, yet relief that he had decided to go.

Phoebe, who had been quiet, appeared as a composition in white. Her mourning drapery, unrelieved by any ornament, her fair complexion made wan by grief, her opaque empty eyes, left only pale gold hair pulled back to a fastening at the neck, and faint pink full curving lips for contrast. "We have become accustomed to your absences," she said. "It is surprising how one can answer the needs brought upon us by loss and change. I, for example, depart tomorrow, also. I will return to Messenia with my children. Marpessa, Queen to fallen Idas, has requested help now that she alone must care for all the business of government."

"Our old father, King Leucippus, has come to her aid," Hilaeira added, her voice retaining its richness, "but he is not well."

Tarsas, Laconia's royal hope for the future, sat at ease between Prince Paris and Prince Aeneas. Their convivial interchange had suddenly ceased, as everyone's attention had shifted to Phoebe.

"We wish you good journey," Prince Paris said to her. "My travel plans take me north to the island of Salamis, before I return to Troy. However, I am in no rush and offer my assistance to you as an escort." His cheerful tone somehow changed the dire mood.

"Thank you, but it will not be necessary. I have many attendants, and travel between here and Messenia is free of danger these days," Phoebe replied.

On our return Menelaus rode at my side. "You have made the correct decision," I told him. I will miss you, but it must be thus."

He looked upon me with a hard expression made of hurt and anger. "I do your bidding, Helen."

INVITATION

Menelaus, Aeneas and his retainers rode out through the courtyard and disappeared down the steeply descending path. Paris accompanied them, and Hermione ran off to play, not knowing that this parting with her father would be much, much longer than the others.

My good-bye to Menelaus had been a hushed grasping of hands, a slight shake of the head as he turned and left. I remained at the open gate reflecting about kings and self-knowledge, as Theseus had explained it to me long ago. Self-knowledge was absent in Menelaus. Would he even recognize the truth when he encountered it? I feared his treks to Delphi and to Troy would be of little use to him. Menelaus would never be able to remove himself from the curse of the House of Atreus and Pelops.

I had selected Menelaus to be King in Laconia when I was very young, yet it came to me that I had understood well my choice. Menelaus had not been my brothers' favorite. That alone should have informed me. I had not even included Menelaus in that small group of princes who stood out as talented in kingly ways. Why had I chosen him? I sighed. I had turned my back on every good choice and had selected Menelaus because he would bring Iphigeneia closer to me.

I closed my eyes tightly and turned quickly. I repeated the facts in my mind: Menelaus continues to be bound to the evil influence of the House of Atreus; he is unable to separate himself from Agamemnon, his blood brother; he is unable to act as our King. "Ah," I said aloud, shrugging my shoulders, thinking how the ancients would have had no such turmoil. Then a king's youth and potency were mixed in with the freshly plowed furrows and newly planted seeds, for in those days a king was sacrificed yearly after each cycle of crops. But, thankfully, the savagery of human sacrifice had long ago been abolished.

"They will arrive in Limera Harbor while you stand here in meditation," Prince Paris said, as he returned from escorting the travelers on their way. "You find this parting very difficult." His troubled voice brought me back to the present.

"Perhaps," I said, glancing at him, then looking about for Hermione, who played a game of throwing stones in the gravel at the side of the courtyard.

"Tell me, Paris," I said, moving quickly along, "your father has been King in Troy for many years. Does he have self-knowledge about his kingship?"

He thought a moment. "People respect him. He cares about his children. My mother, Queen Hecuba, believes he is a good king." He laughed engagingly, knowing his response was inadequate.

"Queen Hecuba would know," I answered. "She seems to me to be endowed with much wisdom."

"She is indeed. You will meet her for yourself one day."

Hermione ran to us. "Come, play with me. Please."

"Yes, darling. I would like to."

"And Prince Paris, too."

"By all means," he agreed.

"I have made some arrangements for this morning." I said to Paris, later, as he jumped from space to space in Hermione's marked-off game. "Two of my counselors will be here soon. I hope you will join us."

"I will be honored," he answered, by-passing the square containing Hermione's stone.

"You understand," I said, catching his eye for a serious exchange before I tossed my pebble onto the drawn pattern, "crucial matters are at hand. I must confer with my counselors to inform them of the King's absence, and we have promised to discuss future amenities with Troy and hear your account of possibilities."

I turned to Hermione. "How can I play your game, darling, with this long drapery in the way?" She giggled as I wadded my skirt in one hand and leaped about the outline. "Oh, no," I said, stepping into the wrong place. "Darling girl, it's your turn."

Hermione deftly hopped from spot to spot, balancing on one foot as she picked up her stone, twirled around and back again. As her marker landed in the last square, she laughed and danced through the course.

Chief Counselor Arneus, solemn and self-contained, joined us in the interior courtyard where high hedges of swaying oleander protected us from a strong breeze that plunged down from the mountain tops. We sat in the shade of an ancient olive tree; its great gnarled trunk was an austere presence in itself, a reminder of the endless past. General Volos, ushered in by Meriandynus, hustled across the garden, his sword banging against his square body.

"I am honored to meet with you," Prince Paris said, after introductions were completed. Paris crossed his bronzed legs casually, the thongs of his sandals interlaced over his muscular calves nearly to his knees. His dark blue tunic was adorned with metal studs, and I noticed that his hands rested easily in his lap; they were competent hands with nimble fingers and clean short nails. When he smiled, creases of laughter appeared at the sides of his mouth. His vibrant presence lent a congeniality to our meeting.

We sipped cups of mint drink and I thanked them for coming together. "Before we commence our discussion," I said, "I must tell you that King Menelaus has gone away."

A frown appeared and quickly vanished from the face of Arneus. General Volos sputtered, "Again? So soon?"

"I know not when he will return," I said. "I believe he seeks answers to difficult questions. He is unable to perform his duties here, perhaps indefinitely."

Neither man appeared unduly surprised at my words. Arneus looked at me as though expecting further explanation, and Prince Paris raised one eyebrow quizzically.

"I believe he will step down from his kingship." I said. "In any case we must continue without him." Both counselors nodded in understanding. "I called you here this morning," I continued, "to also tell you that Prince Paris has words for us from Troy, as we have information to share with him about Laconia. General Volos, will you please summarize our military situation?"

General Volos rearranged himself in his seat, then spoke to Prince Paris. "You know, I trust, of our recent very successful military operation in Kydonia, and of the ignominious crime, the murder of our honored Dioscuri by Mycenean soldiers at the behest of King Agamemnon, himself?"

"Yes, I was told all, I believe," Paris replied. His gaze focused intensely on General Volos. "Is it true that the combined forces from Messenia, Laconia, and Arcadia suffered only minor injuries in the entire operation?"

"Yes, that is correct," General Volos replied.

"And that the killing of the five leaders happened after their return to Laconia?"

"Yes, that is also correct." General Volos sipped from his cup, and when Paris nodded, Volos continued. "The dishonor of the act, the sheer brutality, the searing loss is impossible to describe. It was clearly murder, not in any way an heroic battle killing, man against man. Agamemnon is responsible for this act of unmeasurable shame and will forever be judged for it." His gruff voice took on a doleful tone.

He continued: "We believe our best strategy is to re-group our alliances with Messenia and Arcadia. We have sent envoys to establish these accords. We are also in touch with other countries with strong Goddess worship prac-tices. We look to Aetolia, Boeotia, Locris, and Attica to help us bring Agamemnon down." Volos did not mention Troy, but it must have been in his mind. An alliance with Troy would be a master stroke.

"Then, I am to understand," Paris said, "that you are not defeated by this terrible loss?"

Arneus answered. "The exaltation we felt in the glory of the Dioscuri was a wonderful mantle that fell over all of us; it enhanced us, made us more than we were. We feel something else now. We feel an opposite degree of rage and can no longer be a part of Agamemnon's realm."

"Are you expecting Agamemnon to attack outright?" Paris asked.

"I think not," General Volos answered. "He knows our strength. His expertise at using small striking forces that come in secret may well have to be confronted. But he also knows from our success in Kydonia that we are skilled at repelling such groups. Our thrust will be to organize like-minded states into a potency of our own."

Arneus put a hand over his bald pate as though to smooth his hair and took up where Volos had ended. "Our trading ventures and policies have benefited from the in-formed and intelligent judgment of The Dioscuri, and our activities have not been disrupted with their death." He leaned over to a small table and poured mint drink into his cup, then looked at Prince Paris. "Our policy is more and more one of cooperation with others. Our experience in Troy is our best example. It is not just happenstance that those places with strong Goddess worship are most amenable to peaceful trading ways." He smiled easily. He was an open-minded man and had nothing to hide. "Prince Paris," he added, "I believe the vessel that brought you here has been safely loaded with stone and olive oil, a successful exchange for all."

"Yes, so I understand." Paris said. He stood and walked about as though to expend some pent-up energy. He sat again on the edge of his seat, demanding our attention. "In Troy the King and Queen have long been interested in Laconia. We have long been aware of the moderating influence that has come from here and spreads out to far reaches, calming the rough waters agitated in Mycenae. We knew all about the marvels of The Dioscuri. Polydeuces and Castor were admired everywhere for their strength, grace and style, their bravery and generosity. First, we heard stories from our own harpers, and then from travelers. We knew of their tribal feud with their Messenian cousins and marveled at the untangling of the dispute, and all in the name of The Goddess. Then we heard the story of Helen."

He stopped speaking, sat back in his chair and looked down at his hands. When he commenced again, his voice had lowered and his words came slowly. He looked at me, and his eyes seemed to emit a power of their own, so forceful was his gaze. "We heard of your unbelievable beauty which is even greater in person than in legend. We heard how you brought back the famous Laconian effigy, so grievously stolen, and of your own captivity and your Queenship and the many princes who vied to be your king, and of the agreements made among the many leaders of states in your name."

Again, he stopped and looked off at some distant site. I was relieved to have the intensness of his gaze shift, for it had made me uneasy. He had not before concentrated so fully on me with words of praise and appreciation. I felt a distinct gratification in pleasing him that bothered me.

General Volos nodded his head in glowing agreement. Arneus looked upon me as though I were his well-behaved child. Paris continued, but the intensity of his eyes had dissipated. I could attend him without discomfort. "Queen Hecuba and King Priam invite you, Helen, Laconian Queen, to come to Troy to take part in rites and ceremonies celebrating the Great Mother. Every ten lunar years clans and tribes gather in the valley of the Scamander River for such an event, and you would be the focus. I am to escort you. I invite you in their name to join us in this celebration."

I stood, astonished and honored beyond measure.

Paris stood also. "Helen," he said. "Before you answer, let me say more. You have mentioned how important it is for you to stay here, because King Menelaus is away and your brothers..." His voice lowered without completing what we all knew so well. "Please," he continued, "before you decide, hear me. Troy is the largest holy center for Goddess worship. Our traditions are as ancient as exist anywhere. We have many temples and sacred Goddess figures. This celebration will bring worshippers from far places. It will be an outright announcement of the close ties between our two countries." That powerful force from his eyes was compelling. "You must come to Troy."

His argument was overpowering. How could I refuse to do as he asked? I looked to General Volos and to Counselor Arneus. They were both on their feet, and I could tell that they had seen the vision Paris described. They wanted me to go.

"Helen," Volos said. "This opportunity is important for Laconia. It will reenforce our aims. Those states that are our friends will be more likely to join us against Agamemnon this way than any other."

I understood his reasoning. "I will go for two reasons," I said, looking at Paris and my counselors. "To take part in the reverent ceremony you described, and for another ceremony, establishing the accords between our countries."

"Yes. I understand this mission in that way," General Volos said.

"To have our Queen so honored in Troy," Arneus said, "will mean an open declaration that Troy supports Laconia in our dealings with Agamemnon?"

"Did I fail to make that clear?" Paris said. "Troy supports Laconia in their dealings with Agamemnon. This meeting will prove it. Accords will be made in Troy to formalize our relationship."

The three men stood before me, each looking at me, attending my response. I thought quickly of the necessary arrangements. Lani would care for Hermione. Meriandynus would accompany me as aide. Phiona would be given temporary power as Goddess Incarnate and Protector of the Effigy. Arneus would act in my place as Chief Deputy. General Volos would continue as military leader. I would not be away for long, two lunar months perhaps. I must have some drapery styled. Captain Thaos must be contacted for I would only go to sea with him.

What of gifts? I must take grand gifts. I looked around and discovered the three men still awaited my decision.

"I will go to Troy," I answered. "Yes, yes, I will go to Troy."

NAS

The prow of the ship lifted rhythmically, creating a foamy wake that I watched in lazy fascination. Each day, since passing Cape Sounion, a steady sea breeze filled the sails and idled the oarsmen. Some played at dice, some repaired equipment, some slept. One piped a tune on his flute, the notes hung on the air then skipped away with the breeze. Captain Thaos and the pilot scanned the sky where wisps of clouds appeared around the mountain peaks of an island ahead.

"Look there," Paris said beside me, pointing to a family of dolphins dipping and arching in the sea.

I watched the billowing dark forms and laughed gleefully. "That big fellow turned on his side and looked directly at me," I said to Paris.

"I know," he answered. "I saw him smile." We looked at each other in mutual pleasure.

Captain Thaos came to us, stepping around one sprawling crew member and another. "We will stop early today," he said, the corners of his dark eyes creasing in the brightness. "We expect strong northerly winds to blow up by tomorrow. We'll establish ourselves in a bay in the island ahead this afternoon. This is fortunate timing for it is utterly impossible to enter the Bay of Nas after the strong winds commence."

"I have no doubts about your decisions, Captain," I said. "Though these easy days have been a joy."

"They cannot last forever," Thaos said.

"A few days in a village will be an interesting change in any case," Paris commented.

"Ah, but no village exists in the Bay of Nas, as on our other stops," Thaos answered. "The island is rough and wild, but the small inlet we're headed for is completely protected."

As we closed with the island, I saw sheer cliffs that came right down to the sea and heavy forests that covered the mountainous terrain above. We followed the northern shore around a cape, and suddenly, between two promontories, appeared an entrance into a nearly concealed bay with a yellow line of beach and beautiful calm water. I felt as though a charm had fallen over all of us; the only sound was the dip of the oars and the creaking of the leathern locks as we glided into the cove.

"This is a place of the Goddess," Thaos said in a very low voice behind me.

I nodded, feeling the presence.

"In fact," he explained, "there is an ancient shrine here."

"I understand why seamen construct shrines of thanks to a deity." I put my hand on his arm. "I will never forget that sacred spot where my child received her name blessing."

"Nor will I." His gaze wandered to the approaching shore. "This one is different," he said. "It feels as though it has been here since time before time."

The boat was beached, the oars used to make shelters by burying the handles in the earth at an angle, then crossing the blades to make a frame for hanging skins or cloths. Meriandynus moved our bundles into such a hut that was set amidst some umbrella pines on a rise of sandy ground.

"The sun is still high," I said to Meriandynus. "While you arrange things here, I will bathe in the sea, or perhaps find a pool of fresh water near the river and wash the salt spray from my hair."

"Yes, Queen Helen," he said, standing straight before me. A scatter of freckles overlaid his cheeks and nose. "I will put things in order. My sleeping place will be here where I can guard the entry."

"Yes, and I see the gifts we take to Troy are in that heap of bundles at the back of the hut. Amongst them is a sack of gold beads from the royal storerooms; they must be put into smaller bundles that can be tucked here and there among our things. I brought some leathern pouches for that purpose."

"I understand."

I walked over to where the gifts were piled and recognized the large, tightly bound sack that contained the gold. "There is no rush to make the exchange." I smiled at him for he was very serious.

"You can depend on me, Queen Helen." His earnest voice confirmed my complete trust in him.

My personal bedding and cases were at the far side of the hut for greatest privacy. I searched through the packs and found the empty leather pouches intended for the safekeeping of the treasure. I also retrieved a linen towel and a vial of cleansing nectar. "I will leave you, then," I said, tossing him the pouches. "Why don't you bathe, as well, while the sun is still warm."

"Yes, a good idea," he replied as he held the tent flap for me.

I ducked out, breathing in the spicy air. The sailors and their gear spread out in every direction. I waved at Paris who came towards me. "Are you settled?" I asked.

"Yes, Over on that hillock." He indicated it with his hand. "The Captain and I will share a shelter." He seemed pleased to see me, as though we had not been constantly together recently. "I was about to come for you."

"I plan to bathe in the sea," I said, "or perhaps, as it is so very much occupied right now, I may find a pool in the river. Fresh water would be my preference."

We turned away from the camp and ambled towards the stream that gushed down from the wooded mountains into a narrow ravine. An overgrown path led along its bank crowded with bracken and adorned with cobwebs shining silver in the sun. We followed it uphill where ancient stone walls stood deep into the hillside amongst moss and ivy. Sedge warblers sang in the thickets and swallows skimmed overhead.

"I believe the Goddess shrine must be close by," I said. "With such a source of nurturing water and all the fruitful vegetation, this place is sacred to Her."

"Who knows, maybe—." Paris stopped speaking. We had come to stepping stones in marshy ground that led to a stone shrine. We stepped inside permitting the essence of the holy place to surround us. Light filtered into an oblong chamber, empty except for a few dried flowers on the floor. We saw a second, darker chamber with roof slits directing a light shaft onto a large altar rock.

I stopped suddenly, for behind the altar a shadowy figure sat in a recess. My heart raced, and I raised my arms in awe of the compelling presence. After moments, with my head lowered in veneration, I cautiously lifted my eyes to the figure.

A carver of former days had seen the likeness of the Great Mother in the curving swells of an ancient olive tree. A human-sized form had been hewn from its gnarled clefts. With head lifted, her mouth curved up at the corners in a baffling smile of sensuality, and her eyes were dark hollows of primitive knowledge. A serpent encircled her long neck and curving shoulders, and her arms crossed under projecting breasts. With his simple tools, the carver had emphasized the roundness of thighs, hips, belly, and the fecund triangle of procreation. Every surface was incised with spirals or zigzags.

Her entire figure generated a potency that caused my breathing to deepen and my skin to prickle. I turned to Paris, and our eyes locked. We clasped hands, and, turning back to the Goddess, bowed our heads to receive Her nearly palpable blessing. After a long time of quiet, allowing her essence to enter us, Paris and I backed away from the Goddess and left the shrine.

We continued on along the river bank. An aura of full slanting light embellished each shining leaf of the oleander bush, each of its pale pink flower petals and green rigid stems. I looked at Paris beside me and saw the intricate perfection of the folds of his ear, the strength of the muscles in his cheek, the sun-struck hair that fell so gently on his brow. I yearned to touch the smooth skin of his chest, and feel the ridges of some old scars on his shoulders and back. A golden bloom had fallen over him, and I, too, was included in it. He and I had become a part of the natural wonder around us. Fearful of breaking the spell, we kept our silence and followed the path to a quiet pool apart from the rush of the stream. I smelled the pungent odor of bank foliage and river reed. We untied our sandals and slipped off our clothing and entered the water.

I lay back and the coolness washed over me as light filtered through the branches of overhanging pines.

"Helen," Paris said in a muted voice.

"What is it?" I asked, drawn to his physical nearness.

"Helen." He knelt in the shallows. "Since the moment I first saw you, I knew something special was meant for us."

His words excited my heart, for I understood. "Yes," I said. "I know."

"We must purify ourselves."

I had left the cleansing nectar on the bank and turned to fetch it, but he stopped me with his eyes. "Here is white sand." I knelt facing him and we plunged our hands into the water, grasping handfuls of sand and smearing it all over each other. I felt the gritty roughness on my shoulders and back, breasts and belly. I rubbed it over Paris in whorls and circles, harder and harder, as I felt the stinging pain of the scouring bite into my skin. For a moment we were brutal with each other, but then I felt a vital flame envelop me. It glowed within and radiated out to every part of me; my lips, my breasts, my belly, and my fingers tips were on fire. We reached for each other, our lips touched, first softly, then we clung together, our bodies pressed tightly. This is as it should be, I thought. We belong like this, melded together. My face lifted to his, our kisses were frantic and deep. I could think no more; our bodies joined in a driving ebullience. I felt part of a voluptuous ecstasy that encompassed nature itself. On the mossy banks of the sacred pond, caught by the gleaming rays of the sinking sun, we offered up to the Goddess the erotic rites of copulation, in the profound knowledge that it was consecrated by Her.

The wind commenced at dawn and blew without ceasing for seven days. It raged and tore at the trees, but we were protected from the fury within the confines of the sacred cove. Paris and I felt part of the uproar because of the passion that raged within us. Our offering to the Goddess, that first day, had stimulated a compelling passion between us.

We tried to maintain a semblance of decorum within the compound. I helped Meriandynus move the gold beads into the smaller pouches which we placed here and there amongst our packs. Captain Thaos and I planned our voyage.

"If the winds come strong again, we will seek refuge in mainland harbors," the Captain said, "but I would prefer a direct route by way of the off-shore islands." He smiled broadly. "From now on, each settlement, village, or town we visit is named for the Goddess. I wish we could detour to each one."

I tried hard to catch his vision. "We must not take extra time," I cautioned. "Let us follow your first judgment and keep to the islands, unless the weather forces us to do otherwise."

Paris wore a leopard-skin hood for luck and hunted wild fowl and deer for our feasts around the fire in the evening. He told me he had encountered the great cat when he was a boy. They had faced each other, each poised to kill. Paris had let go the fatal arrow just as the beast leapt from a rock above, crashing into Paris and wounding him with agonizing, clawing death throes until the life-force slipped away. "The leopard is my sign," he told me. "I wear a fearful leopard mask for ceremonial dances." He screwed up his face and danced a few steps to demonstrate.

Inevitably, our eyes would catch across a crowded tract, where sailors played at dice or listened to sea stories, and we would slip away to a prearranged meeting place.

From on high, one day, we caught the full tumult of the wind's voraciousness as it whipped our hair and thrashed our skin, nearly shredding tunic and drapery. We watched the sea boil over in a foaming rampage; it crashed on the rocks in a frantic eruption of spume and spray. Up on the heights the very turbulence that surrounded us excited us. We clung together in its ferocity, then found a sheltered place behind some rocks where we abandoned ourselves to the inflaming ardor that directed us. Satiated, for a time, we relaxed in each others arms and talked about the mystery of our infatuation.

"We must thank the Goddess for permitting us this interim of beauty," Paris said, as I lay quietly, my eyes closed against the brightness of the sky.

"I am content to follow the passions of nature wherever they lead us" I replied. "I know this enchantment will end when we leave here."

"Perhaps not," Paris answered, his voice husky. "Perhaps we are forever destined to hunger for each other. You are always more beautiful when I am with you than my short memory can manage when I am apart from you."

"Which is hardly at all," I reminded him. "We had better return to the camp."

"Yes, after a while."

I heard the passion in his voice and felt his gentle hand smooth my hair and finger my cheek. I turned to look at him and we came together. Just the thought of our sensual pleasures aroused our ardor. I had let go of my grief and my queenship for an unquenchable physical delirium on this isolated island, where the past could not encroach its sadness or the future its responsibility.

The wind moderated at sunset, and the old timers said it was finished for now. Captain Thaos sat on the sand before the fire and chewed on a piece of beach grass. "It is my guess that we should now have four or five days of respite before it starts again," he said.

"The Goddess' will has great power here," I said.

Thaos seemed about to reply as Paris crouched down next to us. "The venison is ready," he reported. "It's baked slowly all day over hot coals in a basket woven of bay tree branches for flavor."

"We appreciate your skill in the arts of wilderness living," Thaos said to him, preparing to rise. "The next time we must sleep in the open I'll remember your way of making a hut frame from crossed branches." He stood and brushed the sand from his clothes.

The firelight flared on Paris's face in the darkening evening. "If only my skills in battle were as apt. I have never learned to kill men as I would an animal for food to eat, or to protect my own life. That is the problem with growing up in the wilds; I'm not civilized in the arts of killing." Thaos and I exchanged a look of wonder as Paris hopped up and the three of us moved towards the other fire.

"Captain Thaos believes the wind has abated for four or five days," I said to Paris.

"Then we will depart at dawn?"

"If our Queen so wishes," Thaos answered, looking at me.

"Yes, we will depart at dawn," I answered.

TROY

"**Q**ueen Helen," someone called. I turned to see Queen Hecuba hurry up the walk. I stood in the secluded sanctuary garden, the sun already on its downward journey for the day. Hecuba's drapery flowed around her ample figure as she mounted the stone steps. Her breath came short, and her color shone high on her cheeks. I smiled my welcome but was unable to reply because of her many questions.

"Are your quarters comfortable, my dear? Will the serving girl be useful to you? You will feast with us this evening, will you not? The entire family will be present. I hope you do not feel isolated. But you will have privacy, and the priestesses are nearby if you need anything."

I nodded my head that all was quite perfect. "And I thank you for Klara. She is a sweet person and takes good care of me," I said, just as the girl limped past at the other end of the garden.

"I am relieved. Come, sit with me," Hecuba said, indicating a bench that looked out to the vast autumn fields below, set amid orchards and rows of naked twisting vines.

"On a really clear day you can see Mount Ida from here," Queen Hecuba said. "But then you have seen Mount Ida from sacred Assos."

"Yes," I answered. "We were forced to abandon our sea journey at Assos. Prince Paris was in a fever to proceed and could not wait for the winds to cease and arranged for horses and a chariot." I thought of how we had left Meriandynus to organize the hauling of our bundles by oxen and cart with a hired driver. When the winds moderated Captain Thaos would bring the ship north to Troy. "Paris and I stopped to see Mount Ida on our way here,"

"No amount of city life will remove his attachment to the wilderness," Hecuba sighed. "Did he take you to the shepherd hut where he grew up?" Hecuba's dark brown eyes narrowed in anticipation of my response. I felt deeply her pain, for she must be reminded of how she had given her new-born child away those many years ago.

"Oh, yes," I said. "He wanted to show me everything. The hut is a roomy house overlooking a lake, with several out-buildings for the animals. The old man's son now manages the flocks. His wife gave us a splendid lunch and afterwards we tramped through the hills."

"Did you see anyone else?" she asked as we both watched a flight of cranes headed south.

We had seen several shepherds whom Paris introduced to me, never flaunting his princely mantel before these simple friends who, in former days, were his equals. I did not mention them. "We stopped to visit Oenone. Do you know her?"

"I know her. She is a high priestess in Assos and lives in a compound with her small son."

"Yes, a pleasant place in a well watered valley. Paris told me how he is always welcome at her hearth."

We had found Oenone with other women at the river, where clothes and bedding had been spread about on rocks and bushes for drying. The women sang and laughed as the sheets billowed in the breeze when they held them at each corner for folding. A small boy, romping about with other children, spotted us as we approached and ran to Paris, who picked him up and threw him high. The happy giggles of the child drew the notice of a slim girl with a long thick braid, who held a huge mound of fresh laundry to her. She turned, put a hand to shade her eyes from the dazzling glare and recognized Paris. Her smile outshone the sun as her bundle fell away, and she came forward to meet him.

He took her hand and introduced us. The radiant look dissolved from Oenone's face; she bowed to me with the respect a priestess should have for a Queen.

"Oenone is gifted in healing and is often here with us in the city." Hecuba commented.

"We have much in common, then," I said, "for I also have interest in the healing arts. I would like to be her friend." My words expressed my true feeling, but I could not help but know friendship between us was unlikely. Oenone had discerned instantly that Paris and I shared a profound physical attraction. Though the winds had ceased in the Bay of Nas, our mutual desires had not.

After leaving Oenone and her son, Paris and I continued alone to the wooded shore of a mountain lake where we spent the night in a simple hovel. The horses had been tethered near rich tufts of grass, and we swept the dirt floor of the hut clean, spreading skins for sleeping and arranging other bundles for easy access. I placed our food sack amongst some rocks near the cool water of the lake and stopped to marvel at the rosy-gold reflection of the sinking sun in the limpid depths. Paris had fanned a beach fire to crackling; I smelled the wood smoke, and a wonderful contentment came over me.

I did not hear his step behind me, but I felt his hands on my shoulders, then his tender touch on my neck and chin and lips. Overwhelmed with a sweet fulness, I turned to him. Our gentle kiss inflamed us to a marvelous passion, a powerful hunger that could not be satisfied until we disrobed and clung in naked twining on the skins in the shelter.

"Tell me of your husband, King Menelaus," Hecuba said. "We remember him with much warmth."

I forced myself back to the present, but not before regretting my separation from Paris. I had vowed to represent the Goddess, Laconia and my Queenship in Troy with all of the authority and energy I could muster. I was relieved to have been given quarters in the sanctuary, removed from the easy charm of our infatuation. Even my boy-servant had to have special permission to enter my living area. I hoped to meditate and prepare myself for the coming rituals and meetings.

I answered Hecuba's question. "Menelaus told me of the genial welcome he received when he visited here. He thought highly of every thing he encountered in Troy." I paused, feeling keenly my disappointment in his weak effort at kingship. "Unfortunately, the growing problems between Laconia and Mycenae made it difficult for Menelaus to serve as our King. I asked him to step down. He is now on a journey of his own, hoping to find direction and strength."

Hecuba had appraised me carefully as I spoke. "I see that Laconia has a strong Queen. King Priam and his counselors are eager to meet with you."

"Yes, I am also eager for these meetings and to participate in Goddess celebrations." I smiled into her bright eyes and found an answering glint of pleasure.

She put her hand on mine. "The autumn rites are nearly upon us. Even now the clans are gathering in the river valley. I hope you will be with us for a long visit."

"It is essential that I leave here while the weather permits a sea passage. I must depart immediately after the celebrations."

"Ah, of course. I understand. Now, my dear," she stood and held her hand out to me, "I wish to guide you through the sanctuaries, this one and another, close by. Then I leave you to refresh yourself for the feast.

Arm in arm we followed the steep path behind the windbreak of cypress trees, across the myrtle-covered terrace to the main entrance, where an elaborately carved wooden ramp led us to a lofty doorway and into the temple interior. I stood spellbound in a shower of gold, for brilliant beams of sunlight poured into the hall through numerous light slits cleverly spaced in the rock masonry. A joyful sight delighted me as I looked about at many welcoming figures of the Goddess Cybele. Near the entry the Great Mother sat in a chariot drawn by two lions; she was about to dash through the open portal, away to her worldly tasks.

Other Goddess forms occupied wall niches and larger recesses. Some were simple carvings of ancient origin. Others were highly crafted and adorned with gold and gems. At the end of the hall she sat in an imposing chair; magnificent emeralds and garnets embellished her rich robe, and a fire ruby centered her tall headdress that, Hecuba assured me, lit up the darkness of night. She looked at me from inset ivory eyes with pupils of black onyx and followed my every move through the temple.

"I will take you now to an older shrine where my daughter Cassandra is High Priestess to the Goddess Hecate. There rests the image most sacred to Troy, for it is believed to have fallen from the sky and it sanctifies our city."

We entered this ancient holy place in the quiet of the afternoon. Hecuba led me into the dark interior of the earth itself. Hecate, a figure of a slender young woman carved of cedar wood, stood upright on a golden stand where lamps burned all through the day, The stone from the sky resided in her high hat. I sensed a most ancient presence and bowed many minutes in respect.

Hecuba led me to the quarters for the young girls who came to live and study, and where the temple guardians practiced their augury and managed the work of the order.

I heard an undercurrent of voices as we entered a courtyard where fifteen or twenty young women stood about in conversation, and older priestesses sat at a table over cups of spicy smelling brew.

Cassandra came to greet us. She bowed to us in courtesy, and I admired her smooth head of long brown hair parted in the center and kept in place with a clip at the base of her neck. "Royal Queen Mother, welcome. And Queen Helen," she said turning to me. "We are happy to see you." She led us to seats in the shade of a plane tree, its yellow leaves carpeted the ground at our feet.

A girl with a sweet smile joined us. "My friend is from Boeotia," Cassandra said. "She will answer your questions. Please forgive me, Queen Helen, but I must take Mother away for consultation." No smile graced her face. "I hope to dine with you this evening."

When they had left, I spoke to the girl. "Are you one of the maidens from across the sea chosen to come here for training?"

"Yes, this is the end of my third year."

"What are your duties," I asked.

"I keep the records of the flocks and visit the shepherds every spring," she said simply. "I enjoy being in the hills and seeing the new lambs."

I liked her friendly way. "Will you be returning to Boeotia soon?" I asked.

"When the new maids arrive, I shall return."

"When do you expect them?"

"We never know, to the day. Anticipating their arrival is quite exciting. One day they simply appear—and then we have a wonderful celebration."

"What do you mean, simply appear?" I asked, confused.

"Haven't you heard about the secret passage? she asked. "Everyone here knows about it, but no one knows exactly where it leads. We come and go in the dark of night and see nothing but lamps that light a tunneled way."

"I have not heard of it," I said.

"The entry is out there somewhere." She indicated the distant sea and line of beach. It is impossible to see, unless you know what to look for. It meanders underground to a stairway and brings the maidens here."

"Right here?:" I asked, turning to inspect every wall for some sign of egress.

"Actually, it leads to the sacred shrine, the very oldest part of the temple."

"Do you mean where the guardian image is? I have just been there. I did not notice a doorway."

"No, you would not. It is disguised by walls of rock."

When Hecuba returned, the girl took us to the Venerable, a blind old seer whose gnarled fingers worked constantly with a basket of colored threads. She painfully untied knots in the discarded weaving so the threads could be washed and used again.

Meriandynus, splendid in his military tunic, escorted me through darkening streets, past large stone houses interspersed with smaller cottages. The palace stood above two tiered terraces from which a stairway led up to a portico. Wearing a handsome tunic of darkest red and gold, Paris ran down the steps to meet us. I wondered if my own eyes so frankly lit up in pleasure at seeing him as did his when they looked upon me.

I nodded to Meriandynus to stay close behind me as we mounted the grand stairway. Paris took my arm and escorted me to his mother and father, who waited within the welcoming room.

Queen Hecuba, regal in a dark blue robe falling free from her shoulders, wore a gold tiara, her gray hair tightly knotted at her neck. "My dear Queen Helen, you have already won our hearts. We welcome you to all that is ours."

King Priam stood tall and thin beside her. His smoothly combed hair was nearly white, and his wrinkled cheeks revealed his many years. His kind brown eyes seemed to understand all about me. "It is time we met, Queen Helen. We have many things to talk of and many things to do. Tonight, I hope you will become acquainted with my family and friends. Tomorrow, we will gather for discussions of a more serious nature."

I held his hands and looked into his wise eyes. "I look forward to our discussions tomorrow."

Paris guided me into a great hall with polished floors of Laconian marble and wood columns painted black with ochre bases. Torches flickered in wall sconces, and servants in long, tightly wrapped skirts and close-fitting head caps passed trays of wine cups and bowls of dried fruits. Meat roasted over a brazier and three-legged tables were set up around the sides of the room for feasting.

Almost at once Aeneas came forward. His short black hair and friendly manner were as I remembered.

"Did you have a successful journey home?" I asked him after pleasantries.

"Yes, except that I could not interest Menelaus in sailing with me. He insisted on his own schedule—off into the wilds somewhere. Ah, here is Hector and Andromache."

Hector stood taller and larger than his younger brother Paris. He had bull-like shoulders and an athlete's grace. Dark hair fell over his forehead, giving him a boyish air despite his mantle of Commander of the Trojan Army. A tall and willowy young woman next to him regarded me seriously.

"Welcome to our city," Hector said, his voice evenly modulated. "We are delighted to have you amongst us, particularly knowing our brother's clumsy, ah, inexperienced manner in diplomacy." He winked at Paris and pounded his shoulder in a show of humor.

I sensed Paris stiffen beside me at this thinly disguised mockery. "But Sir," I said, duplicating Hector's cheerfulness in my smile and happy voice, "a learned demeanor could never match the sincerity and candor of your brother's natural persuasion. Do you not agree?" I asked, turning to Andromache.

"If my son is any judge, I do. Astyanax adores his uncle." Her smile included all of us, and she linked arms with Paris.

"Honors for diplomacy should be yours, Andromache," Paris said. "Astyanax is a good and loyal friend." He smiled.

"Your son is blessed with good judgment," I told her. Is he present?"

"Oh, no," the three of them said in unison, shaking their heads and laughing. "His nurse will be putting him to bed, if she has not already done so," Andromache explained, still amused. "He is just four this month, you see."

I felt a sudden piercing pain in my heart at these innocent words of a loving mother. They summoned up a lucid vision of little Nikko, his hair shining gold in the fire light. I gasped as the true tone of his child-voice called to me, "Mama, come."

"Are you ill?" Andromache asked. "Suddenly you look pale. Let us sit." She took my arm to lead me to a seat.

"No," I insisted. I forced a smile, unable to talk about my dead babe. "I would like to meet your son."

"And I would like you to know him. Please, I hope we can be friends."

Later, Paris walked back with me to the sanctuary, Meriandynus following.

"You have a fine family, Paris, but I have difficulty telling them apart. Except for Andromache and Hector, and Cassandra, whom I met this afternoon as well as this evening, and Polyxena. She is lovely in her first blush of womanhood. The other sons are a confusion for me."

"Even the second son?" Paris asked. Do you not have some impressions of him?"

I thought deeply about the second son. I spoke quietly, not looking at him. "The second son is truly gifted," I answered. "He has an inner strength of self-direction that lights his way and is sometimes visible to others. It radiates around him and draws people to him. He outshines his brothers in his skill in games and his wise understanding of others." I paused a moment, and as he did not reply, I said in a near-whisper, "He has brought me much happiness."

We reached the door of the Temple courtyard, and I nodded to Meriandynus to open the doors and bring a light.

When the boy disappeared inside, Paris turned to me. His voice was urgent. "We must be together. We are fated to be together. You must come to me in my house, stay with me in my house, where we can be alone and touch and kiss each other at any time. I cannot let you be isolated here in the temple."

"It is best for now," I spoke quickly. "I could do nothing in your house but be occupied with you." I spoke again before he could answer. I took his hand and moved close to him. "We will again meet by a sacred pool and give ourselves to each other." He was outlined by the light from the stars and a single torch still flickering on the wall sconce. "We will know when that time comes to us again.

He stared down at me. "I await it with impatience," he said quietly. "Let us get these duties over with quickly."

Meriandynus returned with a lamp, and I followed him into the sanctuary.

AGREEMENT

I waved at the familiar figure of Captain Thaos walking towards me on the harbor path. The gentle breeze rocked some boats at anchor, and I recognized our ship at the docks by its curved-horn prow.

"I thought you would never get here," I said as he drew closer.

"One learns to be patient in these waters," Thaos answered smiling warmly. "Rushing, waiting and rushing —actually, the cycle of gale winds should moderate now that autumn is here."

"I see you are unloading cargo," I observed. "I don't wish to detain you, but I have something important to tell you." I was, sitting on a whitewashed stone wall that looked across the wide bay of the harbor to the headland opposite, covered with beach grass, "If you have to rush off, I will understand" Families of sea gulls dipped and swooped in the sunshine.

"I am honored to serve you," he replied.

"Captain Thaos, you are my advisor and Laconian cohort on this mission. It will be important for you to be at my side at the ceremony today."

"A ceremony? Today?"

In a vain effort to subdue my elation, I told him that the accords between Laconia and Troy would be formalized at mid-day in the palace. "I have been meeting with King Priam and his counselors for the last six days."

"You have made progress," Thaos said. His gaze fastened beyond me.

"Oh, my. I am sorry, but I see I must go." His tone had changed in concern for his ship. He made a hurried bow. "I will meet you at mid-day before the palace." He rushed off. "I'll wear my Captain's mantle and insignia," he called back, waving, and was gone.

"I'll look for you," I said, quietly, knowing he could not hear.

When I returned Klara helped me dress. We chatted amiably as she limped about, performing her tasks efficiently. My royal robes of gold-threaded violet fell in folds from my shoulders. I tied in place a belt of obsidian beads that girdled my hips and kept my skirts in place. A wide gold-encrusted band was wrapped round my forehead. It had ear-dangles made of myriads of gold bits laced on golden wire that swung to my shoulders. The golden necklace Klara fastened for me was as intricate as the head piece and rested heavily across my breast. "Oh, my lady, you are indeed a wondrous queen," she said when I was ready to leave.

King Priam had arranged for a carrying chair, but I had refused it. Prince Paris would escort me to the palace. We had not been alone together for days, and when I saw him in the temple courtyard, our eyes locked in an intimacy that made my breath come short. I looked away to compose myself. During the days of negotiation he had been at his father's side, intelligently stating the Trojan position, sometimes adding insights of his own.

"This is a notable day for us, is it not?" I said.

He smiled, refusing with his eyes to let me turn our meeting into anything other than a personal one between us. "Oh, Holy Mother, you are lovely," he said, his voice so low I could barely hear him. His expression became serious, his eyes darkened and filled with tenderness and yearning as they looked upon me. "Come, Helen," he said. He took my arm, his touch exciting my heart. "We will complete the business in the palace, and then..."

I wanted to touch him and kiss his lips, but I forced myself to look away; I would go with him when the time came.

Captain Thaos met us on the portico of the palace appropriately solemn, his black hair combed back behind his ears. The deep blue mantle of the ship captain was bordered in white spirals that enhanced his solid presence. Glittering on his chest was the gold medallion of his rank. "Thaos, I thank you for being here."

"It is I who am honored," he replied.

Paris led us to the throne room where King Priam occupied a tall carved chair, and a host of visitors flanked him, standing with dignity as we entered.

I stood tall and walked through the length of the room. I could feel my golden ear bangles swaying with my steps. Meriandynus followed and Captain Thaos came directly behind.

I stood before the seat arranged for me, sitting when King Priam indicated. Paris took his place with Hector and his father. I nodded slightly to Queen Hecuba, who sat in another high carved chair near Priam, surrounded by her daughters and women of importance. I was astounded at the strange mix of people in unusual costume and headdress. I recognized the City Elders, wise sages in the long white robes of their rank. I identified ambassadors, some must have come from afar with their brilliant robes and elaborate jeweled caps over their long, crimped hair as black as night. Others must have been loyal allies, Ilium neighbors, and still others, from where I could not guess. This was a spectacle of Trojan strength that would startle Agamemnon, could he see it.

"Welcome, Queen Helen," King Priam said. "I feel almost as though you are one of my own dear children. For the benefit of our honored ambassadors and counselors, most of whom did not take part in our discussions, I would like to say that the Queen of Laconia is an able emissary who represents her country with great skill. She is generous in all things and kind. These particular qualities which ennoble her person have made our discourse a pleasure and have permitted us to craft a remarkable accord." King Priam smiled at me. "Do you have words for us, Queen Helen?"

I felt much affection for him. I stood and spoke: "I, also, have found this process advantageous to our agreement, and find your keen perceptions and subtle distinctions exceedingly helpful. Now, if you please, I introduce to you my colleague, Thaos, ship captain of the vessel which brought me to Troy. He has sailed into your harbor many times, and it is through his intelligent auspices that the first notions of the plan we formalize today took place in our meeting halls and in your council chambers." Captain Thaos bowed to the assemblage, and we took our seats.

The Trojan dignitaries and ambassadors were introduced and I learned that the strangers came from eastern inland cities, from northern Thrace, and southern Rhodes, and from Crete, the eastern province comparable to Kydonia in the west. "...ancestral home to all who call themselves Trojans," Priam explained.

I was acquainted with the royal family by now and enjoyed King Priam's pleasure in bringing forth his numerous sons who were military leaders, and his priestess daughters. Two Amazonian Queens were presented, garbed in beautifully woven chieftain robes with colored feathers in their hair.

"I am honored to be here with these worthy allies of Troy," I said, when all had been introduced. "It is edifying to know people from lands so distant from my own. If it please you, honored King Priam, I would like to tell these visitors why I have come such a long way to be here with them today."

"We would hear you, Queen Helen."

I knew I must keep to the facts. To speak of my brothers would be difficult. I took a deep breath and talked simply of my people and their continual service to the Great Earth Mother Goddess. I explained the rift with the Mycenaeans, our long-time allies, who had become destroyers of Goddess shrines and sacred places. I detailed the problems in Kydonia, and described our cooperative effort with Messenia and Arcadia to dispel Knossos invaders, sackers of shrines and murderers of priestesses, who were aided by Agamemnon's soldiers from Mycenae. In an undercurrent of rejoicing, I exalted our overwhelming success. Idomeneus of Knossos had agreed to withdraw completely and forever. Then my voice dropped. I managed to get out the horror of the assassins and the murder of our leaders. I explained about the prisoners and Agamemnon's clear involvement in their murders.

A fervent hush filled the hall. I breathed several deep breaths and finished. "My husband, Menelaus, brother to Agamemnon, is no longer King in Laconia. Without the Dioscuri, famed and noble leaders, and without a King, my responsibilities have increased greatly. The agreement we formalize today is very important for all of us."

Again there was an emotion-laden silence. Priam waited a few moments, then said, "I call upon Oukalegon, Elder to our city and Peer, gifted with words and judgment. He will read the treaty."

The wise counselor came to the front. His wavy long white hair and beard mingled together and framed a tanned face with creases of age around his deep set eyes. He held before him a tablet from which he read. "Here is set forth an agreement between King Priam of Troy and Queen Helen of Laconia. In so far as both communities serve the Great Earth Goddess in all her many realms..."

I listened to the words in a heady state of excitement, a bringing together of like-minded lands. In addition to the accords offering mutual support for each other, and the efforts to improve trade through the renouncing of piracy on our side and the renouncing of extorting undue tribute for harbor protection and passage through the straits on the Trojan side, we agreed to enlist like-minded neighbors to join the accords. For our part a Laconian League would be assembled on my return. Messenia, Arcadia, Attica, Boeotia, and Locris would be invited to join in this accord. "...It is hoped that these agreements will create peace and harmony forever," Oukalegon concluded.

King Priam spoke. "Ambassadors, Counselors and others here present today are invited to indicate their accordance, which will be incised on this document for greater import. This original treaty will remain here in Troy. Two copies will be made. One to be held in the Amyklaeon Palace in Laconia, to be carried there by courier immediately. The other to be taken by Queen Helen, when she departs Troy after the Autumn Rites, to the above mentioned communities for reading in the public places so all will be informed."

Other formalities took time, but the treaty which had been discussed with the ambassadors in detail earlier was received with enthusiasm.

After feasting and dancing, Paris and I walked slowly through the city streets, gradually finding smaller and smaller walkways until we came to his house on the heights overlooking the harbor. A lamp burned in a wall holder in the welcoming room, and some furs and woven pieces lay strewn about on benches. The leopard mask I had heard about hung on the wall with his hunting spears, mementos of his former life. Colorful textured rugs were spread about on the stone floor. A bed chamber and a bed covered with furs was visible through a partly opened door.

"Is there no servant here to help you?" I asked.

"Someone comes each morning. We are alone here, Helen."

To be in his house alone with him excited me. Should I be repelling this extraordinary attraction? There was no hope of so doing.

Our glance held, and we came together. Paris cradled my face with his hands and kissed me gently on the lips. My breath quickened, and I returned his kiss. I reached up to remove the golden headband, and found it had caught in my hair.

"I will help," he said, standing behind me to carefully untangle the fastenings. "I can undo this too," he said as he unhooked the heavy necklace and put it and the headband on a table. I felt his hands cover my breasts, free now of the encumbering weight of the golden beads. I let my head rest back on his chest and gave in to the pleasure of his caresses. I turned to him, and my knees felt weak as I saw the desire in his eyes. We moved to the bed-chamber, where the furs and our clothes were cast aside. We lay down naked on linen sheets, stretching like cats on the cool fabric, and abandoned ourselves to a luxurious, unhurried, sensual exploration of the beauty the Goddess desired for us.

AUTUMN RITES

Riding a beautiful white Ilium mare with silver bobbles attached to its braided mane and tail, I led the devout train of worshippers into the valley of the Scamander. Sitting side-saddle to protect my exquisite skirt, I followed a guide over the roadway into the hinterland. After several hours, he stopped on the edge of a high plateau above the river, and we saw from afar the conglomeration of billowing tents spread out along the meandering waterway.

"Look at the great open circle," Prince Paris said.

"It's the ceremonial site," a young votary from the Temple to Attis explained. "And beyond is the smaller Ring of Consultation, where tribal chiefs and clan elders meet."

The sheer largeness of the gathering surprised me. Off to one side there appeared to be a place for market stalls. "That must be the bazaar," I said. Even from this distance one could sense the hubbub. I pulled my warm red military cloak around me for the wind blew cold on the heights. I smiled at Paris, glad for his presence.

I thought of Meriandynus and Captain Thaos who had left ten days past to deliver the Treaty to my counselors in Amyklae. Meriandynus, my personal emissary, had a remarkable ability to remember details and explain a nuance or a central idea. "You may have to make some important decisions," I had told him. "I cannot foresee every impasse." I had given him some of the pouches of gold beads in case of unexpected developments. "It will solve a problem when nothing else can," I reminded him.

Captain Thaos had calculated that the northern winds would have quieted by the time he returned to fetch me. The homeward voyage would take us to Locris, Boeotia and Attica with the second Treaty copy. Prince Paris would accompany me, representing Troy. I would confer directly with royal leaders about a Laconian League.

I nodded to the guide, and the holy procession wound its way down into the valley to the echoes of music and singing. We passed camps spread out near the river, and others set back in the hills. Tents, made white by the sun's noon light, billowed in the breeze, and the aromas from cooking fires wafted toward us. Hundreds of people had gathered at the great circle and crowds gave way greeting us with cheers and frantic drumming. I saw Hecuba and Priam sitting before an elaborate tent surrounded by their children. I reveled in the excitement not knowing exactly what was to happen.

Earlier, I had removed my heavy cloak and arranged the golden band with the long ear dangles on my head and fastened the heavy gold necklace over a gauzy bodice. My skirt, made by the priestesses, was a rainbow of color, and all the shiny ornaments carefully sewed into it held Goddess meaning and glistened in the sun. I sat with a straight back on the mare and followed the guide twice around the circle smiling and waving to the welcoming crowds. I noticed the bands of warrior priestesses with feathers in their hair, and a myriad of others dressed in woven materials of bright colors. I dismounted before the royal tent and was led to a seat near the King and Queen, aware at all times that Paris was next to me as we watched the spectacle before us.

I had never seen such skill on horseback. There was whooping, shouting and cheering for each new team, but when the warrior priestesses thundered into the ring the uproar was overwhelming.

They wore leather shorts, wide belts, feathered helmets and carried spears and double headed axes. Their bare feet guided their mounts with a touch of a toe. They hopped to a standing position on the backs of their horses, and with hands on hips, hailed the audience as they made the circuit. They slung their double axes high and lobbed them to each other, the sun glinting on the sharp edges of the polished metal as they whirred through the air. The maidens threw their spears back and forth, and then, galloping full out, they flung them into the heart of a straw-man target, each spearhead embedded deep down. Several did hand stands on the horses back, and leapt from one mount to the other and back again. I shouted and cheered with the crowd as these remarkable, slender girls laughed and showed us how they played their games.

Important matches took place each day of the seven day celebration. Paris competed, thrilling the crowds with his expertise in archery and spear throwing, out-doing his brothers and every other contender. He assisted his parents in entertaining dignitaries in their vast royal encampment and by attending counsel meetings of clan chiefs.

Sometimes we escaped our duties and wandered together through the bazaar, a gaudy marketplace crowded into a maze of narrow lanes. We saw all manner of cloaks and mantels, filmy veils or thick woven robes, skirts, shawls, heavy stockings and leather shoes. Ceramic jugs and bowls brought different clays and glazes together from far greater distances than were represented by this gathering. Cooking odors wafted about as braziers grilled chines of lamb and sausage rolls sputtered. Copper trays, alabaster vases, bronze urns and tripods, and jewelry—gold and silver rings, bracelets, and necklaces, crafted with delicacy or cast for strength. Some inlaid with lapis or amber were breathtaking.

Polished porphory stones drew large crowds to a stall from Lesbos. "The holy essence resides in each one," the stall keeper shouted out to the crowds, holding up the egg shaped stone of greenish shades with golden highlights. "Look, in the light, see the glow of exaltation deep inside," he said with a touch of reverence in his voice.

"Imagine," I said to Paris. "These are Laconian holy stones."

"They are popular everywhere," he said. "Captain Thaos must carry huge baskets of them on all of his trading voyages."

"Yes. Hampers of them. He fits them in anywhere he can."

Paris peered into a slightly opened doorway. "A secluded garden," he said. "Let's go in."

It was cool with low tables and soft carpets arranged around a fish pond. A waiter offered us a drink. We sat on a rose and blue carpet patterned in flowers and vines and rested against bolsters as a pitcher and cups were placed on the table before us. We tasted the fruit juice and wine. "It contains a spice I don't recognize."

"Refreshing," Paris commented.

A feeling of happiness diffused all through me as I admired the nearly perfect blooms and felt part of the enchantment. I sipped from the cup and watched Paris watch me. I reached for his hand. I wanted to express a profound feeling, a deep meaning about the two of us. Our hands rested on the table, our fingers entwined like the vines on the carpet. We did not talk. It was enough to share the moment.

Each night holy rites were held before ceremonial bonfires. The fall planting of grain seed had brought forth the first new growth. Winter rains would nourish it, and the spring harvest would produce fat ripe barley heads for the sustenance of the worshippers. I officiated at different rituals of initiation, fertility, procreation or consecration. The energy of the Goddess was coaxed into our midst by our fervor and adoration. It entered us as we danced, sang, meditated, and chanted. Her magic was her gift of life to growing things everywhere.

Late at night, exhausted from the demands of the day, Paris and I returned to the voluminous tent arranged for my use. It was furnished with low trapeza tables and comfortable sleeping cushions spread about on a handsome carpet, where we fell asleep in each other's arms.

Each morning we awakened to the sounds of spoonbill ducks foraging for breakfast along the riverbank. On the last morning of the celebration I lazily opened my eyes to the now familiar gabble. The early morning sun slanted through a slit in the tent closure and played against the pattern of reds and oranges on the floor. I lay quietly, at peace, soaking up the serenity. I looked at Paris, still asleep, and tried to memorize his face at rest, so that I could conjure it up when we were apart. It was manly in strength of bone and conformation of brow and chin, cheek and nose. His lips curved up at the corners, and I ached to kiss them. My eyes closed as I thought about kissing his lips and about how much I cared for him. I had never imagined such a closeness with anyone. It frightened me to think of leaving him. I wondered how I could be so completely satisfied at this moment when the overwhelming problems in Laconia so burdened me. Prince Paris would come home with me and take the place of Menelaus. It would be impossible for us to part.

I opened my eyes to see Paris awake, looking at me. Our eyes each held the other's, exchanging yearning and passion. He put his hand out and caressed my lips.

"I never tire of looking at you," he said, his voice husky with the morning.

I kissed his fingers. "Oh, my darling," I whispered. We rolled over and reached for each other. We kissed leisurely, and luxuriated in sensuous caresses until the fervor inside us burgeoned into a blazing expression of the power we created together.

Later we slipped out of the tent and into the river for a bath. We quietly swam in a clear pool made by a sand bar and watched the ducks feed and the herons high-step about. A cold breeze chilled me as I emerged dripping from the river, and a shivering overcame me as we breakfasted on fruit and yoghurt. I drank hot mint brew and felt warmed, but before noon there was a dreadful scratchiness in my throat.

The final ceremony of the entire celebration was one of inducing rain, and, as the Goddess Representative, I allowed myself to be draped in the thinnest of veils, and walked down a pathway crowded on either side by cheering crowds. With a wreath of asterion on my head I waded into the River Scamander. Now a cold breeze stirred the water, and an overcast sky hid the warmth of the sun.

Goddess priestesses and priests of Attis accompanied me, and we doused ourselves thoroughly. I led them out, all of us dripping, and we sprayed the water from our drapery around, dancing and chanting the blessing of rainfall. It was an uncommonly fine ceremony, for before nightfall the clouds had darkened, and a downpour commenced. All that night I shivered as Paris held me to him for warmth. The next day we rode back to Troy in cold pouring rain. By the time we reached my temple sanctuary, I was burning up with fever. The priestesses insisted that I be taken directly into their quarters, where I could be looked after.

For days I tossed and turned between fever and chills on a cot in a dark room, unable to think coherently. The entire period was a hazy jumble of hovering women, hateful tasting brews, and aching distress.

One morning a vague disturbance in the outer chambers broke through my confusion. Perhaps it was Hecuba. Her visits always caused a stir. I was glad Klara had just bathed me.

Paris suddenly filled the doorway. Priestesses fluttered around unable to do anything. Some tugged at his cloak. "You are not allowed." Others protested in vain. "No no, you must not."

I saw those intent eyes surveying the room and the bed. His lips curved into a familiar smile. Without further ado he covered me with furs he carried and picked me up out of bed as he would a child. Relaxed in his arms, I felt a tranquility for the first time in days. He ignored the bustling women and walked out of the temple, down through the city and up the narrow walkways towards his house. Curious pedestrians halted in surprise, but he strode by without explanation. I could not guess what to expect, but I cherished his strong arms for holding me close to him. Once inside his house, he did not deposit me on his bed but went to an easy chair where he sat and cradled me and whispered into my hair. "Oh, Helen. I had to bring you here where I could see for myself that you were cared for properly. No one will be allowed to take you away from me." He stroked my brow and kissed me gently. "Now, you will get well," he said. "I have called for Oenone. She will be here tomorrow, she will know what to do."

We sat as we were for a long time. His voice was like a lilting lyre, and his closeness was a happiness that gradually seeped into all parts of me. I did not try to answer him, for it was hard to talk. My breathing, full of rattles and wheezes, quieted somewhat, and I drifted off to sleep.

I'm not sure when Oenone arrived, for my fever persisted despite her ministrations. Dreams and reality became confused. Sometimes I thought I was a child with Mother Leda, and other times I was in the cold fortress at Aphidnae, and my brothers were with me. At the moment that a surge of joy engulfed me, they became their own corpses, and I saw their terrible wounds and decomposing grotesque faces and smelled the vile odor of their death. I found myself thrashing about, and a terrible screeching echoed in my ears, which came from my own searing throat. A quiet girl with a lovely low voice calmed me.

She deftly changed the sheets, damp with perspiration. She fed me a warm elixir which soothed my throat. Yet my fever persisted, and my throat again felt as though it were lacerated.

Paris moved to his room in the palace, and a sleeping pallet was set up for Oenone. One afternoon when I lay awake, quite aware of my condition but too exhausted to make a sound, I listened to Paris and Oenone talking as they sat in the open doorway in the sunshine.

"I believe a crisis will come soon," Oenone said. I felt weak, and the idea of death was welcome. My eyes filled with tears, and they slowly ran down my cheeks. I had not strength for anything. I faded into sleep.

I awoke at daybreak feeling rested. "I believe you are better today," Oenone said quietly. "I cut into the breathing passage and inserted a reed to help you through the crisis." She held my hand so I could feel the willow reed sticking out of my neck. In the next moment she had deftly removed it and held a clean cloth to the wound. "There is little bleeding," she said, "but it must be kept very clean."

Gradually I recovered. I lay in bed day after day looking at the rich hues of the woven rugs on the floor and the coverlet on my bed. I could discern the limping step of Klara before she entered the house when she came daily to help. The familiar footstep of Paris usually brought me to full wakefulness. His presence alone was a cure. Everyday I asked with my eyes a question he understood, for it was a constant worry to me. Everyday he shook his head. "No, Thaos has not returned."

At first, when the time for the Captain's expected arrival had come and gone, I was relieved, for I was much too ill to leave Troy. But later, for at least the last month, I had become more and more concerned, sometimes frantic about him. What was the meaning of his absence? "Winter is full upon us," Paris had said. "It is not the month for sailing. He is waiting for spring. When you are well, we will make the voyage anyway; I will begin now to have a ship readied."

His kind words reassured me, but my mind conjured up unbelievable situations in Laconia or disasters at sea.

A few days later Klara and Oenone led me to the doorway. I leaned on them and watched Paris and his mother walk up the hill to see me.

I had regularly received messages from well-wishers. Townspeople, I was told, crowded into the temples to offer thanks to the Goddess for my presence among them and for my recovery, and priestesses and priests often came from their sanctuaries to present tokens for good health. I liked especially a clay dove and enjoyed rubbing my thumb on its rounded breast.

"Here you are, Helen," Hecuba said when she came near.

"Dear, Hecuba," I said, shifting my weight to Paris who relieved Klara. "And dear Paris," I said to him, feeling his touch and his closeness. "I can not quite stand by myself, but it will not be long." We sat in chairs around a table, and Klara prepared a hot drink. "Oenone, please join us." I hoped she would not disappear, as she usually did. But she had slipped away. While her healing skills were so needed, her reserve went unnoticed. Now it loomed as a dark shadow that slowly filled the house.

Hecuba regarded me carefully, taking in my warm robe, my ashen pallor, my cropped tresses. "Your hair frames your head like a halo, doesn't it Paris?"

"Yes, so it does," he answered. "It grows in swirls."

"And I had hoped it would become straight and silky," I laughed. "But in any case, it is a sign that my convalescence proceeds rapidly. I could almost enjoy all the rest and attention if affairs across the sea were certain."

The following morning Oenone and I breakfasted together. She had not yet braided her hair, and it hung down her back in a beautiful thick fall.

"I do miss my daughter," I said, suddenly. Oenone would understand for she must miss her son. "I had no idea I would be away from her this long."

Oenone's clear brown eyes attended me thoughtfully as I embarked on a description of Hermione.

"I left her in late summer, and I will not see her again until late spring. I must return as soon as possible."

"I know how you feel," Oenone answered. "My son has many mothers in our compound, but there is a particular relationship with one's birth child."

The mention of a birth child and the planned voyage home reminded me of Iphigeneia and my long separation from her. I ate slowly of the bread and goat cheese and told Oenone about her. "She was never told that I am her mother," I said. "I was persuaded it was her destiny to be raised thus. She believes King Agamemnon to be her father." It was difficult to say these words aloud. "Fortunately, she is away from him now. She is a maiden priestess studying in a Temple to Potnia in Boeotia.

"I am sorry for your unhappiness. I see that to be a Queen is not always pleasant."

"Oh dear Oenone," I said. "You have given me so much, I do not ask your sympathy. Oenone had saved my life, but she would not open herself to me. I was not surprised when she told me she would be leaving.

"You do not need me any more, and Klara will look after you very well."

I could hear Klara's step on the walk outside, but I tried to reach Oenone once more. "Please, Oenone, I must tell you. I know it has been difficult for you. Paris is the father of your son and your life-long friend," I stopped briefly, wondering if I should continue. I could see that she became suddenly still. "What is between us is unexplainable. When it commenced, I thought it was temporary, a whim of nature that would end as quickly as it began. It has not been thus. If it were within my control, I would have..."

Klara entered, and Oenone continued to wipe clean the table.

"Ah, me, what a day," Klara said. "The wind is blowing out there as if it were mid-summer, but it carries an icy chill. I wonder, will spring ever come." She hung her cloak on a peg. "You look well. Your skin is regaining its sheen, as is your hair. It has grown some, hasn't it?" She smiled as though I were a product of her own making. "Isn't her robe perfect for her?" she asked Oenone. I had acquired several in different shades at the autumn celebration.

"Yes," Oenone replied. "Helen is always lovely to look upon, even when she is prostrate with illness." Her back was to us, so I could not read her face, but her voice sounded as though she were scrubbing the floor or engaged in some other unappealing task.

"Oenone tells me she will leave me soon," I said to Klara. "She has done more for me than I had any reason to expect. She is a gifted healer." I hoped Oenone could hear me, busy as she was with airing her bed-cover.

"Ay, she is all of that," Klara said, getting into the spirit of my message. "She is generous beyond measure. Do you know that she has asked me to join her in Assos after you leave? She thinks I have talent in healing and will teach me."

"Oh, Klara, that is just right for you," I said. "But I will not leave until the weather improves. I hope you can wait."

"Yes, I can wait. I would not want you traveling yet."

Oenone told me she would leave that afternoon. "When you awake from your nap, I will have gone."

"But, Oenone, I will miss you and your gentle hands. Must you?"

"Yes. I have a chance to ride with the cart driver today."

"I understand, but how can I thank you? Oenone, I owe you so much. I will give you a gift. What will it be? I cannot think. Later, Later I will know exactly what is right."

Oenone considered my words as though she knew the answer. She neither smiled nor hinted as to what it might be. "Yes, later you will know," she said. When I awoke, she was gone.

Andromache arrived in the afternoon, with wool, to help me set up a small vertical loom attached to the wall. "This will be a pleasant activity," I commented. "Oenone says I am to go out for a walk and fresh air only in good weather. Who knows how long I must wait for that."

"It's hard for Astyanax, as well," she said. "He has so much energy. I promised to return soon to play with him."

"Tell me about him," I urged.

We laughed and talked of his antics as Klara served us bread and broth in front of the open fire. "Cassandra should be here soon," I said, just as a knock sounded.

Cassandra, a frequent guest, entered with a gust of wind, then stood before the fire and rubbed her hands together, warming them. "I saw a boat enter the harbor, just now," she said. "It must be a coastal trader."

"It will be another month before we see a foreign vessel," Andromache commented as she prepared to leave.

We said our good-byes as I prepared a hot cup for Cassandra. "I'm glad you came," I said to her. "Maybe you'll tell me more about the Goddess Hecate. I'm intrigued to know why you believe she is so different from other Goddess figures."

"But why are you surprised. She is very ancient, you know."

"Of course," I answered. "But don't you believe, as I do, that though there are many different Goddess names and sometimes ways of worship, they are the same Goddess essence? I think of such differences as Goddess strength."

Cassandra nibbled a dried plum from a tray Klara had placed before us. "That way is careless, Helen. There must be discipline. Hecate is permanent. She has never changed. She is the first keeper of the mysteries. She alone watches over procreation and pregnancies, and endows the seed with life to grow, and blesses the harvest." Her eyes looked beyond me, unblinking.

"That is not so different from Potnia or Phemonoe or Cybele," I said. "They do all those things." I spoke in a conversational tone, ignoring her grim pose.

She spoke again as though she were receiving a message from Hecate directly. "But they do not know the future. Hecate knows. It has always been her gift. She does not want change. She abhors change. She sees change coming."

"What kind of change?" I asked, almost afraid she would tell me, her tone of voice was so dire.

"A blackness will descend on all people, and the winds will blow, and the storms will cause destruction and mayhem. Troy will fall in a war with foreigners, and we will all perish or become slaves." Her eyes grew wider and remained unfocused. This was not her usual bantering prediction. Awed, I gazed at her, unspeaking.

In a moment the hush was over. Cassandra sipped from her cup and smiled at me. "I like to talk to you, for you listen and do not demean my thoughts." She reached for her cloak.

"I would never do that," I said, my pulse still rapid from her total fixation.

In a clatter of opening and shuffling, Paris came in. As I took his cloak, our hands held briefly in a quick intimacy. "Ah, Cassandra," he said, as she threw on her cloak. "Let me walk with you. It is dark and blustery out there."

"No need, but thank you. I'll come again soon, Helen," she said and was gone.

Paris and I looked at each other in silence as it was Klara's time for leave-taking. "Your supper is warming on the brazier," she said. "Wine is in the cooler, and spring water in the pitcher. I hope you'll be comfortable without Oenone. I will stay if you want."

"Thank you, darling Klara. Leave at peace with yourself. I will be fine." I hugged her briefly, and she left.

I turned to Paris standing at the fire. My heart melted as I saw his concern for me . "How are you?" he asked.

"Better than ever, even with constant visitors." I ran my fingers along the edge of the table. "Oenone left." I looked at him.

"I know. I took her to meet the cart driver."

"She could have stayed. I would not wish her to think we did not want her."

"She stayed as long as she was needed. She knew it was time to leave." He stepped close and touched my chin.

"But how?" I asked, taking his hand. He drew me close.

"I told her," he whispered.

I raised my face to his kiss. "It is nice to be with you, alone," I said, feeling weak with his nearness.

"You must not overtax your strength," he murmured into my neck.

"Let us sit down," I said. "I feel a bit giddy with the heat of the fire, and..."

Quickly he gathered up the furs and put them on the floor before the fire. "We can sup here. It will be warm, and you can relax. I'll get our plates and the wine." In the play of the firelight, we sipped the wine and nibbled pieces of lamb cooked with grain and dried fruits.

"It seemed to me you had something to tell me when you came in," I said. "Did the presence of Cassandra put it out of your mind?"

"Oh, yes." He drank from his wine cup. "A ship came in late today. It was not Thaos. You can be sure that bit of news would not have slipped my mind." He reached over to put his plate on the table, then rested back against a heavy chair, holding his wine cup.

I put my plate and cup on the table and lay down on the furs with my head in his lap. He stroked my hair, and I nearly went to sleep. Paris must have finished his wine for I felt him move as he put the cup on the table, then he slid down next to me on the furs, and we held each other close.

"Kiss me," he whispered. I felt his lips on mine, and returned the kiss with an urgency that surprised me. I sighed. I had often fantasized that sometime soon we would linger in bed and that our loving would be gradual and gentle, that I would be fragile and weak. I had not dreamed that we would be nestled down half-naked amid the furs in front of the fire, and that my craving for him would be so strong. My senses were on fire with pleasure. My body was flooded with an unexpected holy energy.

Later, when the fire had died, we carried our warm furs into the bedroom and fell into a deep sleep. The next morning early, there was a hesitant knock on our door. Paris pulled himself out of bed to answer it. I heard voices and wondered what it could mean. In a few moments Paris returned, quietly closing the door behind him.

"It is Meriandynus," he said. "He looks terrible, warn and drawn. I gave him some bread and put water on to boil. I told him we would be right out.

DREAM AND REALITY

Sallow light entered the bedroom window without warmth. In the cold, I washed and rubbed scented oil into my skin and shivered with apprehension, sensing grave tidings. With forced control I wrapped a brightly woven robe over a fine wool tunic. "Keep calm, keep calm," I repeated to myself as I carefully arranged my hair and rubbed a faint bit of color into my ashen cheeks. Finally, I could put it off no longer. I opened the door into the welcoming room.

The slumped figure had no aspect of a boy about him. Meriandynus stood. I noticed his untidy hair, his dark soiled tunic, his miserable torn leggings. Paris, who had returned quickly to the exhausted traveler, poured out hot brew.

"My dear," I said, and went to Meriandynus and put my hand on his arm. "When did you arrive?"

"Last evening, by ship," he said. Paris handed him a cup and placed a plate of honey and bread before him.

Meriandynus wolfed down three pieces then sipped from his cup. "I gave my last gold beads for passage to Lesbos, "he began. "The crossing was terrifying." His eyes widened in memory. "After landing, I boarded a coastal trader as a rower, and when we arrived here, I slipped away and hid until nightfall. I learned at the Goddess sanctuary that you were here."

I reached over and took the boy's hand. "I know, because I know you, that you have conducted yourself with courage and honor."

Meriandynus shook his head, his eyes damp.

"Before you continue," Paris said, "perhaps you would wish to wash or rest."

"Yes," Meriandynus mumbled. "I shall wash."

"I cannot remain calm," I said, when the boy had gone to the washing room. "Why is he so torn and distressed?"

"Relax," Paris said quietly. "We must not upset him. He is on the edge of panic as it is."

Meriandynus reappeared prepared to tell what we must hear. He sat in a chair facing us.

"My voyage home to Laconia with Captain Thaos went well," he began. "The winds were moderate and the rowing minimal. We stopped nightly in island shelters, and waited once for clearing weather to cross the open sea to Limera Bay. We set out at mid-day and rowed all night. The great landmark-rock loomed on the horizon at dawn, but it took half a day more to reach it. I felt the excitement of homecoming when we threw our lines ashore. Our heartfelt return covered the strangeness, for it was only in retrospect that I realized no one returned our waves. Everyone on board was immediately seized. We were led away with our hands tied behind our backs, and the vessel was impounded."

I felt suddenly weak and lowered my head to my hands, willing myself not to faint. Meriandynus had forged ahead almost too quickly for comprehension. I sat straight again in my chair. "Was it Agamemnon?" I interrupted, demanding to know the worst.

The boy nodded. "None of us could truly realize that we were prisoners, that there was not some mistake that would be instantly cleared up. However, I understood almost at once that Mycenaeans were among the strangers. Captain Thaos and I were able to talk to each other then, and he agreed with me."

Meriandynus smoothed his hair back with both hands and drank from his cup. "I will tell you now, not a day by day report of our jail and jailers, our trip in carts to Amyklae, our interrogations and mistreatment, but the situation in Laconia which had transpired since our departure for Troy, even though I did not learn the full import for many days."

Mute with shock, I nodded.

"To be brief," he said, "King Agamemnon had asserted rights of kingship in the name of his brother Menelaus. That he had brought with him a considerable armed force was persuasive, I gather. The word was passed along that Queen Helen had been kidnapped by Prince Paris of Troy and that Agamemnon and Mycenae would help Laconia redress this terrible deed. Anyone who knew differently and attempted to correct the error was either murdered or imprisoned."

"Murdered?" I whispered. My counselors, my generals, my family. "Surely Hermione..."

"Hermione, with Lani and Chief Counselor, Arneus, disappeared. General Trophonios and General Volos are dead. The other counselors are in prison. Some of the governors of distant provinces stayed away and remain free."

"I should never have left," I moaned, taking on to myself the full responsibility of the disaster. My only relief was that Hermione was safe with Lani and Arneus.

"It might have helped if you had been present, Queen Helen," Meriandynus finally said. He looked at me briefly, and I caught a familiar vital spark that disappeared as soon as his gaze focused on something in his mind, far away from me or Paris. "Your presence may have made a crucial difference. At least they could not have said you were kidnapped by Prince Paris. But..." Again he was quiet.

Finally Paris said, "Yes, but—but what?"

"Apparently Agamemnon and his army had been in Messenia before coming to Laconia." Meriandynus spoke quickly, spilling out information. "The old King Leucippus, the new Queen Marpesa, Phoebe, widow of your brother Castor, all of the leaders in the military—all gone."

"Gone?" I nearly shouted. "Where did they go? What do you mean?" I recalled Phoebe's words of reassurance when she left for Messenia. She had looked forward to going home to see her old father, to helping Queen Marpesa with her solitary queenly duties. "It is safe now. I have no need of an escort," she had said.

Meriandynus just shook his head. "Gone," he repeated.

"Do you mean dead?" I demanded. Wanting to know, spitting out the distasteful word.

"Yes." The blank expression on his face did not change. "Word came back from Goddess Temple messengers. Mycenaean soldiers destroyed the royal residences and all royal persons, including children. " His voice was even, and his eyes unchanging.

Confused, I looked to Paris for clarification and saw his terrible expression of disbelief and horror. I moaned, covering my face with my neck scarf, keening my grief quietly. Undulating sickening waves of misery spun in my head. Lovely Phoebe floated before me in her pale beauty as she smiled at her children.

"Is a new king ruling in Messenia?" Paris asked.

"No. A puppet Mycenaean governor is in charge. Many of the Goddess temples have been destroyed. Some priestesses have retreated to secret locations and carry on their work as always. They are the source of information and communication."

"What of Hilaeira?" I asked, dreading the answer.

"She also disappeared," Meriandynus answered, maintaining his icy poise. "She and her children were not found, nor were Phiona and the temple priestesses."

I was mute with shock.

"I have told you the bare facts," Meriandynus said. "Now it is necessary to relay an advisory of the greatest importance for Troy before more time elapses." His tone was deadly serious.

What now? What more can there be to tell?

Paris nodded, and Meriandynus continued. "Fleets of ships, hundreds of them from all of the Mycenaean provinces and allied states have gathered to prepare an attack on Troy."

Paris gasped. "Why? How? Where?"

"In a place opposite Euboea on the mainland of Boeotia."

"Boeotians are our friends. It cannot be so!"

Meriandynus shrugged. "We were too late with the treaty. We were unable to announce it as we had all hoped. It was only luck at all that I managed to escape from prison and travel undetected among the armies gathering on the shores at Aulis. I learned much that I am eager to report to you and King Priam. Agamemnon, Idomeneus from Crete, Nestor from Sandy Pylos, Odysseus, Ajax, Diomedes and many others all have brought ships to Aulis. King Nestor called on everyone and invoked some pledge they had made to support each other. Patroclus comes from the north with his cousin whom they all say is invincible. His name is Achilles." He stopped and pushed his hair back. "They plan a surprise attack as soon as the weather permits. There is no time to waste, even though the throngs gathered in Aulis are restless and fast losing confidence in Agamemnon."

Paris stood, his eyes wild and angry. "How dare they. Yes, we must report to my father at once." He strode about the room, ranting against the alarming turn of events. "This is appalling. What do you mean about the throngs 'becoming restless'?"

Paris's disturbed activity stirred Meriandynus from his trance-like position. He jumped up, following Paris. "They have used up most of their stores just waiting for the wind to moderate, and they dare not raid Boeotian or Euboean host cities and storehouses as they would do here in Troy.

The soldiers get drunk and fight each other all the time. Terrible sickness has weakened the forces and destroyed their purpose. It may be that soon they will be so ill and disgruntled they will all go home. That is what Agamemnon fears. He is so worried he is prepared to make a human sacrifice."

"A human sacrifice?" Paris and I said in unison.

"Yes," Meriandynus replied, suddenly resuming his former seat, his unfocused gaze, his flat unemotional tone. "Agamemnon's seer predicted that the wind will change if he offers to Zeus his daughter, a priestess to the Goddess in a nearby temple."

Meriandynus turned to me, and I saw a terrible look of pity flood his face. I looked to Paris as his hand reached out towards me and a ghastly realization grazed his features.

"Iphigeneia, adored Iphigeneia." Her lovely face drifted before me, her loving, unassuming smile, her bright sea-blue eyes, and a black veil beclouded the day and numbed my mind into all-obscuring darkness.

"I have slept very late," I murmured to Klara, who stood over me. As Klara nodded I began to recall the arrival of Meriandynus and all that he had told us. I screamed. "No, he could not. Even he could not do that."

"You fainted. Here, drink this. It will calm you, please." Klara held me gently and tipped a cup of potion for me to swallow. "Prince Paris carried you in here, and he told me all. He will return when he and Meriandynus have seen King Priam."

Klara's voice droned on, and I ceased to listen. I felt the potion's sleepy effect, and began to drift away. I became a bird and soared across the sea to a great island near the mainland. I saw a narrows with a gulf to the north and another to the south. The currents worked both ways and provided a clever and protected place for fleets to gather. Aulis!

My bird-self flew inland gliding on air currents around a high hill, then circled the Sanctuary where Iphigeneia was a virgin priestess. No one was about but a few old women tending the garden. I returned to the coastal plain and sailed above the hundreds of ships pulled up on the beach. As far as one could see, fires burned here and there, and hordes of unkempt burly soldiers milled about. Colored standards snapped and cracked unceasingly in the searing wind. Huts dotted the entire area, and a foul odor of open latrines permeated the air. Banners streaming from tents in a marked-off clearing indicated the central command. I flew low and recognized kings and princes who once came to Amyklae to offer me their loyalty and now planned my destruction.

I watched everyone move toward a raised platform where a square altar stone glistened white in the sun. The din of voices ceased, the unkempt horde stopped; they stared in prurient concentration as Iphigeneia appeared between two soldiers. In the windy blasts, her dark hair blew about her face, and her simple loose drapery clung to her nubile form. Though her hands were tied, soldiers held firmly to her arms. Some priestesses in the crowd called out protestations and were restrained by guards.

Iphigeneia stopped when she saw Agamemnon, who stood with his head lowered in the front ranks. The power of her gaze forced him to look at her. His mouth curved cruelly, and his defiant eyes did not flinch. "Father, Father, why? Why?" she shrieked, struggling to escape the firm grasp of her captors. As they dragged her off a terrible shame defiled Agamemnon's face, and he looked away.

My daughter's eyes were wild with fright as a priest appeared in a dark heavy tunic. He wore the wreath of sacrifice on his head and carried a double bladed axe in one hand. He nodded to an assistant who forced the girl to kneel before the altar. The assistant gathered her hair in his two hands and tied it with twine exposing her slender white neck. Her head jerked back as a golden necklace was torn off and flung to the group of women still screaming at the sidelines. Suddenly I recognized Lady Aethra. It was Lady Aethra in a purple cloak who had reached out for the necklace.

Prayers of sacrifice were muttered by the priest, and Iphigeneia's head was forced onto the rock, the vulnerable whiteness of her nape exposed, her eyes streaming. The polished metal had been sharpened to glistening, and the axe found its mark with an incisive thwack.

The assistant picked up the head by the hair and held it high for all to see, spraying tears of blood wide around. A great cheer arose from the assemblage while dark red gushes of blood erupted from the headless corpse until it was finally wrapped and bundled away on a litter.

My bird self flew away, injured, falling, down, down, down to the sea, which rushed up to meet me.

"Calm yourself, calm yourself," Klara said over and over, restraining me as I thrashed and struck out in horror and anger. Though I realized, finally, I had dreamed the murder of Iphigeneia, every tortured nerve in my body informed me that I had seen the entire sacrifice in every gruesome detail. "My daughter, my daughter, my daughter."

My whole being welcomed the warmth of the sun. We sat on the roof top terrace and I listened to Paris. "Every year the same armies pirate ships that trade at our ports, raid our fields and sack our cities. Every year we must put our energies into repelling them. That they have organized so many in one place to operate together, that is what is different and so alarming."

"If only our plan had been put to work," I said. "I should not have waited for the Autumn Rites, but left at once for Boeotia to inform our allies. I could have made our treaty work."

"You came here for that purpose. You must not blame yourself," Paris insisted. "King Priam does not blame you. He just sits and shakes his head in regret for what might have been. Then he pulls at his beard and stares off in the distance." The breeze fluttered his hair. "Let us hope they have all died in the sickness of their own filth."

"Did your father do nothing?" I asked, still bewildered.

"He finally called everyone together. 'We will prepare for this expected invasion,' he finally said. 'The boy may be correct. These enemies will bemoan their bad judgment, and rue the efforts they have made and the resources they have wasted. We will prevail.'"

"Allies have been alerted, battalions called up, new weapons turned and forged, old weapons amassed, swords, shields, spears sharpened, chariots repaired, and armor polished," Paris reported.

All day long I could hear the pounding of chariot wheels resounded from the arena, and the cries of the drivers commanding their horses echoed across the fields.

The murder of Iphigeneia, though a dream or vision, stayed with me in all of its gruesome detail. At any time I might smell the odors of cooking fires mingled with the stench of reeking feculence. I watched again the salacious expressions of leering soldiers and the cruel tearing away of the gold neck-chain that wrenched Iphigeneia's entire body. But it was the sound of the axe on that same slender neck, the indescribable slice, blow, thwack, that resounded in my ears in an unending echo. My recuperation lagged, and a gloom possessed me, from which I could barely stir.

"We will force them back and destroy them," Paris said. "You will return to Laconia as a savior, Queen of your people. Agamemnon and his cohorts will be annihilated."

Yet, the first attack was a surprise. Under the cover of darkness a fleet of twenty vessels attempted a landing at dawn on the outer shore of the harbor headland. Guards posted for duty ran for help, and others fended off the debarking enemy with twanging bows. The first of several soldiers who waded ashore was killed instantly by an arrow through the heart. When the arrows were gone, the guards picked up beach stones and hurled them with enough accuracy to keep the invaders at bay until reserves arrived.

After Paris had hastened away with the call to arms, I covered my sleeping robe with my warm military cloak and climbed the stairway to the rooftop. In the growing light of dawn, I watched the dark hulled ships retreat towards Tenedos Island. It was here that Cassandra found me.

She held her wrap close in the morning chill, her mass of hair, uncombed. "You must come. You are needed at once." Cassandra, breathless, insisted. "Hurry."

"But what is it? Why?" I inquired, loath to rush off, feeling too weak to hurry anywhere. "The invaders have been forced back."

"But they will return. More of them will return." She had regained her breath and spoke deliberately.

I could see and feel her power, and knew I must accompany her. "Wait while I robe. Why is it so important?"

"It is the long-awaited maidens! They arrived an hour ago."

"But why must I come? Why am I needed? Tell me."

"A girl named Iphigeneia is amongst them."

I felt the weight of Goddess mystery hanging heavy all around. Light from wall slits played on one single image three cubits high in a central position. I bowed low before her, then Cassandra led me into other chambers through a courtyard filled with sun and the burgeoning buds of spring. "They are in the eating room," Cassandra said.

Fifteen girls sat at a table. A brazier glowed hot with coals, and a spicy aroma from a steaming crock filled the air. Their soft voices ceased as we entered, and all stood but one. My eyes flew by each maiden and stopped at the seated figure. Iphigeneia's startled blue eyes looked back at me, alarmed and fearful as a fawn's.

Suddenly the sun's bright light of day-break filled my dark soul. Joyful, I went to her and took her hands; they were warm. I touched her cheek. It was soft and alive. "My dream," I whispered, "it was false. Darling Iphigeneia, thanks be to the Goddess, it was false." I put my arms around her and felt her slender form close to me.

But she did not respond in any way. "Darling, it is I, Helen. Please, please," I insisted.

"She has not spoken since her arrival," Cassandra said.

"She has not spoken for days," a voice said from behind.

I recognized something about it, a timber, an accent. I turned to see Lady Aethra. Her completely white hair was pulled back starkly from her face, her pasty skin wrinkled and worn, but the boney structure beneath was firm.

She regarded me dully, her eyelids drooping. I thought it strange, for she was wrapped in the very purple shawl of my dream.

We embraced, and I felt her uncontrollable silent sobbing. I gently led her apart, and Cassandra brought us cups of hot brew. I breathed in the pungent steamy aroma and felt a heavy burden slip from me. I took her hand, but her anxious face was unchanged.

"I thought she had been murdered," I said. "I saw a vision or dreamed a dream. I believed it."

"Tell me your dream," Lady Aethra croaked. "Tell me your dream while I compose myself."

"It was terrible, too horrid to repeat."

"The telling will help you forget it."

"I will try."

Lady Aethra nodded, resting back in her chair, looking at me, through me, as I spoke.

"I had been ill, and I am still regaining my strength. A few days ago...," I began, "...and in my dreams I smelled the horrid odors, saw the kings and princes and soldiers and the altar rock..." As I spoke Lady Aethra followed my words, watched my mouth, searched my eyes. When I finished, she waited and pondered.

"You cannot ever have been to Aulis," she stated.

"No, never, though my messenger described it well."

"It was all as you dreamed, except for the final brutal act."

"How can that be?"

"An animal was substituted for the girl. A hind, willowy and small. No one knew. A sack was put over the head of Iphigeneia and another over the head of the hind, something you did not dream. A clever exchange, and quick. The amount of blood was more than sufficient. They wanted to see and smell the blood; the soldiers were thirsty for blood."

"But Agamemnon. He didn't know?"

"No, he did not watch the act, could not, I suspect, for his head was lowered throughout. He saw the priest display the severed head in the sack, spraying blood everywhere, and then Agamemnon left. Menelaus arranged a diversion for which he and the other generals were called away."

"Menelaus? But what of Menelaus? Did he not see it?"

"It was Menelaus who planned the subterfuge, who bribed the priests, who managed the entire trick."

I stared at Lady Aethra in disbelief. Menelaus?

"As soon as it was finished, we were rushed away to join the group of Maidens headed for Troy. Iphigeneia did not know of the planned substitution and was, is, dazed, stunned by the dreadful affair."

She continued. "The wind changed, our crossing went smoothly, and Iphigeneia slept most of the way. When she was awake, she ate a bit but never spoke." Lady Aethra mouthed the words, her voice weak.

"You are exhausted," I said. "You have experienced an outrageous situation, but you are safe now. We have much to talk about, later. I will take care of Iphigeneia."

Lady Aethra did not object, and Cassandra led her away.

I returned to Iphigeneia, who sat as before with two other priestesses. Her cloak had fallen open, and I saw that she wore the gold necklace with the bird-goddess amulet. I could see a raw-red welt on her neck as though someone had pulled the necklace away with such force that the thin chain tore the skin.

"Have you come from Boeotia?" I asked the girls.

"Yes," one of them answered. "With Iphigeneia, we are the three maidens for this year."

"Were you—present—at the..." I couldn't say it.

"We were held back by guards, but we saw it all. We thought—we thought, we all thought..."

"Do not speak about it, please," I urged them, feeling sickened myself with the vision in my mind. "Try to forget it. It is over now." Here I was in a sunny, warm garden, sitting next to my daughter who was alive. I took her hand and felt its warmth and relaxed for the first time in days. "Tell me about her. Is she your friend?" I asked them, keeping Iphigeneia's hand in mine.

"Oh, yes," the girl nearest me answered. "Everyone likes Iphigeneia. She is smart and quick and funny."

"Does she make jokes?" I asked, not surprised, for her humor was well developed when last I saw her.

"She makes us feel good if we are homesick or have performed badly in our studies. She acts out scenes, getting the posture or the inflection of voices perfectly. Although the high priestesses do not always find it amusing."

I laughed remembering how Hermione loved to watch Ighigeneia. In my mind I could hear their laughter echoing all across the garden.

"Will she shake loose of this trance?" I asked.

"Yes, yes, she will," they said in unison. "She has a happy nature and will return to us. After she rests she will be herself."

"She is safe with her fine friends," I said. "I am called Helen. I am her aunt," I told them. "I will take her to her chamber, and help her to bathe and perhaps sleep, if she wishes."

The girls helped me guide Iphigeneia into the sleeping room. "All of her belongings have been put in that chest under the window," one said. "Now we must leave for the priestesses await us."

When they left I stood at the window looking out at the garden, hoping their heartening expectations would not prove to be false.

"You are not my aunt. You are my mother." The words took a moment to penetrate my preoccupied thoughts. "I have been lied to my entire life by the people I cared for the most."

Iphigeneia's statement, so calmly uttered, quaked an alarm through my entire body. She sat as she had before, resting back against a bolster, her hands at ease in her lap. But her eyes were sharp; her accusing, unblinking blue stare regarded me coolly.

"Who told you this?" I asked, walking over to her, sitting on a low bench near the bed.

"You do not deny it?"

"No." I shook my head. "I do not deny it." I returned her look, measure for measure. I restrained myself from grabbing her hands and gushing my tale of woe and grief that had tormented me through the years.

"Your husband told me this." Her mouth curved in bitterness. "He saved me from certain death. He took the sack off my head, untied my hands, and told me that I was not the daughter of my parents."

"Oh, no," I whispered, appalled at the cruel shock. "Menelaus did not mean to hurt you," I said, trying to fathom his action. "He must have thought it easier for you to understand Agamemnon's brutal decision, if you knew you were not truly his daughter."

She turned her head and stared at the wall.

"I will tell you anything you wish to know," I said. "When you are ready, I will tell you about your birth, a wonder story".

Cassandra came in with a potion. "How is she?"

"Iphigeneia has come back to herself, but her experience is almost too much to bear."

"My dear Iphigeneia," Cassandra said, leaning over her. "You are safe here in Hecate's shrine. Hecate will take care of you. Give yourself over to her. She will carry your burdens while you rest. Drink from this cup. It will relieve you, relax you. Perhaps you will sleep. When you awaken, the Goddess will be here with you."

Iphigeneia permitted Cassandra to hold her head up while she drank from the cup. She lay back on the bolster and closed her eyes. In a few moments she spoke, her voice drowsy with sleep. "Aunt Helen, I always admired you, loved you. We had fine times together, but, my mother— I adored my mother—and my father. He took me with him on his business around the city. He was so proud of..." her voice caught. Why did he..?" Tears slid from between her eyelids. "There, darling," Cassandra said. "Go to sleep, go to sleep."

We sat on the roof terrace watching a gentle breeze ruffle the harbor waters below. The open sea beyond the headlands was empty and calm and a few fleecy clouds hung in the sky. Klara passed cups, and Meriandynus followed with cakes and nuts. Iphigeneia's face held a lovely purity with the flawless skin and a mouth that could not be rude, for her lips of a rosy hue curved naturally into pleasantness.

Iphigeneia, I beseeched, silently. All of your life I have longed to be truly your mother. All of your life I have felt close to you, although we were far apart. Now, we are together. You know the entire story of your birth; we need not be strangers.

Iphigeneia, in her effort to sort out the quandary of her identity, had besieged me with questions. Despite an undercurrent of anger at a mother who would abandon her child, an anger that could boil to the surface without warning, she had wanted to know everything. In long sessions in her sleeping chamber, I had told her about her father, and about his kingdom of Attica where I first met Lady Aethra and my servants Pindros and Lani, whom she remembered from childhood visits. She admired Polydeuces and Castor and attended carefully when I told her how they took me from the fortress of Aphidnae and attended her birth on the shores of Argolis Bay.

"Lady Aethra," Iphigeneia addressed her grandmother, "you stayed with me the entire time. We were close, yet you never told me who I was. I knew in my heart that you were more to me than a tutor."

In the shade of a vine-covered trellis, Lady Aethra's hands, seemingly separate beings, stitched colored floral patterns into a woven material spread round her.

"No, I never did tell you," she said. "I had promised, you see." She looked up at us and smiled benignly as though her promise was the entire answer.

I took a cup from Meriandynus and felt suddenly numbed by her words. And Lady Aethra had promised me, I recalled. She had reassured me as much as anyone could when Iphigeneia was a babe in arms, that she would bring her to Laconia. Lady Aethra had promised to bring my child to me, I repeated in my mind. She had not felt bound to do so.

Had I known in my heart all along that Lady Aethra followed her own plan regarding Iphigeneia, keeping what promises she chose, promises made to me or to Clytemnestra or whomever? And now I knew for a fact that it was not my child's fate that determined her life. It was the deliberate manipulations of her grandmother. I set the cup down abruptly on a table near Paris, overcome with the revelation.

Lady Aethra's eyes briefly locked with mine, and I saw in hers an awareness of my knowledge: she had kept only promises that suited her purpose. Lady Aethra quickly sought the safety of her hand-work.

"Tell me again, Helen," Iphigeneia demanded. "Tell me what grandmother said when I was born."

Paris put his hand on my shoulder. "Are you well, Helen?" he asked softly. He sensed my discomfort.

I nodded and girded myself for the telling. "Lady Aethra was injured. She had hit her head in the storm at sea and remained unconscious for a long time. Sometimes she called out mumblings we could not understand. So it surprised us when she articulated clearly: "She shall be called Iphigeneia, the mother of a new race, the essence of the redeemed Goddess."

Lady Aethra smiled. She had taken it upon herself as a primary mission to oversee Iphigeneia in every facet of her development. She had kept my daughter apart from me, and Clytemnestra's mothering must have been as easily wielded. I recalled the pain of separation, and a powerful urge came over me to shake Lady Aethra and pull her hair as I had once done. But I sat quietly, and the feeling left me. I looked at Paris, whose eyes gave me courage.

Meriandynus quietly refilled our cups. Iphigeneia thanked him, and I saw his face light up with veneration. I recalled Thaos, and his ecstatic awe when he encountered Iphigeneia. Dear Captain Thaos, where was he now?

Iphigeneia smiled at me, and I smiled back, our eyes exchanging an intimacy that might exist between a mother and a daughter. I knew then that the fulfillment of my love for Iphigeneia would have strengthened both of us, had she been permitted to be my daughter.

Lady Aethra spoke to her granddaughter directly. "I always believed in you, my dear. I always believed and still do. It is your destiny to bring harmony to the world of Goddess worship."

Iphigeneia's lips parted slightly. Her eyes looked deeply into those of Lady Aethra's and glowed with an uncommon knowledge. "And it is the Goddess Hecate who will instruct me," she breathed.

TEUCER'S MESSAGE

If it had not been for the worry of war, one would have felt at peace amidst the flowering shrubs in the warmth of the courtyard where Priam, his aides, and allies gathered to hear the latest information reported by scouts and messengers. We learned that the treasure houses and food supplies of coastal cities continued to be attacked. Achilles, leader of the striking forces, had gained a fearful reputation for savagery, and just the sound of his name chilled the bones of ordinary folk.

Scouts reported that Mycenaean ships were entrenched along the coast south of Troy. Their closest camp was on the shores of Shelter Bay opposite Tenedos Island. They had started building earth works on open ground between the camp and the citadel but the effort lagged. Mycenaean soldiers lay ill and many died, for the pestilence they suffered in Aulis had not been left behind.

"Our scouts watch closely," King Priam told us.

"It seems the invaders are causing themselves more problems than are we," Paris commented. "Too many men inhabit too small an area."

"Could you not simply chase them away in their weakened condition?" I asked.

"It would be a dishonorable slaughter," Hector explained.

"We will watch and wait," King Priam advised. "In addition to the pestilence, the leaders fight among themselves over captured women. Their original purpose, to attack Troy, has been set aside for petty arguments over hurt vanity. This year's invasion from across the sea is larger and earlier in the season than ever before, but it is not that we are unused to these attacks. They have come as regular as the north wind for many years."

King Priam turned to me. "Can you imagine our delight, Queen Helen, when we learned that Laconia was eager to cooperate, rather than fight?"

"Thank you for your gracious words, King Priam," I said. "But I realize that if I had done my part in implementing our treaty, this might never have happened."

"It pleases us to have you well again. Your presence alone lifts one's spirits," he paused. "It is not for us to comprehend the whims of fate."

A servant appeared. "Sire, a visitor from the Mycenaean camp is at the gate. He says he comes in peace."

King Priam sat straight in his chair. "Did he leave his name?"

"Yes, he is called Teucer of Salamis."

"Teucer, you say? Why, that is Teucer, son of my little sister Hesione. Bid him enter, at once."

Paris and I exchanged a look of surprise. I had not seen Teucer since his time in Laconia, but Paris had been with him recently.

Teucer entered without weapons. His dark red tunic accented his strong tanned legs and ruddy cheek. The boy Teucer of my memory had become a man of stature and poise. He went at once to his uncle and bowed before him. "King Priam, I bring you greetings from your sister, my mother. I have long wished to call on you and regret that it is under these circumstances."

"You are welcome, my boy, under any circumstances," Priam said. "Here are your cousins, Paris, Hector and the other lads yonder, and over here my counselors, and Queen Helen of Laconia."

Teucer went from person to person and spoke a few words. He seemed awed to see Hector, who radiated authority in his military cloak of a Trojan General. Teucer greeted Paris in friendship, for the two had spent many days in Salamnis together before Paris joined our ship for the voyage to Troy. To me he bowed deeply, then looked at me steadily for several breaths before his face broke into a dazzling smile which I could not help but return. I would never forget his eloquence at the meeting of the suitors in Amyklae, when he protested the practice of kidnapping moon priestesses.

"Sit over here, lad," Priam said. A servant had placed a chair next to that of the King. "I do believe you carry a resemblance to my sister about you."

I had never met Hesione, but I could see that Teucer's abundant soft brown hair might someday turn the white of Priam's, and his clear eyes held the same depths of understanding.

"You look as healthy as a high bred steed," Priam commented. "How is it that you have escaped the pestilence ravishing your camp?"

"It must be that our army is small compared to others, and we have camped apart, keeping our own discipline."

"I am glad you fare so well," Priam answered. "But what of the others? I must tell you, it is our greatest hope that things go so badly for them, they will go away some dark night and not come back."

A flash of concern creased Teucer's brow. "It would not surprise me either. Agamemnon, our chief, has cut himself off from his advisers. He sulks like a chastened child because he was forced to return a beautiful young priestess he had captured. Her mother, an eminent priestess seer threatened dire consequences. When the sickness raged again, Agamemnon finally agreed to send her home, but then insisted on taking for himself Achilles's favorite concubine, a girl captured in the raid on Lyrnessus. This so angered Achilles he has refused to fight or even talk to Agamemnon. He stays in his hut, feeling a terrible hurt and nursing a wrath out of all proportion to the situation, or so it seems to me."

"And is that how it is today, as we sit here?" Hector asked, one eyebrow raised in incredulity.

When Teucer nodded, Hector chortled, "Zeus is on our side."

"Oh, but the great seer Calchas must be upset," Paris commented.

"Yes," Teucer agreed. "And, in a way, his concern has to do with a message. When I asked permission to come here, I was given a dispatch to bring to you."

"Let us hear it, then." Priam said. "What momentous words do you have for us?"

Everyone was silent. The counselors stopped their whispering. Diephobus and Troilus came closer. Even the birds stopped chirping.

"I am to propose a single combat. One Trojan and one Mycenaean." Teucer paused as King Priam took in the information.

Hector nodded. "It would save many lives", he said, considering. "We choose our man, you choose yours?"

"No," Teucer said. "They want it to be Menelaus and Paris. It is because of the theft of Helen by Paris that we are here. If Menelaus wins, Helen returns to him. If Paris wins, Helen stays."

"But that is not as it was," I interjected, horrified that a falsehood about me should be authenticated by this ploy.

"Such a surmise does enormous injustice to Helen," Paris said.

Teucer turned to me. "I know you were not kidnapped by Paris. I was with Paris just before he joined you on your ship. How could that be called kidnapping?"

"I am happy for your confidence, Teucer, but is it not possible to tell others in your camp of this fact?"

Teucer looked away, refusing to meet my eyes. "The truth is not so important among them," he whispered.

"Then why should we trust them in this case?" Priam asked.

Teucer looked at Priam, but he could not answer.

Antenor, an aged counselor, intervened. "If Paris wins, your armies will make restitution for all the damage you have caused and go home?" he asked, "and never return?"

"Yes. And if he does not, we take Helen, as well as all rights of passage through the straits."

Compelled by an urgent need for truth, I stood again to speak. "But, Teucer, you yourself said you knew I was not kidnapped. I came here because I was invited. Menelaus had stepped down from his Kingship. I sent him away because he was disloyal to Laconia. Here in Troy we have made an agreement of fairness in trading based on trust because Troy and Laconia both follow the ways of the Goddess. This truth has been ignored. Such a combat between Menelaus and Paris would be a travesty if not a trap."

"But an opportunity," Agenor, another of Priam's counselors spoke, standing from amidst the circle of elders. "Paris, you could win. You are younger, stronger, and skilled in ways he is not. It might be a marvelous chance to end this dreadful situation quickly before we lose even more riches for lack of trade. Few merchant ships come our way with such an enemy fleet clinging to our coast."

Priam listened carefully. "You are suggesting that we accept this offer, although it is based on falsehood?"

"We do not have to accept the reasoning to approve the combat," Agenor replied.

A flame of anger burned deep within me. Was Agamemnon going to succeed at deciding the stakes? Of course it would be assumed that the Trojans accepted the reasoning if they approved the combat. I stood to speak. "To accept this plan for one on one combat is to validate the presence of Agamemnon on your shores. I urge you to reject it. I myself will return with Teucer and confront the invaders and explain to them my mission here. I will put their ruse to the test by offering to return with them. If, indeed, that is the reason why they have gathered here, my departure would be of little consequence in the larger view."

"Queen Helen," Priam said, "my dear Helen, we could not permit you to debase yourself in that way. You are our honored guest. The tribes that gathered in the Scamander Valley to pay homage to you would never understand. We and they know it is a lie, what is said about you being kidnapped. What say you, Paris?" Priam turned to his second son.

"I believe we can correct the lie without Helen having to confront the invaders. This entire plan may be a trick," Paris answered his father. "Yet, if lives could be saved...I will fight if it is made clear to the Mycenaeans the truth about Queen Helen's mission to Troy."

"I say we will meet to talk about it," Hector said. "It matters not the reasoning behind it, as Agenor put it. If it please you, Father, Teucer should return with a message of possibility, depending on the details worked out in a meeting. And the explanation for Helen's presence in Troy should be made very clear to all."

I shook my head in disagreement, seething within, knowing it was wrong.

"Yes," Priam said. "Well put, son. Teucer, my boy, tell them that. We will not agree for certain, but we will meet to discuss the possibility."

He turned to me. "And Helen, when we meet the Mycenaeans, a copy of our treaty will be shown in hopes of convincing these fools that this nonsense is all unnecessary."

I nodded, full of grave doubts, deep feelings of concern for Paris, and surprising old loyalties for Menelaus. Was there no Laconian loyal to me?

"Friend Teucer," I said, "tell me of the Laconian ships. Who amongst my ship captains is here and how many ships made the crossing?"

Teucer stood before me and spoke without guile. "The ships of King Menelaus and King Agamemnon sailed under one banner, Laconia a subject land under Mycenae. Laconians are present, to be sure, but the ship captains are from Mycenae, twenty of them."

My hopes were dashed. No loyal ship captains waited at Shelter Bay for some contact with their Queen.

Two days later, Hector reported to us that the single combat would take place. "Yes, a clear explanation was given concerning Helen's presence in Troy. The Treaty was presented, read from the tablet in their presence."

"How did they respond?" Paris interrupted.

I listened carefully, equally impatient for the answer.

"Agamemnon and the others," Hector said, "they nodded wisely. They did not verbally reply, except for Nestor, later. 'Such a treaty has no meaning. Helen no longer has authority in Laconia.' Moreover everyone knows he is a bag of wind. I think they were impressed with the treaty."

My spirits, already depressed, sank to abysmal depths. Nestor might have been verbose, but he was also Agamemnon's confidant.

Lady Aethra, Iphigeneia and I slowly climbed the steps of the walls above the Scaean Gate where the murmuring voices of King Priam and his aged counselors droned. We had come to witness the one on one contest before the tower of Ilios, site of a shrine and altar, where sacrifices would be made.

The combat was a nightmare for me. I feared that Paris would lose, for he was not a warrior. He had stated the fact often. Yet, he was a mighty hunter and his courage was undaunted. Menelaus, an efficient seasoned soldier, had always left the glory to his brother. How would he handle this moment of prominence? Menelaus and Paris had once shared guest-friendships, which demanded a code of honor between them. Menelaus had been my husband and the father of my children. I would not want him to be killed, especially by Paris. And the mere thought of losing Paris was unimaginable. I could not fathom the armed confrontation about to happen between them, and I felt a fearsome anxiety that I tried to hide.

Iphigeneia, fresh and young, glowed with inner energy. She wore the white tunic edged in gold of the priestess of Hecate. Lady Aethra, dignified and serene in her purple drapery, and I, in shades of amber with gold bands in my hair and the heavy gold-work necklace covering my breast, had prepared carefully. For the ceremonies and the contest we would stand together on the low landing above the sacred lions that watched over the entrance to the tower shrine protecting the citadel.

Cassandra had first noted, and others were quick to agree, that the three of us together personified the Triple Goddess. Grandmother, mother and daughter, three in one, one in three, past, present and future, a sacred combination inspiring awe in the worshipful and a powerful image easily viewed. I wanted my daughter and her grandmother on either side of me, and I wanted Agamemnon to see that Iphigeneia was alive.

For now, we moved toward Hecuba, Andromache, Cassandra and the other women, but King Priam called to me. "Helen, come here, dear child. Sit with me for a moment."

I did as he asked, excusing myself from the women to join him higher on the scaffold seats prepared for viewing. The armies were beginning to gather, and we looked down on the Mycenaeans, their various colors dotting the plain as they approached the open area before the gates. "It is difficult," Priam said, "to have to watch my own son in mortal battle. And you, my dear, how your heart must race. It is unfortunate that you have been put in such a position, as though you are responsible for this strife which has been going on since long before your involvement." He held my hand tightly for a moment expressing his concern.

"Tell me, Helen, you know these enemies. Who is that man out there, who is that powerful figure? He is walking with Menelaus, whom I know from before. He has an arrogant stride. Is he...?"

I saw the familiar form of King Agamemnon, his head held proudly. Menelaus was listening to him as they moved together toward the combat site.

"Yes, you inquire of Agamemnon, grandson of Atreus and great-grandson of Pelops, a worthy inheritor of their evil deeds."

"And over there, who is that officer? The grandson of Atreus stands taller, but this is a ram of a man with great shoulders."

Before I could answer, the elder Antenor spoke. "That is Odysseus. Once long ago he was my guest. I thought him slow of wit until he spoke. His facility with words rival none."

"And who is that," Priam asked, "that other one, so massive that he towers head and shoulders above the Mycenaean troops?"

"That is the giant soldier, Ajax, half-brother to your nephew, Teucer," I said. "And opposite him, among the Cretans," I pointed out, "is tall Idomeneus, talking with his captains. I do not know the famed Achilles, but over there is his cousin Patroclus, with the yellow hair, speaking to Ajax from Locris. 'Little Ajax' they call him.

Priam chuckled. "Little Ajax is as large as Agamemnon himself. About Achilles, we have heard rumors that he wants to leave, to go home. Strangely, my younger daughter Polyxena has met him. She trains her horse in the pastures of the Brothers of Attis. It is outside the walls, a neutral place, as you know. Achilles is often there, alone."

A loud cheer interrupted him. The Trojans had come from the other side of the citadel, Hector blazed in glory at their head. His aides and generals spread out behind. Paris was not in sight.

Criers arrived with sacrificial sheep and goblets with wine for libations. King Priam stood at my side as all the generals faced him from the solid earth below.

King Priam raised his arms for attention and spoke out loudly. "Before we proceed with the sacrifices and the combat, Menelaus and Paris, please step in front for the ceremony."

Menelaus, glowing in a polished plumed helmet, bronze cuirass and silver greaves, stepped forward as people began to look for Paris. I saw him at once as he emerged from one of the recesses in the wall of the citadel. He stood at attention, and a gasp of surprise emanated from the ranks. Wearing his leopard cowl and carrying his long hunting spears, Paris marched boldly to the front. His curved bow hung across his shoulder with a quiver of arrows, and his small sword was fastened at his waist. His heavy leather hunting jerkin was his only armor.

He had not told Hector of his plan for fear Hector would object. Now it was too late for objections. But I could see from above that Menelaus was not pleased. He stared at Paris in alarm; rage flooded his face as he turned to Agamemnon who seemed to think the hunting garb amusing, perhaps an advantage. I had never seen Menelaus openly dispute Agamemnon before. In a moment Menelaus stalked away, back to his troops, and it appeared that the combat between Paris and Menelaus was off.

Hector and Agamemnon together then turned to Paris, pressing him, urging him. I hoped with all my heart that he would not give in, but he shrugged and turned to make some demand I could not hear.

At directions from Agamemnon and Hector, the entire force on both sides began to sit down on the ground with a heavy clatter and banging of weapons and armor. After a hasty nod of agreement, Paris moved into the Trojan midst removing his cowl, throwing off his hunting gear, borrowing armor and battle weapons from one and then another soldier. He buckled on greaves with silver ankle circlets and the cuirass of his brother Lykaon. By a heavy belt, he slung a sword with a silver studded hilt on to his shoulder and over this a shield strap and a many layered shield. Then he drew a helmet upon his head, its tall plume grimly tossing for the chin strap was not quite tight enough. He picked, from the many offered, a solid short battle spear and returned to the front of the ranks where he waited for Menelaus who slowly came to join him.

A wave of terror at the perilous position of Paris washed through me. I returned to Lady Aethra and to Iphigeneia, and we stood as we had planned, a trio representing the Triple Goddess, sacred to everyone, just above the gate in a central position. Their presence on either side calmed me.

I looked out into the mass of military might before me. I raised my arms in Goddess blessing. In the hush that followed, I called out, "The sacred center is here with the Goddess. The mystery of regeneration is our domain, the force of life our potency. Do not embrace the decay, deterioration, and impotence of slaughter."

Prince Paris nodded at us in approval. Menelaus caught my glance. His did not waver. Patroclus and Little Ajax, talking seriously together, noticed us simultaneously, their faces radiant with surprise and awe. Odysseus looked amazed, his eyes bright with admiration. Nestor did not quite know who we were. He squinted as though looking at the sun. Great Ajax seemed confused. King Idomeneus frowned, and Acamas, next to Menestheus from Athens, stared at me, astonished, and proud. Suddenly his countenance broke into joy when he recognized Lady Aethra, his grandmother.

Agamemnon scrutinized me carefully. I returned his gaze steadfastly, as I had done on previous encounters. Then he looked puzzled, not at me, but next to me. His face paled, a terror panicked his eyes. He had recognized Iphigeneia. His mouth slackened and he brushed at his eyes as though to remove a cobweb. He shook his head and put his hand on the shoulder of an aide and walked slowly away.

Iphigeneia trembled next to me. "Have courage," I whispered.

Criers announced the sacrifice and edged a knife hard across the sheep's throats and laid them quivering. Hector, and Nestor, representing Agamemnon, dipped wine and tipped their offerings to their deities.

Menelaus and Paris stationed themselves in the marked-off ring. Paris wasted no time. His spear hurled across the space and hit Menelaus squarely over his heart; the hard armour bent the point of bronze on impact.

I was both horrified and fascinated, unable to remove my eyes from this fight I had no wish to watch. I could almost hear Paris curse. Just one of his own long hunting spears would have broken through the metal layer to find its mark.

Menelaus's spear passed the shield of Paris, shaving his polished metal breast plate, but ripped his sword-arm sleeve.

Now for the long swords. Menelaus swung blow after blow, each parried by Paris until he saw a high swipe coming. Paris lunged under the raised arm of Menelaus, upsetting him, and the misdirected sword came down striking the hard ridge of Paris's helmet, forcing the blade to break from the hilt.

Paris seized his advantage when he saw the broken blade tumble to the ground. With his sword raised, he advanced on Menelaus, now weaponless, who stared with frightened eyes from behind his shield.

I watched Menelaus, the father of my child, a man I had selected to be my King, a man of quiet humor who preferred agreement to strife, a man who had no strength to declare loyalty. A terrible sadness filled me.

"Now your shield is useless," Paris said, cutting through the shoulder leathers. It fell away with a clatter. Paris cut the leather helmet straps and those that buckled on his cuirass, and nudged the helmet off with the tip of his sword; the cuirass fell away by itself.

Menelaus stood helpless before Paris.

"On your knees," Paris said, and Menelaus knelt before him. Paris put the tip of the sword's blade over Menelaus's heart and tore away the leathren shirt and cut his skin beneath so that blood dripped from the wound and spotted the earth.

Paris was about to kill Menelaus before me. I gasped and covered my eyes with my hands. All I could hear was the occasional clang of soldier's armor as they moved for better seating.

"Oh," Iphigeneia said next to me.

"Amazing," Lady Aethra breathed.

I looked. Menelaus knelt with his head bowed, expecting the killing blow. Paris paused for long moments, then put his sword in its scabbard. Having brought Menelaus to the ultimate moment of humility, he turned his back on the scene and walked away.

Menelaus, raising his eyes, suddenly realized that he was not to die. He leaped up and, just as Paris was about to step out of the marked-off ring, grabbed at the helmet's loose chin strap and yanked it back, hard. Upset, Paris nearly lost his balance and his face turned bright red, then purple. The Mycenaeans shouted with blood lust. Suddenly the chin strap broke, and Paris fell out of the ring, his hand to his throat, gasping. When his breath returned, he took an offered drink, then pushed away through the crowds.

The contest was over, the match called a draw. Menelaus had broken rules, but Paris had stepped outside the zone of combat. The battle lines were set. The armies would meet on the plain tomorrow. My instant relief changed to anger and disappointment. Paris was clearly the victor in every way, but he had not won.

In mid-afternoon the drawn shutters cast slatted patterns on the rugs and coverlet. Paris, stripped of his tunic, rubbed some salve into the wound on his neck.

"Let me help," I said, examining the injury. Relieved to see it was not deep, I took the balm and gently applied it to the lesion.

"I honored him as a guest friend." Paris's voice was strained and tight. "I should have killed him. When he pulled my helmet by the strap, I looked right into his face and saw a fearsome anger. Where was his honor? The code of the wild is tame compared to the code among men."

I put my arms around him. "You are safe," I whispered. "You are alive."

"No, that is not important," he rasped. "What matters is that I did not kill Menelaus when I had the opportunity. I defeated him. Honorably. Any judge would agree. He groveled in death and I freed him. My guest-friend," he said scornfully. "He is nothing but a spineless coward." He coughed, putting his hands over his face; his shoulders shuddered. "Now we have to fight the battles. Why, oh why, did I not destroy him?" His hands dropped from his face and I saw a bitter expression, his eyes empty of the vitality and exuberance of life.

HUBRIS OF HECTOR

I walked with Polyxena to the shrine of Attis. "The Brothers gave me the colt a year ago when I turned fifteen," she said. "I come here nearly everyday to see him."

"I hope not yesterday," I replied, concerned, for ever since the Trojans had encamped on the other side of the Scamander, runners had brought reports of terrible fighting, and yesterday we heard clearly the cries of battle.

"No, not yesterday," she answered. "But the battle on the plain was nowhere near here. Mama is such a worrier." Polyxena's golden hair flew out about her as she tossed her head like a spirited filly. "Oh, Helen. There he is—the gray one—Gespari." Her sullen mouth broke into joy and her slate-blue eyes shone suddenly azure as she ran off to an enclosed grassland where a band of yearlings frolicked.

The eunuch priests of Attis had built their shrine within a grove of alder trees on the edge of a deep pond beyond the pasture and barns. Its aged walls of white stone had weathered the winds and scorching sun for years too many to count.

I watched Polyxena as she called to her colt. Gespari's ears twitched, and he stood still as she went to him, her hand held out in gentle welcome.

"She has a way with animals, has she not?" A man I took to be one of the dark-robed temple priests leaned against a pasture gate.

"Yes, but she has little regard for the dangers of war raging all about," I said, my eyes fixed on the girl placing a halter on the animal. "Her brother Troilus was injured badly yesterday, not to mention others who were not her kin."

"I like her for that," he said. His voice was very deep for a eunuch, but then they were not all castrated as boys. Physically mature men regularly offered their procreative power to the Goddess in fervent rites of self mutilation and adoration.

I looked at him more closely. He had sleek black hair pushed back from his face, and his black eyebrows slanted toward prominent cheekbones. The bridge of his nose arched slightly, and his fleshy lips curved sensually. He turned to me, and I saw deep-set eyes of the darkest brown. He returned my gaze, straightening up from his leaning position, and I realized it was a long dark cloak he wore, not a robe of Attis. He pushed it behind his shoulders and I saw his battle tunic and belted sword. He was a massive man of enormous strength.

"Oh," I said, "I thought you were a priest of Attis."

He laughed shaking his head. "And I thought you were a servant maid. But your ethereal golden glow tells me you must be the beautiful Helen."

"And you are the famed Achilles." He towered over me, but I did not feel menaced. "I hoped I would encounter you today," I said. "Polyxena has told us that she often meets you here."

"Yes. I came first to see the Brothers' renowned horses." Achilles looked out across the pasture at the grazing band of handsome beasts. "But now I must admit I come to be with Polyxena. Just look at her."

We both watched as the girl and the horse played together in the fresh grass. Caught by the sun, her long hair glistened as it splayed out around her. The pale gray horse answered her prompting whistle, swerving one way and another to her command. When he stopped, she patted his muzzle in appreciation and rubbed her own cheek against his.

"That Gespari," Achilles said, "he has a good life."

Polyxena had jumped on Gespari's back and rode off toward the far end of the pasture.

"Come," Achilles said, leading me to a bench under a great oak tree at the side of the path. "I imagine you have something to say to me. Let us sit in the shade and be comfortable." He smiled and I noticed a wide gap between his front teeth, otherwise strong and even.

We sat side by side, his dark blue tunic edged in gold against my fine linen, patterned in complicated openwork.

"This is why I came here this morning," I said, getting right to the point. "Polyxena told us you were leaving, giving up the battle here to Agamemnon. She told us you were taking your Myrmidons home. Is this true? It will boost the Trojans' chances beyond measure if you go, and as you refuse to fight along-side Agamemnon, you must feel little allegiance to his cause. I assume that you are not compromised by discussing this issue."

Achilles made a sound of pleasure deep in his throat, which may have been a laugh. "Queen Helen, there is nothing I would not discuss with you." He smiled his gap-toothed smile. "Patroclus, the man I care for most in the world, my best friend and cousin, believes you are not only the most beautiful woman anywhere, but also divine and trustworthy. Yes, I plan to leave, take my Myrmidons, as you say, and return home. But..."

"You have changed your mind? I asked.

"It is Agamemnon who has suddenly changed," he said. "He has offered me marvelous gifts in apology for his insults. It is an unexpected development, as though he must atone for a terrible wrongdoing. He wants me to forgive him and to join him in battle against Troy."

Achilles turned to face me more directly and chuckled . "I am to receive gold beads, bronze kettles, copper cauldrons, six pairs of race winning chariot horses, and beautiful girls taken at Lesbos."

"How extraordinary," I gasped.

"But that is not all. He offered to adopt me and let me marry his daughter, with no bride price, and a dowry larger than any ever settled before."

"But..."

"There is more. He will give me seven towns near the sea."

He named them and told me they abounded with lush meadows, and their inhabitants were rich in flocks and would bring him worthy gifts in allegiance. "Ah, yes," I answered, a dark shadow falling over me. "I know of these towns. They are all in Messenia, the neighboring land to my own Laconia. After Agamemnon slew King Idas and his brother Lynceus, he occupied Messenia and murdered their heirs and supporters. That is how he has come to have dominion over those towns." I did not expect sympathy from Achilles upon learning of such brutal acts. I knew full well of his own list of similar atrocities.

"Rest easy, Queen Helen. I have no wish to provide Agamemnon with atonement for whatever terrible deed is eating at his heart. I have refused his offer, even though my soldiers fight with Patroclus today. My cousin borrowed my soldiers and my armor. He believes the mere sight of it will frighten the Trojans away." Achilles stood and strutted about. "Also," he said, more to himself than to me, "I could never forgive Agamemnon's attempt to humiliate me before the entire Mycenaean force."

A Brother of Attis walked by leading a pack horse with baskets bulging with onions strapped to its back. The priest's rough robe was tied with a woven belt, and his dusty sandals showed beneath his swaying skirt.

"It is another reason that keeps me here, one day or many," Achilles said, after the graciously nodding priest had passed. "I want to take Polyxena with me when I leave. I want to marry her and take her home to Phthia where she can cavort endlessly with the horses, if she wants, and live with me and be my wife." He stood before me in silence, searching my face for my approval. "Will King Priam and Queen Hecuba agree to this?"

Polyxena on Gespari raced towards us from the far end of the pasture. "You must ask them," I answered. "It is my guess that, if you left at once, they would honor you as their own son. Does Polyxena agree?"

Achilles did not wait to respond. He hurried to the gate and opened it enough to slip through. Polyxena halted the galloping Gespari at the last instant, and throwing aside the reins, she slid off the horse's back and into Achilles' waiting arms.

Later in the day Achilles drove us to the citadel of Troy in his chariot. He told us about the fighting.

"We heard Agamemnon himself has been wounded," Polyxena said."Is it true, Achilles?"

"Yes, but the wounds are not serious. What is serious is the burning of the ships. Your Trojans have already destroyed five."

I hoped in my heart they would succeed. Surely, if enough ships were burned the Mycenaean effort would be devastated.

At the walls of the citadel, Achilles and Polyxena went through an outside portal to the shrine within the sacred tower of Ilios. Guarded by six lions, it enabled pilgrims to offer sacrifices or tokens to the Goddess without breaching the walls.

I hurried to King Priam who conferred with counselors in the throne room of the palace.

"Forgive me for interrupting," I said.

"What is it, Queen Helen?" Priam asked, his tired eyes regarding me under a weary brow.

I paused only an instant. "It is Achilles. He is with Polyxena. They await you in the tower shrine. He wishes to take her with him when he leaves these shores and has come to ask your permission."

"Oh, Great Mother," King Priam said, rising to his feet. "I will go at once." He beckoned to a counselor. "Come with me, Antenor. Hecuba, someone fetch Hecuba," he called as he left.

"I shall find her," I said and hurried up the stairs to the Queen's apartment, barely permitting a maid time to announce me before rushing in to her. She sat at the window, looking across the rolling land that stretched south to the battlefields.

"I have lost two sons to this despicable war. Two more are badly wounded. Why have you come, Helen? What is the urgency? Is it death, more death that cannot wait for the telling?" She gripped the arm of her chair so that her knuckles shone white. Her head was held high and proud, prepared for whatever the fates had in store for her.

"Queen Hecuba. It is not death news I bring." I went to her and took her hand which had relaxed its hold on the chair arm. I held it and put it to my cheek feeling profound affection for her. "You are so very brave, Hecuba, so formidable in the face of this calamity."

"You are mistaken," she said, shaking her head. "I am filled with dismay and horror most of the time. I wait daily in trepidation for the messengers to bring us the tally of dead and injured. I cringe at the sight of them and tremble with each report." She turned in her chair. "Now tell me of your news that does not hint of death."

"King Priam has gone to the tower shrine where Polyxena awaits with Prince Achilles. Hecuba, Achilles wishes to marry her, to take her with him to Phthia at once. Achilles is here to ask your permission. Come. I will escort you."

"But Polyxena, what does she say?" Hecuba asked.

"She seems agreeable," I said as we rushed off.

We entered the shrine and paused in reverent respect before a seated wooden Goddess figure. Light from high-up played on the well known features, altering her holy gaze to a questioning ambiguity.

Achilles and Polyxena bowed low to Hecuba. "Welcome, dear Mother," Polyxena said. "Queen Helen will have told you of my wishes. Here is Prince Achilles. He is our reputed enemy, but in truth he has not committed a hostile act on our shores."

King Priam's eyes shone with hope. He nodded his head, giving Hecuba some message that only they understood.

Achilles stepped forward. "Honored parents of Polyxena, great leaders of Troy, hear me for a moment. I am tired of sacking cities and robbing storehouses. I am exhausted with killing. My commander is so full of abusive arrogance that I cannot stomach any more of him. Let me take Polyxena home with me, where we can live in peace in the quiet countryside."

"And what do you say to this, my Poly?" Hecuba took the hand of her daughter and searched her eyes as though to feel and see her response as well as to hear it.

"I will go with Prince Achilles, Mother," the girl answered; a tremulous elation lit her face. "I have accepted these gold bracelets as his pledge, unless you tell me to return them." Polyxena held up her arms so we could see the wide embossed bands of gold above her elbows.

Priam and Hecuba exchanged looks. "You may keep them," Hecuba said.

A commotion at the gate, a clatter of chariot wheels and excited calls interrupted the meeting.

"Sire, it is Prince Hector come from the battle front," reported a servant standing at the entry-way.

King Priam rushed out with Antenor. Queen Hecuba and Polyxena followed. Achilles seemed hesitant, but I nodded to him, and we left the shrine together.

Hector, brilliant in glowing armor, jumped down from his chariot and threw the reins to his driver. He saw his mother and father and called to them, "We have routed the Mycenaeans in mighty combat. Many Myrmidons have been killed, and I slew Prince Patroclus with a single blow." Battle dust still smudged his cheeks but could not dispel the conquering pride that emanated from him like a holy aura.

A terrible fear grabbed my heart. Achilles had told me that Patroclus wore his armor today, armor illustrious in itself for its unique beauty and strength, recognizable to all soldiers as belonging to Achilles.

I turned and saw realization spread across his face. Patroclus, his gentle brother-in-spirit, was dead. A wave of grief engulfed me, for I too, had experienced the particular grace of Patroclus when he was my suitor.

The eyes of Achilles widened and filled with hate as he looked upon Hector. His jaw rose in defiance, and his mouth hardened into a scythe of cruelty. Achilles' powerful form seemed to grow before my eyes as he pulled himself together, every muscle taut. I understood the racking pain that must be tormenting him.

And here was Hector, a considerate, moderate man most times, now bragging and posing, unaware of his audience. I willed Hector to stop, but he kept on with his boasting. In a resonant voice he described in detail how he had des-ecrated the poor dead body of Patroclus, stripped it of its armor and put it on himself. In truth, the armor fit Hector as though it were forged for him, and he turned this way and that so we could all admire it.

Achilles stepped forth. His deep voice compelled attention. "Who are you to flaunt the sacred armor that was made for my father by Hephaestus himself? You brute, who will never know the loyalty or recognize the excellence of such a man as Patroclus. I die a million deaths in his death. I challenge you, Hector of Troy, to single combat tomorrow. I will wait for you before these gates at sunrise."

In a puzzled dawning, laced with fear, Hector recognized Achilles.

When Achilles had finished speaking, he walked steadfastly to his chariot and climbed in. As he thundered away, his terrible scream of grief and anger echoed back to us, who stood in ghastly silence before the Scaean Gate.

At dawn I stood with Andromache on the walls of Troy and saw in the distance the dust of an approaching chariot. As Achilles' drew closer, I made out a military escort behind him. Below, Hector waited, with Paris and Diephobus silently attending.

"My father, King in Cilicia, and my brothers, all seven, were ruthlessly slain by Achilles," Andromache said, her voice trembling with emotion. "He cut them down like a mad woodsman might fell trees in a forest, without consideration of anything other than his skill at hacking." Her voice dropped in fear. "And this morning this same mad man will battle my husband."

Her terror flared within me. "Come," I said. "We need not stay."

"I must," she answered.

My eyes fastened on Hector standing quietly next to the bright shield that leaned against the tower buttress. The rest of his armor, Achilles' armor taken victoriously in battle from Patroclus, was in the care of his brother Diephobus.

"Hector is not prepared in spirit for this fight," Andromache whispered. "He has convinced himself that Achilles is soft, that he has lain about in indolence while others battled these past months. Hector believes he can out-run Achilles," her voice quavered, "and he plans to race him on foot."

"It is not like Hector to avoid a contest," I said, thinking the strategy strange.

Achilles, in battle dress from helmet to greaves, jumped out of the chariot before the driver had come to a full stop; he advanced like a war lord, brandishing his lance.

Hector turned suddenly and, with great speed, sprinted close under the walls of the citadel.

"Oh," Andromache whispered. "There he goes." In silent fear we watched Hector speed by with nimble feet and Achilles, encumbered with armor, follow. Achilles soon threw down his shield and spear, ripped off his helmet, and managed to unbuckle and discard his metal breast plate. The runners disappeared from view, and in my mind I saw the long outside path wind past the gates, where the fig tree grew and past the springs of fresh water on the north and on to the impregnable solid western battlements. To our surprise and horror Achilles had gained on Hector when they reappeared.

After the third circuit, Hector stopped to grab his shield and fast took up an ashen, bronze-pointed spear handed to him by Diephobus. Poised to throw, he heaved it mightily as Achilles came into view behind him. Quick Achilles dodged the flying shaft and picked up his own spear from where it had been dropped, all in one smooth movement. As Andromache cried, I felt a ghastly premonition.

I could not breathe as Hector advanced, his sword inhand, Achilles's own shield covering him. It was a fine heavy shield, I thought, so fabricated as to be admired by every soldier anywhere. But hold it up a little higher, I silently instructed Hector. I could see an unprotected spot where his collar bones divided his neck and shoulders. Achilles stood with his feet solidly apart, his lance raised, and as Hector's sword came close Achilles drove his spear-point straight through Hector's tender throat.

Andromache screamed as he fell. Stunned, I led the sobbing girl away. We went to Hecuba's quarters, where the Queen, who had just received the deplorable tidings, embraced the inconsolable wife of her dead son. I spent the rest of the day with baby Astyanax.

Much later, when I entered his house, Paris stood in the doorway to the bedroom in a linen sheet wrapped around his hips, having just bathed. "It was grotesque," he said.

Exhausted with despair, I sat in a chair in the welcoming room. What is in store for this man who stands now before me? I wondered. Will he die on the battlefield, this man who holds my very essence in the curve of his cheek or the light in his eye?

"After killing Hector," Paris said, "Achilles walked around and collected his armor, that taken from the corpse of Patroclus. He handed it piece by piece to a retainer and spoke to the several soldiers who accompanied him. He told them they would now, with Hector's death, be able to honor Patroclus in funeral rites and games.

"Then he addressed Diephobus and me, we two who waited to take our poor brother's lifeless body away for bathing and laying out. Achilles had only outrage and shame planned for poor Hector. 'Such an honor will be denied to him,' he said, his voice full of hate as he pointed to the pitiful corpse stretched out on the sand. The drawn swords of his cohorts stood between us and our fallen brother.

Unable to act, we watched Achilles kneel down and pick up Hector's feet. He drew out a sharp knife and made a slit behind the tendons at the ankle and drew a rawhide cord through the hole, tying the feet together and then to his chariot. Without another word he drove off. King Priam's son, General of the Trojans, was dragged behind, his head bumping on the ruts, his black hair streaming in the dust."

I listened to this horror tale and envisioned it clearly. I understood the immensity of the insult; it could not go unrevenged.

Paris looked godly after his bath, with his clean hair uncombed on his forehead and the solemn expression of concern on his face. "Father Priam will not rest until we have Hector back."

I put my hand lightly on Paris's arm, and my fingers were on fire. Suddenly all of our pent-up grief and anger for what had happened and what was to come focused on that touch. We held each other and each touch demanded another. I put my hands to his head and felt the damp hair as we continued kissing, kissing, kissing. We clung together, caressing each other in a frenzy of mating passion as though it alone would make everything right.

OENONE'S GIFT

As a man possessed, King Priam demanded the return of Hector's remains. With cold determination he selected items from his treasure house to be used as ransom for the corpse, and I watched with others as gold goblets, precious weavings, robes, mantels and white cloaks, tripods, cauldrons, and more were placed in wicker hampers in a cart.

His faithful herald drove the rig, and Priam himself took the reins of the royal chariot. As they rode off Polyxena ran after them, her slender young form touchingly vulnerable.

"Stop. Papa. Wait. Stop," she called.

A hush fell over us. King Priam pulled his team up short. "What is it, Poly," he said kindly.

She handed her father the golden arm bands pledged to her by Achilles. "Add these to the ransom," she said. Her voice was strong enough to carry across to us, and a murmur of approval rose up.

When the same two vehicles were sighted the next day, we rushed to the ramparts. And when it was determined that Hector's body was in the cart, it was as though he returned victorious from battle, so magnificent was his welcome.

Later, King Priam told us that when Achilles heard that Polyxena wished to return the bracelets, he nearly wept. "Until then he had disdained the ransom," King Priam said, his voice full. "He agreed and his servants washed Hector's body and prepared a bier, but he would not take back the bracelets." Priam turned to Polyxena. "Here, my darling. Here are your arm bands." He handed them to her.

Polyxena rubbed her fingers over the embossed design. "I will put them in Hector's tomb," she said, brushing at her eyes.

"A full ten days of armistice has been declared," Priam told us. "We will have time for funeral rites for our fallen son and general."

Cassandra and I walked together to the Temple of Hecate. "Paris tells me that help is expected," I told her. "This period of truce will provide time for the Hittites and Amazons to get here."

"Won't they ever understand—only more killing will come of it?"

"But Cassandra," I pleaded. "How can you be certain?" In truth, I felt crushed inside, with little hope, but I could not admit it. It seemed to me wrong for her to always speak in terms of defeat.

Cassandra looked on me with pity in her dark blue eyes. "Come along then. I wish to take you to someone."

I followed, curious as we entered the sanctuary, and, after offering respect to the sacred figure, we continued into the dark depths and stopped before a hidden recess.

"Is this the entry to the way of the maidens?" I asked her in a whisper. She nodded and opened a creaking door.

"Come," she said, handing me one of several oil lamps burning on the wall of a narrow passage.

In silence I followed her down ranks of steep steps cut out of the rocky floor. The path went on and on, until she moved to a side passage leading to old chambers of some other time, some other city. "What is this, Cassandra. Where are we?" I looked around, startled, for a figure moved and a huge shadow rose and lurched towards us making my heart pound.

"I brought her," Cassandra said.

"Good." A deep voice echoed through the chambers.

Lamp light cast eerie streaks across Cassandra's face, and a cold chill made me shiver. I looked into the face of the stranger—I knew him. It was someone from the Mycenaean Camp—Ajax—the Locrian, Little Ajax with his pet serpent wound around his shoulders.

I put my hand on his arm to steady myself. "Oh, this is too much. Please tell me what it is all about."

"Come—over here," Little Ajax said. "Daylight breaks through just above. We are not far from the exit. Put out your lamps to conserve oil, and relight from this one I will keep burning."

We blew out our lamps and sat on a ledge. I was freezing cold.

"Here", Ajax said, handing us some skins. "Cover yourselves."

Confused but grateful, I warmed up quickly wrapped in the deer skin. Water dripped in a far off corner.

"Long ago Little Ajax served as a leader in bringing Maidens to Troy," Cassandra explained. "He recognized the peculiar arrangements of rocks on the shore that hides the entry."

"It is well concealed," Ajax said, "and impossible for a stranger to discern. I recognized it by accident. Not wishing to alert Odysseus, my companion, to my discovery, I ignored it then, but returned later with lamps and oil."

"But why?" I asked.

"I felt compelled to visit the ancient Hecate," he said.

"I found him kneeling before the Goddess image," Cassandra said. "I thought his ghostly presence a demon, then a god. Finally, I realized that he adored Her as I did. After that, he came often, and we have spent hours and hours together. He is a holy man."

"All this time?" I asked, alarmed.

He nodded. "His serpent coiled around his arm."

"It makes me sad," I said. "Why must you be among the invaders."

"We were obliged," he replied.

Cassandra interrupted. "We must tell you. We plan to take the Maidens away soon."

"Troy will fall," Little Ajax said.

I gasped at the boldness. "You cannot be certain," I said.

"Cassandra has received the devine spark of Hecate, she sees the future. It is the curse of those who have this gift not to be believed." His deep voice resounded through the rocky cavities.

In nearly total blackness his words were sharper, my mind clearer. Had a truth been pronounced? Awed, I spoke of something else. "What of your seer, Calchas. What does he say?"

"Oh, Calchas. He likes to please Agamemnon. He is obsessed with some idea Palamedes conjured up. He is building a great war horse."

"What does that mean?" I asked.

"It is a contrivance to scale the walls of the citadel," he says.

The very idea seemed absurd. Yet, upon hearing his imposing voice describe the activity in the darkness, a frightening image of a strange wild beast came to me. "Is Calchas, too, a seer whose gift of prophecy goes unheeded?" I asked.

"He is usually listened to," Little Ajax laughed, "which must mean he sees unclearly. But enough of Calchas and his nonsense. We will take horses and supplies and carry the girls to safety. You must come with us."

Leave Troy! I had never considered such a choice, though now reviewed, I could easily see myself at home. Could I leave without Paris? "Why must I come with you?" I asked.

"It is important to protect the life of Helen, Queen of Laconia, Potnia's essence."

"Do these titles still mean something? They are hollow honors."

"No one has ever carried them, as do you. Your presence before your people will speak truth to them as nothing else could."

I imagined being with Hermione—and Phiona, Arneus, and Hilaeira, dear sister and wife of my brother now dead, and her children. And Lani, faithful, Lani. Once put in motion, it was difficult to return to other thoughts in this dank dark place. Finally I answered. "I must consider what it might mean for Troy."

"We cannot wait long for your decision," Little Ajax replied.

"Now, we must go," Cassandra said.

"Yes." Little Ajax stood. "Listen to Cassandra, Helen. She is wise and knows more than we do."

As we climbed up into the blackness, I looked back and saw the light of Ajax's lamp moving away from us. I imagined the long shoreline outside and the endless sea that stretched all the way to Laconia.

"Paris, I dreamed I went home to Laconia." He had come back exhausted with war and unable to think seriously about my remark.

"Dreams are ways of longing," he said.

We relaxed on the roof terrace, protected from the summer winds by a flowering vine entwined in a lattice.

"But, it is the dreams of battle and death that haunt me," he continued. "They rob me of sleep and shatter any moments of calm." His eyes found mine. "If it were not for the thought of you when I am not with you, I—I do not know—"

His voice frightened me with its pain. I could never leave him. "The killing is savage." He paused. "I have become as cruel as any." He turned his face from me, but I saw his look of revulsion. "The killing of Penthesileia..." The vision had stirred him. "Out there on the battlefield the warrior priestesses rode with a sublime spirit." A frown creased his forehead. "They disdained protection. Their helmets and corselets were of leather. Anyone's spear could penetrate them easily. But they were superb, dodging spear thrusts, and forcing Mycenaeans off the field. Penthesileia was a match for Achilles. She forced him several times to retreat before injuring his thigh. When one woman fell and then another, it was tragic in the extreme. For their enemies it was, I think, exciting. They took unusual pleasure in slaying these wonderful girls."

I visualized the battle scene and could clearly see Penthesileia and her followers. I felt a tremor of horror at Paris's next words.

"Achilles finally speared Penthesileia through. She fell off her horse, and as she lay dying Achilles fell on her and raped her."

I had known of the defeat and the death of Penthesileia, but not of this bestial defilement. Horror-stricken, I did not speak.

"We retreated." His voice had again taken on the earlier pain. "It was a carnage beyond belief. The plain out there— it reeks of blood."

I had strong misgivings when Paris and Meriandynus, now his aide, returned to battle. I spent most afternoons with Andromache finding solace in weaving, and Astyanax never failed to amuse me.

Most evenings I went to the Shrine of Hecate. Cassandra admonished me when I told her that I would not leave Troy.

"You make a great mistake," she had said. "Why, oh why can you not see the right way?"

I ignored her plea. "Will it be soon?" I asked.

She nodded without comment.

I called on Lady Aethra who lived more and more in a world of her own, and I looked in on Iphigeneia. The Maidens had not been informed of their coming departure.

"Mother Helen, enter."

"Am I interrupting?"

"No. We are practicing the sacred dance of honor to the Goddess."

"Queen Helen, will you help us?" the girls asked.

"Oh, yes," I answered. "To dance for the Goddess expresses total adoration, for in dance alone the mind and the body work in harmony to create beauty."

The three pair of eyes looked upon me as a wise teacher.

"Come." We pushed aside cots for space and holding hands I took them through the steps. When we rested, I told them the story of how I danced before the stolen Goddess effigy in the moonlight while thieves slept. Their eyes never left my face.

"But weren't you afraid?"

"It was something she had to do." Iphigeneia said.

When I left Iphigeneia went out with me. She took my hand, and I felt a surge of joy. All of the devices of fate and contrivances of humans that had kept us apart seemed to have melted away. When we reached the gate-yard, I turned to my daughter in the joy of our closeness. "Are you content, my darling?" I asked.

Her Theseus-blue eyes scanned the roof-tops below us, and then her face broke into the radiance of her lovely smile. "Yes, yes, I am," she answered. She looked into the distance, listening. Had she heard a voice or a ringing bell or the trill of a flute? The only sound was the rustling leaves of the oak trees in the court-yard. "I have been chosen," she whispered.

"No," I mouthed silently and shook my head, but she did not notice. I recalled Lady Aethra's premonitions and the rancid wild smell of the she-bear. I could never forget the awed sailors and fisher-folk at her birth ritual, or Captain Thaos's wide-eyed adoration when he saw her as a new born babe, and later in Amyklae.

I thought of all the simple folk who confused the power of the Goddess with the bringer of her message. A stab of fear penetrated my heart. Iphigeneia believed herself to be a part of the divine power rather than its tool.

"I was saved from sacrificial death for a purpose," she went on. "I have been selected! I am the light! I will follow Hecate as Cassandra told me!" She no longer seemed aware of my presence. A slight frown of concentration creased her forehead and her eyes took on a luster of certainty as she turned and left me.

The next evening they were gone; the Maidens had left without a trace. I felt an urgency to commune with the sacred image fallen from the sky, but it, too, had disappeared. Another, nearly as old, had been put in her place. It was wooden, carved with care and plentifully endowed with mystery. Its presence enhanced my worship, and I remained amid her tranquil aura until time had no meaning.

One evening my mind floated to a place where Iphigeneia and her companions sat around a camp-fire, cooking fish on skewers over the coals; Iphigeneia joked with her friends, but something was missing. Little Ajax sat in the flickering light sharpening a knife blade to prepare the fish, and a net and lines were strewn about. It was Cassandra who was missing.

At that moment the door to the underground passage creaked open, and Cassandra herself stepped forth into the chamber of worship.

"Oh, Cassandra," I said, immensely relieved. "I feared some evil had befallen you."

Cassandra smiled. "It was not meant for me to go with them. I saw them ferried across the straits and onto a safe trail to the north. I will join them later."

I was alarmed. "Why are they to travel north and not west towards Boeotia?" I demanded.

"Their destination is the Black Sea land of the Taurians."

"But it is far too distant," I cried.

"In Taurus they will join the ancient order of Tauropolus, and reestablish the old ways, the mysteries of the sacred bull. We had wanted you to be with them, to supervise and help them."

"Never," I protested. "I would never have made such a distant journey for such a purpose. It is my responsibility to return to my own land. I would have insisted!" I spoke in a very low controlled voice to keep myself from shouting out.

"But Little Ajax guides them, and I will join them soon. Also, they carry with them the most powerful Goddess figure in Troy."

"And what of Troy?" I wondered aloud.

"Troy will fall! They have rescued the image by taking it. This is the beginning, not the end." Cassandra's voice had taken on a shrill note. Her flashing eyes were wide and frightening.

Later, that very night, Meriandynus rushed into the house where I slept. "I have brought him back," he called to me in alarm.

I rushed to the welcoming room, fully awake. I knew at once he spoke of Paris. "Is he dead?" I asked, expecting the worst.

"No. It is a deep and ugly wound. The surgeons could do little for him on the field. He is outside in the chariot." The boy's eyes were wide with shock. "He killed Achilles and then was gored."

I rushed to the chariot, and a terrible fear shook me when I saw Paris unconscious. He lay with his head thrown back, his face utterly pale. His breathing was faint and his heartbeat was slow.

"It's his side," Meriandynus croaked.

I removed the battlefield bandage and saw a deep stab wound in the groin. I made a supreme effort to hold off panic. "I can do nothing but tend the external wound," I said. "I have no remedy for the internal damage, which is no doubt major." I thought hard.

"There is one person who might save the life of Paris, Oenone. Meriandynus, we must take him to her." My even voice surprised me.

"But it will take all day in a cart, even if we leave at once. It might be too much for him." He was frantic with worry.

"You know the way. You drove it just last autumn. Can you find a cart, prepare it for his comfort, and bring it here as soon as possible? We must leave while the dark of night protects us."

As Meriandynus left to do my bidding, I called to him again. "Stop to leave a message with Cassandra or at the palace. Tell them Prince Paris is gravely wounded, and we are taking him to Oenone."

I packed food and water, some clothes, clean rags and all the medicines I had. When the boy returned, we wrapped Paris in a sheet and dragged him to the cart, placing him on a straw pallet. Meriandynus had even thought to arrange an awning overhead for shade during the hot day to follow. I found a place for my bundles and we left well before dawn while the town was quiet.

I sat next to Paris's still form and leaned against our packs as we lurched along. The cart was pulled by a strong mule Meriandynus borrowed from the palace stables. "Were you able to leave a message?" I asked him, after we had exited the gate in the eastern wall.

"I did," he said. "A messenger told King Priam of our journey. The King thanks you, and will send his own aides to follow."

We deviated around the battle area, and soon were safely away. By the light of early morning, I bathed Paris's forehead, saying all the while, over and over, "You are going home to Mount Ida."

We stopped to rest near a rushing brook in the shade of a birch wood. The sound of bubbling water was pleasant to the ears. I redressed Paris's wound and saw with dismay that it was oozing blood and some other fluid, thick and yellow. I held his head and tried to give him a drink of water, but he did not swallow it. I washed out some of the soiled dressings in the stream and spread them out on the grass. We ate a hurried meal of bread and goat cheese, and when I climbed back into the cart, I rejoiced to see that Paris lay with his eyes wide open looking up at the swaying branch above.

I did not try to explain our whereabouts to him, or why he was in the back of a cart. "You're awake, my darling," I said softly. "I have a drink for you. You must be very thirsty."

He drank, finally, greedily. We started off again, and he closed his eyes. I took his hand and sang softly as to a child. Gradually the rolling hills became more forested. The high ridges of Mount Ida rose up ahead of us. Paris awoke again late in the day. I could see the expression of pain contorting his face so that, along with a drink of water, he took the pain reliever I had brought. He looked at me as though he knew me. I think he may have smiled.

It was evening when we arrived at the compound where Oenone lived with her son and other priestesses of the Sanctuary of Assos. The sun was low on the horizon, radiating hues of orange and yellow across the sky. This magnificence seemed to me a sign of hope.

"Meriandynus, find Oenone. Tell her we have come to her for help." He tied the reins around a tree and went off, but the tired mule was not likely to wander away.

"Oh, Paris," I said, putting my arms around him, holding his head up a little so he could see. "Look at the sky. It's putting on a show for us."

I could see that he noticed the marvelous array above, for his hand lightly pressed mine and he whispered my name. The golden light fell across our place, onto the mule and the cart, onto Paris and me, gracing us before it disappeared. A redish after-light throbbed and glowed a brief moment in reflected beauty, then faded.

I suddenly felt Paris's head slacken in my arms. Oh, no, no, I said to myself as I searched his face for life, for that gentle humor and intelligence that was Paris— but they were absent. My tears welled, and in the dusky twilight they fell on to his still, still face, so that my tears streaming from my eyes seemed to be his tears rolling down his cheeks. It was as though he, too, grieved at losing the ineffable beauty we shared.

We buried Paris high on Mount Ida where flocks grazed on rich grass and wild flowers. "I know of a cave," Oenone had said, "where he liked to sleep out at night and watch the stars." Five days later we put the final rocks and stones in place to seal the tomb. Oenone and the priestesses from Assos led us in the ritual ceremonies, and eight-year-old Corythus danced with the trees in farewell to his father. My throat ached as I noticed the tilt of his head and his gift of movement so like that of Paris.

A party of four Trojan house guards, sent by King Priam, had carried the tightly shrouded body on a litter to the cave and stood by at attention during the rites. King Priam's herald, who had been sent as an envoy, stood with Paris's foster brother and other shepherds, Meriandynus and me.

Oenone led the mourners back down the mountain, but I stayed on by myself for many breaths. I sat in a grassy spot among the wild flowers and listened to the breeze rustle the oak leaves and thanked the Goddess for Paris.

A fire burned in the council ring and lamb carcasses roasted over hot coals. Oenone, always polite, never intrusive, had kept a distance that I respected. It surprised me when she came and stood before me, her eyes clear and her message direct. "Let us move apart for a moment. I have some words for you."

"Of course Oenone. Let us walk down to the lake and sit on the rocks at the shore?"

"I have been thinking," she said, when we had settled ourselves on round boulders still warm from the day's hot sun. "I remember how you had hoped to return to your homeland and how your illness prevented you from doing so." She looked to me for confirmation. Her long black plait fell over her shoulder on to her bodice.

"Yes, that is correct," I agreed. The lake reflected the sky and wavelets lapped gently at our feet.

"You can leave tomorrow, from here—to Lesbos with two of our priestesses. In Lesbos you can wait until someone from there goes to Chios or Euboea, then continue on, always with priestesses where their tasks take them. You will make your way, gradually, do you see?"

The idea appealed to me. The heady feeling of going home to Laconia came over me again. Would it be disloyal to go now? I wondered. "How did you happen to think about this?" I asked.

She had picked up a stick and drew a design in the wet sand at our feet. "I promised Paris I would help you, back when you were so sick. I do not mean just in nursing you, but in other things as well. I want to honor him and his request of me." She looked at me and I saw her sincerity, even as her mouth curled in bitterness. How hard it was for her, I thought.

"Thank you, Oenone." I wanted to call her 'sister' but I did not. I must think hard about the possible reasons why I should not follow this plan. "The idea is a good one. I will tell you my decision tonight."

We returned to the feasting where I sought out Meriandynus, but he was busy helping to carve the lamb. It was at that moment that King Priam's envoy came to me.

"Excuse me, Queen Helen. I have been wanting to speak with you, but I have been reluctant to interrupt you during this time of honor for Prince Paris."

"Do you have words from the King or Queen?" I asked.

"Yes," he said. "My message is from the King. I was told to give it to you if Prince Paris should not recover from his wounds. He said I was to wait until you were free to hear me—when you could attend his words with care." The herald smiled in sympathy. "Is this such a time?" he asked.

"Indeed it is," I answered, "but should we not seek privacy?"

"The message is short. I can relay it now, if you like."

"Continue. What is it?"

"The King wishes you to know that if you have an opportunity to depart our shores for your homeland, you must not return to Troy for reasons of loyalty or obligation. He said that it would be easy for you to set out from Assos. He urges you to do so."

King Priam had given me permission to leave. "You have been considerate in all ways during this time of burial for Prince Paris," I said. "Please tell King Priam and Queen Hecuba everything you can about it, so that they will know that their son was honored and celebrated and is buried in a tomb that would please him and them. Also tell them," I added, "that the suggestion that I continue on from here came at just the moment that an opportunity presented itself to do so. The coincidence makes it decisive. I shall leave tomorrow."

TAYGETUS RETURN

We set sail in the dark of early morning with priestesses bound for their sister shrine in Lesbos. A surge of grief for my poor dead Paris overcame me as the mellow light of sunrise hit Mount Ida's peaks. I felt a brutal despair that his life had been lost to the fruitless killings of war.

Soon sunlight flashed on sparkling wavelets, and in my heart and mind, I placed Iphigeneia within the care of the Goddess throughout her perilous journeys: one north to the land of the Taurians and the other back in time to the Tauropolian mysteries. I shivered in the growing warmth, imagining her innocence amidst the old savagery.

The Sanctuary to Cybele in Lesbos occupied a rustic spot in a woods on the western hills and became my cloistered haven from worldly activities. Meriandynus lived in the village and came daily, amusing me with tales of the country life around us. We sat in the courtyard shaded by a giant plane tree, and it was here that he brought me the first dire news of Troy.

"The citadel has been sacked by the Mycenaeans," he called as he dashed through the open gateway. When I heard his words, I knew the inevitable had happened; Troy had fallen.

Mycenaean soldiers soon became commonplace in Lesbos ports. They drank heavily of Lesbos wine and bragged about their deeds as they waited for portents of fair winds to take them home. Meriandynus repeated their exaggerated tales, imitating their voices.

"King Priam and all of his sons were cut down the same night. Blood flowed in the palace. The Mycenaean generals took turns choosing the women they would take home as slaves and concubines, as though they played a game of jackstraws."

"Not Hecuba," I asked, aghast. "Not Hecuba, who carried herself with light and life, the mother of mothers. Not Andromache, who had already suffered so grievously from their deeds."

"No man or boy related to the Trojan royal family was left alive," he reported having heard.

"Oh, impossible," I moaned. "Certainly not Astyanax. Certainly not that sweet, clever babe," I cried.

"Hector's son, they threw him from the ramparts," Meriandynus repeated. "Hecuba, the old Queen—she has gone with Odysseus. The young one, the youngest girl, she was sacrificed, stabbed and cut up on the grave of Achilles."

I put my hands over my face in horror as I visualized Astyanax catapulting through the air and brave Polyxena's blood spurting over Achilles' grave. "This must be all fabrication. How could it be anywhere near true? How could it be true?"

"It must be false," Meriandynus agreed. "I am just repeating their drunken babble. They told me that Great Ajax killed himself. He was driven mad when Achilles' armor was not given to him."

He, of all men, would care mightily about that, I realized. "I wonder what happened to Lady Aethra. How could she have managed amid such terror?" I visualized her long white hair flowing about her as she roamed in a daze amidst the slaughter.

"Here, at least, is something you would want to believe," Meriandynus explained. "Her grandson from Athens rescued her. He took her away. Oh, and here is another bit of news that you won't believe, but it may amuse you. They talk about a giant wooden horse, a war machine. It sounds preposterous, doesn't it?" he asked. "The Mycenaeans supposedly used it to climb over the walls at night."

My relief in the salvation of Lady Aethra vanished. In those next words I recognized the contraption Calchas was building. Little Ajax had said it was nonsense. Yet, it must have worked. Calchas must have made it work. I felt horror and disbelief. I could have warned them. But Cassandra warned them; she talked about the downfall of Troy all the time, and no one listened.

"Does it make any more sense than another story they tell about Odysseus slipping into the city through a secret tunnel and opening one of the gates?"

Again, I cringed in anguish. Little Ajax had told us of Odysseus being with him when he discovered the entrance to the way of the maidens. Odysseus, of all men, would have been able to do this daring deed. My mind whirled in confusion.

"They spoke of you," Meriandynus said.

"Me? Well, tell me. What did they say about me?"

Meriandynus, his cheeks bronzed, his hair bleached and grown long, had become apt at mocking the soldier's drunken speech. I could have laughed if the subject were not so grim.

"'The Queen, you know, Helen, who was kidnapped by Paris?'" he mimicked. I waited impatiently for his next words. "'Menelaus, her husband, was about to cut her down.'" Meriandynus lowered his eyes.

"Yes, yes, carry on. What was said?" I insisted.

His speech had lost the flavor of his drunken reporter. "They say he saw Helen naked. She was so beautiful he could not do it. He took her back. Forgave her."

I was strangely moved by the story, as was Meriandynus. A slight rosy tinge mingled with his sun-browned complexion.

"Ah, finally!" I said, looking across to the gardens, "here is a statement we know to be false. Thus, the others must also have been." Yet, the sound of my voice was not convincing. I had known enough brutality at the hands of the Mycenaeans to realize it was nearly all possible.

After months of waiting, we left Lesbos for Euboea, then Aulis, Delphi, and the Peloponnesus. I accumulated information about priestess work, and I learned that their knowledge intertwined in a complicated web that stretched outside, around and underneath the everyday lives of others.

In Aulis, I was reunited with my old friend, High Priestess Macaria. After supper she and I sat together in her quarters, a fire burning in the brazier as the cold winter months were upon us.

"She told me," I said to Macaria, "Iphigeneia told me that Menelaus had intervened—bribed the priests."

"Yes. That is true," my friend answered, handing me a steaming cup. "He and I spoke often together, planning the rescue. Menelaus was decisive," Macaria said. Her lovely face glowed in the firelight as she sipped the brew.

"Oh, but I was relieved to see her in Troy," I told Macaria. "I had dreamed the sacrifice in every detail and cannot think of it even now without dredging up the full horror. For Iphigeneia," I continued, "she was numb with shock. She had experienced every ghastly moment of decapitation but the final one. It was too much."

We sat silently until I spoke again. "Iphigeneia looked to Cassandra for solace, to Cassandra and the Goddess Hecate."

Macaria did not need to hear the disappointment in my voice to know my feelings of desolation when my daughter turned away from me.

"I remember Cassandra," Macaria said. "We were in the same priestess year when I was a Maiden. Cassandra believed herself to be divine. We mocked her behind her back."

"Iphigeneia harbors the same delusion for herself," I said with regret. I felt Macaria's surprise, though she did not reply. "She has gone to the land of the Taurians. On the Black Sea," I continued. "Little Ajax secreted them out one night and Cassandra was to join them later."

"I know of Tauropolus," Macaria said. "It is a primitive order devoted to ritualistic practices of blood-letting, animal augury and human sacrifice."

"I know, I know," I said. "It is not what I had hoped for her." I had difficulty not crying out my fears.

"Helen, we cannot always understand the ways of the Goddess. Her meanings may not be clear to us," Macaria reminded me, but I barely attended her words. I had grown tired of advice about Iphigeneia's destiny, always the same. I longed to be home.

Macaria stirred the fire, and as I watched the glowing charcoal, an idea came to me. "Now that I am safely on the mainland, perhaps Meriandynus and I will continue on by ourselves," I said. "It takes altogether too long to wait for a group of priestesses to decide to travel in our direction."

"There is no need, Helen," Macaria said. "A pilgrimage to Delphi leaves from here in three days. Why don't you join them?"

"But Delphi is not on my way, Macaria."

"But in Delphi you are certain to meet many others who will be."

As I stood among the great trees overlooking the vast panorama of Delphi, I understood that if Menelaus had never come here to consult the Pythia, he would never have traveled to Troy, and Paris would never have come to Laconia. Standing in the sacred waters I felt the gushing springs of purification splash over me, and I recalled the Lake at Nas where Paris and I were purified together. Drops on my eyelashes reflected the sun in glistening brightness. Paris's face swam before me in its perfection. I ducked my head in the cold water washing away the tears but never the memories.

Crossing the Corinthian Gulf, Meriandynus stood in the bow of the boat and helped the pilot identify the approaching headlands. I sat in the back with the Priests of Apollo with whom we traveled. The rowers relaxed at their positions, for the breeze carried us splendidly. I rested my gaze on my young servant and realized that he had grown tall this last year, as tall as the pilot next to him.

Meriandynus and I returned to Laconia together, as we had left together. Never could I have foreseen the tests of character and endurance the boy would be forced to undergo. Never could I have imagined the extent of his loyalty, good judgment, and intelligence. I had begun to think of him as a son. Yet, a son would be bound to me in filial memories and intimacies that were not present with Meriandynus. It was a relationship as none other that I could think of, yet equal, I decided, only to that of son.

The priests from Delphi were on a mission to the Temple of Hyakinthos-Apollo in Amyklae. When we landed, they provided horses for us, and we moved rapidly. At night we sat around a camp fire and I learned of their work in Delphi. The priestesses guarded the flocks in the high meadows or cared for the grain and olives below, while priests became expert craftsmen in gold-work. Their omphalos stone amulets were sought after by pilgrims, and the gems and gold beads taken in exchange made them rich. They served the Pythia by organizing the flow of visitors and arranging the meeting with the Oracle herself. The priestesses supervised all spiritual activities, and I believed a harmony existed between the orders.

One priest with bright red hair and prominent teeth did most of the talking. He asked me questions about Asia, so one night I told them about the great tribal meetings on the Scamander River. I described the warrior priestesses and the eunuch priests of Attis.

"The tradition of Attis is ancient," he said. "But we know no eunuches." He looked to his companions for verification. "We are celibate by choice," he added, his fellow priests nodding avidly.

We followed a series of river valleys to Tegea, and from there it was an easy trip to Amyklae. One morning we passed the camp-site of the thieves who had stolen the famous Laconian goddess image so long ago. A short time later I felt a quickening of my heart when I saw a dry stream-bed winding up into the high rocks. Did it lead to the niche where I had slept with the sacred effigy wrapped tightly in my arms? A few hours later we saw the massif of mighty Mount Teygatus and the city of Amyklae spread out below. I felt a lump in my throat, my eyes stung—I was home.

At the banks of the Eurotas River, I trilled to some swans, and though they seemed fewer in number than I remembered, I was rewarded by some who made a fuss and took bread from my out stretched hand.

We looked for signs of Mycenaean soldiers, but saw none. A few houses needed repair and many fields and orchards were overgrown. Could it be simply the bleakness of winter we noticed?

People milled about in the streets, but no one paid us particular heed. I had wrapped a dark cloak over my head to keep out the cold, and certainly Meriandynus did not draw attention in his warm hooded skins. Perhaps we were taken for retainers of the priests. We dismounted from the horses, and bade our escorts farewell at the Royal Palace, our destination.

A desolate air pervaded the place, and we entered cautiously. We walked through empty rooms that had once glowed with color and went down into the vast basement storerooms, now vacant and still.

"The occupiers have left," I said, convinced.

Meriandynus set out to find someone in charge, someone to tell that we had returned. I wandered again into the welcoming room and then, reminded of that earlier return when I found old Tyndareus lonely and nearly mad, sitting in his chair, staring out the window, I entered the King's quarters.

Tyndareus's chair was in the same place, and it was almost as though he were present, for a plate of half-eaten bread and cheese was on the nearby table, a cup of wine next to it. It could not be Tyndareus, but I felt someone was in his chair. I tiptoed around it—empty. Had I sensed a ghost? I turned to the window to reassure myself with the familiar view.

The vineyards and orchards fell away to the river, which would soon reach its flood. My throat ached with a fullness of nostalgic longing, and a marvelous, unexpected happiness surged through me as I noticed the buds on the fruit trees burgeoning with new life, a sign of spring, of renewal.

"Helen, I did not hear you."

I turned, startled by the familiar voice, my eyes still brimming with the joy of nature's regeneration.

Menelaus stood in a shadowed recess, so that I did not notice at once the deep fatigue etched in his face, or how lean he had become. As he stepped into the light, he reached for a staff that rested against the wall, and I winced when I noticed the purple scars on his arm. We regarded each other in silence. Despite the outward signs of frailty, I sensed strength in his presence. Amidst dark shadows like bruises, his eyes glowed forth a kindliness that touched me.

"I looked for you in Troy." His voice was so low I had to listen keenly. "They told me you had left."

"Yes." I heard myself answer, my own voice catching as I explained. "It took us a long time to get home. We, Meriandynus and I, traveled with priestess groups from temple to temple."

He nodded, leaning on his staff. "For a moment I thought I was seeing a beautiful ghost that appeared to confuse my weary brain."

"I, too, felt the presence of ghosts," I said. "And Hermione?" I asked in a whisper, holding my breath.

"She is well, Helen." He spoke naturally, a tired smile accompanying his good news. "Lani took good care of her. Hilaeira and her children were with her the whole time, as well. Phiona is still High Priestess. Arneus performed a noble act by hiding much of the palace treasure before it could be stolen."

"But where did they go?"

"Hermione and the others were in the country at first, mainly at Father Tyndareus's place, but they are back here now. The Mycenaean soldiers left gradually. There was not much for them to do with all their chiefs in Troy."

"How long have you been back, Menelaus?"

"I arrived five days ago. I was lost at sea, blown far off course. It took all this time to return." He stood quietly. People live simply," he said. "They have had little contact with other provinces. The family moved into the new palace," he paused, "our summer home. They put in some stoves and chimneys, and it is quite adequate. Here, where we stand, was the center of the occupation."

"Menelaus." I spoke his name in a near whisper. "What happened in Troy? I have heard so many stories."

A bleak look of hopelessness washed over his face. He rested against the table, still holding the staff, and shook his head. "I cannot speak of it now," he breathed. "Later, later, I will tell you, if you insist." Deep creases at either side of his mouth made him look very serious. His hair at the temples was white and his beard too contained hints of silver. It had been recently trimmed in the way he preferred.

"I know about Iphigeneia," I said. "I know of your part in saving her."

His glance shifted to the window, which he studied before returning his attention to me. His voice, now strong, his words precise. "I could not permit it. I had to intervene. It was worth it all to keep Agamemnon from carrying out such a shameful act."

"You were brave."

He shrugged his shoulders. "It was not a matter of courage or choice." We stood in silence as I pondered this man, Menelaus.

"Helen." He turned to me. "I had hoped you would be here when I returned. When I entered this room today and looked out the window, across the groves and down to the river, it occurred to me that you might not be coming home. The thought was devastating."

"Menelaus," I said. "We have both returned, and I believe you have the right to resume your kingship. By saving the life of Iphigeneia, you have earned it." I thought of how Agamemnon had always been able to influence him and wondered how much Menelaus had actually changed. "Just think," I said. "Now you can have control, rebuild a fortune, lead an army." I heard my voice take on a sharp note and felt ashamed.

"Helen." His eyes saddened. "Helen," he repeated.

I turned to the window again, unable to speak for the moment. The panorama before me quieted my soul, and I heard the husky voice of Menelaus continue.

"You sent me away. You sent me into the wilderness. I had never felt desolation before. I was hopeless, despondent, nearly out of my mind with grief. I had left everything I cared about, everything that had any meaning for me. I left it all without even an argument or backward glance."

"Aeneas, poor soul, insisted that I board ship with him in Limera Bay, but I could not even bare to be civil to that nice fellow. I had no destination. I wandered, and to be sure, I did wander in the wilderness. The wilderness of wild lands and the wilderness of my wild mind."

I turned back to Menelaus and saw his tortured face reliving that time. His expression did not change as he continued.

"I never thought of food or shelter. I became uncombed and unwashed. My clothes eventually shredded to rags by thorns and briars. I slept in the open when sleep overcame me. I ate berries, raw fish, or even dead birds if they were not too rotten.

"Finally, I awoke one morning when the sun hit my eyes with its brightness. I had slept near a stream of fresh flowing water. I scooped up a handful for a drink, and as the cool water splashed my face, I noticed some beautiful pebbles in the sandy bottom. They reminded me of my time at Delphi." Menelaus was not looking at me any longer. He stared past me. "I could not take my eyes from their irregular shapes and subtlety of color—beige, umber, pink"—He stopped speaking for a moment, and his eyes returned to my face.

"A gentle peacefulness began to spread through me, and my body relaxed in a bliss of restful sleep. When I awoke, I looked at once for the pebbles, and they were as I remembered, even though the sunlight had changed and they were now in shadow. New dimensions of their beauty were revealed to me. I resisted an urge to collect them and take them with me for ever and ever. I left them, for they belonged where they were.

"The awareness of beauty restored a balance to my tortured mind and permitted me to put myself to rights and plan my future. Clearly, I had to break once and for all with the House of Pelops and Atreus. It was this tie that undermined me." His entire face brightened, and I rejoiced for him.

"And did you?" I asked.

"Yes," he replied, with certainty. "I returned to Mycenae to confront Agamemnon. In my heart I knew I had gathered the inner strength to face him. It was a long journey back to my boyhood, and all along the route I reflected on my life. Eventually I was able to articulate the naked truth."

I watched wide-eyed as Menelaus spoke. I waited, wondering.

"I became aware of two codes of behavior in my world. One was inherited from Pelops and Atreus: the complete subjugation of everything to personal power. The man who controlled such power became hugely important in the eyes of others, and in his own. It gave to one man an unreal sense of himself and an unjust control over others. It was for this pleasure of self-importance that men seek power. I am sorry to say that my grandfather Atreus and my great-grandfather Pelops lost all sense of balance in their effort to acquire power to make themselves important. My brother, Agamemnon was of their pattern."

I quietly thought about these words of Menelaus. He watched me, silently, waiting for some response.

"What is the second code of behavior?" I asked.

"Let us walk out into the garden," he said. "It is overgrown, but we can find our way."

He used his staff to ease a slight limp, and we went into the courtyard that had once bloomed with carefully cultivated roses. They had been left to grow wild, a tangle of rambling thorny vines with smallish yellowy-red flowers browned in the winter cold.

"The second code is that of the Great Mother Goddess," Menelaus said. "Helen," he turned to me, "I must tell you, as I have before, I will never be part of her magic. It is not in me to give myself over to such mysteries."

I thought of his revelations of beauty both in Delphi and in the wilderness, but I did not voice my thoughts.

"Hers is a way by which to live," he continued. "Her adoration of procreating, nurturing and caring is the opposite of those who lust for power by killing, demeaning and hating. Hers is the way, especially for a king."

"I like your truths, Menelaus."

"Of course, when I reached Mycenae, Agamemnon was not even there. But the damage had been done. You had gone to Troy, and the word was passed that you had eloped with Paris. I knew that could not be true, but I was helpless to change the rumor. Mycenaean soldiers moved into Laconia. My new-found insights were of little use. I caught up with Agamemnon in Aulis, where the armies of invasion were to meet. You know the rest."

We strolled around the garden in silence, he using his staff to push aside debris as we walked over or around tangles of trailing plants, stirring up a wafting aroma of forgotten blooms.

"The fight with Paris," Menelaus said. "By then it was clear to everyone that you and Paris..." His voice faded. "I was beside myself with anger and humiliation."

My eyes stung, remembering. "Menelaus," I said after a while, "Paris and I...it was completely unexpected. It was a bit like you and the peace and release you found with the pebbles. We both felt it was a gift, something beyond us to understand."

Menelaus shook his head. "I was livid," he said. "I had redeemed my life, discovered a new way, your way, only to have it muddied. I would have murdered him had I been a bit luckier."

I could not speak. I felt his degradation. We continued walking, the sound of his staff marking our steps.

"But then," he continued, finally, his voice quiet and strong, "I slowly realized that balance and insight remained in my soul. It had withstood a trial. I sought beauty and found it. I grieved for your suffering and rejoiced in your strength. I saw my own betrayal and my weakness."

Again we were silent as I took in his words. "Menelaus," I said, stopping, grasping his arm, "you have clearly freed yourself from the curse of the House of Atreus." We looked at each other, our eyes communicating a message deeper than any we could have spoken. I felt esteem for him, and I saw, deep in his eyes that glow of kindliness kindle and spread until it lit up a reciprocal feeling in me.

We turned and continued our stroll, his limping gait and my even one. "The treaty with Troy would have been wonderful for Laconia and our allies," he said. "It was a masterstroke."

"If Agamemnon had only listened, it would have ended your brother's need to capture and control so many states," I said.

"Yes, Helen, all is as you say, except that it was Agamemnon's interest to amass power, not to agree with others. He would never have accepted a bargain, but our allies would have, if they had known of your work before Agamemnon cajoled them to his side with sham and lies. Well, we will not worry about him any more."

"What do you mean?" I asked.

"You have not heard? My brother was murdered, stabbed, the very night he returned home. It was Aegisthus, our cousin who carries the same evil of the House of Atreus as do I—or did. He was aided by Clytemnestra. They are lovers, your sister and my cousin."

Oh, my poor sister, I thought, to have been brought to such an act. Before I could think further on it, voices came from inside. I could hear Meriandynus and a woman talking. It was Lani. Then it was Hermione I heard.

"Mother. Mother Helen. Where are you?" Her clear, young voice carried through the empty halls. My heart began to pound.

"In the garden, darling. Out here in the garden," I called.

In a moment she appeared in the doorway lithe and alert. She stood poised just long enough for me to see her entirely. She had grown, of course. Her auburn hair, held back by a wide gold band, fell to her shoulders. Her hazel eyes lit up as we exchanged a long look. I was overwhelmed with a glorious happiness. "Oh, my dear girl," I cried, as her face broke into a joyful radiance and she rushed into my arms.

As I held her close, I watched the sun and cloud shadow sweep the sharp mountain ridge. The rocky heights shown golden one moment, then dark as death the next. Iphigeneia's lovely smile came into my mind, then changed to an expression of fanatic rapture as I imagined her journey into the shadows. I heard, as though she stood beside me, Cassandra's dire forecast of gloom and slavery for all of us. Suddenly, the sunlight illuminated the sharp crags with a brilliant clarity. It revealed degrees of exquisite color and sublime solidity that banished the bleak vistas ahead, filling me with hope.

CHAPTER NOTES

Chapter One - Laconia is in the south eastern Peloponnesus comprising an area from the Taygetus Mountains to the Aegean Sea, and from the upper reaches of the Eurotas River to the Laconia Gulf. In the environs of present day Sparta are found the Mycenaean Age archaeological ruins of Amyklae, the Menelaion, Vapheio, and several religious sites. I have walked the ground of nearly all the places in Helen's story.

The descriptions of this Laconian site have followed the archaeological information in the *Blue Guide*, Michael Wood's, *In Search of the Trojan War*, *The Peloponnese, A traveller's guide to the sites, monuments and history*, by El Karpodini-Dimitriadi, and others. *Greek Art and Archaeology* by John Pedley was helpful for detailed archaeological information of the Mycenaean Age.

See R. Graves, *The Greek Myths:2*,110.1 for a reference to the girls' foot race.

H.B. Willoughby, in *Pagan Regeneration; a Study of Mystery Initiations in the Greco-Roman World*, provided ideas for the virgin fertility initiation.

The desecration of religious shrines by roving Kings is borne out by Mary Renault in her *Author's Note for The Bull from the Sea*, (Penguin Books), p.231.

Chapters Two - Three - Four - Five. *In Plutarch's Lives*, "Theseus", 31,33, we learn of the kidnapping of Helen by Theseus, her imprisonment in a fortress in Aphidnae, and her rescue by her brothers. In an earlier version preserved in Pausanias,ii.22.7, and attributed by him to sources including the lyric poet Stesichorus, (640-555 BCE), Helen became pregnant by Theseus and was delivered of a daughter at Argos where she dedicated a sanctuary to the goddess of childbirth. The daughter was Iphigeneia, who in later stories appears as the daughter of Agamemnon and Clytemnestra, but according to Stesichorus, was only their adopted daughter. Plutarch also tells of Aethra, the mother of Theseus, as companion to Helen. Robert Graves, *The Greek Myths*, (103,104), cites several other works that include this version of Helen and the birth of Iphigeneia. Hyginus, *Fabula* 79; Pausanias, ii. 22.7; Diodoris Siculus, v.63; Pindar, as quoted by Pausanias,i,18.5,

The Mycenaean Age was a time of religious conflict between worship of the Earth Mother and the patrilinear religions brought by invaders. Kings were inferior to queens in a culture that honored the mystery of the life-giving female. The king of the patriarchal invaders was in direct contact with the sky gods.

The old customs lingered amidst change. Before the institution of marriage, procreation took place in ritual celebrations centered around women of the goddess shrines and men of various totem bands organized for the community welfare. That these procreation rituals, and other religious customs did not cease, expressed the on going practice by indigenous peoples in the old religious ways.

Invader kings found it necessary to abide by the tradition of marrying a goddess priestess to verify kingship. Thus, it was not until Tyndareus married Leda, a moon priestess, that his kingship was secure from his brother Icairus and half-brother Hippocoon, who had dethroned him earlier. It was common practice to kidnap priestesses rather than win them through contests or courtship.

Marija Gimbutas, in *Civilization of the Goddess*, pp.345-346, 399, and *The Language of the Goddess*, pp.316-319,346; Erich Newmann, in *The Great Mother*, 14,15; Riane Eisler, in *The Chalice & The Blade*, 4,5,6,7,8; Merlin Stone in *When God was a Woman*, 2,3,4,7, discuss and explain indigenous prepatriarchal traditions and cultural clashes with alien Indo-European religious forms. Robert Graves summarizes this change in his Introduction to *The Greek Myths.*

Giving Helen an important place in the goddess oriented religion fits in with what we know about her in myth and what we know about the Earth Mother religion through mythology, archaeology, history and literature. As quoted from H.J.Rose in *The Illustrated Dictionary of Greek and Roman Mythology*, even a "glance beyond (Helen's) mortality...and the evidence is there of someone who was probably a goddess in origin...her non-Greek name suggests an ancient pre-Hellenic goddess connected with vegetation and fertility."

The importance of the Earth Mother deity and her presence during the Mycenaean era, is verified by Linear B texts, a written record found on clay tablets in several Mycenaean sites and decoded in 1952. John Chadwick, wrote in his *Mycenaean World*, "The cult of the Earth Mother dominated religious life all over the Aegean world...under a variety of names. The conclusion that Potnia was the Mycenaean name for this figure is inescapable."

His conclusion supports archaeologist Marija Gimbutas and her major works on the presence of female deities in the culture of old Europe. It also gives credence to the many scholars who found the female religion present in the study of ancient literature. Foremost amongst them is poet Robert Graves. See his *Greek Myths*:1, pp. 11-24.

M.I. Finley, not one to accept Graves'ideas, nevertheless says in *The World of Odysseus, Revised Edition*, p.136, "That we are faced here with a new creation, a revolution in religion, can scarcely be doubted. We can be sure that a sudden transformation had occurred, not a slow, gradual shift of beliefs...It is no understatement of the magnitude of the revolution to add that it was far from complete... More precisely, it was not universal...the pre-Olympian cosmological myths had a long life ahead. All the more remarkable...that the traces in the Homeric poems (in contrast to Hesiod) are so few as to warrant another reference to Homeric expurgations. Most notable of all is the indifference to Demeter, the Goddess of Fertility. Homer knew all about Demeter (she is mentioned six times in the Iliad and the Odyssey) and that is just the point. He deliberately turned his back on her and everything she represented."

Martin P. Nilsson discusses Helen as an old vegetation goddess akin to Kore, in *The Mycenaean Origin of Greek Mythology*, c.1932;1972, pp.74-76.

Chapter Four. The bear sequence in Chapter Four came from Gimbutas, *Language of the Goddess*, p. 116. "The appearance of a bear in a village brought good luck for child birth..." A bear had healing powers and sick people were made to lie on the floor so that a bear could step over them. Bear masks were worn by virgins and dances were per-formed in honor of the bear mother.

The work of Greek archaeologist, John Papadimitrou, discussed in *The Sanctuary of Artemis at Brauron*, tells of the sanctuaries of Artemis Tauropolos and Artemis Brauronia, located close to each other on the coast of Attica east of Athens. They honor Iphigeneia, a personification of the great mother goddess, whose cult survived the desertion of the sites around 1300 B.C. where Mycenaean ruins, shards, and tombs were found. Celebrated here was the festival of Arkteia, derived from the Greek word *arktos*, meaning bear. Young girls called *arktoi*, imitated bears, wearing bear masks and saffron-colored robes. Many statuettes of arktoi were found near the retaining wall.

Chapter Five. In myth, The Dioscuri have many special gifts. One of them is to be guardians of sailors at sea.
The Curse of the House of Pelops carries its shadow on through his descendents, particularly Agamemnon and Menelaus. See Graves, *Greek Myths*:2, 110.111.

Chapter Six - The archaeological studies of the citadel of Mycenae are described, illustrated and mapped in *Mycenae-Epidaurus; a complete guide to the museums and archaeological sites of the Argolid*, by S.E. Iakovidis.

Chapter Seven - A harbor on the east coast of the Peloponnese would be a preferred destination, when coming to Laconia from the north or eastern Aegean, to the protected, yet distant ports in the gulf of Laconia. The idea of adding many miles of voyage by sailing around the Laconian Peninsula, and especially having to round the most treacherous cape in all of Greece in doing so (Cape Malea) encouraged me to look for a possible alternative. Epidauros Limera, just north of Monemvasia, seemed a likely harbor. I was pleased to discover that it is a known archaeological site of the Mycenaean period. Drews, Robert. *The End of the Bronze Age.* p.24.1993.

Lynceus and Idas, brothers from neighboring Messenia, are the mythological adversaries of Castor and Polydeuces, and persistent enemies of Laconia. In Chadwick's discussion of geography using Linear B from Pylos, 'the further region' of Nestor's realm included a small part of the Messenian plain and coast. The Messenia of Lynceus and Idas could include most of the Messenian plain, the eastern coast of the Messenian Gulf, the central peninsula of the Peloponnese and the area east to the Taygetus Mountain border with Laconia. The mountains and terrain are particularly difficult in the southwest Peloponnese. Pylos was quite isolated from this region.

Indeed, the later Mycenaean take over of Messenia as advanced in Helen's tale, instigated by Agamemnon, would have had no resistance from Nestor in Pylos, a distant cousin of Lynceus and Idas. (see Chapters Thirteen and Fourteen).

The two pair of brothers are descended from the same Queen. Several generations back Gorgophone, daughter of Perseus, married kings of both realms and was Queen in both lands. In this interpretation, under the influence of Queen Helen, the idea to reunite, as in the "days of Gorgophone," appeals to all of them. Martin West's, *Hesiodic Catalogue of Women*, was helpful in tracing the generations that were used in the mother line recited by Lynceus to prove to Helen who he was. Marija Gimbutas discussed the mother-line concept in *Civilization of the Goddess*, p.344. Her work was a constant resource to Bronze Age matriliny in the Aegean area.

Chapter Eight - In Goddess lore, swans were an important source of food, and a symbol of well being. They were often considered magical. M. Gimbutas, *The Civilization of the Goddess*, p. 234.

Chapter Nine - I have interpreted the agreement of marriage between The Dioscouri and the daughters of Leucippus, acting King of Messenia, as a sign of reconciliation between the neighboring countries. It is in the interest of both to cooperate.

Chapter Ten - The suitors mentioned in this account were taken from the list of suitors in M. West's, *The Hesiodic Catalogue of Women*, with the addition of Lynceus and Teucer.

Chapter Eleven - The Linear B tablets are mainly accounts of goods relating to storage, places where materials, animals and persons were to be sent, and the people responsible. No information about accords among princes and kings is noted. However, written agreements between Egypt and the Hittite Empire, as well as other kingdoms of the same period, are well known.(see Chapter Nineteen)

Chapter Twelve - Thirteen - Fourteen - Hesiod: *Catalogue of Women*, Fragment 70. Loeb Classic Library, translated by Evelyn-White. Helen and Menelaus had two children, Hermione and Nicostratus.

Michael Wood, *In Search of the Trojan War*, p.153, relates the trade in "Spartan stone," from Laconia. Overgrown quarries above the Eurotas valley produced a mottled porphyry stone. It was widely sought and ranged from dark green flecked with yellow to a reddish color, and particularly used in decorating holy places. A pile of this unworked stone was found in Knossos by Evans, ready for use, a clear example of the sophisticated trade practices of the Mycenaean era.

John Chadwick, *The Mycenaean World*, pp. 48-60, tells of the Linear B tablets in Knossos. They indicate the presence of a powerful monarchy in the north central part of the island, which had no influence in either the most eastern or western sections of the island, separated geographically by natural mountain barriers. "The incursion of Mycenaean culture and religion in Crete is documented in all accounts of the Mycenaean age," M.I. Finley, *Early Greece*, p.43, and by the presence alone of Linear B tablets found in Crete.

Kydonia, now Khania, and Aptarwa or Aptara, site of an ancient sanctuary high on a hill, settlements in the western section mentioned on the tablets, were supported by Laconia in Helen's version. The efforts to crush the reawakening of female religious manifestations in western Crete, as in Helen's account, is not inconsistent with what history we know of Crete or the information found on the Linear B tablets.

I have assumed an easy access between Crete and Laconia by way of islands, perfect stops for ancient boats. From Grambusa Island, just off the northwest coast of Crete, it is fifteen miles to Adikythira Island, twenty miles to Kythira and seven miles to Elafonisos, or the reverse. All are easy day runs in fair weather, and with a favorable breeze the trip could be made in one.

Coming from Crete, the presence of the mouth of a great river (the Eurotas) at the head of the Gulf of Laconia would be a natural destination. The ultimate citing of a settlement up the river in the highland valley indicates a natural pathway between Amyklae, which is almost completely isolated from the rest of Greece by high mountains, and Western Crete.

Chapter Fourteen - The death of The Dioscuri in myth suggests that Lynceus and Idas, and Castor and Polydeuces killed each other in an argument over Arcadian cattle. The eminence of The Dioscuri is celebrated throughout Greek mythology. They are saviors and benefactors to mankind. e.g.Their only request in Athens, after becoming masters of the whole city on their expedition to rescue Helen, was to become initiated into the Eleusinian Mysteries.(Also a clue in myth to their loyalty to the Goddess). They were adopted by their supposed enemy, Aphidnus, after rescuing Helen. Plutarch, "Theseus", 33.

To trivialize their death demeans both sets of heros. I have put forth another explanation. When Agamemnon learns of the success of Laconia, Arcadia and Messenia in protecting the shrines and villages of western Crete against the raiding parties of Idomeneus and Agamemnon, he murders the victorious military leaders in a sinister scheme.

Menelaus's visits to Delphi and Troy during the tangled web of intrigue fostered by Agamemnon, and the military activities in western Crete, are mentioned in Graves, *Greek Myths*, 2,159,9.

Chapter Fifteen - The visit of Paris and Aeneas to Laconia is told in the *Cypria*, as well as the departure of Menelaus at this time. It also gives the reason for Paris's visit to Laconia as a desire for purification. R.Graves, *Greek Myths*:2,159,q. (The *Cypria* is part of the "Epic Cycle" a succession of narrative fragments, excluding the *Iliad and the Odyssey*, pieced together to complete the story of the Trojan War. The *Cypria* is attributed to Stanus of Cyprus.)

In the *Cypria*, the story of the death of the two sets of brothers falls between Menelaus's departure, Helen and Paris's elopement, and Menelaus's plans for revenge. It seems completely out of place, perhaps indicating a different original version, a further clue that the death of the Dioscuri had a place in the drama above. That the famous Vapheio Cups should have belonged to the Dioscuri and found in their tomb is an imaginative leap on my part.

Chapter Sixteen - Menelaus leaves his home while Paris remains. *Cypria* 1.

Paris describes Troy to Helen as being "the largest holy center for Goddess worship. Our traditions are as ancient as exist anywhere. We have many temples and sacred Goddess figures." From Michael Wood's, *In Search of the Trojan War*, p.141; "The description of Ilios as 'holy' is notable...the finds of cult idols around the gates of Troy VI on Hisarlik, including six at the southern gate alone, could suggest that the place was remembered as having been uniquely sacred."

Chapter Seventeen - In *Cypria*, 1, Helen and Paris set sail for Troy. They are detained on an island in a great storm, where they mutually acknowledge their incredible attraction to each other. In Helen's account the island refuge is the Bay of Nas on the island of Icaria. A legend of an ancient Goddess sanctuary is known there. The Bay of Nas exudes a mystical charm and would be a logical place to wait out a change of wind, as many ancient voyagers did indeed do. *Ancient Icaria*, by Anthony Papalas.

Chapter Eighteen - The archaeological findings of Troy VI are declared to be Homer's Troy by the excavation currently underway by the University of Tübingen and the University of Cincinnati. I have used The Plan of Troy, 1994, from this archaeological project. John Fleischman, writing in the January, 1992, Smithsonian, says of Manfred Korfmann, director of the current fifteen year reexamination, "His investigations focus on the explosive mix of geography, piracy, and aggression that might explain the rise and fall of so many Troys." He tells us that the imposing citadel looked out towards the Aegean Sea, as at that time the sea was much closer to the fortress.

Michael Wood says: "Troy was a major port at the mouth of the Dardanelles which, like Miletus and Ephesus, eventually silted up and lost its *raison d'etre*. This crucial discovery makes sense of the whole history of Troy. Michael Wood, *The Search for the Trojan War*, p.142.

Helen's tour of the shrines is her introduction to the 'secret way of the maidens'. She learned of the maidens who came from other places to study in Troy from Macaria when she was in Aphidnae, but this is her first knowledge of a secret way into the Temple. Robert Graves, *Greek Myths:.* 2, 168,3.and note 13.

Chapter Nineteen - The accords reached between Laconia and Troy or Ilium are possible in light of the many treaties made at that time in Egypt and the Hittite Empire. e.g. in 1269 BCE a Treaty of Mutual Assistance between the above kingdoms said, "good peace and good brotherhood worthy of great friendship forever." It is on display at the Archaeological Museum, Istanbul. Michael Wood describes other treaties. "The Greeks frequently had friendly relations with the Hittites, evidently governed by the kind of treaty we find all over the Near East at this time: ... the Greek lands around Miletus were marked by a frontier agreed by treaty. The literacy of the Late-Bronze Age world is something almost totally forgotten by the Homeric epic, but—that King Priam could have corresponded with Hattusilis III or Agamemnon for that matter —is at least conceivable. See pp.169-185 of *In Search of the Trojan War*, for more discussion of treaties with two and three copies, and other correspondence between Hittites and Greeks.

The Amazons as horsewomen is described by Norma Lorre Goodrich in *Priestesses*, 2, as well as a complete review of their origins and culture.

Chapter Twenty-One - The sacrifice or attempted sacrifice of Iphigeneia by Agamemnon at Aulis is told in two dramas by Euripides. *Iphigeneia at Aulis*, and *Iphigeneia at Tauris* are basic to the action of Helen's account regarding Iphigeneia.

The arrival of Iphigeneia and Lady Aethra via the 'way of the maidens,' refers to the sources given for Chapter Eighteen.

Chapter Twenty-Two - The duel between Menelaus and Paris follows the action of the *Iliad*, with the addition of reasons why Paris behaved so oddly, appearing in a leopard cowl, and having to borrow armor from fellow soldiers. Homer, *Iliad,* III.

Chapter Twenty-Three - The Temple of Thymbraean Apollo is the neutral place in the usual telling where Achilles saw Polyxena and fell in love with her. Robert Graves, *The Greek Myths.* 2,163,a. I believe a Temple to Attis is more in keeping with the lore of the Earth Mother. Attis, an ancient deity, founded a shrine to the Mother Goddess. Attis unmanned himself under a pine tree and bled to death, sacrificing his virility to the new growth in the spring. The priests of Attis regularly castrated themselves on entering the service of the goddess. For more on Attis, see James Frazer, *The Golden Bough.* "Attis".

The breeding of horses by the Brothers of Attis is consistent with Homer who singles out Troy for its fine horses, and archaeologists have found an abundance of horse bones in the excavations for Troy VI. M.Wood. *Search for the Trojan War,* p.166.

"The seven cities which Agamemnon promised to Achilles are not identified, with two exceptions, but relying upon those identified places scholars believe them all to be situated around the (Messenian) gulf." Martin P. Nilsson, in *The Mycenaean Origin of Greek Mythology,* p.80 (Berkeley, Univ. of Calif.,1932;1972)

The south gate of Troy VI was flanked by a great tower ('The great tower of Ilios' Iliad, XVI, 702) of finely jointed limestone blocks; more over it was built round a major altar, and outside it were six pedestals, and a cult house for burnt sacrifices. It was certainly the main gate of the Late Bronze Age City, the Scaean Gate." Michael Wood, *In Search of the Trojan War.* p.143.

The combat between Achilles and Hector, the death of Hector, the desecration of Hector's body, and the retrieval of Hector's body is told in the *Iliad* XXI, XXII, XXIII, XXIV.

Chapter Twenty-Four - That Little Ajax is a Goddess follower and an accomplice in stealing the Goddess effigy, The Pallidium, guardian of Troy, is important when one uses the information that he is from Locris and strongly tied to Goddess traditions. (Graves, *The Greek Myths* v.2,168,2, with references to Strabo, Dionysius of Halicarnassus and others)

The importance of the theft of the sacred image that protected Troy from invaders is explained in Helen's account using the secret passage to the sea. Robert Graves includes a discussion of the secret way in *The Greek Myths*, 2.159,9, and cites many references in 168, note 13.

Iphigeneia's departure with the maidens and with the sacred image, protectress of Troy, feeds into the Euripides drama, *Iphigeneia in Tauris*. In Helen's account the maidens are bound for Tauris and to a more ancient Goddess worship involving human sacrifice. Euripides drama centers on Orestes, brother of Iphigeneia, who seeks a sacred stolen Goddess image in Tauris. He finds his sister, a Goddess priestess in a shrine where she oversees rituals of human sacrifice due any Greek man who comes to that shore. With her help, he escapes. The brother and sister flee with the image. In the museum at The Sanctuary of Artemis at Brauron, dedicated to Iphigeneia, described in notes about Chapter Four, is a very ancient wooden statuette found preserved in mud and unique in Greece." *The Blue Guide, Greece*, 1977, p.203.

The slaying of Achilles by Paris is reported in a fragment of the "Epic Cycle", *The Little Iliad* by Lesches, Trans. by H.G. Evelyn-White. The death of Paris on Mount Ida is reported by Tzetzes: *On Lycophron*, and by Apollodorus:iii.12.6